THE BERINFELL PROPHECIES
BOOK ONE

Curse
of the
Spider King

Other Books by . . .

Wayne Thomas Batson

The Door Within Trilogy

The Door Within
The Rise of the Wyrm Lord
The Final Storm

Pirate Adventures

Isle of Swords
Isle of Fire

* * *

Christopher Hopper

The White Lion Chronicles (series)

Rise of the Dibor
The Lion Vrie

To those in hiding, lost far from the Light
Swift wings are summoned to bear you safely home.

Published in Nashville, Tennessee, by Thomas Nelson. Thomas Nelson is a registered trademark of Thomas Nelson, Inc.

Scripture references are from The King James Version of the Holy Bible.

Thomas Nelson, Inc., titles may be purchased in bulk for educational, business, fundraising, or sales promotional use. For information, please e-mail SpecialMarkets@ThomasNelson.com.

Page design by Mandi Cofer.

Library of Congress Cataloging-in-Publication Data

Batson, Wayne Thomas, 1968–
  Curse of the Spider King / by Wayne Thomas Batson and Christopher Hopper.
    p. cm.–(The Berinfell prophecies ; bk. 1)
  Summary: With mysterious Sentinels revealing breathtaking secrets of the past, and dark strangers haunting their every move, seven young Elf Lords must decide whether to remain on Earth or return to their homeland of Allyra.
  ISBN 978-1-4003-1505-5 (pbk.)
  [1. Fantasy. 2. Christian life–Fiction.] I. Hopper, Christopher, 1979– II. Title.
  PZ7.B3238Cu 2009
  [Fic]–dc22

2009026149

Mfr: World Color / Fairfield, PA / June 2010 – PPO #109899

THE BERINFELL PROPHECIES
BOOK ONE

Curse
of the
Spider King

By WAYNE THOMAS BATSON
and CHRISTOPHER HOPPER

THOMAS NELSON
Since 1798

NASHVILLE   DALLAS   MEXICO CITY   RIO DE JANEIRO

contents

CONTENTS

Principal Cast

Allyran Elves: All Elves who live in Allyra.

Tommy Bowman: Curly-haired seventh grader at Thurgood Marshall Middle School in Seabrook, Maryland.

Autumn Briarman: Petite, blond seventh grader who lives outside Depauville in upstate New York. Sister of Johnny Briarman.

Johnny Briarman: Burly seventh-grade student who lives outside Depauville in upstate New York. Brother of Autumn Briarman.

Annelle "Nelly" Brookeheart: Gift-giving owner of A Likely Story Book Shoppe in Depauville, New York.

Flet Marshall Brynn: Second-highest-ranking Elf military officer.

Mr. Charlie: The custodian at Thurgood Marshall Middle School.

Children of the Light: The ancient name of Allyran Elves.

Cragons: The monstrous black trees of Vesper Crag.

Dreadnaughts: Elite warrior Elves who practice Vexbane, a profoundly effective form of combat.

Drefids: The Spider King's ghoulish assassins; Drefids have four deadly claws that extend from the knuckles of each hand.

Elves: One of the ancient races of Allyra; Elves are known for their books of prophecy and their woodcraft.

Anna Rosario Delarosa Espinosa: The Simonson family's new housekeeper, who picks up Kat from school.

Miss Finney: Lochgilphead school's new reading teacher and part-time librarian.

Sarron Froth: One of the brutal and bloodthirsty Drefid assassins for the Spider King.

Eldera "Elle" Galdarro: The mysterious librarian at Thurgood Marshall Middle School.

Jett Green: Seventh grader in Greenville, North Carolina. Rides motocross bikes and plays football.

James "Jimmy" Lewis Gresham: Redheaded seventh grader who lives in Ardfern, Scotland. Lived in an orphanage until he was adopted at six years old.

Guardmaster Olin Grimwarden: Commander of the military forces of the Elves and their allies.

Gwars: One of the ancient races of Allyra; Gwar are known for their brutish strength and their affinity for spiders.

Cathar Indrook: Gwar field commander.

Varuin Khelgast (Vair-ooh-in Kell-ghast)**:** The Gwar overlord.

Lyrian Elves: A very strong race of Elves. They are dark skinned and have violet-colored eyes.

Regis McAuliffe: Gresham family friend, who works at a local pub.

Mobius: The Spider King's most decorated Drefid assassin.

Mr. Ogelvie: Jimmy Gresham's new neighbor.

Mr. Phitzsinger: Physical education teacher at Thurgood Marshall Middle School in Seabrook, Maryland.

Edward Rengfellow: A tour guide for Dalhousie Castle.

Sentinels: They are very wise, very traditional Elves who are rumored to still follow the "Old Ways."

Mrs. Sherman: Kiri Lee's chaperone in Scotland.

Kat Simonson: A seventh grader in North Hollywood, California; she has polycythemia vera, a condition that gives her skin a bluish color.

Sophie: Kiri Lee's friend; she is an art prodigy.

Mr. James Spero: English teacher at Jett Green's school in Greenville, North Carolina.

The Spider King: The ruler of all Gwar, who harbor an ancient grudge against the Elves. Lives in Vesper Crag.

Vendar Stonebreaker: Berinfell's third flet marshall, superior to all in command except the Guardmaster and Flet Marshall Brynn.

Sir Travin: Clever warrior for the Elves.

Tyrith (Tier–ith): The Drefid's high commander.

Mr. Charles Wallace: Kat's American history teacher.

Warspiders: Spiders that are so large they can be ridden like horses; red Warspiders have lethal venom.

Wisps: Enemies of old. Vapor-beings, shape shifters.

Aaron Rothchild Worthington: Wealthy seventh grader in Tommy's school. Lives in Tommy's neighborhood.

Kiri Lee Yuen: Seventh grader in Paris, France. Musical prodigy.

ALLYRA

The world where the Elves, Gwar, and Spider King reside.
Locations on Allyra include:

Berinfell

The capital of the Elves, who once resided across
the many continents of Allyra

The Forest Gate

The western gate to enter Berinfell

The Gap Gate

The eastern gate to enter Berinfell

The Garden Gate

The southern gate to enter Berinfell

The Tree Gate

The northern gate to enter Berinfell

The Great Hall

The throne room and master chamber
of the Seven Elven Lords of Berinfell

Moonlit Crown

A secret place known only to the Elves, where the Sentinels
and other Elves who follow the "old ways" meet

Nightwish Caverns

A vast network of caverns beneath the Thousand-League Forest,
used as an emergency home by the Elves of Berinfell

Red Coast

Allyra's tempestuous coast

Vesper Crag

Volcanic home of the Spider King and his minions

Whitehall Castle

Ancient training facility for the Elves,
far to the northwest of Berinfell

EARTH

The world where the humans reside.
Locations on Earth include:

Ardfern, Scotland
Dalhousie Castle, Scotland
Depauville, New York, USA
Edinburg, Scotland
Greenville, North Carolina, USA
Lochgilphead, Scotland
North Hollywood, California, USA
Paris, France
Seabrook, Maryland, USA

1

Eight-Hundred-Year Echoes

CONCEALED IN a grove of alder trees, two cloaked figures waited, their whispered voices lost in the soft rustle of wind-stirred leaves.

"Commander, I had forgotten how brilliant the moon is."

"I know, Brynn," the burly warrior replied, absently rubbing a whitish furrow on his cheek, one of many scars on his face and neck. "Since we are allowed only rare views . . . I, too, drink it in." He sighed.

"How many hundreds of years since we could gaze our fill?"

"Too many," he said, more than a hint of bitterness in his tone.

They waited, not ten paces away from the flat side of a massive boulder. Beyond that, the silver moonlight shone down on a clearing framed by trees. It was a haunting view of their once glorious city, now in ruins.

Suddenly, the sheer face of stone radiated a dazzling blue light. The two crouched lower beneath the trees. Brynn raised her bow and drew the bowstring back to the feathery red sideburn near her right ear.

"Hold," whispered the leader. "If it is the enemy, we are done." The wall of stone rippled like a vertical film of water. It began to pulse and bulge as if the stone had turned to some elastic fabric or web. Something was struggling to break out.

Neither warrior breathed as a hand broke through, then forearms and a torso. But the light intensified, making it impossible to see beyond the form's black silhouette.

1

The portal snapped shut, just a boulder once more. They couldn't see much of anything as their eyes readjusted to the moonlight.

"Sir . . . should I—?"

"Brynn, stay your bow," the commander said, relieved to give that order. He strode forward from the cover of the alders toward a female draped in a heavy cloak. His archer followed close behind.

"Elle, what have you learned?" he asked.

"They are on Earth," she replied.

"Can you be certain?" he asked.

She removed her hood, shook out long blond hair—silver in the moonlight—and nodded. "There can be no doubt. I felt the tremors among the humans."

"I cannot believe it. . . . Froth told us the truth," said the commander. "I will gather the others still here for the mission. At last, some hope—"

"It will not be easy," Elle interrupted. "They have been scattered."

"Among how many?" he asked.

"Billions," she replied. She stared at her feet.

The commander was thunderstruck.

"Billions?" Brynn gasped. "But that would be like—"

"Looking for a green coin in a sea of clover." The commander rubbed his temples.

"And that is not the worst of it," Elle said. "The enemy is there."

"Then he knows," said the commander. "Froth thought as much. Elle, you and the others already on Earth must prepare for battle. You must not let the enemy get to them first. Do whatever is necessary."

"I understand," she replied. "The humans have swords there and other weapons."

"Good," he said. "Their weapons won't match the quality you're used to. Do what you can. But no matter what, you must continue to blend in."

Elle replaced the hood of her cloak and turned toward the portal. "If our race has become skilled at anything these bitter, long years, it's hiding."

"Elle?" She heard the urgent questioning in her commander's voice and turned. "We must not fail."

Elle crossed her wrists and bowed. "We will not. Endurance and Victory."

"Endurance and Victory."

2

A Surprise Gift

HUH? TOMMY Bowman didn't know why his parents said yes. They usually said no—unless, of course, it was to chores. To chores, they said yes, each and every time. But to come back to school, at night, on short notice, and drop him off without going through their usual check-list. *Unbelievable.* Just the other day, he'd wanted to ride his bike up to the regional park only two miles away. His parents had made him wear a watch, a helmet, a walkie-talkie, and a cell phone in case the walkie-talkie's battery died. *Almost a teenager and they treat me like I'm seven.*

As his parents drove away, Tommy glanced back over his shoulder at the looming menace of the school. Thurgood Marshall Middle was all columns, statues, white stone, and red brick. Stained and weathered over many years, the façade looked more like a police station from Gotham City than a middle school.

An engine growled, tires squealed, and Tommy whipped back around. He watched as a sleek black sports car pulled into the parking lot and stopped directly under the streetlight by the curb just thirty feet away. Like most twelve-year-olds, he loved sports cars—and he couldn't wait to see which one of his classmates got out of that car. *One of the rich kids probably,* Tommy thought. *Coming to the meeting to steal the show. Give all the answers.* Tommy stared at the car and waited . . . and waited. No one got out. All Tommy could see was the blazing orb of the streetlight's reflection in a sea of dark-tinted glass. The longer Tommy waited, the more uncomfortable he felt. A chill slithering up his back, Tommy rushed inside the school building.

There was no one in the main hallway or in the front office. His sneakers squeaked on the newly waxed floor as he looked around. Tommy glanced at his watch. He wasn't really early, so where was everybody? He rocked back and forth on his feet, wondering if the meeting had been cancelled and no one had told him. *That would figure*, he thought. But he hoped he was wrong. Mrs. Galdarro, the librarian, had selected Tommy personally to be a part of the group. He still didn't know why, but it felt good to be asked.

Tommy had always thought of himself as a rather unremarkable boy. Few teachers ever seemed to take notice of him. He just floated through their classes with straight Bs and an occasional A. Tommy wasn't a bad kid, the sort who would leave a handful of centipedes in the teacher's desk drawer. Nor was he an exceptionally good kid, prim and proper, whose precocious nature drew all sorts of attention from his teachers. In fact, the only meaningful thing Tommy could ever remember a teacher saying to him directly was, "Oh my, what a wonderful head of curly hair you have."

Yep, that's me, Tommy thought. *Curly hair and unremarkable.*

And yet Mrs. Galdarro had still noticed him. "Tommy Bowman, please see me after the bell," she had said.

Tommy had wondered what he had done wrong, so he was more than a little surprised when Mrs. Galdarro said, "You have talent, Mr. Bowman. Extraordinary talent, yes. One of the reasons I came here to Thurgood Marshall Middle School is to spot talent. And I see that you have it."

That had made Tommy wonder if the years had finally caught up with Mrs. Galdarro. Though, honestly, Tommy wasn't sure why he thought she was old. Her hair was not gray. Her skin was not wrinkled. But there was something about the depth of her green eyes and the richness of her voice that spoke of many years and a long history.

"I'd like to invite you to a meeting here in the library," Mrs. Galdarro had continued. "Tonight at eight. This is an important meeting, Tommy. Only for those with talents like yours. And there will be cookies, delicious cookies. But better still . . . everyone who comes will receive a gift. Don't be late."

Well, Tommy thought, *even if she is a bit cracked in the head, it still felt good to be noticed by someone*. And everyone liked gifts, especially Tommy. With that in mind, he decided he'd better at least check the library to make sure the meeting was indeed cancelled. He certainly wasn't in any hurry to go back outside.

Not that being in the school after dark was all that pleasant, either. Half the school's lights were off or dimmed. The halls became shadowy corridors. The empty classrooms . . . pitch-black caves. And the windows . . . dark eyes whose stare Tommy could not escape. *No cookies, no gift could be worth this.*

Then Tommy heard a squeaking sound, and Mr. Charlie, one of the school's custodians, appeared wheeling a cart out from the eighth-grade hallway. But Mr. Charlie didn't say a word. He just grinned at Tommy and stared. Even in the shadowy hall, Tommy could see Mr. Charlie's eyes. He had dark skin but very unusual dark blue eyes. They almost looked purple.

Mr. Charlie winked and rolled his cart toward the cafeteria. Soon, his cheery whistle floated back from the hall, that and the squeak of his cart. Everyone knew that Mr. Charlie had a few screws loose, but he was very nice and he smiled a lot. As a matter of fact, he always said good morning to Tommy.

Tommy hesitantly walked down the half-lit hall. Something small darted out from under one of the classroom doors. Tommy swerved to the right side of the hall. *Get a grip, Bowman!* he chastised himself. *It's only a spider.* The quarter-sized, brown and black arachnid stopped about two feet from Tommy's left foot. A myriad of tiny black eyes stared up at Tommy. Small or not, Tommy didn't like spiders. He lifted his foot to squash it, but it skittered back under the classroom door.

Tommy hastened up the hall to the school's library. He turned the corner, walked out into the cavernous book-filled room, and called out, "Hello?" There was no one there. He reached into his jacket pocket for his cell phone and flipped it open.

He never dialed.

There was a book that caught his eye from across the room.

The room was full of books, of course. But, in the exact center of the third shelf of the middle bookcase on the far wall, one book stood out. It was as if a bright spotlight shined upon its golden binding, and all the other books dimmed.

Tommy put his cell phone away, dropped his backpack on the floor, and strode slowly over to the bookcase. When he touched the book and felt it slide into his palm, he had a strange nostalgic feeling, as if he were about to open an old family photo album. He could almost smell the years of memories on the pages.

He turned the book and held it so that he could see its title. *The History of Berinfell*. And beneath it, in smaller script: *The Chronicles of the Elf Lords and Their Kin*.

From behind came a powerful voice: "Well done!" Tommy spun around, and there was Mrs. Galdarro. Only . . . she looked different. Gone was her normal librarian garb: the plaid skirt, ruffled cuffed blouse, and thick glasses. Instead she wore a long, dark hooded robe. It might have been deep purple or blue. In the shadows, it was hard to tell, but it was not black. Embroidery that bordered the hood and the sleeves shimmered, even in the dark.

"Mrs. Galdarro?" Tommy looked at her.

"Yes, lad." She lowered the hood, gave a warm smile, and nodded. ". . . and I say again, well done! You found your gift . . . or, perhaps I should say, it found you."

Tommy looked down at the book and back up to the librarian.

"All who come to the meeting get a gift," said Mrs. Galdarro. "Isn't that what I told you, Tommy?"

Tommy nodded again.

"The book you hold . . . is your gift. Though I must confess, it is not a right regular gift since it was yours to begin with."

"I don't understand," Tommy said, feeling like he might have blown a fuse in his brain.

"Of course you don't, my boy," Mrs. Galdarro replied. "I know that it is all very sudden and confusing for you. Why don't you come sit down?" She gestured to the round table on her right. Upon it lay a platter laden with piles and piles of cookies.

Tommy wondered how Mrs. Galdarro entered the library and put the tray on the table without him noticing. He shrugged. He wasn't about to turn his nose up at the cookies. Still hugging his book to his chest, he took a seat. Mrs. Galdarro sat across the table from him, and the cookies waited between them. He looked at her, the question forming on his lips.

"Go ahead, Tommy, have one."

Tommy picked one up. "It's still warm."

"Yes," she replied. "Just took them out of the oven."

The smell was delightful, sweet and fruity and something else Tommy couldn't quite put his finger on. Tommy took a bite, a big one, and began to chew. The flavor was so rich, so intense that it seemed to melt into his tongue as he chewed. Tommy took another bite and mumbled, "These are . . . *mmph* . . . these are . . . *mm, mmph,* delicious. I've never had anything like it."

"No," said Mrs. Galdarro, "I don't imagine you have."

Tommy was into his third cookie when it finally dawned on him that none of the other kids had shown up yet. "Mrs. Galdarro . . . um, where are the other kids?"

"Let me put it as simply and directly as I can. You are the only one in this . . . this meeting—for now—though others will come in due time. This gift is yours to explore. Oh, I do wish I could be with you when you read page 17. Yes, yes, and page 77 is wondrous, too. And I mustn't forget page 140 . . . ah, those were amazing days."

Tommy stuffed another cookie in his mouth and, forgetting his manners, mumbled, "Sounds like a cool story."

Mrs. Galdarro smiled. And for a moment she was lost in deep thought, staring beyond Tommy.

"Mrs. Galdarro?"

She blinked and looked back at Tommy once more. "Ah, yes, it is a *cool* story . . . but not yet finished." She paused. "Now, lad, listen to me. Reading this book will be quite an experience. Unsettling at first, I should imagine. Just remember, you will be safe. If it becomes too much, you simply close the book."

"Uh . . . okay." Tommy had read creepy books before. No way this elf book was going to scare him. "No problem."

The librarian raised an eyebrow. "I wonder."

"So are we going to meet at lunch to talk about the book? I mean, how much do I have to read? I'm not going to get quizzed on this, am I?"

"When the time is right," she replied, "we will indeed sit and talk about this special book. You have a birthday coming up, don't you, Tommy?"

"Ah, next month . . . November twelfth, why?"

"That's what they told you, is it? Of course, they wouldn't know, would they. Hmm."

"What *who* told me? Wouldn't know . . . huh?"

"Let's just say"—she paused and consulted a small notebook— "let's say we'll need to talk again in two weeks."

"Okay," said Tommy. "I'll read as much as I can by then."

"So clear now," Mrs. Galdarro muttered to herself. Tommy felt like she was staring at the side of his head. "This is a new haircut, isn't it, Tommy? Last year in sixth grade, you wore your hair long, over your ears."

"Yes, ma'am. My mom got tired of it and made me cut it off."

"Hmm, that was fortunate," she said. "I might not have noticed otherwise."

"What?"

"Nothing at all, Tommy."

"Oh."

Mrs. Galdarro stood up. "This meeting is hereby adjourned. Your parents should be here to pick you up soon."

"Over? Already?"

"Yes, dear boy. I called them and suggested they come right back. Wouldn't want you stuck here with the bad weather coming in, you know."

"But I kind of liked being here. It kind of . . . well . . . feels like being at my grandma's house."

"I understand," she replied kindly. "Why don't you take a few more cookies with you?"

"Okay!" Tommy selected three of the largest cookies and then looked down at his new book. "So this book is for me? I can keep it, right?"

"As long as you live," she replied. "It's a gift. Now I think it is time—"

"Mrs. Galdarro?"

"Yes?"

"Do you still think I have talent?"

"I don't think, Tommy, I know."

"Why me?" he asked finally.

"Read, dear boy," she replied as she walked with him from the library into the hall. "The book holds all the answers . . . even to the questions you have yet to ask. Now go. Your parents will be along shortly."

"Thank you, Mrs. Galdarro. For the book, the cookies, and . . ."

"You are quite welcome, lad." She put up her hood once more. Tommy started to walk away.

"Tommy," Mrs. Galdarro called to him, "there is one more thing. When you come to the section called 'Red Dusk,' page 277 I believe, wait until daylight to read it." Muted thunder rumbled outside. The few lights that were on flickered.

Tommy didn't know what to make of that. *Red Dusk.* He gave a half wave and walked up the hall toward the main office. As he turned the corner toward the school's front doors, he could still hear Mr. Charlie whistling a tune from somewhere in the quiet school.

As soon as Tommy left the building, he realized the thunder had not been an empty threat. Great waving sheets of rain rode gusts of howling wind. Tommy wiped a few spattered raindrops out of his eyes and immediately knelt on the sidewalk beneath the awning. He didn't want anything to happen to the unusual book Mrs. Galdarro had given him. He unslung his backpack and swiftly put the gift inside. He stood and swung the backpack up over his shoulder and took a bite of one of his cookies. Then he looked out into the school's parking lot and stopped chewing.

The black sports car was still there, parked under the same streetlight by the curb, and leaning against the side of the car was a tall man. A curtain of rain fell between them, and the man wore a wide-brimmed hat, so Tommy could not see the man's features. The collar of his dark gray trench coat was turned up, his hands were buried in the coat's deep pockets, and he stood very still and seemed content to wait. Rainwater ran off the brim of his hat and down his shoulders.

Tommy didn't see his parents' car anywhere in the school's parking lot. He felt panic rising up inside like a bubble. Though the strange man made no movement toward him at all, Tommy felt such an over-whelming sense of impending doom that his knees started to buckle.

Suddenly, the man in the dark gray coat stood up straight as if he'd just been startled awake. He spun around before Tommy could see his face, clawed at the car door, got it open, and leaped in. The sports car roared to life, fishtailed once on the wet pavement, and sped out of the parking lot.

"Good riddance, Mobius," came a musical voice from behind. Tommy wheeled around and found Mr. Charlie standing by the door right behind him. He held a mop in one hand. His smile was broad . . . almost triumphant.

"Do you know that guy?" Tommy asked the school custodian.

"I'ze just came to make sure you was safe," said Mr. Charlie.

"But that man—"

"I didn' see no man." Mr. Charlie turned to go back inside. "Looks like your folks is here," he said over his shoulder as he and his mop disappeared back into the school.

Blue Girl

KAT SIMONSON had colored her hair the night before. It was the fourth time she had changed her hair shade since school began—and it was only the second month of the school year. Kat Simonson stood in front of her floor-to-ceiling mirror and played with a few of the long pink strands near her ear. She twisted them restlessly around her index finger. The truth was that no hair color went with *poly*.

"Whatever," she half spoke, half sighed. She opened her drawer and searched among the boxes of dye anyway.

"Kat, let's go!" her mom shouted from downstairs.

"Right there, Mom," she replied as she closed the drawer. Maybe next she'd try natural medium ash blond. She grabbed her backpack, slipped out of her room, and began the winding trek though the house.

Kat's home—a sprawling compound of windows and terracotta—rested on an exclusive bluff in North Hollywood overlooking Los Angeles, California. Her friends could scarcely contain their jealousy whenever they came over. They were fascinated with the voice-activated, house-wide stereo system, the plethora of HD flat-screen TVs in multiple family rooms, and her 4,500-square-foot game room. Kat's parties were not to be missed and they rarely were . . . by anyone.

But the gatherings were never her ideas, always her parents attempting to get their reclusive daughter to "connect" or "nurture relationships." But Kat knew better. She saw the looks from her so-called friends. She knew they were the same ones who talked about her when her back was turned, called her Blue Girl and Smurf. They just liked her house. Her stuff.

After navigating the halls and the three flights of stairs, Kat set the alarm code on the keypad by the front door and went outside. She threw her bag in the backseat of their Escalade—the green one—and jumped in.

"You can sit up front, you know," said Mrs. Simonson.

Kat slammed the door. Silence from the backseat at first. Then a hesitant, "Thanks, but I like to spread out." Then silence from the front seat. The huge SUV crawled down the driveway.

"Kat, I was thinking—" Too late. Kat slipped in her earbuds, hit play, and bass-heavy rock blasted away at once.

Mrs. Simonson heard the static buzz of the music. *So loud,* she thought. *That can't be good for her ears.* But she wasn't going to tell Kat to turn it down. It would just be another negative thing to say . . . another few inches of distance between her and her daughter. She glanced in the rearview mirror.

Mrs. Simonson remembered the first time she saw her daughter, just a photo at the adoption agency. She'd fallen in love right there and then. And when she first got a chance to hold Kat, they seemed to bond in such an immediate, powerful way. She just never thought things would turn out as they had.

The poly had come out of nowhere when Kat was seven. Her skin turned blue. *Polycythemia vera* was the doctors' diagnosis. Her body carried too much blood, limiting its oxygen-carrying ability and giving her skin that otherworldly blue tone. Once the poly hit, Kat was never the same. Withdrawn. Sullen. Combative. Her mom winced and stared straight ahead. Kat seemed so unreachable now. Every reply was clipped. Every suggestion shot down. Every compliment ignored. Mrs. Simonson wished they could go back to the easy rapport they shared, especially on those blessed vacations to the beach house. She sighed. Melancholy washed over her like waves over a sandcastle.

Kat stared through the side window. She tried to keep her mind numbed by the blare of distorted metal guitars and thunderous drums. But just before the scene was swallowed by palm trees and gated communities, Kat glimpsed a flicker of sunlight on the Pacific Ocean. Her mind went to her parents' summer cottage in Newport Beach. Despite their incredible wealth, the Simonsons' "escape home," as they liked to call it, was much smaller than most on the shore. But that was why Kat liked it so much. Simple. Picturesque. Little more than a two-room bungalow with kitchen and attached dining room—but a broad view of the ocean from every room.

On its quaint patio, Kat and her parents used to sit and have endless conversations about memories and dreams. From the house, it was only a few strides into the surf and the vast expanse of ocean—Kat's favorite thing in the entire world. She would spend all her time there wading, swimming, snorkeling, and surfing. It was the only place, in fact, that she really felt at home.

She wished she could go there now. *Any place but here*, she thought, glancing up at her mother. It wasn't that she didn't love her mom. She wished she could spend more time with her the way they used to before the poly. Kat's feelings stemmed from the fact that, no matter what Kat did, she always felt like she was a disappointment to her mom. Kat wanted her mom to approve, to applaud, to accept her, but Kat always felt like she had let her down . . . like she wasn't the daughter her mother wanted her to be—even though her mother often said she was proud of Kat.

Kat caught her mother glancing into the rearview mirror and then giving Kat a longing stare and a heavy sigh. She'd been doing that kind of thing a lot lately: sighing, staring, shaking her head. Kat knew why. *I'm a failure*, she thought. *I don't get the grades. I'm not in any clubs. And I don't have any good friends.* Kat turned up the music.

Mrs. Simonson reached over the seat and tapped Kat on the knee. "You ready for your American history test?"

Kat frowned and took out one earbud. "What?"

"I said, are you ready for the American history test?"

"I guess," Kat said, watching one mansion after another pass by. They'd be getting on the highway in a few more blocks.

"Did you need help studying? We're still early. We could pull over at Starbucks and just—"

"No, Mom. Thanks. I'm good." Kat stuffed the earbud back in. Kat growled at herself internally. She knew she'd been rude. *How can I tell her how I'm feeling? She won't understand.* Kat laughed with exasperation. Besides asking for things and quick yes-and-no stuff, did she even know how to talk to her mother at all anymore? Kat stole a glance at the rearview mirror and saw her mother's furrowed brow. *One big, happy family.*

They rode the rest of the way without talking, Kat engrossed in her music and Mrs. Simonson tuning to a satellite talk-radio station. When they finally arrived at Sierra Valley Middle, Kat turned off her music, slipped out of the SUV, and showed a weak smile to her mom.

"Don't forget, Dad will be picking you up from school today because—"

"Because you guys just fired the third housekeeper this month."

Her mom sighed. "Honey, she made some serious mistakes."

"I guess our family rubbed off on her."

"Oh, Kat." Her mom looked down and fidgeted with the steering wheel. She looked up. "I love you."

"Thanks. Can I go now?" Kat watched her mother's shoulders sag as the tinted window went up. *Mom says I love you, and what do I do? I kick her to the curb. Real nice, Kat.*

Kat turned to walk away, then suddenly stumbled. Disorientation came on so fast she almost got sick. She doubled over. Her vision blurred. A loud ringing came to her ears and slowly faded. Voices came next. No, it was one voice. It came in and out like a radio station not quite in range. It sounded like her mother's voice, but just snippets. *Oh, Kat . . . why . . . so much . . . I can't . . . anymore.*

Kat could almost feel her mother gripping the steering wheel harder and harder. She could almost feel the tightness in the muscles of her mother's neck and shoulders. She could almost feel the wetness of tears on her mother's face. Kat reached up to her own cheek. No tears at all. *What's happening to me?*

It passed as quickly as it had come on. Feeling like she'd just awakened from a strange dream, Kat continued up the school's front steps. She refrained from looking back as she jostled between other students and squashed through the school's front door. She ignored the whispers:

"Blue girl."

"Now she has pink hair."

"What's wrong with her?"

When she'd climbed the stairs to the second flight, Kat looked out of the gum-wad-speckled window to the teeming lot in front of the school and then to the glittering city beyond.

4

Manifest Destiny

THE AMERICAN history test packet glared up at Kat from the desktop. *What a screw-up*, she thought. *I could have studied with Mom and had Starbucks to boot.* She signed her name on the top and nervously flipped the pages, looking at the questions and assessing her complete lack of knowledge. *This is a disaster.*

She tapped her pencil on the desk and looked nonchalantly around the room; everyone was already leaping into the first question. She looked back to her test, took a breath, and read the first question again:

1.) Define the term *Manifest Destiny* and give one example in American history.

Kat felt a wave of anxiety spread through her chest. *Manifest what?* She tried to break the question down. *Manifest means something like obvious or easy to see, right? And destiny was like some great big mission or a goal you were meant to reach . . . right?* She decided to skip it and come back later, a technique she remembered hearing her teacher talk about for taking tests like this.

2.) List two ways that the transcontinental railroad affected the economy.

You've got to be kidding me, Kat thought. Sweat beaded on her forehead. Someone definitely needed to turn up the air conditioner. Kat ran her fingers through her hair and took a deep breath. *Question three?* She could only skip so many before she'd be out of questions.

She looked out the window to her right and watched the palm leaves stir above the playground. The cloudless blue sky normally brought her some peace, reminding her of the sea, but not today. This test and her fam—*Huh?* There was a man leaning against one of the slender palms. He wore one of those Indiana Jones hats, but gray, more like a detective. He had a long gray detective-coat, too, and dark sunglasses that hid most of his face. It wasn't unusual for the police to have a presence at the school. But the way he just stood there, leaning against the tree and staring. If Kat didn't know any better, she'd think he was looking right up at her.

Kat caught her breath. Her heartbeat stuttered. She looked down at her test, then up at her teacher, Mr. Wallace, as he paced the front of the room. She tried to breathe, but found she could inhale just short breaths. The fringes of her vision grayed out. Kat turned side to side. No one else noticed. They were focused on their tests, oblivious. Kat turned back to the window once more.

The man—there just moments ago—was gone.

Heat and cold fought for her shoulders and arms, and her chest tightened. But there was something else, too, a new emotion, something like anxiety but more potent . . . a panicky sensation of fearful anticipation. But anticipation of what?

Kat couldn't shake the mounting drama in her heart. Something was happening. And somehow she knew it wasn't the test. And who was that man? Did she imagine him?

Something was very wrong.

The first thing she thought was heart attack. But at thirteen? She had most of the symptoms she'd learned about in health class. But Kat never touched red meat and avoided fast food like the plague.

Maybe it was the poly, some new symptom the docs didn't know about. She gripped the desk and felt a wave of dizziness wash over her. Mr. Wallace finally looked in her direction.

"You okay?" he mouthed from up front.

Kat nodded and looked back down to her test. Her hands were trembling. Why did she lie to Mr. Wallace? Why not tell him she needed a break? A restroom pass? Anything! Kat closed her eyes and tried to keep from being overwhelmed. Her head was swirling. *Focus!* She tapped her foot, trying to give herself something to think about other than the mounting sensations that were overpowering her body. *Focus!*

"Miss Simonson"—a hand touched her shoulder—"are you all right?"

All at once she was composed. The panic was gone. Kat looked up to Mr. Wallace standing beside her. "Yes, Mr. Wallace," she said, blinking a few times. "Everything is fine."

"I know my tests inspire dread and apprehension, but you didn't look so good," he said. "I thought—"

"No, I'm fine, really. Just thinking about my next answer." She watched Mr. Wallace's eyes glance at her blank test sheet and then back to Kat.

"You mean your first answer."

"Ha." She laughed nervously. "Yeah, that one." She turned back to her test and waited for Mr. Wallace to walk back to his desk. *That was close*, she thought. But then wondered, *What was close? I'm not hiding anything. I thought I was going to die–*

Manifest Destiny was the policy of U.S. territorial expansion beginning in the 1840s. It was the belief that the settlers had the right to take possession of land and resist anyone who threatened them, including the Native Americans. One example was the massacre at Wounded Knee with the U.S. 7th Cavalry's complete disregard for the welfare and land ownership of the Lakota Sioux.

Kat flinched and looked over her shoulder. She couldn't believe it. Someone had just whispered that answer to her. *Who?* No one looked back. All eyes were riveted to test papers. Well, except for Sean Pinkerton in the corner. He was staring at something on the classroom wall and moving his head like a bobblehead doll. *No,* Kat thought, *he wouldn't know the answer anyway.*

Someone had given her the answer. Maybe a secret admirer? Her face flushed. She looked around again. Except for Sean, they were all still working. Maybe it had come from inside, some repressed memory from watching the History Channel while half asleep. It had been like earlier when her mom dropped her at school—sounding more inside her head than an audible voice. Besides, Kat didn't think anyone in class liked her enough to give her an answer.

She looked back at her test, and a different sort of fear gripped her. She reviewed the answer in her mind and thought about writing it down. Perhaps it was her own answer after all; perhaps it was her brain just communicating an answer in a time of extreme need. She had talked to herself before, right? This was just like that . . . but not at all.

Kat muttered under her breath and doodled something in the margin. The answer sure sounded like a good one. But was it hers? She glanced up at the clock. Five minutes had already gone by, and the only thing she'd written on her paper was her name and the doodles on the side. She could feel Mr. Wallace's eyes on her. She had to put something down. She took a deep breath and then put her pencil to the paper and started writing.

Done.

One down, nine to go.

She read the second question again and drew a blank as before. But a moment later another voice, this time clearly male, spoke in her head:

The transcontinental railroad provided new jobs for immigrant workers, specifically Irish and Chinese foreigners seeking to create a new life. It also provided a fast means of transporting raw materials from one part of the country to the other, which perpetuated capitalism by starting new small businesses.

Kat stared at her desk. What was going on here? She put her pencil down and rubbed her temples with her fingertips. *I'm going crazy*, was all she could think. She glanced to her left and her right to see if anyone else had heard what she did. But no one seemed the least bit distracted. She could hear the *tip-tap* of their pencils.

"This is madness," she whispered to herself. Then Kat picked up her pencil and wrote down the answer she'd heard.

Kat again doodled as she glanced at the third question. No sooner had she finished reading it when another voice spoke an answer into her head. Only this time she could have sworn it was the voice of Erin Freeburg. Kat looked forward and to the left where Erin was busy scribbling away on her test. Then she looked up at Mr. Wallace. There was no way Erin could have spoken to Kat that loud without Mr. Wallace noticing.

Kat chewed lightly on her pencil. Maybe it was some kind of subconscious recall. Maybe Mr. Wallace had spoken about these things, and maybe Erin had said that answer aloud in class. That would explain the familiar voices. It was just some bizarre recall of what her classmates had said in class. That was it. That had to be it.

Kat had a troubling thought: What if she wasn't listening to her own mind? But just as fast she shot down the idea, citing it as something you'd see on the SyFy Channel, not something that happens in real life.

She filled in question three. In fact, Kat wrote down the answers that she heard for the next seven questions until the test was done. She flipped through the booklet and checked her work. She stood up to hand in her book but stopped, staring at the design she'd doodled on the front page. She flipped to the second page. She'd scribbled the same thing on that page, too. In fact, Kat had drawn the same image on every page of the test. It was a peculiar thing: curvy, shaded . . . kind of like a circle with tiny lines branching out from the inside and spiraling around decoratively. An even smaller circle adorned the top.

Kat shrugged. It was strange, but not as strange as the other events of the morning. She looked at the class, most of whom were still working, and realized she'd finished as fast as Molly McMillan, easily the smartest girl in the seventh grade. When Kat met Molly at Mr. Wallace's desk to deliver her test at the same time, Molly seemed indignant.

"Just because we finished at the same time doesn't mean you aced it," Molly said with a sneer and then turned abruptly away.

Mr. Wallace looked up, surprise spreading across his face. "Why, Miss Simonson, finished already?"

"Yes, Mr. Wallace," she said, avoiding eye contact. "I think I did pretty well on this one."

"Really?" He stretched the pronunciation. "I must admit, I had concerns. You looked ill."

Kat blushed. "Just a little bit of test anxiety, but I calmed down."

"You sure you don't want to review your answers? Just to double-check?"

"Yeah, I'm sure. Thanks though."

Mr. Wallace smiled and took the test from her. Kat walked back to her desk and sat down, playing with her hair. She looked at the clock on the wall and watched the second hand click by. More and more students turned in their papers until the last student returned to his desk and Mr. Wallace declared that the test was over.

"You have two minutes to chat before next period," he announced. "And Miss Simonson?"

Kat looked up.

"Can I see you for a moment?"

The whole class *whoa-ob*ed her, guessing that Kat was in big trouble. Kat blushed and went forward. Mr. Wallace silenced the class with his famous "move and I'll vaporize you" look while Kat waited nervously at the side of his desk.

He turned sideways and said, "It seems you were accurate in your self-appraisal. You did quite well, Kat."

"Really?" Kat asked, perhaps a bit too surprised. "I mean, I thought I'd gotten most of it right, but that one on continentalism— whew! I'm sure I messed something up on—"

"No, Miss Simonson," he interrupted. "As far as I can tell, you didn't miss a point. Granted, I'll take a closer look later tonight when I grade the rest, but it sure looks good."

All Kat could say inside was *And?*

"Anyways, I just wanted to let you know I am very impressed, Miss Simonson. This is a welcome change for you. I hope it continues."

"Thanks," Kat said. "It's coming more natural to me," was all she could think to say.

"Well, hard work does pay off."

"Yeah, it sure does," Kat said, now feeling incredibly guilty for passively lying. But they were her answers. *Right?*

Mr. Wallace was a sharp guy. He might suspect something. If he did, what would he do about it? Kat hardly slept that night, and dreaded the ride into the school the following morning.

5

Red Dusk

TOMMY SAT on the edge of his bed in a narrow cone of golden lamplight, the book Mrs. Galdarro had given him early in the evening on his lap. The rest of his bedroom lay cloaked in shadow. He could hear his mom downstairs, talking to his dad. "I think it's wonderful that Tommy's taken such an interest in reading," she said.

"That librarian is something else," Mr. Bowman replied.

Tommy glanced at the clock—9:30. On most nights, he'd be in snoozeville by now. But tonight he just couldn't fall asleep. He wanted to read. He slid his hand across the smooth surface of the book's cover, letting his fingers ride up on its gilded trim and down around the binding. *Wait.* Before he opened it, he stood up and parted the curtains of his window. The streetlight was bright and yellow behind the now bare crab apple tree in his front yard. Tommy half expected to see a black sports car parked there, but there wasn't one.

Tommy dropped back to his bed and opened the book. A detailed sketch emblazoned the first page. *Cool artwork,* he thought. Tommy studied the sketch of a partially collapsed stone wall, and beyond it a white pedestal upon which a cobweb-shrouded book lay. There were shelves behind it, shelves full of other books and artifacts that Tommy did not recognize. And perched on the arm of a statue was a huge bird of prey, like a falcon but much, much larger.

Tommy carefully turned past the art and came to a kind of table of contents. There were page numbers, but rather than chapter titles, this book seemed to be divided in sections and subsections by some kind of date. And the dates descended on the page from top to bottom.

9680 Founding of Allyra

8015 Golden Age of Elves

7252 Construction of Berinfell

5807 The Nemic Wars

4297 Alliance with the Saer

4021 The Bloodless War

3927 Invasion of the Taladrim

3811 The Gwar Revolution

3108 Age of Peace

2222 The Fall of Berinfell

2220 The Age of Hiding

Beneath each of these main headings, in smaller script, was at least one subheading. There, Tommy found what he was looking for: *Red Dusk.* Given Mrs. Galdarro's warnings, Tommy reasoned that it had to be the most exciting chapter. *Of course, she'd said not to read it at night. But come on . . . how bad could it be?* Tommy flipped through the pages until he arrived at page 277.

Cool! The text was in the same calligraphy as the table of contents.

It almost looked handwritten. Tommy touched the ornate first letter . . . and something went terribly wrong.

The lights dimmed. The temperature dropped twenty degrees. And the door blew shut, sending the curtains fluttering. Something on the page poked Tommy's finger. With a yelp, Tommy jerked back his hand and let the book fall open to the floor. He watched as a dark twig emerged from the book. No, it wasn't a twig. It was the beginnings of a large tree, rising now as if the pages were a bed of soil, and centuries of growth were happening right before Tommy's eyes. Red light began to shine out, surging around the trunk of the still-growing tree as if a setting sun hid somewhere in the pages. Tommy's room filled with the smell of leaves and grass wet with dew.

Tommy shrank back to his headboard as the tree continued its ascension. Its narrow trunk thickened, and broad boughs strewn with foliage rose up and penetrated the ceiling of Tommy's bedroom. But rather than cracking the painted drywall and bursting beams of lumber, the tree pushed up the ceiling as if it were a huge tent canvas. Soon there was nothing but night sky, stars, and a red glow to the east.

More trees spread upward, followed by great grassy hills, and then . . . magnificent castle towers! From the towers, small flag-adorned turrets rose that soon grew beyond the confines of the room. Trees dotted the landscape from near to over the far hills. The castle towers were part of a magnificent fortress that sprawled to the edge of a massive, distant forest. Tommy could see no more of his room. His bed was gone, and now he sat on lush grass with his back against the trunk of a dark tree. But there were other things waiting to escape the pages.

At first Tommy thought he was watching yet another tree branch emerge from the book, but it was not. A black limb with barbs and a claw came up, grasping until more of its segments became visible. Tommy rolled onto his side and ducked behind the tree just as the first giant spider broke free from the pages. There were more to come. Many more. And on their backs rode creatures Tommy had never seen before: brutish, gray-skinned beasts wearing armor on their barrel chests, thick shoulders, and short, stocky legs. These creatures were armed with all manner of weapons and held the reins of their arachnid steeds in huge, meaty fists.

Tommy had seen enough. Remembering Mrs. Galdarro's warning, he dove for the book, slamming it shut.

Whoosh!

It was gone. Once more, Tommy was sitting alone on his bed. He was breathing heavily. Curious, he crept out of his room to the foot of the stair. "Mom, Dad? Did you hear anything strange just now?"

"Strange?" Mr. Bowman asked. "An ambulance went by."

"No," Tommy said. "Stranger than that?"

"Not a thing, Tommy," his mother said. "Are you all right? You sound upset."

"I'm fine," Tommy replied. Then more to himself, "I think." Scratching his head, he wandered back into his room and stared at the book. He hadn't imagined it all. No way. But there was only one way to find out for sure.

Tommy opened the book, turned to page 277, and once more put his finger to the text. Again, the entire environment in his room changed as a living world surged up from the pages of the book. Faster and faster—forests, hills, stone walls, and creatures—gushed up like an eruption. Three giant spiders, each one as big as a truck, burst above ground and came right at the hill where Tommy stood. This time Tommy couldn't get out of the way fast enough. Their burly riders driving them hard, the massive, black eight-legged beasts came upon Tommy. His field of vision filled with hairy mandibles, pincerlike jaws, and eyes—so many blank, staring eyes.

Tommy screamed as the creatures drove their legs deep into the soil, the sounds of armor clanking above him. Tommy covered his head and rolled sideways, screaming louder. As they passed, Tommy dared a peek from between his arms and slowly let down his guard. *I'm not dead*, he thought, feeling around to confirm that all of his limbs were still whole and in place. *I'm not even hurt. . . . It never even touched me*. Even with all those eyes, the spiders hadn't seen him. In fact, they had passed right through him. Tommy turned the page and touched the script. At last, he understood. *The History of Berinfell* was unlike any other book on Earth. It was a living history . . . and Tommy was right in the middle of it.

Like a deep wound in the dusk sky, an angry sun bled crimson from behind the hills east of Berinfell up into the shreds of high clouds and the falling curtain of night. Against the darkening blot of red, a pair of long, segmented limbs of a Warspider tentatively reached over the top of a black hill. Convinced of its safety, the Warspider quickly clambered over the crest. The creature's armor, as well as its Gwar rider, was draped in gray and sable shrouds to blend in with the twilight. The oversized arachnid was visible for just a moment before disappearing into the shadows of the valley. Hundreds more followed—the bulk of the Spider King's mobile army. Each approach timed so that only one could be visible upon the hills at a time, and only for an instant. If observed, it could easily be dismissed as a trick of the eye.

The rolling hills that guarded the eastern flank of the Elven capital city of Berinfell had seen its share of would-be invaders throughout the ages. Armies of the Nemic, the Saer, the Taladrim—all had tested their mettle against the Elves—and failed. For just a hundred yards from the walls of Berinfell Stronghold, a treacherous cavern yawned. The Gap, as the Elves called it, curled protectively around the city. Atop the immense stone walls of the fortress and hidden in the tall trees on the east side of the

Gap, the finest archers from the legions of the Seven Elven Lords fingered their bows and waited.

No one would dare assail the Elves on the western flank, tucked deep in the Thousand-League Forest. For in the wooded realms in the world of Allyra, the Elves were perilous.

So in spite of the open hills and shelterless valley, in spite of the deep ravine, and in spite of the biting rain of arrows that could whistle in at any moment, attackers always approached from the east.

And so they did on this night.

The Elven archers—stationed on wide, open platforms called *flets* in the few towering trees on the east side of the Gap—had been watching, but their keen eyes had not seen the stealthy invaders. Swiftly, the Warspiders advanced on the trees. Their Gwar riders, who could see clearly in darkness, were deadly accurate with their heavy crossbows. Arrows flew. The Elves fell from their perches.

When he was certain that no Elven sentries had survived, Gwar Field Commander Cathar leaped from his Warspider. Going from spider to spider, he signaled all Gwar generals to dismount. Once gathered, they stepped as close to the brink of the Gap as they dared. Cathar leaned forward and looked down at the bottomless blackness. *One wrong move*, he thought morbidly, *and a Gwar could die of starvation before he hit bottom.*

But he knew there would be little concern for falling once the spiders had finished their job. He turned to his generals, three teams of six, and nodded. Each one removed an odd, oblong flask from a very tight shoulder holster. Cathar held his bottle as far away from his body as possible, pointed it toward Berinfell, and slowly wriggled its stopper free. There came an undulating hiss and then something like a loud, painful sigh, and Cathar felt the bottle warm in his hands. Then tendrils of luminous smoke began to leak into the air. But unlike common smoke that unravels and dissipates in the slightest breeze, this vapor held its form. It poured forth and curled to and fro like an airborne serpent. It collected in a swirling mass that presently became a hideous, leering face.

"Go on," commanded Cathar. "Be off with you." The face twisted into a snarl before dissolving back into its serpentine form. With another hiss, it raced away, across the gap and into the darkness.

"Blasted Wisps," Cathar muttered as he stoppered the bottle. The other Gwar generals released their captives as well. In all, nineteen Wisps slithered invisibly toward the walls of Berinfell.

The Gwar commander strode back past the lines of Warspiders, placed the flask back in its holster, and removed a pouch from his side. He shook the pouch until two small stones rolled into his palm. He took one in each hand and struck them together, producing a blue spark. The light flared for a second and glistened on Cathar's greasy sideburns that spilled out from his oak-leaf-shaped ears and ended with an unruly patch on his chin. Scouts lying prone atop the hills saw the signal and answered with a brief flash of their own. Cathar grinned. The rest of the Gwar infantry would come now, followed by the Drefids. The Elves would never know what hit them.

The first stage complete, Cathar led his battalion of Warspiders to the eastern edge of the Gap. The Gwar riders dismounted and removed the reins from their mounts. The Warspiders, now spread across a quarter-mile span along the Gap, rose up tall on their gangly legs. They curled their abdomens beneath them and aimed their spinnerets high toward the walls of the Elven city. Nearly in unison, their great bodies shuddered and launched fist-sized globs of sticky webbing in a high arc over the Gap. Each one had a long strand of gray filament trailing behind it, still connected to the spider's abdomen, the web-anchor easily clearing the Gap and landing safely on the other side. Strand after strand sailed silently through the night air until enough anchors were in place to support the weight of the Warspiders. The beasts crept heedlessly over the edge. Following their guide webs, they began to weave. In less than an hour, the Gap of Berinfell would be bridged by an enemy force for the first time in its long history.

6

The Fall of Berinfell

Elden Hemlock had seen thousands of beautiful sunsets in his days, but he thought this one topped them all. He gazed east from the high wall of Berinfell and marveled at the deepening crimson on the horizon.

Wait!

He stood stone-still. He'd seen movement atop one of the distant hills . . . or at least, he thought he had. There was nothing there now but black hill and blood-red sky. Elden began to relax.

Ah, getting punchy after a long watch, he thought.

Then he heard a strange gurgling hiss behind him. He turned and came face-to-face with . . . himself! Elden opened his mouth, but no sound came forth. There was a strange burning under his ribs, spreading rapidly over his chest. He looked down and saw the *other* Elden's hand holding the haft of some strange blade that had been broken off but for an inch. Elden's knees felt suddenly weak, and he leaned on the parapet for support. His sight withered away as he collapsed. The second Elden yanked the body of the first off the stone and, with very little effort, heaved the real Elden over the wall.

———————— ··•····•·•·|··|··•·•······| ————————

"The bridge is finished," said Cathar, dropping to one knee.

"You are behind," stated Varuin Khelgast, the Gwar overlord who had

32

arrived with the legions of infantry. As overlord, Varuin wielded the Spider King's authority in battle, and, as Cathar well knew, he was not to be questioned. Varuin lowered the hood of his cloak and looked up. The sickle moon reflected in his black eyes as he scanned the trees to the west. "It is a wonder that the hive of Berinfell has not released a swarm of Elves upon us. The Wisps have done their part, no doubt."

"No doubt," Cathar replied.

"Quite useful, they are," said Varuin. "But they will not stand long in the path of the Elven Lords. The time has come. Send the spiders and legions. At first resistance, light up the sky."

"Yes, sir," Cathar said.

"When the walls are breached, the infantry will ascend by the spiders' tag lines. And then . . . then the Drefids will come." Varuin motioned with one of his massive hands.

Cathar looked beyond several rows of Gwar soldiers and saw tall figures, shadows in their hooded cloaks. *How many times had Cathar seen the Drefids revealed?* And yet their presence—even the very thought of them—always sent a tremor through his body.

"Be swift, Cathar," said Varuin.

"Yes, sir."

Cathar climbed back onto his Warspider, removed a finger-sized whistle, and blew it three times. It emitted no sound that men or Elves could hear, but at once, the Warspiders crept over the edge of the Gap. The webbed bridge held strong as the eight-legged combatants picked their way across. Their riders, the Gwar generals, watched the dark walls for movement and readied their arc rifles.

Farther back, the Gwar infantry unlaced and removed their usual boots, and strapped on boots that were half-height and wide, more like heavy black shoes. The soles were padded with a slick, dimpled material called *kassek*. Only kassek-woven footwear would allow warriors to march safely across the incredibly sticky spider filament needed to create the bridge. Even with the kassek-woven boots, warriors took great care not to fall or touch the web with any other part of their body. Such a clumsy soldier would be hopelessly ensnared in the web and perhaps fall victim to a hungry arachnid.

As the spiders neared the walls, the infantry and crossbowmen began their slow, perilous march. Cathar's own spider worked its way past the midpoint of the bridge when a haunting, sonorous tone came from one of the many high towers. *The first war horn. The element of surprise has been lost!* Cathar thought. But no other war horns picked up the call.

Elven archers sprang up on the parapets and took aim. Their bows sang as long-shafted arrows surged into the coming ranks of the Gwar. Dozens fell dead. Still more careened from their saddles and found themselves sprawled on the webbing and unable to get up. It had only been a moment, but Cathar had seen enough. He drew back the firing cord, raised his arc rifle, and fired. Even as the black arc stone sped into the night sky, it kindled to a fiery blue. But as it plummeted toward the Elves, the arc stone flared such a bright white that Cathar averted his eyes. The stone exploded in a ball of white flame, which consumed several Elven archers.

Soon it seemed that falling stars filled the sky over Berinfell. The Gwar expected that each blazing stone cast would kill tenfold Elves.

The Warspiders claws delved into thin crevices of the mortar walls, their Gwar riders gripping sturdy tethers. Arrows aimed precisely at the joints of the spiders' legs glanced off or broke on the spiders' armor. The giant beasts clambered up in spurts, pausing to dodge falling rocks and arrows, and reached the parapets virtually unhindered.

But not for long. Elven flet soldiers slung their bows and loosed their siege axes. The first spider to crest the walls lost its forelegs to the lethal blows of the Elves. Their axes bit between and behind the plate armor, cracking exoskeleton and severing sinew. With horrible shrieks, spiders fell away from the walls and plunged into helpless masses of Gwar infantry below.

As the second wave of Warspiders climbed the wall, they released strands of a darker, almost black web from their spinnerets. The web trailed to the ground—where the Gwar infantry, spread all across the base of the keep, took hold, and began to ascend. Swords and axes met as Gwar and Elf came face-to-face. The Warspiders successfully crested the walls in greater numbers, and their Gwar riders directed them through the melee deeper into the city. They were searching for doors, and each they found—be it wood or iron—the Warspiders tore it from its hinges and tossed it away. Gwar infantry surrounded each new entry point and dispatched Elves as they issued forth. But a Gwar horn blast summoned their attention back to the eastern wall above the Gap.

Larger Warspiders with long, red forelegs clambered over the walls. Their riders, hooded and robed, sat impassively in their saddles. For a moment, an eerie hush fell over the area. The huge Warspiders stopped and raised themselves high on their limbs. As one, the Drefids removed their hoods, revealing shadowy figures with long white hair, burning embers in otherwise empty sockets, and knife blades extended from their boney knuckles.

———————— •········•···•·····•···· ——

Flet Marshall Brynn stood transfixed in the dancing shadows of torchlight at the top of the inner wall's curving stairway.

Screee! The Warspiders' talons scraped the outer stonework of the stronghold. Brynn froze, but not because of the battle raging outside. She had seen an Elven warrior, one of her own flet soldiers, draw a blade and strike down another Elf in cold blood right before her eyes.

"Elden!" she cried, rage bursting free at last. "Elden, drop your sword!" Agile, even in full armor, Brynn raced frantically down the stair.

Elden never glanced up at his commander. His cold stare lingered on a more immediate threat. Another Elf leaped over the fallen flet soldier and brought his curved blade crashing down on Elden. Elden blocked, barely. His enemy's sword had come within an inch of his scalp. And before Elden could recover or counter, his enemy slid off the weak parry and drove his sword through the armor protecting Elden's ribs. The blade went deep and up, surely into Elden's heart. But Elden did not collapse.

He grinned at his attacker with a sickly, misshapen kind of smile. Then he brought his sword down hard on his enemy's helmet. The Elf fell away dead just as Flet Marshall Brynn stopped short three steps above. She flashed her rychesword, her movements a blur. Elden countered and attempted to duel for a moment, before Brynn slashed his weapon from his hand. It clattered to the stone, but before Elden could reach it, Brynn wheeled her blade around and carved a gash into Elden's neck. But there was no blood. There was no wound. Elden vanished, leaving only swirling eddies of thin black smoke.

"What devilry is this?" Brynn cried. She stood out of breath on the bottom stair and held her rychesword as if she might drop it.

"That was not Elden." Guardmaster Olin Grimwarden strode to the foot of the stair and knelt at the side of the fallen Elf. "It was a Wisp."

"A what?"

"A Wisp." Grimwarden's broad shoulders sagged, and he shook his head. "They are enemies of old. Vapor-beings, shape shifters. We thought they had all died out generations ago. But now they reemerge, loosed by the Spider King to wreck our defenses." Grimwarden stood, hefted his spear menacingly, and took Brynn by the hand. "The Wisp you dispatched is not dead. He will quickly take on another form. And there may be others within our ranks."

"Can't they be killed?"

"Only by the two-edged sword," replied Grimwarden. "Speak the Words as you strike, and the Wisp will be sundered." He looked with regret at the familiar phrases inscribed along the haft of his spear. "If only we still forged all our weapons as we did of old—"

Grimwarden flinched as bone-chilling shrieks tore through the clamor.

Flet soldiers froze in mid stride and clutched their ears. "Drefids have come. That means—"

"Our archers have failed."

"Then our defenses are undone," he said. "Fall back, flet soldiers! Fall back to the west wall. Alert the Sentinels! Protect the lords!"

— •••••••••••••••••••••• —

The Elvish High Council in Berinfell was the nerve center of the Elves, who resided across the many continents of Allyra. In the Great Hall of the Western Stronghold, the Elven Lords usually held court—but on this night there was a special celebration. Seven children had been born to the Elven Lords in the same year. It was considered something of a miracle. Now each of the children had reached the first-year mark, and it was customary to have a public ceremony.

The ceremony took place in the center of the hall, a grand, white marble room resembling an arboretum. The sweet notes of harps mingled with the music of flowing water passing through leafy tree branches into dappled pools around the wide chamber.

Among the marble columns and living trees that grew in the midst of the hall, more than one hundred guests had gathered. Knights and female warriors, flet soldiers and flet marshalls—all who could be spared from their duties on Berinfell's walls. Among them stood Gwar attendants, those whose families had long ago allied themselves with the Elves. There also stood Berinfell's mighty Sentinels. Descended from an ancient Elvish bloodline, the Sentinels were known to follow the old ways. Their woodcraft was second to none, and their usual missions took them far and wide on tasks considered too dangerous for the typical knight. Sentinels rarely gathered together in one place, but even they would not miss the historic events of the ceremony.

Elrain Galadhon, the high cleric, emerged from the back of the hall.

He stepped between the tall white thrones of the Seven Lords and approached a white altar marbled with bright silver. He turned around just as the Elven Lords and their spouses approached. They were dressed in white and gird with ceremonial golden swords. And in their arms, they carried their precious children. All eyes turned to the children.

Perhaps it was the pageantry of the event or the special splendor of the setting; perhaps it was the pristine innocence and beauty of the children; or it might have been the location of the Western Stronghold, almost entirely surrounded by thick trees, two and a half miles—nearly a full league—from the eastern wall and the front gate. For whatever reason, no one in the hall heard the distant sounds of battle. In fact, it wasn't until just after the high cleric had waved the ceremonial scepter over the last lord's child that one of the Sentinels noticed something was amiss.

Elle stepped down from the dais and walked curiously toward the arched entryway of the Great Hall. The Sentinel glanced out the window. The trees outside were still. *Odd*, she thought.

Then she heard a steady cadence of boots on a stone floor. And when the shadows appeared at the end of the hall—broad, brutish shadows, perhaps numbering in the hundreds—Elle knew. She turned to warn the others just as Warspider limbs crashed through the stained glass windows in the back of the hall.

———— •••••••• •••••••• •••••••• ————

Flet Marshall Brynn and Grimwarden rushed to the long passage leading to Berinfell's Great Hall. But as they neared it they knew something was wrong. "No music," said the burly Grimwarden, his square jaw taut.

There'd always been sweet music cascading from the Great Hall into the surrounding passages. Brynn turned and signaled to the flet soldiers behind her. They silently drew their short swords and siege axes and approached the Great Hall in formation.

They needn't have bothered. The massive chamber—normally alive with warm light and sparkling colors—was now darkened by smoke and night. Columns toppled, broken, and charred; ancient trees hewed and burned; once-magnificent windows shattered. And everywhere, corpses. Twisted, broken, burned, or bleeding bodies were piled in great heaps and strewn wildly about the vast chamber. It seemed a legion of soldiers had met their fate.

Grimwarden entered the hall and stooped at the smoldering hulk of a dead soldier. "Gwar," he muttered. "One of ours, by the silver armor."

"Yes," Brynn agreed. "Many of our own Gwar attendants were slain. But see, the sable armor is most numerous. Most of these Gwar bodies are from the Spider King's legions."

Grimwarden nodded as he scanned the carnage. "And yet I fear we will still be counting Elven dead long after the Gwar have been removed."

"This was not just a battle of iron," Brynn muttered. "Rarely have I seen such carnage brought by fire." She pointed to a bulbous shape surrounded by segmented legs, curling in rigor. "Warspiders, too, they came through the windows. They would need such a force to assail the—" She never finished her sentence. Through the smoke and debris, she could just barely make out the white thrones in the back of the room.

"The Elven Lords?" Brynn whispered. "Olin?" She almost never used Grimwarden's first name, but the scene before her somehow made conventions of rank irrelevant. Their entire world as they knew it was about to change forever.

The flet soldiers filed in behind Grimwarden. "Search the room!" he yelled, fighting to suppress the panic rising within him. "Find the Elven Lords!"

The flet soldiers fanned out and began the grim work of sorting through the rubble, made all the worse in that some of the bodies they found were friends. But it was Grimwarden and Brynn who first dared to venture into the back of the Great Hall. They passed by the altar and tried desperately not to think about the horrors that might have occurred during the ceremony. But when at last they stood at the bottom of the wide steps before the dais, their world seemed to spin out of control. The Elven Lords were all seated in their thrones, propped up as if alive. But no breath stirred in their lungs. And there was no sign of the children.

"Why would they do this?" Brynn asked.

"They are taunting us," Grimwarden answered.

"Grimwarden!" one of the Elven knights called as he stumbled up the stairs to the dais. "We've found one of the Sentinels, and . . . she's alive!"

Tommy closed the book and found his mom standing in his doorway and smiling strangely. "How long you been standing there, Mom?"

"I'm not sure," she replied. "I don't think I've ever seen you read like that before."

"Read like what?"

"Well, you were so focused, that's all. I actually made faces at you, and you never looked up. It was like you weren't even here."

Like I wasn't even here. . . . Tommy wondered.

"Anyway," she said, "you should get some sleep. It'll be morning before you know it. And tomorrow is your last practice before Falcon Day."

"Okay, Mom, thanks." But in his mind, he thought, *Sleep. Yeah, right.*

Curious Customers

WHEN THEY heard about the bookstore reopening on Market Street, in Depauville, New York, Johnny and Autumn Briarman were far from impressed. Although they didn't live far away, bookstores were about as useful to them as washing machines. Why wash a perfectly good pair of jeans when you could wear them all week? No, reading was something they had to do, but never something they did— even in school—if they could avoid it. They were alike in that way.

But on the bus ride home from school, Johnny and Autumn saw that the plain, little store had been repainted. Now it looked a bit like a gingerbread house, and its old sign had been replaced with a thick, wooden placard that hung over the sidewalk: A Likely Story Book Shoppe.

Johnny shrugged and turned around.

Autumn looked a little closer. There was a handmade sign in the window: TODAY ONLY! A PRIZE FOR EVERYONE WHO COMES IN!

Autumn tapped her brother on the shoulder repeatedly. "Johnny, did you see that?"

"'S a bookstore, Sis," he said. "So what."

"But there was a little sign. Said anyone who comes in gets a prize."

"Yawn," he replied, patting a hand over his mouth. "Big deal. Probably just some book. What's a guy need a book for?"

"I dunno. Maybe to learn how to use all those power tools?"

Johnny chuckled.

"I think we should go check it out," said Autumn.

"You can."

"You know, . . ." said Autumn, a twinkle in her bright blue eyes, "the prize could be candy."

Johnny scratched his chin. "I guess . . . it wouldn't hurt to go in, just this once."

❊

"Where are you both going in such a hurry?" called Mrs. Briarman as two blond streaks whooshed out of the house and the screen door slammed shut.

"We'll be back before dinner!" Johnny yelled.

"I know," she replied, stepping to the door. "But where are you—?"

"To the new bookstore," was all Johnny said as they peeled out of the driveway on their bikes.

Bookstore? thought Mrs. Briarman. *Well, that can't be a bad thing. Can it?*

❊

Johnny would never admit it, but he was a bit nervous as they approached the entrance to A Likely Story Book Shoppe, although he didn't really know why. The door was propped open to welcome the mild afternoon air, as well as any passersby who might wander in. Johnny folded his hands once or twice—bike-chain grease from a little repair on the way and sweat making his hands slippery.

Johnny stopped a pace in front of her.

"What is it?" Autumn whispered.

Johnny jerked around. "Why are you whispering?"

"Why are you stopping?"

Johnny shrugged his shoulders, and Autumn nudged him on. "Just go, would ya!"

"What's the hurry?" he asked.

"Oh, brother," she said, blowing an S-shaped strand of blond hair out of her mouth and shouldering past him into the store.

Johnny was broad and muscular for his age. Though his own lack of courage made him feel anything but strong, he frightened some of the smaller kids at school and was even thought of as a bully. But he dutifully followed her into the store.

Once inside, the two squinted in the low light and found themselves enveloped in scents, a strange combination of musty old house, fresh-cut flowers, and warm sugar cookies. There were couches and easy chairs. And, of course, books. Books everywhere: books filling shelves, book towers climbing haphazardly from tabletop to the ceiling, books spilling off reading desks, books in stacks on the floor. The crazy organization reminded Johnny of his room at home . . . minus the books, of course.

Brother and sister walked down the first aisle and scanned row after row of bound editions and paperbacks. They didn't see too many titles they recognized. A lot of the books looked really old.

"Can I help you find something?"

Johnny and Autumn spun around. A woman smiled at them. The woman had red hair, freckles, and the most wonderful green eyes. She wore a white and yellow sundress and a white ribbon in her hair.

"We're just . . ." Autumn couldn't think what to say.

"Reading," said Johnny. "Err, looking."

"I see. Well, you've come to the right place for that."

Autumn stared at the floor. Johnny let his eyes trace along the tangled path of books as if it were a maze.

"Oh, I see," said the woman. "You don't really like to read much, do you?"

"We did come to the old store a couple of years back," Johnny jumped in, saving them both embarrassment. He thought the bookstore lady was pretty, in an older-person sort of way. "It used to look kinda . . . uh, lame, but now I almost feel like I like the place."

"Almost feel like you like the bookstore?" the lady replied. For a moment she had a misty, faraway look in her eyes and wore an odd smile. "That's good," she said. "That's uncommonly kind of you."

Autumn asked, "So do you own this place, Mrs. . . . um?"

"Annelle Brookeheart is my name. But call me Nelly," she said. "Look after it, I suppose you could say. I just watch and make sure customers find what they need."

"A fine thing for a business owner to say," Johnny said, trying to sound older.

"Why, thank you," replied Nelly with a chuckle. "But 'owning' is such a misunderstood term. I'm more like a guardian or . . . or a steward. Yes, a steward, that's it." She paused. "I like to think I introduce people to their dreams."

Something about the way she spoke these last words made Johnny and Autumn feel odd. Not threatened or even uncomfortable, just different. It was as if Nelly had some unique authority, a peculiar confidence, or perhaps a secret that only she knew.

"And only young adult fiction, to be exact. No grown-up novels here."

Just then three kids came bounding in through the front door.

"Would you excuse me?" Nelly asked, and then turned to greet the other children. "How was school, Sam?"

Listening enthusiastically to their school-day tales, Nelly went to work helping the new kids find a few books, making her own suggestions of course, and answering questions. The most urgent one seemed to be: "Do we get a prize again today, Miss Nelly?"

She smiled, went back behind the counter, and bent down. Johnny and Autumn couldn't see what she was doing, but they heard a muted thump. In a few heartbeats, Nelly returned with several ice-cream cones. She doled them out, each child happily getting his or her favorite. Then Nelly turned back to Johnny and Autumn.

Autumn raised an eyebrow. "Have they gotten prizes before?"

Nelly put a hand to her lips. "That's kind of an inside joke here. The sign says, 'Today Only,' but every day is kind of a prize day."

"It's a good day for ice cream," said Johnny.

"Indeed it is," she said, going back behind the counter. "So, what can I get for the two of you?"

Looking through the choices, Autumn said, "Cookie dough would be nice."

"Chocolate-chip cookie dough in a waffle cone. Mmm . . . good choice." Nelly wrinkled her nose. "But . . . are you sure that's all you want, Autumn? A bit of sugar and frozen milk, melted and gone in moments? I might have something much better."

"Really? Hey . . . wait a second—how did you know her name?" Johnny asked. The two kids looked at her, confused.

"Come with me," replied Nelly, looking first to Johnny and then to Autumn. "You may find I know many things about you and your . . . brother."

8

Geographical Anomaly

NELLY LED them behind the counter, through a door, and into a round sunlit parlor. Overflowing bookcases leaned against the walls that didn't have windows. Dust particles whirled and danced in the sunbeams, giving the room a strange quality.

Nelly motioned for Johnny and Autumn to have a seat on one of the dark wood benches by the windows. She walked over to a large chest on the other side of the room.

"Autumn, look at that picture!" Johnny pointed to a large oil painting hung in a thick gilded frame just above the chest. It depicted a spectacular red bird perched upon a tall castle turret. It was not red like a cardinal, but a richer, deeper red. And it was not a common yard bird but an extremely large bird of prey.

"Pretty," said Autumn.

"Pretty?" Johnny shook his head. "You ever seen a red eagle before?"

"It's not red. It's burgundy."

"'S a type of red, Autumn." Johnny grunted. "You ever seen a bird like that? A hawk? Falcon?"

"No."

"It's a scarlet raptor," said Nelly, closing the chest, turning, and sliding something the kids couldn't see behind her back. "Very rare. You don't find them at all in this country."

"Cool," said Johnny.

"You like unusual creatures, do you, Johnny?"

"Sure, I guess."

"Hmmm," Nelly replied. "That's good to know. This is my private reading room. After closing up for the night, I come here and read for hours and hours." As she spoke, she seemed to be searching for something.

"Something wrong?" asked Autumn.

"No . . . no," said Nelly. "All's . . . well. Now, are you two ready for your prize?"

The siblings nodded and leaned forward. They hadn't seen what Nelly took out of the chest—but, if it was better than ice cream, it had to be good.

Nelly hesitated a moment more, and then took the hidden item from behind her back. She held out a very old book bound in dark leather.

"A book?" asked Autumn.

"I told you," said Johnny. He huffed and leaned back, putting his hand behind the bench. "Whoa!!" He jerked his hand back out. At the same moment, and from the same general direction Johnny had put his hand, there came an odd, trilling squeal.

"*Eww*. What is it?" Autumn stood up and backed away from the bench.

"A mouse, a rat? I don't know." In an instant, his face morphed from surprise to curiosity. "It was furry and really warm. And it squeaked."

"Oh dear," said Nelly. "I think you'd better go."

"What–what is it?" asked Autumn.

Nelly put the book in Johnny's arms and ushered the kids hastily from the room. "Dreadfully sorry about that," she said. "But I can't have one of you going home with a bite or scratch."

"*Eww*. It was a mouse," said Autumn.

"Well, not exactly, my dear," said Nelly as they neared the store entrance. "Now, I wish I could explain more. Just take the book home. Read it thoroughly. We will talk again."

"I'd rather have ice cream," said Johnny.

"I'll tell you what," said Nelly, "if you don't like this book, next time you come in, I'll give you two free scoops of ice cream."

"Deal!" Johnny said.

"Now, I need to go, and so do you. Everyone else has already left."

Johnny and Autumn looked around. Everyone had left. The door to the bookstore closed behind them with the ringing of a little bell. A Sorry, We Are Closed sign appeared in the window.

❋

Nelly Brookeheart raced back to the parlor. "Where are you?" she demanded.

A soft trill came from behind a bookcase.

"I hear you," she said, storming across the room. She reached back behind the case and felt around. "Come on, get over here. Ah, there you are . . . gotcha."

She gently pulled her hand out. Something fuzzy and very warm nuzzled between her fingers and around her hand. It looked up expectantly with very large dark eyes.

"Shame on you," said Nelly. "You know better than to scare the humans. I'm sending you home tonight!"

❋

"Some gift this is," Johnny scoffed as he gave the book back to Autumn. They stashed their bikes inside the old hay barn and walked back to the house. "I'm looking forward to those extra scoops of ice cream."

"Well, I think it's cool," Autumn said, fingering the old leather cover.

"It's a book," Johnny said, grabbing the book from her and holding it up in front of her face. "You know, a book for reading?"

"I know, but it looks old. Don't you wonder what it's about?"

"What I wonder is how that lady knew your name. Maybe she's a stalker or something."

"Johnny!"

"I'm serious. There are crazy people out there these days."

"Johnny, she's not a stalker."

"I'm just saying."

Autumn shot him a stare and he knew better than to press further. "All right, she's not a stalker. Here, give it to me."

"No, you don't want to read." Autumn pulled the book from Johnny and turned back toward the barn. She opened the cover and flipped the first sheet to a page with a beautiful ink drawing of a thick forest. The scene captivated her immediately, so much that she stopped walking. The leaves of the trees were amazingly detailed, almost as if she could see them moving in the breeze. Birds sat on tree limbs, and insects fluttered about. A brook meandered around rocks and a fawn stood alert in the distance. And there, peering around a tree, was a strange face—

"Give me that!" Johnny yanked the book away.

"Hey! Give it back!"

But Johnny was too quick and too strong and folded the book against his chest. Autumn beat on his back relentlessly as Johnny passed her and jogged toward the barn.

"All right, all right! Enough!" Johnny raised his hand to stop the assault. "I'm not giving it back unless we can both read it."

Seeing as how she couldn't get the book back by any other means, Autumn said, "Okay, we'll both read it."

"I can't believe we're fighting over some stupid book. Don't tell my friends."

The two stepped through the barn doors and climbed the ladder to the loft, brushing away newly formed cobwebs that clung to their faces. Amidst the ruins of stale hay, they found a place to sit and laid an old piece of canvas in front of them. Afternoon light poured in through the wide cracks of the planks behind them, and a small spider slowly descended from a thread affixed to a beam up above. The siblings placed the book in front of them. Then Autumn opened to the drawing once more.

"Where'd he go?" Autumn burst out.

"What? Where'd who go?"

"There was a face." Autumn pointed to a tree in the drawing. "It was right there! I saw it."

"A face?" Johnny examined the tree.

"Johnny, there was a face right there. I promise. Just before you pulled the book away."

"There's a deer and some birds. Autumn, you're totally imagining stuff."

"I'm not! I'm serious! There was a face of a . . . of a . . ."

"See, you're crazy."

"Johnny!" She punched his arm. "You have to believe me! It was like an elf or something."

"An elf? One of Santa's?"

"It's not funny." Autumn turned and folded her arms, hot tears welling up in her eyes. He never trusted her.

"Aw, look, Autumn. I'm sorry. I didn't mean it." He grabbed her shoulder. "C'mon, let's turn the page."

She didn't budge.

"Autumn . . ."

She lifted her chin up further.

"I'm sorry," Johnny breathed out. "There, happy?"

"Mean it," she said.

"I'm really, really sorry. I shouldn't have said the Santa thing."

"And?"

"What else do you want?" Johnny threw his hands up.

"For not believing me, Johnny?"

"All right! I'm sorry for not believing you."

"Really sorry?"

"Yes, really, really sorry. Autumn, can we please read the stupid book now?"

She turned to face him. "It's not stupid."

"Autumn," he pleaded, completely exasperated with her.

She looked down at the drawing. "Fine." She reached for the book and flipped the page.

In the center of the next aged sheet of paper was the title, *The History of Berinfell*, and beneath in smaller print, *The Chronicles of the Elf Lords and Their Kin*.

"See! I told you there were Elves!"

"The Elves of Berinfell actually." Johnny smiled and turned the page. They flipped past what appeared to be a table of contents, laid out with big numbers and strange titles, then turned to a second drawing with the title *9680 Founding of Allyra* and a section of text. A path bordered by briars lead to a gentle waterfall adorned by a thicket of tall pine trees—*amazingly lifelike for a drawing*, they both thought. And beneath the waterfall, a cave. More like a narrow mouth set to one side of the falls than a fairy-tale cave entrance.

"Huh." Johnny sat back. "That reminds me . . ." *No, she'll think I'm nuts.*

"Of the cave in the woods!" Autumn finished.

"What? Hey, don't finish my sentences. That's not even what I was going to—"

She ignored him. "Johnny, think about it. The path, the briars, even the waterfall and the pine trees! That's exactly like—"

"You are nuts, Autumn!"

"No, I'm not!" She'd had enough of his insults.

In a flash, Autumn flipped the book shut, picked it up, and leaped from the loft.

"Autumn!"

She landed with a soft thud in a stack of square bales that tumbled over as she scampered down.

"Where are you going?" Johnny yelled and started down the ladder. Once out the barn door, Autumn was almost to the house. "Autumn!"

"I'm telling Mom!" she yelled and then stormed through the screen door into the kitchen.

Mrs. Briarman stood at the counter, marinating chicken for dinner, her hands dripping with Italian dressing. Her brown hair was pulled up, and she wore a paint-smeared sweatshirt with the sleeves cut off at the elbow.

"Mom!"

"Autumn, inside voice," she said without looking from her work.

"Mom, Johnny is being—is being . . ."

"Have a seat, dear."

Just then Johnny burst in through the door. "She's lying!"

"Autumn hasn't said anything yet, John," Mrs. Briarman countered.

"But she's going to! And it's not true!"

"You don't ever believe me!" Autumn blasted him. "And you know it's true about the cave!"

Mrs. Briarman turned. "The cave?"

The room grew silent.

"Now you've done it," Johnny said through clenched teeth.

"Oh, I wish your father had never given you permission to go there. You know it makes me nervous. You shouldn't have gone there alone," Mrs. Briarman said.

"But we didn't, Mom!" Johnny retorted.

"I don't want to hear it, John."

"But, Mom, he's telling the truth," Autumn defended. "I'm talking about this book." She offered it up. "It talks about the cave in our back woods. I'm sure of it."

"Where did you get that?" Mrs. Briarman asked.

"At the bookstore," Autumn said. "A Likely Story Book Shoppe."

"And with what money?" Mrs. Briarman was growing more concerned.

"It was a gift from the owner, Nelly," Autumn explained.

Mrs. Briarman looked to Johnny.

"It's true, Mom. She was really nice and gave us the book."

Mrs. Briarman accepted the answer, although still wary. "Well, it looks a little old to be describing our property, my gems. Of course, the cave has been there a long time." Mrs. Briarman washed her hands and dried them on a kitchen towel before joining Autumn at the table. Taking the tome in her hands, she flipped open to the first page. Johnny slid into the chair beside his sister.

"Let's see what we have here," Mrs. Briarman said, flipping the thin sheet and examining the drawing. "Fine work."

Johnny and Autumn looked on eagerly. It was their cave. Autumn had voiced the conclusion Johnny had been too skeptical to verbalize. But he knew what he had seen. There was no mistaking the landmarks and the way they were described in such amazing detail. Unless, of course, every waterfall-hidden-cave appeared in the woods the same way.

"*Pioneers of the Western United States*"—Mrs. Briarman began—"by M. S. Ward, Esquire."

Thinking their mother had made one of those jokes that adults thought were so funny, Johnny and Autumn stared at their mother. If she was joking, she hid it awfully well.

"Foreword: Those who braved the treacherous journey westward, leaving their homes in search of destiny, wealth, and the unknown, faced many hardships. . . ." Mrs. Briarman looked up. "Impressive. This is some fine reading you two are doing. I'm thinking you can go to that bookstore anytime you wish."

The siblings were speechless, mouths agape.

"And where's this section about your cave?"

Autumn stood up cautiously and sidled next to her mom, flipping back to the opening section. *9680 Founding of Allyra* had been replaced by *Foreword*, and the text was completely different. It was as if an entirely different book sat before her. Even the drawing was not the same—now a grand vista of the Rocky Mountains.

"I—I don't understand," Autumn said, perplexed.

"What is it, sweetie?"

"It's not there." Her mind was racing, trying in vain to sort it out. Johnny, too, was perplexed, thinking as fast as he could.

"Go ahead and show me," Mrs. Briarman instructed.

"No, I mean it was right here," Autumn stated. She flipped the pages back and forth.

"Let me explain, Mom," Johnny said, a bit distantly, Autumn noted. "She thought our cave was formed the same way the Rockies were, with the plates in the earth and all. But I told her no. This is upstate New York, not Colorado. She's nuts."

Autumn looked to her brother and then to her mom, then back to Johnny. *Thanks, bro*, she thought. "So . . . our cave *wasn't* made by the same gee-o-more-phical—"

"Geographical," corrected Mrs. Briarman.

"*Geographical* am-o-mally—"

"Anomaly," she helped again.

Autumn laughed in spite of herself. "*Anomaly* that caused the Rocky Mountains to form?"

"Not at all, sweetie," Mrs. Briarman said. "The Rockies formed through the collision of tectonic plates. The cave on our back property was probably formed through erosion as glaciers receded, or just from runoff as is the case with the softer sandstone."

"Oh, thanks, Mom," Autumn said absently.

"Thanks Mom," Johnny added.

"That's it?"

"Yeah, thanks." Autumn folded up the book.

"Wait a second." Mrs. Briarman put her hand on the cover. "What's going on with you two?"

"What do you mean?" Johnny asked, getting nervous.

Mrs. Briarman eyed them both for a second. "Are you playing a trick on me? Where is your father?" She stood up and looked out the window smiling.

"No, Mom. Everything's cool," Johnny assured her. "Argument settled."

She looked to him. "You two never resolve things that fast."

"I guess I just wanted to hear you say it, Mom," Autumn clarified. She pulled the book away and made for the door. "Thanks, Mom!"

"Yeah, thanks, Mom!" Johnny echoed as they let the screen door slam behind them.

"You two are up to something!" Mrs. Briarman hollered after them. "Wait, you aren't thinking of going into that cave, are you?"

"Uh, well, no . . . not unless . . ."

But Mrs. Briarman knew better. "At least take the dog!"

9

Lighting the Blue Beacons

"MISS SIMONSON, see me after class," Mr. Wallace said as Kat walked in. *It's about my test*. She just knew it. What else could it be? But the uncertainty ping-ponging around her mind for the remaining forty-nine minutes of American history was what Mr. Wallace wanted to say about her test. His first take was that she'd gotten all the answers correct. Maybe all he wanted to do was congratulate her for her unprecedented success. But that was just it. Kat hadn't broken the "C-barrier" in American history the whole marking period. Surely Mr. Wallace would be suspicious. *But he couldn't think I was cheating. It was all in my head. Ah!* It was maddening.

Kat fidgeted with her hair incessantly, so much so that Darren Lions behind her smacked her in the back of the head.

"Ow!"

"Cut it out, would ya, Smurf? You're annoying me!"

Instead, Kat rested her elbows on the table, leaned forward, placed her chin just above her elbows, cupping her ears with her hands.

When the bell rang and the classroom emptied, Kat was both nervous and relieved . . . nervous for the conference with Mr. Wallace, and relieved because her next class was study hall. Alone time. No matter the outcome with her teacher, Kat needed time to think. The voices in her head had not returned, but there was no disputing that they had been there. Voices in the head weren't exactly healthy; this much she knew.

"Miss Simonson?"

"Yes, Mr. Wallace?"

"Have a seat," he said, pointing to a chair next to his desk.

Kat put her backpack down and braced herself. She hated confrontation. "If it's about my test—"

"Yes, it is."

"I can explain—"

"Kat, I believe this is your first one hundred since, well, since I've known you."

Kat sat speechless when she saw the bright-red A-plus on the test cover.

"Well done."

"Thank you, Mr. Wallace."

"But I do have a certain discrepancy I'd like to discuss with you."

Great, here it comes. "Discrepancy?"

"Your answers were exactly like another student's . . . in fact, like ten other students'."

"Excuse me?"

"It would appear that either you spontaneously copied off ten of your friends across the room without me noticing, or each one of the other ten students copied off you for one of their answers, again, without my noticing."

Kat was beyond nervous now. "Uh . . . Mr. Wallace . . . I-uh . . ."

"Miss Simonson, I really don't have a choice here."

She looked down into her lap, hands clammy and folded. *I'm getting expelled. No more Blue Girl to freak anyone out.* "I understand."

"No, I don't think you do."

Suddenly, a massive, leather-bound book plopped into her lap. She was so startled she almost jumped out of her chair. "What is this? I . . . I mean . . . what are you talking about?"

"I believe you have what some of us would call a gift, Kat."

Kat was completely dismayed now. *What? No lecture? No detention?*

"A gift?"

Mr. Wallace peeked over his shoulder to make certain no one else was in the room. "Just read the book, Kat. I think you might connect with it in more ways than one."

"So you're not kicking me out of class?"

"Read the book, Kat. You have study hall next, right?"

"Uh, yeah."

"No time to start like the present."

Kat got up and tucked the book under her arm, all the while eyeing Mr. Wallace as if he'd just escaped a mental ward. "Thanks." *I think,* she added to herself.

�֍

Kat shoved her backpack under her desk in room B24 and sat down as far away from the other students as possible. Ms. Reedley sat at the monitor's table and graded papers. Kat's cell vibrated and she pulled it out, seeing she had an incoming text from her mom: *new bskeeper pickn u up aftr schl. name Anna. drvn the tahoe.*

Great, she thought. *Another one.* Kat frowned and crinkled her nose. Room B24 was one of three rooms constructed from the old gym locker room when the building was renovated a few years back. Now carpeted and repainted, B24 still smelled like a locker room. The bell rang, and the rest of the students filed in. Ms. Reedley removed her glasses and glared at them until they stopped talking. Her stare could be best described as somewhere between a rabid German shepherd and the warden at the state penitentiary. A hush fell over everyone in the room.

Kat settled down and laid the heavy book from Mr. Wallace on her desk. *The History of Berinfell. Great,* Kat thought. *History.* She squared her shoulders and flipped open the worn cover. *And old history at that.* It even smelled old. She flipped a few pages. There wasn't any of the usual publisher and copyright stuff, but she paused to admire the next page: an amazingly detailed sketch.

Kat loved to draw. She was a natural with charcoal, pen and ink, or even just pencil. But she had never seen a sketch such as this one. It was an orchard of tall, broadleaf trees laden with blossoms and fruit. Splendid patches of grass and long-stemmed flowers wavered at the base of the dark trees. It was as if the trees were wading waist-high in the middle of an ocean of foliage. Kat felt like she could almost smell the fragrant pollen from all the blossoms and hear the muted buzz of the bloom-hopping bees. *I want to go there*, she thought. After a long look, she turned the page.

She leafed through several pages until she settled somewhere in the middle of the book. *Hm*, she thought. *This text looks kind of raised, as if it has its own texture.* She brushed her thumb across the first letters. The lights in the study hall flickered, the temperature climbed well past the 78-air-conditioned degrees, and the smell of smoke filled the room. A lick of fire appeared on the page and began to grow. Kat shut the book in a hurry. The lights stopped flickering. It was a comfortable temperature again, and the room smelled like gym socks once more.

Kat looked around. But to her astonishment, no one was staring at her as she thought they would. They carried on as usual—reading, passing notes, whispery giggling—completely oblivious. *Didn't they see?* Even Ms. Reedley still sat grading papers, without so much as an eyelash flutter from her lethal gaze. Kat opened the book once more, found her page, and touched the text. No sooner had her fingertips brushed the lettering than the temperature rose, the lights dimmed, and the air filled once more with the smell of smoke. Fire leaped up from the page, but still no one in the room so much as flinched.

This time, Kat didn't close the book.

More and more fire burst through the pages. It danced along the ceiling of the classroom before dropping to patches on the floor, some right at the feet of her classmates. Kat held her breath as huge marble columns rose up from the pages, followed by shards of broken glass, streams of water, and pieces of timber. Room B24 melted away.

Kat found herself sitting next to a huge basin of water, like a fountain, in an enormous hall. She could even feel the cool spray from the trickling water. But there was something terribly wrong in this scene. Dark smoke rose from many fires and swirled on the ceiling. It was hard to see clearly or breathe. But everywhere she looked, things were broken or burning. And there were lifeless forms strewn about the hall. Bodies. But other forms entered the scene. Some crowded around the bodies. Others ran from one place to another as if on urgent errands. Kat heard voices, turned, and saw that someone nearby was wounded and others were tending to her.

"What?" Kat muttered to herself. "They . . . they have pointed ears!"

"Please, Elle!" Flet Marshall Brynn prompted, wiping the excess saliva away from the wounded Sentinel's lips. "I'm sorry to press you, but we must know what happened here. Tell us what you know . . . anything you can remember."

Elle lay on a litter surrounded by Elven warriors. She tried to speak but coughed harshly through the first few syllables. Fresh blood trickled from the corner of her mouth.

"Break out the rest of those windows on the other side!" Guardmaster Olin Grimwarden yelled at the flet soldiers who milled about the ruins of the Great Hall.

Flet soldiers exchanged pained glances as they trod into the wreckage. They hoisted large pieces of marble and charred wood and hurled them through their beloved windows.

"Now," said Brynn. "Tell us, Elle, what did you see?"

"They came up the main hall"—whispered the Sentinel—"and through the glass: Warspiders, Gwar soldiers, Drefids . . ." Her voice, now thin and weak, fell away. Her ceremonial robes were torn and her ribs badly bruised and broken. It was all she could do to stay conscious. "We had no time." Elle coughed. Brynn offered her another sip of water, but she denied it. "The guards barely had time to draw their swords . . . many were cut down right where they stood."

"Go on," said Grimwarden, his own fear making him impatient.

"It was so sudden. We had no time." Elle coughed and scowled. "They just kept coming."

Grimwarden frowned. "Surely the Seven Lords fought."

Elle's eyes grew large and fierce, and for a moment her strength seemed to return. "They fought like lions," she said. "Galadhost was the first to recognize the danger. His twin blades took many a Gwar head! And Tisa, she nearly sent the hall up in flames. In spite of the overwhelming numbers of Warspiders, Gwar, and Drefids, the lords might have still turned the tide of the battle. But they could not advance on the enemy without leaving their offspring unprotected. The lords were slain as they defended their children."

The children? Grimwarden looked sadly up at the thrones. Something troubled him. Behind the thrones, hidden and unknown to all but the most elite Elves, was the tunnel entrance to the ancient Nightwish Caverns. *Why hadn't the Seven Lords taken their children and escaped?*

"Elle, what became of . . . of the children?" asked Brynn. "They are not here among the dead."

Elle winced at the memory. "After the Seven Lords fell, it was only a matter of time before the Gwar gained control of the hall. We were overwhelmed. The Drefid commanders took the infants. They placed them in satchels on the Warspiders, and the war party left through the windows."

"Why would they leave?" asked Brynn. "Had they stayed, they could have cut into the heart of the city and hemmed us in."

"They accomplished their mission," muttered Grimwarden.

"What?"

"They came for the children," he said. "Why? I cannot say. But a growing fear gnaws within me. The Spider King now holds the end of the lordship bloodline in his hands."

Elle groaned. Her voice came out in an agonized wail. "I failed them!"

"You have not failed," Brynn consoled her, placing a hand gently on her shoulder. "You live to tell what the Spider King wanted known only by the dead in this room. He is the one who failed. You are strong."

"Neither strong nor smart enough," she whispered. "Ah, treachery!"

"Treachery?" Brynn stood, sympathy vanishing from her expression. "Treachery in Berinfell? I don't believe it."

"How else could they get past the Gap? The walls? How could they know just where to hit us . . . or that the Seven would all be here?" Her eyes narrowed. "It was the Gwar attendants, I'm sure of it."

"Come now, Elle, surely you don't believe that!" Brynn bristled. "We've come too far as a people to go back to antiquated notions and judg—"

"Who else, then?" Elle asked. "One of our own?"

"Just as likely," said Brynn.

Grimwarden cleared his throat. "I would be inclined to agree with Elle," he said, "but there might be a third possibility."

"Wisps," Brynn muttered.

"Precisely." Grimwarden gripped the pommel of his rychesword, his knuckles whitened. "We ignorantly believed they were all dead. How simple it would have been for the enemy. Just lie in wait for one of our scouting patrols and replace a true Elf with a treason-minded Wisp."

"Guardmaster Grimwarden!" a flet soldier yelled from the hall's entrance. Grimwarden raised a hand. The Elf approached at once, delivering his news as he came. "The east gate of the city has been breached!"

"What?" Grimwarden spun around, furious. "But we have more than a battalion there . . . and archers."

The soldier at the entrance was clearly beside himself, growing paler with his commander's response. "The gate itself is thrown down," he said. "But our forces were able to waylay the enemy in Sentinel Garden. There, we hold the higher ground. But for how long, I cannot say. What are your orders?"

Thrown down? Grimwarden rose slowly, eyeing the messenger and then surveying the body-strewn hall with great sorrow. So much loss, so much death. If he did not act quickly, even more innocent lives would be lost.

Brynn sensed Grimwarden's distress.

"Sir"—said the soldier again—"your orders?"

Grimwarden still did not answer. The Gap had been crossed . . . the city walls overrun. The Seven Lords murdered, their infant children taken to some horrible end. And now, the final gate thrown down. The Spider King had not come to defeat the Elves; he'd come to wipe them from the face of Allyra.

Grimwarden glanced once more past the thrones. He knew what he must do. But he shuddered to think what it might cost, what dire destiny he would bind his people to. And if they survived, he knew that history would not reflect his decision kindly. He would be known as the coward who led the Children of the Light into the abysses of the deep . . . and what of the light? If he could not find a way to get his people sunlight . . . he shuddered to think.

Grimwarden straightened his back. "You are Xander, aren't you? Belarius and Thenna's boy?"

"Yes, sir."

"Then, Xander, gird yourself for this task. For never in the long history of our beloved city has this command been spoken, and it makes my heart heavy to do so." He waited a deep breath and said, "Light the blue beacons."

Xander's mouth hung slack. He muttered in shock, "The blue beacons . . . but that means—"

"I know very well what it means," Grimwarden barked. His prominent jaw jutted out even more as he spoke. "But we will not be wiped like a stain from this world. We will live to fight another day. Light the blue beacons, NOW!"

Xander sprinted away. Grimwarden turned to Brynn. "Can you get to your remaining commanders and order them to gather reinforcements to Sentinel Garden? We must have time for the women and children to get here."

"I will make it happen," she replied. "But we cannot allow the citizens to travel unguarded and by open ways. The enemy will slaughter them."

Grimwarden was thoughtful. "No, we cannot. Brynn, you must lead them. See to it that your commanders take a full battalion or more to the garden, but muster at least a troop for yourself. Shepherd our people here by whatever concealed ways you can find. We are going underground."

Brynn crossed her wrists and bowed. "I will bring our people here safely."

Grimwarden bowed. But even as he watched Brynn depart from the hall, he thought more on what she'd said. *We cannot allow the citizens to travel unguarded and by open ways. The enemy will slaughter them.* If the enemy saw their route of escape, they would pour after them like a pack of wolves trailing a wounded gazelle. Grimwarden's eyes flared, then narrowed. A final piece to the puzzle had fallen into place.

10

Leaving the Sunlight

Grimwarden stood alone behind the thrones of the seven slain lords. The doorway leading to the Royal Chambers was half torn from its hinges. There was no escape that way. But to the left of that arch, the wide stone wall had been emblazoned with an etching of a great tree. He studied the tree: its thick, tapering, gray trunk; sprawling limbs; and vast canopy of foliage. He strode up to a certain leaf. It appeared no different from the others. But when he touched the leaf, it slid away from his fingertip and receded an inch into the wall. One by one and in the proper combination, he pressed seven leaves. From somewhere behind the wall there came a light tinkling of notes as if from a wind chime.

Dust fell away from the outline of a wide arched doorway in the wall. Taking with it the roots, trunk, and thickest branches of the etched tree, the door slid backward until it was lost in shadow, revealing thick, gaping darkness . . . but not for long. A green torch kindled on the inner wall. Grimwarden stepped back and raised his spear. Nine yards into the passage, another torch sprang to life. Then another. Soon a long, curling tunnel was revealed.

"*Humph,*" Grimwarden muttered to himself as he lowered his spear. "I didn't expect torches." Then he called back over his shoulder to one of the flet soldiers attending to the bodies of the Seven Lords.

The young Elven soldier came and stood by his commander and gaped when he saw the passage.

"Graylan," Grimwarden said. "Soon, all living Elves of Berinfell will travel this passage, and we will depart from our homeland. It is only fitting, however, that the Seven Lords lead the way one final time."

"Sir? The lords knew of this passage?" Graylan shook his head.

"Yes, . . . they knew." Grimwarden's voice became strained. The rims of his eyelids reddened.

"But why didn't they . . . I mean, couldn't they have . . ."

"So I thought as well, lad. But the lords were far wiser. The horde the Spider King sent here was an assassination force. They would have pursued our lords to the ends of Allyra. Had our lords fled, the hidden passage to Nightwish Caverns would have been uncovered. Our only real escape would have been lost, and the race of Elves might have been blotted out forever."

"May Ellos rest their souls," said Graylan.

"He will, but now the lords shall enter. Do what you can to quickly prepare the bodies. Then you and your men take the Seven Lords and follow the path. Go past the Guardian, over the Jade Bow, and through the Hall of Echoes."

"The Jade Bow? Hall of Echoes? How will I—?"

"You'll know." He took Graylan by the arms. "Bear them safely at last to the Nightwish Cavern. In due time, we will lay the Seven Lords to rest among the only flowers in Allyra that bloom in the dark."

"Yes, sir, but ah . . . how soon until you and the rest follow?"

Grimswarden looked past the thrones to the entrance of the Great Hall. "I wish I knew."

As Graylan went back to the team of flet soldiers preparing the Seven Lords, Grimwarden searched the hall for a certain warrior. At last he spotted the Elf he wanted. In the smoke and shadow, there was just a burly silhouette, but it had to be him. No one else could heave such heavy debris around like him. "Travin!" he shouted across the hall.

The silhouette stopped, looked up, and then rushed over to the commander. Travin was a head shorter than Grimwarden but much broader across the back and chest. He had such huge forearms and fists that he never wore bracers or gauntlets. His ears were pointed like all Elves', but his skin tone had more gray than most. He was, in fact, the offspring of a Berinfell Gwar and an Elf maiden. But Grimwarden had no doubts about this warrior. Travin had proved himself faithful to Berinfell and sturdy in battle.

"Sir?" Travin was still out of breath.

"The blue beacons are lit," said Grimwarden. "Flet Marshall Brynn is even now seeking out women, children, and all citizenry not fit to fight. She will do what she can to lead them here safely. She'll need to stay hidden, keep the enemy's eyes off them. But for such a large group, moving at once, that will be terribly difficult. The Spider King's main force is yet held at bay at Sentinel Garden, but likely not for long. We need to buy our people more time."

"You will need a diversion," said Travin.

"Yes," replied Grimwarden, his voice more like a growl.

"Tell me what you want me to do."

Grimwarden took Travin aside and told him the plan. Travin listened carefully and let out a low whistle. "I will need at least two hundred," he said.

Grimwarden scanned the hall. "Leave only the flet soldiers necessary for our task here. Take the rest. That will give you about seventy-five."

"I will scour what's left of the defenses between here and the marketplace and find the others I need." Travin turned to leave. "We will make the enemy turn his head."

"I have no doubt that you will, but you must be swift," said Grimwarden. "If the garden defense fails before your diversion, the Spider King will drive our people like cattle to a slaughter."

"The battle is far from over, Grimwarden." Travin looked up and crossed his wrist over his armored chest. "Endurance and Victory."

"Endurance and Victory," Grimwarden replied. He grasped him by the arm. "Travin, one more thing."

"Aye?"

"Should the enemy discover our ruse, I want you to seek the trees and, by the hidden ways, at last enter Nightwish Cavern. Whatever you accomplish, do not pursue the enemy back here. Dead heroes do nothing to protect their people tomorrow."

——— •·······•·•···•··•··• ———

Bleak, uneventful hours had passed. The painstaking search through the debris of the Great Hall was now complete. Only a handful of flet soldiers and Grimwarden, their commander, remained impatiently waiting. He stared beyond the jagged frame of the windows. A cold wind out of the northwest howled outside and bent the dark trees. They creaked and groaned. Limbs fell and leaves swirled, but no tree fell. *Like us*, Grimwarden thought. *We are battered and bent but not broken . . . not yet anyway.* A soft but perilous sound came from the main passage at the entrance to the Great Hall. It was the marching of many feet.

"Gulrain, Jissick, Arrador, into the tunnel," Grimwarden commanded as the steady cadence of footfalls grew louder.

Jissick hesitated a moment. "Will we not fight?" he asked.

"It cuts against my spirit as well," said Grimwarden. "But should we linger and fight as lions—even should we each slay fifty Gwar—we will still die, and the enemy will gain access to our underground. We must retreat for now, collapse the tunnel, and join the others in the caverns."

Jissick nodded and joined the others at the mouth of the tunnel. They, like their commander, turned to watch the entrance to the Great Hall.

"Ready, flet soldiers!" Grimwarden called over his shoulder. "I will wait only long enough to see them in the moon's light."

The march rose until it was like rolling thunder in the mountains, and the first dark forms entered the Great Hall. The group did not spread out, but marched behind one leader. Grimwarden watched him, saw the plate armor, the iron helmet, the long blade of—*Wait!* Grimwarden sprang up from behind the throne. "Brynn, thank the Highest you've returned to us!" He ran up to the flet marshall, but her expression stole the joy from the moment. Grimwarden stared at the train of Elven women and children funneling into the Great Hall. "How many?" he asked, but seeing the haunted look in his people's eyes he immediately regretted the question.

Brynn looked up as she continued to direct her people between piles of debris across the chamber. She wouldn't risk answering the question while the already terrified Elves might hear. She led Grimwarden into the shadows at the end of the thrones. "We searched every district, Olin. A few we found hiding in basements or church sanctuaries. A few in culverts or sewers." Her eyes were wet, and her jaw trembled. "Near five thousand, as best we could count. We found ten times that many . . . dead."

Five thousand? Grimwarden fell to one knee. *How, in just one night, could the thriving city of Berinfell be reduced to five thousand?* "Were you seen?"

"Yes, several times, but the lips of those Gwar sentries are now forever still. Teams of flet soldiers and archers protected our retreat."

"Five thousand," he muttered. He watched as Jissick and the other flet soldiers escorted them into the tunnel. So few, and yet it might well prove to be a number too large to evacuate in time if the enemy is at their heels. "What of the garden?"

"The battle at the garden is desperate," said Brynn. "The enemy pours unopposed through the east gate. Soon they will overwhelm the garden. Our defenses may hold another hour, perhaps two."

Grimwarden shook his head. "Brynn, I want you to get our people below."

"But if our defenses and diversions fail?"

Grimwarden did not reply. In truth, he wasn't sure of the answer. The two walked in silence back to the tunnel entrance. A small Elf child looked up at Brynn. "Flet Marshall?" The child's eyes were enormous with fear. "Will there be any spiders in our new home?"

Brynn glanced at Grimwarden and then knelt to be at eye level with the little one. "No, there will be no spiders," she said. "Guardmaster Grimwarden will see to that, won't you?"

Grimwarden realized Brynn was not asking only on behalf of the child. He hefted his spear and patted the war hammer at his side. "Yes, Elfling, you may sleep in peace tonight. You are going to a wondrous place where no spider has ever trod."

Brynn smiled. "You see? No spiders." She put an arm around the child. "But come, I will show you the prettiest flower in all of Allyra."

Brynn looked to the dust-filled opening and then regarded her commander one last time. "Endurance and Victory."

"Endurance and Victory," he said.

Flet Marshall Brynn ducked under the arch and he watched her pass by one green torch, then another, and then she was gone. Behind her followed a seemingly endless train of Elves: a woman carrying a pair of small infants, two gray-haired warriors whose fighting days had long been over, a small clan of children and a grandmother. On and on they went, Grimwarden's men counting and keeping track of each and every person who disappeared into the underground. Surely the standoff at the garden had collapsed by now. And if the diversion also failed, the Spider King's forces would come upon them in the Great Hall. Then Grimwarden, now the senior military officer of Berinfell, would have a terrible decision to make.

"Endurance and Victory," he muttered to himself. He thought the Elves might endure, but there would be no victory today.

11

Lifeflight

EVERYONE WHO followed the Greenville Raiders football team in the Pop Warner twelve- and thirteen-year-old division knew about number twenty-eight, Jett Green. His father, Austin Green, had played tailback for Clemson University and for the National Football League's Carolina Panthers. The way Jett played the game, it seemed inevitable he would follow in his father's footsteps.

But on the morning of November 4, Jett for once wasn't thinking about football. He stared into the small section of the mirror in his room that hadn't been covered up with newspaper clippings and photos. He flashed his large, almond-brown eyes and grinned like a Cheshire cat. Because today . . . today was riding day. Two weeks prior, Jett's thirteenth birthday, his parents had finally given him the new dirt bike he'd been dreaming of for two years: the Tanaka Thrasher. Single cylinder, four-stroke, liquid cooled, 400cc's of ridiculous power! In a straightaway, it could do more than 80 miles an hour. Who knew how much air it could get on a dirt track with hills? And it was all Jett's now.

As Jett walked to the bathroom, he visualized himself riding his new motocross bike, tearing around corners, sending loose dirt spraying into the crowd. As Jett stepped into the shower, he imagined gunning the throttle and launching himself off the biggest hill he could find. And as the hot water poured over Jett's scalp, he saw the cameras flashing as he pulled off the midair tricks his freestyle motocross hero

Dak Metzger always did: the Tsunami, the Helicopter, the No-Footer Can-Can, and the mighty SideWinder with a scissor kick.

"Ah," Jett sighed. Football and school had kept him so busy he hadn't even been able to ride his new bike. *That will change today*, he thought. It was a Saturday, and his football team had the weekend off. His father had promised to take Jett to the track in nearby Simpson.

Jett stepped out of the shower, dried off, and wrapped the towel securely around his narrow waist. He stood in front of the fogged-up bathroom mirror and began gelling his close-cropped hair to its usual flattop perfection. As the mirror cleared a little, he put down his pick and comb and began a little personal ritual.

He flexed his chest muscles. Then he pressed his thumbs into his waist and flexed his wide back muscles. "Lats, baby," he muttered under his breath. "Now for the guns," he said. In turn, he held up each arm and contracted his biceps. "One hundred percent, all-natural muscle—"

His arms dropped to his sides. He leaned forward. *What in the world?* he thought. *Maybe the mirror is still fogged from the hot shower.* He yanked up a washcloth and wiped it down. *It can't be.* The washcloth wiped away nothing and only served to make the reality all the more clear.

"Ma, Dad, come quick!" Jett was frozen with disbelief. "My eyes!"

Jett's father, still fast after all the years, arrived first. He wore socks, a dress shirt, and boxers, and somehow managed to button his shirt as he slid to a stop on the hardwood floor outside the bathroom. "What's wrong, J? You get gel in your eyes?"

"Nah, Dad, look!"

Mr. Green took Jett by the shoulders and stared. Then he lifted Jett's chin to get a little more of the bathroom light. "Well, I'll be. Never seen such a—"

"Austin?" Jett's mom asked as she walked up the stairs. "My baby okay?"

"Ah, Ma!" complained Jett. "I'm not your baby."

"Don't you sass me. You'll be my baby even when you're forty and have babies of your own. *Humph*, not my baby. Now, what's all this yellin' about?"

"Look at his eyes, Hazel," said Mr. Green.

"What's wrong with 'em," she said, looking over her son. "Still look as pretty as ev—" She put a hand to her chest. "I . . . I can't believe it."

Her son's big brown eyes, which had always been striking with his dark skin, were now deep violet.

"Can you see okay?" asked Jett's father.

"Does it hurt, baby?"

"I can see fine, and no, Ma, it doesn't hurt at all. In fact, I feel really good."

The next twenty minutes were a flurry of activity. Mr. Green searched furiously on the Internet. Mrs. Green called several doctors' offices and even jumped on an online ophthalmology chat room. But no one thought it would be anything worrisome. It was rare to have eye color change during adolescence, but not unheard-of. Even so, Mrs. Green made an appointment with their general practitioner for Monday.

"Looks like the Lord gave you a special birthday present," said Mr. Green as they sat down to a large breakfast.

"*Mmm, mmph*," said Mrs. Green. "Now those girls in school will really be driving you crazy!"

"I don't think so, Ma," Jett said. He put his plate on the counter and struck a Heisman Trophy pose. "They won't be able to catch me."

"Boy likes his speed," said Mr. Green. Jett grinned.

When Jett went up to his room to get his motocross gear on, his parents sat at the table and hovered nervously over steaming cups of coffee. "Do you suppose one of his birth parents had eyes like that?" asked Jett's mom.

"Don' know, Hazel. The agency didn't say anything 'bout that. Didn't say much about anything. Every time I asked something, they said it was 'a violation of confidentiality.'" He mimicked the social worker in mock form.

"Austin." Hazel put her hands on her hips. "Be serious. You know we've got to tell him one day."

"I know," he replied, taking a sip of coffee. "Just not yet."

Jett's father released the straps and cinch cords, and Jett rolled the Thrasher off the trailer. They both waved to Carl at the front desk of the Simpson Motocross Park. He waved and said hi, but no one heard him over the roar of the bikes already tearing up the track. Once inside the perimeter barricades—bales of straw stacked six deep and eight high—Jett mounted the Thrasher.

"Remember, Jett!" Mr. Green's powerful voice penetrated the staccato blasts of the bikes. "Take it easy at first, 'til you get used to it!"

"No problem, Dad!" Jett yelled back. He hit the electric ignition. The Thrasher growled to life and purred like a tiger on steroids. Jett grinned at the sweet sound and dropped the visor on his helmet. Mr. Green watched the track until a few bikes went by, and then gave Jett the all-clear signal. Jett flexed his wrist to turn the accelerator. The bike responded like a rodeo horse out of the chute and surged forward into the center of the dirt track.

Jett did take it slow—at first. He cruised on the straightaways, caught little hops of air off the small hills, and skidded around corners. He avoided the freestyle hills for a while, which were much higher . . . and more dangerous. The main track was pretty easy to navigate, and soon Jett thought he had a feel for his new toy.

He waved to his dad and gave the Thrasher a little more throttle.

It responded like a dream, and once again the images of Dak Metzger poured into Jett's mind. He got a little more adventurous on the next couple of hills, getting more air and performing a simple version of the Heel Clicker he'd been doing for years. While in the air, Jett let his legs rise up behind him, kicked his heels together, and quickly seated himself just before the bike landed.

"Whoooo, yeah!" Jett yelled. He had ridden dirt bikes since he was seven, but this was just a whole new level.

Jett's confidence surged. As he passed the grandstand where his father sat, he motioned toward the freestyle hills. Taking his cue, Jett's father left his seat and hurried around the perimeter of the track to a better vantage point. Jett hit the first freestyle hill and launched the Thrasher sixteen feet in the air. This time Jett was able to clench his knees to the bike, release the handlebars, and lean back. Not exactly a real Lazy Boy like Dak did, but it was good enough to draw cheers from the spectators scattered in the stands. Jett landed perfectly and roared around the base of the biggest hill, affectionately nicknamed "the Monster." "See you soon," Jett mumbled to himself as he passed through the Monster's massive shadow.

Jett gathered speed and courage on the next two laps, each time perfectly executing jumps and stunts off the lower freestyle hills. He heard more cheers, saw his dad pumping his fist, and decided it was time. Jett zoomed calmly around the track until he hit the eighty-yard straightaway before the Monster. There he stopped. A couple of the other bikers stopped there as well. They flipped their visors or took off their goggles and looked at Jett as if to ask, "You gonna' do it?"

Jett nodded and hit the throttle.

He'd done the Monster once before on his old bike, but the Thrasher had far more horsepower. Jett felt all 400cc's roaring beneath him as he streaked up the hill.

It was too fast.

At the crest of the Monster, the bike took Jett airborne and started to get out from under him. All Jett saw or heard from that point was . . .

flashes and sounds . . .

the sky . . .

a shadow . . .

the whine of the motor. . . .

Just before the crunching sounds of metal and bone.

His heartbeat throbbed in his ears and at his temples, he coughed, tasting something coppery, and he felt something warm on his chin.

Suddenly, lots of faces were looking down at Jett, and his ears rang so fiercely that he couldn't hear anything else. Jett tried to speak, tried to move, and failed. A strange, icy coldness crawled across his brow and around his eyes.

His vision grayed in and out. Then his dad was there. Jett had never seen his father scared . . . until that moment.

The loud ringing faded, then came back with a vengeance, and short clips of voices came through.

. . . "still alive" . . . "flipped" . . . "Son, you hold on!" . . ."They're here." . . .

Then there were two guys and one woman dressed in yellow jump-suits with belts and cords wrapped and draped every which way. *Paramedics.* The two men knelt and looked down at Jett. One of the men shone a penlight into Jett's eyes. Another spoke something into a walkie-talkie. The woman came over very close to him.

. . . "ck" . . ."could be broken" . . . "internal injuries" . . . "fatal" . . .

Jett coughed and again felt heat on his chin but cold over his eyes. *Fatal?*

The woman tore open a plastic bag and took a strange foam cylinder out. She knelt next to him. For a moment, Jett was afraid she was going to cover his face with it. At the last moment, her direction altered and she slipped the foam brace around Jett's neck. He didn't feel it exactly, but his frame of sight through the helmet shifted as if he'd been turned on his side. Out of the corner of his eye, Jett saw his father pacing to his left. He had his cell phone snug to his ear, his face grimaced and twisted, and his free hand gestured dramatically.

Jett felt a heavy throbbing on his face, and suddenly, a black helicopter appeared over Jett's father's shoulder. The craft seemed to fall out of the sky. He blinked, and for a moment, he thought a gigantic spider was about to descend upon him. It disappeared from Jett's sight, and more paramedics appeared. These wore helmets bigger than Jett's motocross helmet, and huge tinted visors.

"Your going" . . . "okay now" . . . "little tug" . . . "ride with us" . . . "hang in" . . .

The paramedics lifted Jett and carried him beneath the chopper blades. They slid him into the helicopter like a school lunch tray into a return slot in the cafeteria. Most of the light vanished when the chopper door shut.

Dad! DAD!! Jett thought he was screaming but wondered if anyone heard. Then his father's face appeared. He mouthed something Jett couldn't hear. Jett watched his father lift and squeeze Jett's hand, but felt no comforting touch, no warmth, nothing at all.

The helicopter cabin rocked. Jett saw the sky wobble and a brief glimpse of trees. Then he felt dizzy. To this point, he'd been able to move his eyes, but now it seemed he had lost control of everything. His vision now fixed, he saw nothing but his strapped and blanketed chest rise and fall. *At least I'm breathing*, he thought.

But there was precious little relief. Gray mist like woolen blankets crept in from the corners of his eyes. He screamed silently as everything went dark.

12

Mr. Miracle

JETT WASN'T sure when or if he actually woke. There were moments, otherworldly and vague, when images came and went. At one point, he was in a blue room with three suns. Or at least these blazing white lights seemed like suns. Masked faces flitted in and out between drifting gray veils.

Once Jett found himself in some kind of long white tube. There was a strange whirring noise that seemed to spiral around his head. His mother's face appeared next, and three nurses gently pulled her back away from Jett's bed.

Ma? he mouthed. *Ma, come back.*

❋

A shrill beeping sound and squeezing pressure around Jett's upper arm woke him. He blinked a few times and stared at the inflating black cuff and realized that he could feel it squeeze his arm. "I feel—" He tried to speak, but gagged. A plastic tube was in his mouth and down his throat. Jett tried to swallow and gagged again.

Other tubes ran along his arms. Still more curled around the bedrail and disappeared over the side of the bed. With all the tubes and wires hooked up to him, Jett felt like a bug tangled in a spider's web. He could even imagine the IV monitor with all its small, red lights as the face of a huge spider, red eyes gleaming as it came to claim its snared prey.

As Jett faded in and out of sleep, it seemed his parents weren't there one minute and the next they were asleep, each with head and arms resting on the sides of Jett's bed.

�֎

Jett awoke with the blood pressure cuff inflated again. It seemed to be on some kind of timer set to go off every hour or so. His parents were gone.

Jett tried to blink away the sleepiness, but drifted off time and time again. Even when awake, Jett felt disoriented and weak. He lifted his right arm an inch off the bed; he could hold it for a second or two before it flopped to the sheets like a dead fish. He started to close his eyes when a doctor came to the foot of his bed.

He was a short man with dark skin and a mustache so thick it looked like a woolly bear caterpillar had decided to rest on the man's upper lip. The doctor looked at Jett for a few moments as if he were an exhibit at the state fair. He lifted up Jett's sheet and exposed Jett's feet. The doctor glanced again at Jett and took something that looked like a sewing needle from a little case. Then the doctor took the sharp end of the needle-thing and ran it under Jett's foot. He did it twice on each of Jett's feet.

To Jett's horror he felt nothing.

The doctor put Jett's feet down. He took the needle-thing and began to poke Jett's lower leg. Jett's fear increased. He wanted to kick his legs, wanted to jump up and kick the doctor for poking him, but he couldn't move his legs, not an inch. But Jett felt nothing, not a single one of the doctor's small stabs. The doctor shook his head and wiped a few beads of blood from Jett's leg.

✳

"Jett, can you hear me?"

He opened his eyes and found a different doctor staring down at him. She had dark coppery hair tied back. Large, intense blue eyes gazed out from behind thin glasses. She had a nice smile.

"Yes . . . yes, I can hear you." Jett realized that he could swallow now. The tube was gone.

"I'm Doctor Creighton," she said, smiling. "And you, I'll just call you Mr. Miracle."

"What do you mean?" Jett asked groggily.

Dr. Creighton smiled. "Well, for one thing, you're still alive."

"I wrecked my bike . . . right?"

"You wrecked more than your bike," she said. "What do you remember?"

Jett thought a moment. "I went too fast . . . I think. I—"

"Oh, my baby!" Jett's mother came around the curtain to Jett's bedside. She began to reach out her hands, but turned and looked questioningly at Dr. Creighton. "Can I . . . can I kiss my baby?"

Dr. Creighton laughed. "Of course you can."

Jett had never been showered with tears before, but his mother leaned over, smothered him with kisses, and cried all over him. Mr. Green wasn't far behind. He didn't cry on his son, but softly said, "I love you, Son. You don't know how worried we were."

Mrs. Green finally stood up and wiped her tears.

Jett lifted his arms one at a time. Then his legs. "I . . . I think I'm okay," he said.

Mrs. Green gasped. "Praise the Lord!"

"Doctor Creighton," Jett's dad stammered. "How?"

"Like I was telling Jett," she said, "he's Mr. Miracle. The CAT scan, the MRIs showed no broken back, no broken ribs, no broken bones at all. The paramedics swore Jett had broken just about every bone in his body. I know a couple of those paramedics, and they're not often wrong."

Jett's parents shook their heads. Jett wasn't sure what to say.

"That's not all," said the doctor. "You may remember that Jett had more than a few scratches, cuts, and bruises."

"It was horrible," said Mrs. Green, nodding.

"Well, some of the doctors are convinced that those wounds spontaneously healed."

"Spontaneously?" asked Mr. Green.

"We even have some documentation from the intake nurse," said Dr. Creighton. "A wound here"—she pointed to a spot on Jett's arm—"on arrival, but gone this morning."

"Praise the Lord!" exclaimed Mrs. Green. "My baby's been healed."

"Yes, well, . . . it certainly seems that way," said Dr. Creighton, a thoughtful expression lingering on her brow. "Now, we were just trying to find out what Jett remembered, if that's all right."

"Go on, Jett. What do you remember?" his father asked.

Jett sat up a bit, glad to have most of the tubes and wires gone. He felt a lance of pain and rubbed his wrist. Then, with silent fascination, he watched as a pink scar disappeared from his wrist.

"Jett?" Dr. Creighton looked at him curiously. "You okay?"

"What? Uh . . . yeah, fine . . . good." Jett scrunched his brows trying to recall what had happened. "I remember taking some jumps off the freestyle hills. And I guess I didn't expect how fast that bike would take me up the Monster. I knew something was wrong as soon as I went off the edge of the hill. I felt off balance. I . . . I don't remember much else. Next thing I knew, I was already on the ground, on my back."

Dr. Creighton said, "I'm surprised you remember that much. You were wearing a good helmet . . . but not that good."

✳

Jett stayed in intensive care through the night, but by Sunday morning, all the feeling had returned to Jett's limbs. He was walking by lunch. The pediatric doctor and the shift nurse gave him a thorough physical at two o'clock and pronounced Jett completely healthy.

It was hospital policy for patients to be taken by wheelchair to the curbside. Dr. Creighton herself wheeled Jett down to the entrance, where his father awaited beside his truck.

Jett stood up. "Thank you, Doctor Creighton, for everything."

Dr. Creighton smiled. "I'm glad we could help." She turned to Jett's mom. "You better watch out for this kid. With eyes like those, girls will be chasing him all over school."

"See, baby, that's just what I told you," said Mrs. Green.

"Awww, Ma!" Jett complained as he slowly lowered himself into the backseat of the truck.

"And by now, half the town'll be talking about my miracle boy."

13

The Cave

JOHNNY AND Autumn walked through the woods as if it were their first time. Everything seemed fresh, new, and exciting. Their faithful black lab, Sam, ran alongside them, sometimes darting farther down the trail . . . other times letting them walk past as he stood motionless, sniffing the air, or ears up at some elusive sound. Sam had gone on every one of their woodland adventures since he was a pup, which is to say, he was a very experienced adventurer.

They followed the dirt path that divided their family's property from that of their neighbor's, Mr. Rizzo. With well over a hundred acres of forest and wild fields, the two kids found the untamed expanse full of countless places to explore, including the mysterious cave that straddled the two plots.

Preferring the Florida winters, Mr. Rizzo only came up for the summers, leaving his vast acreage untouched the rest of the year. "As long as youse don't get hurt, I don't care what youse explore," he'd always say before leaving for winter. It was his habitual send-off. Of course, the kids loved to hear him talk with his heavy Brooklyn accent. And Mr. Rizzo didn't mind them playing on his property as Johnny kept his grass cut, and Autumn was in charge of collecting any unforwarded mail. Having them tromping through his fields was a small price to pay for a few extra eyes keeping his home safe during his absence.

"It's just a little bit farther," Johnny said, pointing to a large wooded area and then a peculiar cluster of pine trees set back even farther. "Through there."

Autumn switched the heavy book to her other arm. "What do you think this book has to do with our cave?"

"I don't know," Johnny said, spotting the stream up ahead that led into the heart of the forest and eventually flowed right over the very mouth of the cave they sought.

"Maybe we should read the book."

"What, now?" Johnny stopped.

"Why not?" She took it from underneath her arm. "It might have some instructions or something."

"Let's just keep going, Autumn." He started forward again. "I think the cave is the place to read it."

"You think too much," Autumn quipped. "It's going to get you in trouble one day."

"Oh yeah? Well, you're too impatient," he said over his shoulder. "And it's already gotten you in trouble. More times than I can count, that's for sure."

Suddenly Sam barked up ahead. "He's found something," Johnny pointed. "Come on!" They raced through the brush to where Sam stood, snarling at something in the tall grass.

"What is it, Sam?" Autumn asked, drawing near.

"Careful, Autumn."

There, cradled in the tall grass, was a thick piece of rolled parchment about as long as her arm, bound with thin, translucent thread. Autumn reached down and picked it up. Sam barked.

"What is it?" Johnny asked.

"Dunno." Autumn took her finger and touched the thin threads that held it shut. "It's sticky."

"Sticky? Lemme see." Johnny took the parchment and noticed that the strings were wrapped numerous times around the document, seemingly unending, without start or finish. "That's weird . . . it's not tied or anything."

"Think you can snap them?"

"Sure." Johnny shoved his finger underneath the threads and instantly noticed just how sticky the things were. He pulled.

But they were stronger than they appeared.

"What's the problem?" Autumn chided.

Johnny grunted. "These things won't budge." He pulled again.

"Maybe you can slide them off one of the ends?"

Johnny yanked his finger from the threads, wiping it on his pants once free. Then he tried to slip the threads down the length of the roll. After some effort he pulled them right off the end as a bundle in his palm. "That's weird," he noted. "Almost like spiderweb."

"Here, let me see that," Autumn said as she grabbed the parchment from his hands. She started to unroll it as Johnny looked over her shoulder. His jaw dropped.

"Think it's a treasure map?" Autumn asked.

"A treasure map? Sure, Autumn, and I suppose you think Bartholomew Thorne, infamous pirate of the Caribbean, has been tramping around in Mr. Rizzo's backyard." Autumn shot him a lethal stare. "You can't even tell what it says, Autumn." He pointed to various markings. "It's written in some sort of gibberish. And look at all these weird symbols. It looks more like a maze or tunnels or something."

"Well, whatever it is, it's ours now."

"You don't know that, Autumn. Suppose it's Mr. Rizzo's or something?"

"Oh, please. It looks like it was just dropped there yesterday! It's not wet from rain. . . . It was practically sitting on top of the grass. No way it's Mr. Rizzo's."

"Then whoever it is will be coming back, if it was dropped yesterday."

"Like I said, you think too much." Autumn crouched, layed the book on a tuft of tall grass, and put the scroll into her backpack. She stood and grinned triumphantly. "Finders Keepers."

Sam started barking his deep "there's a stranger" bark. Autumn's smile vanished.

"What'sa matter, boy?" asked Johnny. But their pet rushed toward the base of a gnarly, black-barked tree at the edge of the woods. Sam sniffed at its roots, squealed as if he'd been hit, and then barked some more. He repeated the process, darting close and racing away, barking all the time.

"What's gotten into him?" asked Autumn.

"I dunno," said Johnny. He started to chuckle. "Maybe another dog peed on the tree, and Sam smelled it."

"What is it with boys that makes pee, poop, and snot so funny?" Autumn glared at her brother. "Be serious. Something's really spooked Sam."

"Come here, boy!" called Johnny in his lowest "I am master" voice. Sam turned a few tight circles before racing over to Johnny. "There's my good boy," said Johnny, scratching the fur on Sam's neck. That earned Johnny several sloppy licks on his cheek.

"That tree is kind of creepy," said Autumn. They both stared at it for several thumping heartbeats. Taller than the white pines that surrounded it, the dark broadleaf swayed and creaked in the breeze.

Johnny was the first to speak. "I still think it was just—"

"Don't say it!" She whacked him on the shoulder. "Now, let's go. We don't have a whole lot of daylight left." With that, the three of them bounded toward the cave.

When they arrived at the stream, Johnny said, "I can take the book across."

"I can do it," Autumn answered, placing it securely in her water-proof backpack with the scroll.

They rolled up their pant legs and took off their sneakers before crossing the fast-flowing water. Once on the other side, they put back on their shoes and started down the steep slope into the ravine where a waterfall emptied, carefully picking their way through fallen timbers and giant rocks until they arrived at the face of the falls. And there before them was the subtle, black cave mouth hiding behind the flow of water.

Autumn quickly retrieved the book, swung her backpack on, and flipped the book open to the first page. "See, Johnny. Look at it. I told you it looks just like the book."

"Sure does," he mumbled.

Autumn closed the cover and looked at her brother. "Well?"

"Ladies first." He smiled. But Sam beat them both to it, skirting the main flow of water and ducking into the darkness.

"Sam!" Autumn yelled, tucking the book under her arm and heading after him.

"Wait for me!" cried Johnny. The two of them followed Sam into the cave, ducking so as not to hit their heads on the low-lying ceiling of sandstone. Once inside they heard Sam bark up ahead.

"I can't see anything," said Autumn.

"Here." Johnny flicked on a flashlight he had stuffed in his belt for just this occasion. The beam washed over the walls and centered on the floor up ahead. The cave was more like a tunnel, stretching on out of sight, its floor damp with puddles of cold water. "I don't see Sam."

"He must be really far ahead. Let's go."

They plunged on into the blackness, dispersed only by their meager flashlight. The dampness sent chills up their spines . . . or was it more than the change in temperature?

"It feels funny in here," Johnny said.

"Don't be silly." They both heard Sam bark again from up ahead. "See? Sam says it's fine."

"He just barked, Autumn."

"I know; that's his 'everything's all right' bark."

Johnny hesitated but moved on anyway. "I'm not so sure."

They walked through the ankle-high water, Johnny watching for water snakes, Autumn being careful not to trip. Soaking the book would be a horrible mistake. With the sound of the falls now far behind them, Sam let out another bark, this time closer. Slowly, the floor began to rise, and soon Johnny and Autumn were on dry ground. They examined smaller offshoots of the tunnel splitting from the main cave but chose to stay to the larger route. They skirted around large stalactites formed by hundreds of years of dripping minerals, and eventually entered a large chamber. Sam stood at the far end by a wall—the very back of the cave. He barked at them.

"What is it, boy?" Autumn inquired, walking toward him. Sam turned his head toward the unusually flat wall.

"He's such a dumb dog."

"No, he's not," Autumn contested as she drew near her pet. "Johnny, look! Footprints!"

"What?" Johnny moved forward and shined the beam on the dry silt floor. Sure enough, there was a series of fresh footprints. "It looks like two sets," he said examining them. "Don't look like sneakers."

"No funny lines," Autumn noted. "Boots?"

"No. They're more like socks or something."

"Moccasins, like the Indians?"

"Maybe."

It looked as though one set of prints led into the cave, all the way to the wall, and the other led back out of the cave.

"Huh," said Johnny. "They came in and turned around just like we are." Then he noticed something else, something so peculiar that his first thoughts made no sense at all. "Autumn! Look!"

They both knelt down where Sam was standing and examined the spot where the wall met the dirt floor. One of the footprints that led away from the wall was cut exactly in half. "That's impossible," Johnny blurted out. Sam barked.

"It's like the back of the cave was built after . . . after whoever it was walked through here."

"Maybe it's a prank."

"A prank? Out here? On who? Us?"

"Well, maybe it's a fake door or something." Autumn immediately pounded the wall, but she stopped as soon as her hand throbbed.

Johnny used the flashlight to search for a secret lever or a hidden button. He had seen it plenty of times in the movies. "I dunno. I just can't explain it."

"Neither can I," Autumn said, scratching her head. They both knelt and puzzled over the strange sight, until finally Autumn sat down and set the book on her lap. "Hold the light up for me, would ya?"

"Why do I feel like we shouldn't do this in here?" Johnny asked as he sat down next to her.

"Because you worry too much?" She sat cross-legged, Sam sidling up beside her. "We showed the book to Mom. We told her we were going to read. What could happen?"

"Y-e-a-hh, I g-u-e-s-s," he said slowly. "But it wasn't the same for Mom. She thought it was some kind of Old West book. What'd she call it?"

"*Pioneers of the Western United States*," Autumn replied.

"How'd she get that, Autumn? Look at it! *The History of Berinfell: The Chronicles of the Elf Lords and Their Kin*. There's something messed up with this book. Maybe we shouldn't read it in here after all. It's getting late, and who knows how long this battery will last."

"Ah, you worry too much. Of course we should read it in here," Autumn declared with know-it-all finality. "How else are we going to figure out what's going on?"

Johnny didn't have an answer for that. He stared down at the book. The beam of his flashlight shone down, setting the gilded title ablaze. "So where do we start?"

"At the beginning," Autumn said, opening the book and flipping past the artwork to the table of contents. She scanned down the page. ". . . or maybe not right at the beginning. This "Fall of Berinfell" chapter sounds cool. Lessee . . ." She began to flip through the pages. "Here we are, page 287. Man, look at this fancy writing . . . like an invitation to a prince's ball." She reached out a finger to touch the script.

"Autumn, the chapter starts on page 277, not—"

Johnny never finished the sentence. The temperature in the cave dropped even colder, so low he could see his breath. Dust on the cave floor began to swirl in small eddies like miniature tornadoes, and Johnny's flashlight dimmed, then went out. A foul smell filled the air. Then a lick of flame leaped up from the book illuminating the back of the cave, and the wall seemed to ripple like water.

"Fire!" Johnny yelled, backing away. Sam jumped back, too. "Close the book, Autumn!"

Her face an odd mixture of frozen shock, utter disbelief, and blank confusion, Autumn shut the book. With a flanging *whoosh*, the cave went back to normal, including the flashlight coming back on. "What . . . what happened?" she asked, for once without an answer.

"It all came from the book," Johnny whispered. "When you touched the page, I smelled something weird. Did you smell it?" Sam sniffed the air. "It's gone now."

Sam whined.

"But how can a book—?"

"Open it up again," suggested Johnny.

"I don't think we should."

"You even said it's the only way to find out."

"Yeah, but that was before . . . before . . . before all that fire and stuff!"

"Oh, come on, Sis. Here, lemme do it." Johnny took the book out of her lap, but before he could blink, Autumn had it back. Lightning fast. Johnny sat stunned. He had never seen hands move so fast! "How'd . . . how'd you do that?"

Autumn blinked, again at a loss . . . but only for a moment. "If anyone's going to open this book back up, it's me," she said. "'Cause I want to be able to close it before we burn ourselves to death." Autumn cracked open the book and flipped back to the same page. Nothing happened. "I think you're right," she said. "I must need to touch the page."

No sooner had her fingertips brushed the text than the temperature dropped, the flashlight went out, and wind swirled. The air filled once more with the peculiar, unpleasant odor, and fire leaped up from the page.

Autumn looked questioningly over her shoulder to her brother.

He shook his head.

This time, Autumn didn't close the book.

The fire was merely the top of a torch. It rose out of the book and was held in a gloved hand. Autumn dropped the book and edged away. The torch-bearing hand belonged to a soldier. Other warriors followed the first one. The cave shimmered and changed before Autumn's and Johnny's eyes. Strange, curving stone walls emerged from the book and began to curl and twist. No, they were tunnels . . . tunnels beneath a huge castle city. Within the tunnels these soldiers moved at great speed, as if on some urgent errand. And yet not far behind—clambering across crenulated walls, on rooftops, and along the streets—was another army.

Travin led his warriors through the underground network of Berinfell's sewer tunnels. Scores of torches cast flickering shadows against the brick walls, and every sound echoed faintly. Even though they were only thirty to forty feet down, it felt like they were miles beneath the surface.

The flet soldiers sloshed through the mire, stirring up a horrendous smell . . . the reeking by-products of every teeming city.

Finding the way north to the marketplace had not been difficult, as the largest pipelines followed the main avenues above. But going farther south, away from population centers, the tunnels narrowed. They had to stoop as they trod along, and of course, it was much more difficult to move with all the additional layers of clothing they now had on.

Despite the clothing, they were chilled to the bone, exhausted, and reeking of sewer filth. The men arrived at a large metal grate where the refuse continued on and fell over a ledge that plummeted into a crevice connected to the Gap in the east. Travin began searching the walls of the area, waving his torch around. "It's around here somewhere," he muttered. He received a few odd looks from his team. "Not like I come down here every month or anything." The soldiers who overheard him smiled, but dared not laugh out loud.

"There we go!" Travin sloshed toward a rusted iron ladder that followed the contour of the sewer wall, and climbed it to the metal grate above. Shoving his shoulder up into the bars, he loosened the cover from its seat. Making very little sound, he eased the grate to the side. Travin raised his head slowly above street level and looked for enemies. He doubted the Spider King's forces would be interested in anything this far south; all attention was clearly fixed on the east gate and Sentinel Garden. *That will have to change,* Travin thought as he clambered slowly up the ladder. And then . . . he froze.

An incredibly strong grip clutched the hair on the back of his head, and a cold blade pressed against his neck. "Felgost Gwarfrigen," a harsh, deep voice from above growled, "Atten logas e' Feithrill! Feithrill na entracan Allyra, mara wy blakkir na vex clarisca met!"

14

Battle at the Tree Gate

 "What?" Travin asked, in response to the ancient Elven words. His voice came out thin as the knife pressed against his throat, "I am no Wisp!" The pressure of the blade lessened. Travin swallowed, thinking he might know that gruff voice. "Vendar?" he asked. "Vendar Stonebreaker, is that you?"

"Sir?" came a tentative voice from the tunnels below. "Sir, what's wrong up there?"

Travin couldn't answer, for he was hauled by his shoulders up out of the sewer and set on his own two feet. And there, in front of him, was a longtime friend. "Beyond all hope . . . Vendar, you live!"

"Sir Travin!" The voices from below were more urgent.

"It's okay," Travin said. "It's better than okay!" Travin clasped his friend in a crushing hug and then held him by the shoulders at arm's length. "I thought I saw you fall to a Warspider on the west wall!"

"I fell all right," laughed Vendar. "I put my spear through the spider's torso, and the blasted creature let go of the walls. One hundred feet, we fell. I landed on its ghastly, bloated bag of a body. The thing burst beneath me like a bad wineskin. You may have noticed the uh . . . pungent aroma."

"That I did!" Travin laughed deeply once more and hugged Vendar again. "I thought it was me from tramping around in the sewer. But I don't care—so glad am I that you live!"

Vendar was Berinfell's third flet marshall, superior to all in command except the Guardmaster and Flet Marshall Brynn. His skill at arms and aptitude for strategy had made him Berinfell's most renowned tactician. He stood with his sword in one hand and spear in the other, always preferring two weapons over the standard blade and a shield. Never defending, always attacking. His once immaculate green cloak, gilded on its fringes, was now stained and hung heavy against his jointed armor.

Travin shook his head, still in disbelief. Then his eyes narrowed and he smiled wryly. "'Wisp, bondservant of Gwars,' you said?" Travin laughed. "'Hear words of light. Light has come into the world, and the darkness has not overcome it'—that was very dramatic, don't you think, Vendar?"

"Using the words of Ellos, our mighty God, is the only way to inflict harm on a Wisp."

"Still, you gave quite a speech!"

"Laugh if you want, Travin, but once you've dealt with a Wisp yourself, you won't be so smug."

"Smug? Nay. I feared for my life! I think you nicked my neck."

"Can't be too careful. Wisps are perilous."

Travin's smile disappeared. Then he leaned down into the hole. "All clear," he announced. "Those in standard battle dress, get up here now," Travin ordered. "Those cloaked, stay put."

A chorus of ayes rose from below.

"Cloaked?" asked Vendar. He watched as one soldier at a time poked up from the sewer hole and climbed into the street. Then the flet marshall knelt on the road and ducked his head into the hole to see for himself. His head popped up abruptly. "What in Allyra's stars—?"

"It is Grimwarden's idea," interjected Travin. "And I could use your help."

"I don't have to dress as a wom—"

"No, no! But yours will be the most vital task." He took Vendar aside and explained the details.

The flet marshall's face grew ashen gray. He stepped back a pace and looked to the east. "We are that bad off, and so quickly?"

Travin nodded. "If we fail, the Elves of Allyra face extinction."

Vendar clenched his jaw for a moment. "Then we will not fail."

— •••••••• •••••••••• •••••••• —

Cathar Indrook sat back in the saddle of his Warspider and smiled as he looked over the ruination of the Elves' Southern Gate. It was a shame that Overlord Varuin Khelgast had taken an Elven arrow in the eye. Of course, not such a shame. That made Cathar the new Gwar overlord, second in command only to—

"Cathar!" rasped Tyrith, the Drefid high commander. "Why do your forces linger?"

Cathar turned in his saddle. Tyrith removed his helmet. The moonlight gave the Drefid's long white hair and pale skin eerie luminescence, and his dark eyes fathomless depth. Cathar swallowed. "Sir . . . they are merely finishing off the Elven wounded. The Spider King said—"

"The Spider King said you are to pursue the enemy until every last Elf is dead. Did you miss the word *pursue*? Tell me, Cathar, what do your spies tell you about the remnant fleeing north?"

"North?" Cathar stifled a laugh. "The spies must be mistaken. We've secured the northern quarter of the city. The marketplace, the tenements, the ramparts are void of life. If any Elves survived our second wave, they would more than likely have traveled farther west, perhaps to the Forest Gate beyond the Great Hall."

Tyrith turned his void eyes to Cathar and extended a hand, resting his long, knifelike extensions on the Gwar's shoulder. "Hundreds, perhaps thousands, of Elves are at this very moment pouring up from the sewers north of the marketplace and racing for the tree gate. You did scour the sewers, didn't you, Cathar?"

Cathar felt chilling tendrils, like some icy growing thing ripple across his shoulders and down his spine.

━ •◦◦◦◦•• ◦••◦••◦•• •◦◦◦◦• ━

Travin paced the cobblestoned street. He kept one eye on his warriors who filtered up from the sewer, traversed the road quickly, and vanished through the northern tree gate. Travin knew they'd march eighty yards into the trees before descending the spiral root stair and doubling back beneath the trees to the sewers.

He turned and looked impatiently to the empty streets that curved south toward the center of Berinfell. Vendar and his team had been gone too long. If they could not attract the enemy's forces . . . all would be lost.

━ •◦◦◦◦•• ◦••◦••◦•• •◦◦◦◦• ━

"There they are," Cathar muttered. He spurred his Warspider to greater speed as he watched an armed troop of Elves fleeing the desolate Berinfell marketplace. Cathar's armies: thousands of Gwar infantry, hundreds of Warspiders, and a *trivium* of Drefids had long ago forsaken stealth. Recklessly firing arrows and arc stones, they clambered across the rooftops, along the walls, and up the narrow road. Some of the Elves in the rear fell, pierced with black shafts. Others vanished in spectacular flashes of blue fire.

Cathar exulted, "Now, we'll have you!"

━ •◦◦◦◦•• ◦••◦••◦•• •◦◦◦◦• ━

In an almost silent cadence, the Elves marched on the road north of the marketplace toward the tree gate.

Unexpectedly, blue flashes, punctuated by explosions, lit up the road barely a mile away. A desperate horn blew in the distance. Travin could hear screams, clashes, clangs, and thuds. Running toward the middle of the marketplace avenue, Travin saw in the firelight his kindred fleeing up the road. Following the retreating Elves, there poured an ominous, surging, indistinct black horde stretching across the horizon like the tidal waves on Allyra's tempestuous Red Coast.

Travin took an involuntary step backward. Even he was unprepared for the size of the Spider King's full invading force. Watching the oncoming threat confirmed what Travin already suspected: this battle would bring death for him and all those who dared to stand against it.

Well, Vendar has led them here, he thought. *Now, will they take the bait?*

— •••••••• •••••••••• ••••••• —

"What's this?" Cathar blurted aloud. He watched the fleeing Elven soldiers split like the parting of a curtain and scatter into alleys and side streets. "Do they think they can hide fro—?"

Then he understood. It was just as Tyrith had said.

Cathar looked again to the Elves dispersing into the side streets. "They seek to divide us . . . to take our attention from their escaping kin." Cathar loosed a blast on his war horn. *Fools!* he thought. *Divide us all you wish, but conquer nothing. Our numbers are staggering.* Cathar sounded his war horn once more and yelled to his generals, "Rax, take your group of Warspiders left! Gorim, take the right! All other forces, FOLLOW ME!"

— •••••••• •••••••••• ••••••• —

Flet Marshall Vendar grinned when he heard the clamor of the pursuing Warspiders and Gwar. He'd led his soldiers into a winding alley where he knew the Elves would have the advantage and could decrease the enemy that would cut into Travin's defenses at the northern tree gate. But the enemy caught up with them quicker than Vendar had expected.

"Take to the high points!" he yelled. Those who heard sprinted into tight side streets or found ways to clamber up the sides of buildings.

Vendar wasn't quick enough. Three Elven warriors were thrown crashing into him. Vendar fell beneath them with a grunt. Two of the soldiers rolled off, but one was dead. Vendar heaved him over to the side. He looked up just in time to see the pointed leg of a massive Warspider plunge down at him. Vendar threw himself out of the way as the clawed limb crashed onto the stone beside him, sending up sparks and debris. The other two Elves were not so fortunate. The spider crushed one and impaled the other.

Vendar screamed in rage. He leaped to a crouch and thrust his spear up into the exposed thorax of the Warspider hovering over him. The beast let out a terrible, keening screech. Three flet soldiers ran to Vendar's aid, and together, they finished off the creature.

Vendar sneered, wiping globs of spider innards off his breastplate. "To think I started this day off with clean armor," he muttered.

Vendar rallied those nearest him, and they went to the walls. Fortunately, Elves could climb with even the slightest handholds: a crevice between stones, a drainage pipe, or a low-gabled roof. When he and the others reached the highest rooftops, they joined the rest of the Elves and opened fire with their bows. In a storm of arrows, Vendar's archers took out ten times as many Gwar as the other archers.

Dead Gwar carpeted the street, but more kept coming. And while the Gwar couldn't climb very well, their spider-mounts could. Each one now bearing two or three soldiers, the Warspiders began to scale the walls.

Vendar nocked and fired at the first Warspider he saw crest the roofline.

The shaft went straight and true but sprang uselessly away. *Armor. The Spider King has covered his beasts in some new armor!*

"The eyes!" Vendar yelled to his archers. "Your arrows cannot pierce the armor! Aim for their eyes!"

Vendar took aim but could not get a clear shot at the creature's eyes. He watched helplessly as the Warspider swept a young Elf soldier off the roof. Then it turned in Vendar's direction. He pulled back on his bowstring, even past his ear . . .

Shoonk!

The arrow buried right through the spider's eye and deep into its braincase. Immediately, the Warspider went limp and slid off the roof, taking its riders with it.

But that was just one.

More and more spiders came. And the Gwar riders drove them into the Elves or leaped off and assailed the Elves with their Gwar-made hammers and spikes. The well-trained flet soldiers fought back relentlessly, but were overrun.

And so it went on, Elves with the enemy pursuing at their heels, leaping from rooftop to rooftop. Many Elves wielded their siege axes to cripple the spiders but were struck down before they could finish their tasks.

Two Gwar leaped down from their mounts and came at Vendar. The flet marshall was wise to their methods. He rolled inside one hammer blow and dragged his sword swiftly across one Gwar's stomach. The huge warrior crumpled. Vendar stepped up onto the doubled-over Gwar and dove, spear first, at the second enemy. The Gwar was slow to react, and Vendar's spear punctured the center of his breastplate. The Gwar fell to the roof like a rag doll.

But as Vendar loosed his spear from the enemy's chest, a Warspider came from behind. Its clublike foreleg sent Vendar sprawling near to the edge of the roof. As he rolled over, a hammer fell on his right forearm. It was a sharp, stunning hurt that shivered up into his shoulder and rendered his arm useless. His spear tumbled off the roof.

Vendar somehow got to his feet and found himself in the unpleasant company of three Gwar. He took his sword in his left hand and tried to keep his attackers at a distance with jabs and quick thrusts. He ducked a blow that would have taken his head, and sliced his sword into the throat of that Gwar. But the other two attacked. Vendar could not deflect a hammer blow with his sword. It spun him sideways, and he began to slide. The other Gwar seized the opportunity and thrust Gwar spikes into Vendar's upper thigh. Vendar grunted, crumpled, and with a desperate scream fell backward off the roof.

———— •••••••••••••••••••••••• ————

"Autumn!" Johnny shook her, holding the shut book in one hand.

"Autumn, it's time to go."

"What?" She was in a daze. Astonished. Confused. Sorrowful.

"It's almost seven. Mom's going to be furious with us if we don't get back before sundown."

"Sundown?" Autumn snapped out of it. The thought of walking away from this cave in the dark was enough to motivate anyone.

"We gotta go, now!"

"I know," she said, standing up. Both of their feet were freezing from their wade through the water. "Hey . . . where's Sam?"

15

Eency Weency Spider

"ATTENTION, MISS Yuen!" A conductor's wand rapped against Kiri Lee's music stand.

"Pardonnez-moi, Madame LaMoine." Kiri Lee's attention snapped away from the open window. The fall day was much too beautiful to be stuck in the apartment practicing Beethoven's Cello Sonata No. 5. She'd much rather spend it roaming around the palace in the Jardin du Luxembourg, smelling the flowers, and watching the ducks move across the grand pond.

"Alors, measure twenty-three," Madame LaMoine continued in her heavy French accent. "And. . . ." She waved her baton.

Kiri Lee blew a long strand of straight, black hair out of her face and began to bow the notes before her, wishing for a moment that she were not a child prodigy. At times it felt liberating . . . exciting to have such skill, but now it had become a cage, one that she desperately wished she could escape. Hour upon hour of endless practicing, moving from professor to professor, concert to concert. It was never enough. She watched all the other kids playing in the grand square behind her family's apartment. Just playing. She wanted to be like them. Carefree.

But it was not meant to be. Kiri was the adopted daughter of two aspiring musicians who pushed her relentlessly to reach some standard of expertise they never defined exactly. Kiri Lee knew it was somewhere between the clouds and perfection. She knew because her parents were never satisfied—not with her practice, not with her compositions, not with her performance. Never. She was bound for the great orchestras of the world whether she wanted it or not.

Kiri Lee's music lesson stretched on into the afternoon, taking up most of the precious few hours of remaining sunlight until at last Madame LaMoine stuffed her baton into her leather satchel, rose, and went to the door. On her way out she turned and asked, "I will be seeing you tomorrow?"

"Oui, tomorrow at one," Kiri Lee said, wincing as she did.

Madame LaMoine paused. "You know"—she said with a pensive tone—"there might come a day where you grow to love the music as your parents do."

"The music," Kiri Lee looked back out the window. "The music in my head is not the music here." She blindly poked her bow at the pages on the wireframe stand.

"But first you must learn the music—"

"I know. I know. I must first learn the music on the page"—reciting Madame LaMoine's too-often quoted verse—"so I can play what's in my heart."

Madame LaMoine sighed and shrugged her shoulders. "Miss Yuen, you are completely hopeless. Never have I met a child so gifted, and yet so . . ."

"Unhappy?" Kiri Lee finished her thought.

"Oui," her teacher sighed. Silence hung between them. "Bonsoir," Madame LaMoine said and left the apartment.

In a flash, Kiri Lee traded her cello for her violin, and her slippers for a pair of low-cut boots. She put on her jacket, quickly wrote a note to her mom to tell her where she would be, and counted to ten, giving her teacher enough time to walk out of the lobby . . . and if she timed it right, she'd miss her mom coming in. Then she rushed out the door.

Outside, the late-afternoon Paris traffic clambered down Rue

Boissonade, each car trying to squeeze past the next on that skinny road. Kiri Lee never understood why people would struggle for one more car length only to be halted a moment later, no better off than the previous vehicle. She turned right down the sidewalk and headed north for the Jardin du Luxembourg.

The restaurants were reopening for the evening, their delicious smells filling the street around her. The aromas of coffee and warm bread wafted by, making her wish she had grabbed a baguette before leaving so hastily.

She continued up Avenue de l'Observatoire, passing the colonnades of trees and statues to her right, until the park entrance gates welcomed her onto the beautifully mowed terraces. Once on the grass, she slipped her boots off and allowed her bare feet to feel the cool grass slide between her toes. No one else would have taken their boots off on an October day, but Kiri Lee took every chance she could to enjoy the beauties of nature.

She turned left and ventured into one of the many manicured folds of trees, following a meandering pavement path to a playground. Among the many children playing on slides, swings, and jungle gyms, Kiri Lee spotted her friend Sophie. Younger than Kiri Lee, Sophie was born in Paris, spoke French, and was fluent in English. Like Kiri Lee, Sophie was a prodigy, but Sophie's gift was in art. Sophie had taken to drawing with colored chalk as a toddler. After one of Sophie's early chalk landscapes had fetched more than five hundred euros at auction, her parents enrolled her in the famed Académie des Beaux-Arts.

"Bonjour, Sophie!" said Kiri Lee.

The young artist with bouncy brown pigtails looked up from her latest sidewalk creation. "Bonjour, Kiri Lee!"

"The Notre Dame Cathedral?" Kiri Lee asked, looking at the drawing.

"Uh-huh," she replied. "Like it?"

"Like it?" Kiri Lee beamed. "How could I not? C'est magnifique!"

Bright green eyes, rosy cheeks, dimples—Sophie's whole face lit up with joy. Then she went back to her drawing.

Kiri Lee left the playground and followed a meandering path to her favorite spot . . . the mysterious Medici Fountain.

The long rectangular pool seemed as though it were cut off from the rest of the world, covered by arching trees and bordered by carved stone vases. Plants overflowed into the water, and lily pads speckled the surface like tiny islands peacefully ignorant of their neighbors. At the far end was the fountain itself, a massive stone edifice adorned with statues in smooth coves and intricately sculpted terraces. If they ever moved back to the United States, Kiri Lee would miss the fountain more than anything else in Paris.

She leaped to her favorite chair, amazed at how long she could stay airborne. Then she sat, thinking of how this place was almost four hundred years old, the rock green with algae and weathered with age. Four hundred years was a long time. It outlived kings, wars, revolutions, plagues, . . . even the modern age. The very fact that this work of art had endured so much gave Kiri Lee great comfort. *Some things*, she thought, *don't change*.

She sat back in her chair and listened to the water trickle over the layers of rock and splash into the pool. Her eyes closed as the melody of the water mixed with that of the air and of the birds singing above her. It was in this place that she could escape the endless lessons and performances, demands, tests, and reviews. No more Beethoven, no more Haydn. It was here that the music of man died, and the music of life resumed.

She opened her eyes, laid the case across her lap, and unlatched the lid. With violin and bow withdrawn, she let the case slip onto the ground. She tucked the instrument under her chin, took a breath, closed her eyes, and began to play.

All at once she felt her spirit carried away on the wind, countless shapes and colors prompting her onward through a myriad of settings, each with its own mood, its own shades of light and feeling. No one could possibly write this on staff paper or record it in a studio, the way she saw it now. The Master Conductor was at work here, crafting the song of life without being seen . . . without any accolades . . . without any recognition. He was far greater than any conductor she had played under to date.

Here there was no one to critique her, no one to judge if she was living up to her potential. The music that poured from her violin soaked her soul and soothed the tension in her hands. Her arms relaxed. Here Kiri Lee was sure she could fly.

She allowed the melody to fly her far, far away. She slipped into a thunderous crescendo, imagining storm clouds around her. She could feel herself floating among them. But a sense of a lurking menace assaulted her. Brilliant flashes of light ripped through the sky and made the billowing cloud formations glow. Yet strangely, the ominous feeling in her chest did not seem to come from the storm; it was something below the storm . . . something that gave cause to the storm.

But what?

It was then that the melody of the rains came. The music of each droplet rose in harmony with the orchestration of the piece, as if the Master Conductor knew the placement for each one. Kiri Lee tried to drop below the storm, but the winds would not let her. She wanted to see . . . wanted to know what was down there. The music built in her head—swirling shapes and colors all poised on creation.

Then a flash of light.

Kiri Lee opened her eyes. There, only a few yards from her, was a strange-looking man leaning against a tree. He was wearing a trench coat, his wide-brimmed hat pulled down over his eyes. She blinked to get a better look, and he was gone. The sun was dipping below the cityscape. She sat up abruptly, looking at her watch. It had been more than forty-five minutes since she had sat down by the fountain. Her mother and father would be waiting for her at the dinner table by the time she ran back to the apartment. *Not good.*

꙰

Sophie had heard the rumbles of thunder and stopped drawing. She glanced toward the sky and then looked around. She saw a tall man leaning against a tree on the opposite side of the sidewalk. Sophie didn't think she had seen this man before, though the shadow of his wide-brimmed hat hid his face almost completely. Like the twin serpents carved into one of the nearby statues, the man's eyes gleamed now and then—but he never turned his head.

Sophie wondered who he was watching. It might be any number of kids in the area. A blur of boys and girls sat cheering from the merry-go-round even as it made them too dizzy to walk, while others jumped rope, played on the monkey bars, and some preschoolers sat learning a song in English.

Eency weency spider went up the water spout,
Down came the rain and washed the spider out,
Up came the sun and dried out all the rain,
So the eency weency spider went up the spout again.

The man remained motionless, Sophie intently watching him. Something floated down from the tree limb a few feet above his left shoulder. It was a big spider—one of those orange and black ones that built the big webs in the eaves of the apartment! The spider dangled on its web, descended past the brim of his hat, and stopped very close to the man's ear . . . as if it were talking to the man. The man nodded and tilted his head this way and that . . . almost as if he were answering back. Sophie giggled and quickly started sketching the man and the spider. Only minutes later the rain began to fall.

"Come along, Sophie," her mother said. "Get your chalk. A storm is coming."

"Mais Maman!" Sophie said. "That man, he talks with spiders!"

"What?" Sophie's mother asked. "A man who speaks with spiders?"

"It is true, Maman! I saw him."

Sophie's mother nodded to her friends and was leading her imaginative daughter out of the playground, when a police officer approached.

"Pardonnez-moi, Madame."

"Oui?" said Sophie's mother.

The policeman explained that he had received a call about a strange man loitering around the playground and was investigating. Had they seen anything? No, her mother answered, they'd seen nothing unusual.

"Oui, Maman. That was the man I told you about. Come look!"

Sophie walked her mother and the policeman to her unfinished sketch of the man. It was all deep browns, blacks, and grays, a very dark image of a ghostly figure. "He is the one who speaks with spiders! I saw him there," Sophie said pointing to where the man had been standing.

The policeman and her mother laughed. "A man who speaks with spiders? I'll make note of that," the policeman said as he walked away.

16

The Tartan and Tiger

RAINING AGAIN. It almost always rained in Ardfern. And when it wasn't raining, it was about to. But that didn't bother twelve-year-old Jimmy Gresham. Quite the contrary, he felt a kind of kinship with the waterfront of Craignish Loch in the Scottish Highlands. The turbulent sky—jagged clouds, some white, some gray, some deepening blue, churning and drifting high and low, at different speeds and even different directions—was part of it. Sailboats tied to their mooring balls rose and fell in the changing tides like giant swans paddling in a ship's wake. Now and then a ship's bell rang, its melancholy tone hanging in the air seemingly forever. That was part of it, too. Even the lush green hills that ran up from the town of Ardfern were—like Jimmy—quiet, alone, and perfectly sad.

It is better than being back in England, Jimmy thought as he sat, dangling his legs off a rock ledge and tossing pebbles into the sea. Each toss, each splash, brought more life to his hesitant smile. Ardfern wasn't so bad. Sure, his adopted parents seemed to despise him. Oh, they never said it outright, but they didn't have to. Jimmy knew. But anything was better than St. Jerome's Home for Orphans on Paddock Street. Nothing would make him go back there. Nothing.

Thunder announced its presence with a slow, angry roll that rumbled down out of the foothills. Its deep voice penetrated flesh and bone, and Jimmy felt suddenly very strange, almost nauseated. There was a flash of light. Or at least that's what Jimmy thought.

But in that briefest of moments, Jimmy saw something, almost like a superquick movie clip in his mind. He had seen himself pick up a large, flat stone and sidearm it into the water. It skipped seven times. Jimmy blinked and shook his head. The nausea was gone. He waited, but there was no thunder.

The rain came down in earnest now, and Jimmy pulled his slicker tight around himself. He didn't mind that it was a couple years old. He sure hadn't grown much. The slicker still fit.

Of course, Geoffry got a new one. *Geoffry.* Jimmy made a clucking noise in the back of his throat, twisted loose a melon-sized rock, and heaved it into the loch. It landed with a deep *SPLOOSH*. When Mr. and Mrs. Gresham were told they couldn't have children, they decided to adopt. That had been six years ago, and Jimmy's arrival to the cobblestone house overlooking the loch had been a happy one.

They picnicked together on the hillside above their house, took car rides on the weekends to Oban, and frequently rode the ferry to Iona. New shoes and clothes seemed to come every other week, and nothing could have stolen his joy. Then came the news that Mrs. Gresham had miraculously become pregnant, an event that baffled the doctors and the family alike. Jimmy was ecstatic. A little brother to show the ropes to, go for walks with in the highlands, and fishing in the loch. Then Geoffry was born. Their "natural" son, as his parents liked to say.

In the blink of an eye, Jimmy went from the apple of their eye to the core . . . barely more than a tolerated houseguest. Mr. and Mrs. Gresham never blatantly mistreated Jimmy. They met his basic needs for food, clothing, and shelter. Love was another thing entirely. Jimmy just could never compare to a blood son. A "legitimate son," the grandparents had whispered. They, too, favored Geoffry.

Jimmy was almost thirteen now, Geoffry five. The only pleasure Jimmy seemed to take was in the fact that he could wander down to the docks alone while Geoffry whined endlessly to his mother, demanding to tag along. Being doted upon came with a price, and that was Mrs. Gresham's terror that anything should ever happen to Geoffry.

"H'afternoon, wee Jimmy," said a tall man, snapping Jimmy out of his thoughts. The man carried two crates of soiled paint cans. He wore blue coveralls stained with grease beneath an open yellow rain slicker much like Jimmy's. A thick wool hat adorned his head, and he perpetually clenched a pipe between his teeth.

"Hello, Mr. McDougal," said Jimmy as he picked up a rather perfect stone—round and flat, fitting perfectly in the C of his thumb and forefinger. He flung the stone and looked up to the visitor. Jimmy never saw the stone skip seven times.

Mr. McDougal stared down at Jimmy, a bit of blue peeping out between bushy gray brows and the wrinkly, weathered bags earned in a lifetime working on the water. He owned one of the two marinas in Ardfern. But unlike the upscale one with nice yachts—even one or two of the royal family's grandchildrens' sailboats—Mr. McDougal's establishment was for those who lived in the area. Hardworking and never sitting idle for a moment, Mr. McDougal was a diligent soul, even if a bit hard at times. "Yu're workin' to catch a cold there, Jimmy boy?"

Jimmy stared out over the water, watching the rings expand from his last throw. "Think anyone would notice if I did?" He instantly regretted speaking his raw feelings like that.

"There now, we cannot have one of Lochgilphead's finest students absent from the annual science fair, can we?"

Jimmy turned and looked up. "That's kind of you to say, but I'm barely gettin' by with me marks."

"Don't yu be skirtin' the issue now, lad. I know you're a smart one."

"But me marks are——"

"Yur grades are not a reflection of what I know's inside yur head there, lad," he said tapping a finger to his own greasy forehead and then quickly reaching for the crates again so they wouldn't fall. "Keep yur chin up there, Jimmy. Yur best days are commin'."

"Thanks, Mr. McDougal." Jimmy looked up, and the tall man just smiled and went on his way. *Perhaps Mr. McDougal would miss me if I were gone,* Jimmy mused.

Jimmy glanced at his wristwatch. It was time to go fetch his father at the pub and then head home. His mother hated when his father was late, and she would take it out on Jimmy. He stood up and threw his remaining pebbles. For a heartbeat, they dimpled the surface among the raindrops and disappeared into the murky loch.

Rather than walk around a large puddle swirling with oily rainbow lines, Jimmy chose to splash through it feeling the cold water soak his socks. He walked past the general store and continued on down the main street until coming to the hotel, home of Ardfern's only pub: The Tartan and Tiger. While the locals stayed clear of the establishment in the summer months, they returned in force after the tourists were gone. And Jimmy's dad could be found there every evening, laughing with his friends and always good for a game of darts.

Jimmy opened the old wooden door and slipped in unnoticed. Short for his age, not many people ever saw him coming or leaving a place. Just once, he wished everyone would notice he'd entered and say, "Hey, Jimmy boy!" or "Look who it is! Jimmy Gresham!" or even "Join us in a game a' darts, me boy."

He took a look around the pub and pulled off his hood to reveal a damp tuft of red hair above matching brows and hazel eyes. A quartet of men sat around a table drinking their pints, while another pair threw darts. The lights were low, and only a dim gray light seeped in the narrow windows. A few more men sat at the bar, but Jimmy's dad was nowhere to be seen. He walked over and hopped up on one of the empty bar stools.

Behind the bar was Regis McAuliffe, raven-black hair cut just below her jaw line and beautiful dark eyes. Regis always noticed him. But then again, it was her job to notice people when they came in. "Lookin' fer yur da?" Regis asked.

"Aye," said Jimmy, slightly blushing. If he were ten years older, Jimmy would propose to Regis on the spot. Why she wasn't married was anyone's guess. *If someone didn't propose to her soon*, Jimmy thought, *I could afford a ring by my sixteenth birthday.*

"Funny thing is, Jimmy, I've not seen him today."

"Worn out, I bet," Jimmy replied. "His back's been givin' him what for."

"Probably so." Regis gave him one of her trademark winks and then went to washing some glasses. "Shall I be getting yu somthin' in the meantime?"

Several replies came to mind: *A great big hug. Maybe a kiss on the cheek. I know! How about your hand in marriage?* But what Jimmy said was, "A cola is fine." She nodded and walked to the cooler.

Waiting for his drink, Jimmy let his eyes wander over the familiar room. Music pumped out from a jukebox in the corner. He had heard every song in there a hundred times and wished someone would put new music in it. The two guys with darts were yelling at each other, and the men at the table burst out laughing at them. Jimmy laughed for a moment, but stopped abruptly. A man sat alone in the far corner, just out of reach of the nearest table light. Jimmy hadn't noticed him before and tried not to stare. He certainly wasn't a regular. He wore a long gray coat, an expensive-looking fedora hat with tufts of white hair protruding out the side, and had a cane leaning against the table. He leaned over a drink. Jimmy couldn't see his face.

A tourist, he thought. *But a strange tourist.*

"He's a new 'un," Regis whispered, leaning in close. She pushed the cola toward Jimmy on a napkin. "Been sittin' here all h'afternoon. Ordered a pint, but hasn't touched it."

"What's his name?"

"He didn't say, Master Jimmy." He loved when she called him that. *Master Jimmy*. "Ah well, probably just a migrant moving through town."

"Aye, probably," Jimmy said, looking back over his shoulder. Just then a chill shook his body. It must have been obvious because Regis said something about it.

"You catchin' a cold?"

"Nah, is justa' shake to keep me warm."

He looked back to Regis, but she was staring at the man in the corner now, too. And there was something in her eyes. Something fearful he had never seen before.

"I think you best be a-gettin' home, Master Jimmy."

"But me cola—"

"It's on me," she said looking back to him. "Yu'll have a fresh one next time. But the rain's pickin' up and I wouldn'a want yur ma pinnin' yur sickness on me."

"Nay, that yu wouldn't." He smiled, wishing he was old enough not to have her talk about his mother, except for maybe in meeting her when Jimmy introduced Regis as his future bride.

"Run along now, Jimmy," Regis said, her voice hushed. Jimmy slid off his stool and cast one glance around the room, looking last at the man in the corner. He got another shiver and opened the door, but not before walking through a thin net of a spiderweb. He frantically wiped it off his face and pulled the slicker's hood over his head.

In the open air once more, his ears filled with the loud pounding of the rain as he turned back down the road. The main street was flooding and the puddles were now unavoidable. He kept to the shoulder mostly, taking his time. Regis ushered him out rather abruptly, Jimmy thought. What had made her do so . . . *the man in the corner*. That had to be it.

Feeling a sudden panic, Jimmy turned to look back at the pub. Lightning flashed, and a man stood in the middle of the street. Jimmy's heart leaped. *It couldn't be.*

He kept walking, trying to look as if nothing was wrong. His legs felt heavy, his footfalls awkward. A chill climbed up his back and spread across his shoulder blades like a glacial frost. Everything in him screamed *run!* But he held back. *It's justa' tourist or a migrant, that's all,* he assured himself.

He casually glanced behind him again, only this time the man was walking . . . toward him.

Jimmy wanted to remain calm, but it was no use. His heart pounded, and a chill surged over his flesh like bolts of electricity. A moment later, Jimmy blasted down the road, water shooting up from beneath his feet.

Heavy footfalls sounded behind him. The chase was on.

Jimmy's hood flew back, and the rain soaked his hair. He squinted against the water streaming down his face and willed himself blindly down the street. He screamed for help, but the wind seemed to swallow up his voice. It was very unlikely anyone who could help would be out in this weather anyway. He could feel the man gaining on him. Jimmy's legs were just not long enough.

His frantic mind spun to any possible hope of safety. Home was too far up the hill. Mrs. Landry's general store was closed up for the night. Farther away was the marina. Mr. McDougal might still be down there doing maintenance. That man never seemed to quit working.

He had no choice. He'd have to leave the main road and sprint down the slope to the marina. *Mr. McDougal will help . . . if he is there.*

But as he jagged to the right, his shoe caught on the edge of a pothole, and Jimmy went splashing to the ground. He felt his chin dig into the asphalt and his palms burn. Cold water filled his shirt, his trousers soaked to the core.

A hand grasped the back of Jimmy's arm and began to pull.

"Here, let me help you, Jimmy," came a woman's voice. Though Jimmy's vision was a blur at first, he knew the voice. But from where?

He felt the pull even stronger and regained his feet. He rubbed his eyes and looked up. "Miss Finney?" It was Lochgilphead's new reading teacher. "What are yu—? I mean, why—?"

"Run home now, Jimmy," she said. Her dark hair was soaked with a few sodden strands matted against her ivory forehead and cheeks, but there was no mistaking the intensity of her eyes. "Are yu listenin', boy?"

"But I don't—"

"There is no time. I'll handle this. Yu get home, *now*." The urgency of her last word was clear, but still Jimmy hesitated.

"Din' ya hear the lass, Jimmy?" came another voice, this one back down toward the pub. *Regis? What was she doing outside?*

Jimmy blinked once more before Miss Finney shoved him down the road and yelled, "Run!" Jimmy took off at full speed. Between his hammering heart and the drenching downpour, Jimmy could barely breathe.

Bright light flashed from behind. Jimmy winced, waiting for the thunder that would no doubt follow. But there was no noise . . . no *crash* or *bang*. Just a flash of bright bluish light . . . and at street level, too.

Curiosity got the better of him, and he spun around in time to see . . . Miss Finney? There were three figures—two light, one dark—ducking, dodging, lunging, swiping . . . fighting in the street. Jimmy wiped streams of rain from his face and stopped running.

A very dark-haired woman wearing a flowing white cloak stood her ground against something Jimmy couldn't quite understand. It looked human, but crouched like a beast. Through the rain, its face looked skullish, and its fingers seemed more than twice as long as a normal person's. It leaped up from its crouch, much higher than a person should be able to jump, and plummeted toward the woman. But she, Jimmy realized, was not unarmed. She whirled a staff upward and struck out at the dark thing like a child smacking a ball. There was a guttural screech. The thing crashed to the ground, rolled, and was back in its crouch in a heartbeat. It flung something toward the woman in white, and there was another blinding, blue flash. The woman tumbled to the ground and was slow to get up.

The second woman, dressed in a similar cloak—but dark blue—stepped in front of the first, and went on the offensive, stepping forward and raining down blow after blow against their enemy. The beast, whatever it was, took a jab in the abdomen and then a cracking blow to the cheek. It went down and stayed down this time.

The woman in white was up and racing after the fallen thing. She raised her staff as if she might deliver one final crushing blow to finish it off. But with her arms raised, her body was defenseless for a moment. And in that breathless pause, the beast lashed out, scraping one hand at her midsection. She nearly dropped her staff as she covered her stomach with one arm and backed away. The woman in blue stepped in to finish the task.

Suddenly the woman in white looked in Jimmy's direction. "Get home, Jimmy! Now!" Jimmy jumped back at the sudden sound of his name. It was Miss Finney, he was sure of it . . . but her voice had changed; there was more power in it. More authority. But who was the . . . other? *The dark hair . . . Regis?*

Jimmy stumbled backward and turned, running past the general store and then turning up the lane to his home. With every step Jimmy realized he had no idea what he was going to tell his parents when he burst through the door out of breath. They would never believe this. In fact, he didn't know if *he* believed this!

His lungs burned, he gasped for air as he rounded the corner into the driveway and took the stone steps two at a time. He glanced behind him to make sure he wasn't followed.

Nothing but rain and a street lamp.

He stood on the porch and gasped, watching his breath in the cooling air. His chin burned from hitting the pavement, as did his palms. With his heart beating loudly in his ears, Jimmy tried his best to calm down and control his panting. But the images that played over in his head were too extravagant. Too unusual.

He took one more breath and then walked inside. To his surprise, both his father and mother were seated on the sofa beside the fire, with a platter of tea and cookies on the low table. A man sat across from them on the other sofa. Geoffry was busy playing with something in the corner.

"Jimmy," his mother piped up. "Whatever took yu so long?"

"What?"

"Yu're late gettin' home, boy."

"I—I was—"

"Yu was fixin' to catch a cold is what yu're doing," said his mother. "And now yu're drippin' all over the carpet. Mind yurself!"

"Do as yur mutha' says," added his father.

Jimmy looked between them. Something didn't feel right.

"Don't just stand there like a doe in the headlights, take off yur wet things and com'a sit down," his mom commanded. Then her tone softened a bit. "We'd like ta introduce yu to Mr. Ogelvie. He is our new neighbor comin' for a wee chat."

Jimmy turned to the man and got a clear look at him. What he saw stopped his heart cold, and only one thought came to mind: *Get out, now.*

17

Stolen Thoughts

"BUENAS TARDES, Senorita Simonson!" called the new housekeeper from the open window of the blue luxury SUV. Kat's parents had bought the vehicle especially for the housekeeper to use for errands.

"It's Kat. Just Kat," she said, closing the rear passenger-side door to the SUV. "So, uh, what should I call you?"

"Well, my full name es Anna Rosario Delarosa Espinosa," the petite, Latino woman replied. "But my friends call me Anna. So please, Kat, call me Anna."

"Okay, thank you, Anna." Already she liked Anna much better than Mrs. Braithwaite, the last housekeeper. She was an English lady who served tea and condescending insults three times a day—if not more.

Kat smiled at Anna in the rearview mirror. Anna smiled back.

Anna had long black hair pulled back in a bun and wore a non-descript black dress coat and a white-collared shirt. The Tahoe moved slowly forward. The bus lanes were full of cars and, of course, buses.

Kat put her earbuds in and clicked play. No sound came out, but she heard a whispered voice. *I know who you are.*

Kat tore the earbuds out. "Anna!"

The housekeeper put on the brake and turned round. "Sí, Kat?"

"Did you just say something?"

"No."

"Nothing at all?"

"No, Kat, nada." Anna looked at her. "You okay?"

Kat nodded. "I'm good," she said. "Just thought I heard something strange when I put my earbuds in."

"I know de kind of music you kids listen to," Anna said and laughed softly. "And it es strange."

Kat laughed. *True.* Some of the bands she had on her player were pretty weird. Spiked, multicolored hair. Nose rings, eye rings, lip rings, . . . leather everything, studs, chains, the works. The singers often screamed or growled, but Kat hadn't remembered any of her song downloads beginning with someone whispering.

In a flash, the earbuds were back in and she fast-forwarded to another track. This time, the music came on right away: a long drum fill concluding with a thunderous double bass drum and a scorching guitar riff. But above the music came the same raspy, whispering voice: *I know you, Alreenia.*

Kat rewound the track. Same song, but no whispering. She took out both earbuds and leaned across the backseat to look out the other window. And there he was, the creepy detective man standing at the driver's side of a black truck. And, based on the direction of his sunglasses, he was staring right at Kat.

You need not steal my thoughts. I will give them to you freely. I am coming for you, Alreenia . . . coming to correct an ancient wrong. You are going to die today. Or . . . perhaps, I will take you to my home where there is fire and lightning. And you will dine on the black fruit of Vesper Crag. Such a slow, painful death. Yesssss.

The man slid a very pale hand from his pocket. He pointed a long, bony finger at Kat.

"Anna!" Kat shrieked.

The housekeeper spun around. "What es wrong?"

"There's a man over there!"

"What man?" Anna ducked and bobbed, trying to see around cars and between busses.

CURSE OF THE SPIDER KING

"He's there," she said, poking the glass. "He's standing next to that black truck. He's been staring at me. And just now he pointed at me. *Eww,* he has really long fingers."

"Did you . . . did you say this man, he have long fingers?" Anna's expression changed as if her face had been erased and redrawn.

"Yes, Anna, it almost looked like a claw."

"Was he wearing a gray hat, coat, and sunglasses?"

"How did you know that?"

Anna turned back to the wheel and revved the engine. "Senorita Simonson," she said, "again, fasten your seat belt."

"Anna, what are you doing?!" Kat wailed from the backseat. The housekeeper ignored her, stomped on the gas pedal, and swerved between a parked car and a slow-moving bus.

Kat slid hard to the other side of the backseat as Anna yanked the SUV around the school's pickup circle and then out into traffic. Kat pried herself away from the side panel and climbed into the passenger seat next to Anna, somehow feeling safer up front. She put on her seat belt and then wheeled around to look out of the back window. With dread icing the bottom of her stomach, Kat watched a black truck jump the curb, tear across the grass island in front of the school, and blast onto the road. It sideswiped a small convertible and surged forward. "Anna, he's coming!"

"I see him!" she replied. She made a swift left turn, barely missing oncoming traffic. The black truck followed, and a silver pickup clipped its back end. The truck fishtailed but regained control and pursued.

"He's still coming!"

"I must get us to the freeway. We lose him there."

"Anna!" Kat turned around again. "Lose who? Who's after us?"

"Not now, Kat!" Anna swerved around a car trying to parallel park in front of a florist, and then darted onto a four-lane highway. "We are almost there!" She paused and then said, "Ah, these will help."

Kat heard tires squeal. She watched the black truck race out behind them, maybe five car lengths back. Then she turned and saw the traffic light ahead of them was turning from yellow to red. Anna barely made it, but no way the black truck would. The light turned. Cars from both sides began to cross the intersection. But the truck did not stop. Kat watched it barrel through the intersection, slipping between a slow-moving van and a tractor-trailer that was screeching to a stop. The truck had swerved so suddenly to avoid collision that it went on two wheels and seemed likely to roll. But somehow it righted itself and tore after them.

"Oh, no, he made it!" Kat growled. "Gun it, Anna!"

Anna watched the speedometer needle pass sixty, but there was too much traffic to go any faster. She saw the sign she was looking for: Rt. 101 Hollywood Freeway—1 mile. Anna surged ahead and muttered, "He drives well for a . . ."

"What?" Kat hadn't heard Anna's last word. She leaned forward, but Anna said nothing more.

Anna was grateful that no cars were immediately in front of them as she took the freeway on ramp at high speed. She raced onto the six-lane superhighway and looked to pull away. The black truck came up behind them much faster than she anticipated.

Thud! The Tahoe lurched forward. Kat's head snapped back against the headrest as the tires barked against the highway asphalt. She screamed.

"Hold on tight and keep your head down!" Anna shouted, glaring into the rearview mirror.

Kat grabbed the hand brace, but continued to look out the back window. The jet-black truck trailed right behind them and, from the looks of it, intended to ram them again. For the first time, Kat considered the possibility that she might not survive the afternoon. As foreign and frightening as that thought might have been, it only served to infuriate Kat. *Who is this idiotic, detective-looking, maniac?* And why was he coming after them?

The second impact jolted Kat harder than the first. It made her swallow her gum and bite her tongue. "That hurt! What's happening, Anna?" Kat looked up at her, surprised to see how calm Anna seemed behind the wheel.

"Don't be afraid, Kat. Everything will be all right."

"Don't be afr—are you crazy? What's going on? Do you know this man?"

The third impact shattered the back windshield. Kat screamed again and covered her head. Fragments of glass shot forward and scattered all around Kat. She instantly thought of shows she had seen on TV where criminals had abducted children from high-profile, wealthy families in order to secure a steep ransom. Hadn't she seen a movie on that? Denzel Washington was in it . . . something about Mexico. *What if Anna is doing the same thing? What if the guy in the truck actually is a police detective?* Kat took out her cell phone and was about to dial for the police. She stopped. *No, that doesn't make sense. A policeman wouldn't ra—"*

The black truck smashed into them again. Kat's phone flew from her hand and slid somewhere under her seat. She reached for it frantically but couldn't find it.

"Do something!" Kat shouted, overcome by fear. She did not want to be taken. She did not want to die.

"They will not bring harm to you, Kat. I won't let them."

Kat watched Anna pull hard on the steering wheel and felt the vehicle swerve, careening across three lanes of heavy traffic. Kat looked back again. The black truck followed but was forced to drop back behind some cars.

"You're doing it!" Kat exclaimed. She was excited at first, but one chilling thought persisted: *Anna could be the villain here.* "Anna, please!"

"Kat, *por favor*, stay down."

Kat turned back around and watched the exit signs fly by. She glanced at the speedometer: ninety-five miles per hour. Had she ever gone this fast before? Her heart raced, and sweat dripped down her left temple. Pictures from the TV news flashed through her head. She had seen highway pursuits on all the police shows loads of times, but she never actually thought she'd be in one. Here she was, flying down the highway with someone she didn't really know and with someone in dangerous pursuit. Just like on TV, except no police. At least, not yet.

"There!" Kat pointed at a big sign for Hollywood Boulevard West. "Our exit!" But Anna didn't acknowledge her. "Aren't we going home?" Kat became more nervous, her suspicions mounting. They were still one lane away from the exit-only lane.

"Sí, Kat. But this is going to get rough. You will want to hold on."

In a matter of moments Kat and Anna passed the exit; a thin berm of concrete now separated the highway from the descending exit ramp. Kat's eyes grew wide in panic. "Anna!" She glanced over at the driver. "You missed it!"

"No, but he will." And with that Anna pegged the steering wheel hard to the right and sent the SUV across the lane and over the concrete berm. The shocks jolted in the wheel wells, and Kat felt as if her stomach had been wrenched up into her chest. Their SUV dropped into the exit lane below with a loud crash, cars honking behind them. The chassis ripped across the roadway and sparks shot up from underneath. A moment later, Anna slammed on the brakes in order to negotiate the sharp turn of the exit ramp. The tires squealed as they flew around the corner, their vehicle scraping against the side railing.

Kat looked to Anna. *This is crazy! How are we going to explain this to Mom? Oh, and Dad's not going to like what's happened to the Tahoe. Not at all!*

"Look out!" Kat yelled, her eyes fixed on the intersection ahead, red lights aglow. But Anna did not reply, she merely veered into the shoulder and slipped by the cars to the right, turned into traffic, and bolted toward Kat's home.

Kat looked back again. "You lost him!" she said with a wide smile, half-excited, half-delirious.

"We can hope," Anna replied. "But they will guess where we have gone soon enough."

"How can you be so sure?" Kat asked, snapping back to look at Anna.

"Because, niña, I know them. They will not give up so easily."

"What do you mean, you know these people? What are they, like Mexican Mafia? Is that it?"

"Oh no, senorita."

For a second, Kat was semirelieved.

"They are far more dangerous."

Kat just stared at her blankly. They were racing down the road at more than seventy miles per hour, Anna weaving through traffic as if she were a veteran NASCAR driver. Confused, Kat rubbed her head. Anna turned off onto Laurel Canyon Boulevard and started up the winding road toward home. Kat thought she might be sick with all the twists and turns, the wheels complaining with each switchback.

Kat's heart rate had just about returned to normal when she heard Anna mutter, "Mi Dios nos ayude."

"What?!" Kat cried.

"He es back."

Kat turned to see a battered black truck shoot around the corner and charge up the hill after them. "Go, go, go!" Kat tapped Anna on the shoulder as if it would help her.

"We're almost home," replied Anna calmly.

Kat glanced back and forth between the SUV behind and the road up ahead. She counted the houses, watching the prestigious gates whiz by.

"Almost—" But Kat couldn't finish her sentence. The next drive-way was hers, and sitting square in front of the gate was yet another black truck.

"No!"

"Hold on!" Anna yelled.

Kat looked at her, now frantic. "What are you going to do?"

"Brace yourself!" was all Anna said before swerving completely off the road and tearing through the bordering hedgerow. The SUV ripped through the foliage like a tank, the plant stalks snapping underneath. It bounced along on the freshly cut lawn, wheels digging ruts into the soft earth. But they had not faced the worst of it; up ahead was the cobblestone wall that bordered their entire property, meant to keep out intruders. Kat shot Anna a terrified glance.

"You're not going to drive through the wall, are you?" she yelled.

"It is the only way!"

"You're going to kill us, Anna!" she screamed. "Anna, I—" Kat held on to the roll handle and squeezed her seat belt. She looked at Anna, then to the wall.

Anna stomped on the accelerator. The Tahoe raced forward, tires spinning up grass and dirt. Kat could feel the vehicle pick up speed.

"Mom's not going to like this—" Kat's body jarred into her seat belt as the SUV burst through the rock wall. The concussion of the exploding air bag knocked her back into her seat, stars spinning amongst the white powder in the air. The sound of steel colliding with rock was horrific. Deafening. Rocks smashed the windshield. The wall's jagged base ripped the axle from beneath the chassis and nearly flipped the vehicle right over. The SUV careened through the wall, skidding to a halt a few feet into the asphalt driveway.

18

Elfkind

"SENORITA SIMONSON?" Anna said as the engine chunked to a stop.

Kat sat, blinking. Confused.

"We must get you to the house," she continued.

Kat watched Anna's hands reach for her buckle but did not respond. Everything felt like a strange dream . . . hearing voices . . . a car chase . . . racing through traffic . . . blasting through the wall. *Who is this woman? What's happening?*

"Senorita Simonson?" she heard Anna's voice call. Kat looked to her right. Her door was open and Anna was reaching for her, pulling her out of her seat.

"We need to move now!"

Kat's feet stumbled over the debris from the wreck. Her ankle twisted, and the sharp pain brought her mind racing back to reality. She looked back to their SUV, now a semimangled specimen of automotive engineering, and then she saw something moving farther down the driveway near the front gate: The black truck.

"Don't look back, senorita," Anna instructed, pulling on Kat's elbow. "Keep moving. Keep moving."

"Anna, who are they? Why are they after me? It's the money, isn't it? Tell me the truth." Every step she took on her ankle sent searing pain up her leg. But she hardly noticed. Her heart was beating too fast.

"Es not the money they are after, niña."

"Then what? What would drive them to chase me down like that?" She limped along, now much closer to her family's home, and glanced behind her. The window was rolling up, and the black truck was pulling back onto the main road. Her heart skipped a beat. What if it followed their path through the hedgerow? "Anna!"

"Kat," Anna said softly, "you must keep up."

The two briskly made their way to the house, Kat limping, Anna helping her along. They made it inside and to Kat's bedroom. Once inside Kat's private bathroom, Anna helped her wipe a bit of blood from her head. "It es not very serious, but I wanna' clean it." Anna dabbed it gently and held Kat back. "Are you all right, senorita?"

Kat fingered the cut and winced. "I told you, just Kat. My ankle is throbbing, but I think I'll be okay." She took a deep breath, her hands still trembling.

Anna examined Kat's ankle. "It es a bit swollen, a slight sprain."

"Anna, who were those people?"

"You wouldn't believe me if I told you."

"Try me."

"Did Mr. Wallace give you anything today?"

Kat froze. *Is she talking about the book? How did she know?*

"Kat?"

"Uh, Mr. Wallace?"

"Did he give you anything?" she asked again.

"Yes. But how did—?"

"A book?"

Now Kat was freaking out. "What's going on here? Who are you?" Kat pushed Anna away. Kat could feel herself getting dizzy. She got up and made it to the bathroom door before she blacked out.

Kat woke up on her bed, Anna holding a cool cloth to her head and looking very concerned. "I am glad to see you awake so soon, senorita. You were out just a few minutes. It es shock, that's all."

"Anna," Kat whispered. "Who are you?"

Anna studied Kat's face. "Kat, do you really want to know what es going on?"

"With all my heart. I'm so confused. Mr. Wallace said . . . and now you . . . and this crazy thing happened with a book he gave me . . . and I'm hearing things!"

"Easy, child." Anna placed a hand on Kat's arm and insisted she lie back down. "There es much to explain, but one thing es sure: you are not safe here anymore. The good news is that we have found you; but the bad news es that they have found you, too."

"Who's they?"

"Do you remember reading about a ruthless group of warriors, the Spider King's assassins, known as Drefids?"

"Yes. Why?"

"Are you curious about how the book comes to life when you touch the text?"

Kat froze. Things had gone way out of control. There was no way Anna could have known. No one else in the study hall had seen anything. No one but Kat.

"Oh, Anna, you've got to be kidding me!" But Anna just sat there on the edge of her bed. Kat started scooting up toward the headboard as if trying to get away from a spider crawling toward her on the comforter. "That's—that's not possible!"

"Those men are no men at all. They are Drefids, sent here to earth to find you."

"Earth. You mean, like, they're from another planet?"

"Another *reality*, you might say."

"Aliens?"

Anna laughed. "Not quite." Anna tilted her head to one side, revealing a slightly larger-than-normal ear. Nothing seemed to be amiss. Until Anna grabbed ahold of a piece of fake skin and ripped it away.

Kat gasped. Things were getting weirder by the second. "You're—you're—"

"An Elf. Mr. Wallace es, too. But we're part of a special team of Sentinels, sent here to bring you back."

Kat's mouth hung wide open. "You're . . . an Elf."

"Please, Kat, focus. I know this is a bit much. But you are just going to have to trust me."

"You're an Elf who speaks with a Mexican accent?"

"I could have picked any nationality, now couldn't I, lass?" she replied in a flawless British English. "That's rather pointless, you do understand. But when Mr. Wallace contacted me that he had found you, I needed a way into your family. This was no simple thing, and for a time, we were at a loss. But I believe Ellos—er, God—opened the door. Your parents fired your housekeeper, so with my flawless Spanish and English, and my sterling résumé, I stepped in. You Simonsons are far too high profile of a family to approach at school. Mr. Wallace risked everything just to give you the book."

"I don't get—what do you mean, 'found me'? Why were you looking for me?"

"Well, Kat, it began long before your power manifested—"

"My power?"

"How else do you think you could read people's thoughts?" Anna's voice now reflected a typical American dialect. "You've reached the Age of Reckoning, the age when your true nature reveals itself."

"What do you mean, my true nature?"

"Why . . . don't you see? Have you never suspected?" She paused. Kat held her breath. "You are an Elf, too, my dear."

Kat was breathing heavy. Anna doubted whether this was indeed the right time to give so much information. But when was a better time? Things were escalating far too quickly. They had to act. Fast.

"So, what you're telling me is that I'm an Elf . . . from another world . . . with the ability to read minds, and you've been sent to bring me back to that world, while those things are out there stalking me, trying to keep me from going back?"

"Correction," she replied. "They are trying to kill you."

"Oh," she replied blankly. "So that's your story?"

"Yes," replied Anna nodding, realizing she was losing Kat. "It's the truth."

"Look, Anna," Kat began. She searched the room for her purse and then remembered her cell phone was back in the SUV wreckage. She glanced at the landline phone on the bedside table, six feet away. She began to scoot slowly across the bed. "The ears are impressive, and I have no idea how you could know the things you know, but you . . . you and Mr. Wallace could be the kidnappers." Kat put her hand on the phone. "Just let me call my mom. If you're on my side, you'll let me call."

Anna hesitated. Her eyes darted. "Kat, if we were kidnappers, why would I risk bringing you back here?"

Kat started to dial.

"If the Drefids who chased us were actually good guys—police even—then why would they try to ram us? Why wouldn't they use sirens? Why wouldn't they have stormed the house?"

Kat stopped dialing at the last digit. She had wondered the same things about their pursuers . . . police wouldn't drive so recklessly, especially without a siren. "Anna, I want to trust you, but . . . but . . . I just can't. This is all too crazy. Just let me call my mom."

"Oh, Kat, I am so sorry to put you through all of this. And your parents, too. They are victims here—and you doubly so. Believe me when I tell you, I would not wish this on anyone. But, like it or not, we are all in the middle of it. If you make that call, you will just bring more innocent people into danger. I can think of only one thing that might convince you that I am for real."

Kat put down the phone. "You want me to try to read your mind."

"There is no other way."

"But I don't know how . . . before it just kind of happened. Do you know how to do it?"

"I don't know either, Kat. You've just recently reached the Age of Reckoning. Your gift is untrained and very unpredictable. Maybe just close your eyes, focus on me, and try."

Kat glanced once more at the phone, but then closed her eyes. At first she saw nothing but darkness and weird, random patterns. She heard nothing except the birds outside and the hum of the air conditioner. But then she began to feel dizzy. Visions and voices streamed into her mind. She saw a castle-city burning. There was a great battle . . . the same she remembered from the book. She saw the Elven children stolen, saw the grief-stricken Elves traveling a long, shadowy tunnel. Kat saw a gathering of Elves, Anna with them, in a candlelit chamber. She heard their plans to get the children back. She heard the desperate hope in their voices. And then it was gone.

"I did it, Anna! I read your thoughts . . . and this time, I could see them, too!"

"Good, Kat. Your gift is gaining strength. Do you believe me now?"

"I . . . I guess I have to," Kat replied, squinting and shaking her head. "But why . . . why are we so important that you want us back and the Spider King wants us dead?"

Anna's lips trembled slightly, and Kat could see tears welling up. "Kat, you and the other lords are our only hope for survival. The

Spider King's power has grown immense. There is some power waxing in Vesper Crag where he dwells—some power we do not understand. But it has enabled him to build a matchless army. He has gained the allegiance of the Drefids and has somehow brought Wisps back from oblivion. The Elves that remain in hiding are too few to oppose such wicked strength. And even the Sentinels and Dreadnaughts have no such power to stop the Spider King. But we cling to hope in you."

"We're just kids," said Kat.

"Nay! You are descendants of a royal bloodline, unblemished and unbroken for thousands and thousands of years. You and the others have powers beyond reckoning—especially if you use them together, those powers will magnify, and we will rally around you. And . . . and there's something else."

"What?"

"I'm sorry, Kat, but I cannot speak openly about this until I consult with Eldera, the leader of our team. But I can tell you that long ago, at the founding of Berinfell, prophecies were uttered . . . prophecies concerning you. Without you and the other lords, the Elven race will perish from Allyra. Will you come? Will you come . . . back home?"

Kat put her head in her hands. "Leave? Leave my family? Leave Earth? I just don't—I mean, maybe my parents could come."

"Kat, I'm sorry, but I don't want to put them in harm's way. In fact, the longer we dwell here, the more danger they are in. The Drefid who chased us will gather others, and they will descend upon your house in force."

"But if my parents think I'm in danger, they'll have an army of police to guard the house!"

"It will not be enough, Kat. And more innocent lives will be lost. The people of this world will not know what they are facing. You've got to decide now. Sooner or later, someone will notice the crashed

SUV and call the police. We must be gone before the police or the Drefids come back. We must leave right now."

"Leave? For this other world?"

"No. For Edinburgh, Scotland."

Kat looked at her in disbelief. "You're kidding, right?"

"No, I'm quite serious. Mr. Wallace will be joining us soon. But we have got to leave . . . for your parents' sake."

"Would the Drefids really try and kill my parents?"

"If they think they need to in order to get to you . . . yes—but if we escape now . . ."

This changed everything. There was no mistaking those men's . . . those *Drefids'* . . . intentions. And bringing her parents into this was the last thing she wanted. And having read Anna's mind, as far-fetched as it was, it had to be true. Then she had no choice but to go . . . as far away as possible.

"What about when the authorities start looking for me? I'm not exactly hard to miss, you know," Kat said, gesturing to her blue skin.

"Leave that to me."

"And my parents? I can't just leave." Kat thought about how guilty she already felt by not reaching out to her mother more.

"I've left them a note."

"A note? Somehow I don't think a note is going to help."

"It will be much more convincing than you could ever imagine. This note, written with the same craft applied to your book, will not convince them of your safety. They might still call out the National Guard to search for you. But it will at least give them some sense that something otherworldly is going on. Regardless, we must leave right now. Mr. Wallace will have your passport. He is waiting for us at the airport now."

"What, you have some sort of ESP communication technique?"

"No, Kat. We have e-mail."

19

Off Target

IT HAD been more than a week since the meeting with Mrs. Galdarro and, other than a few whispered admonitions to keep reading the book, the librarian hadn't made any contact with Tommy. And when Tommy went to the library at lunch, he found Mrs. Galdarro surrounded by other students and far too busy to talk to about the strange things he'd been reading in the Elf book. But this day, Tommy wasn't worried about trying to catch a moment with Mrs. Galdarro—he had other things on his mind. No matter how hard he willed the second hand on Mrs. Collen's clock to stop, it ticked relentlessly on toward the twelve and the end of math class. Gym was next, and Tommy's hands were already cold and clammy.

The bell rang. Brock Eastman stood up from his desk by the window and whooped. "Fear the seventh grade, Mrs. Collen! We're going to take down the teachers on Falcon Day." The rest of the class, minus Tommy, hooted and cheered.

Mrs. Collen didn't stand up. She lowered her glasses and grinned. "I'd say the odds of the students defeating the teachers this year are about one in a trillion." The class *ooooohhh*ed. "To put it less mathematically," she continued. "The chances of students outshooting teachers in the archery meet are slim to none . . . and slim just left town."

"Boo-yah!" shouted Caleb Scrandis, wagging a finger in Brock's face. "She toasted you, Brock!"

"Actually," said Aaron Worthington, "if you consider the fact that the seventh graders have never defeated the teachers, in combination with a few other select variables, then I calculate the odds to be—"

"Quit, Aaron!" Brock complained, his face reddening. "Yeah, well . . . say what you want. It won't seem so funny after all my bull's-eyes tomorrow. Besides, Haley Shoop's our ringer."

"Well, Brock," said Mrs. Collen with playful glee, "if you want to have any chance of defeating the teachers—a feat that has not occurred in the history of Thurgood Marshall Middle School—I suggest you hurry on to gym. Mr. Phitzsinger won't take kindly to anyone being late."

Chairs and desks scraped on the floor, and twenty-eight seventh graders hurried like blood cells into the steady stream of students already coursing in the hallway.

I feel like some kind of leprechaun, Tommy thought as he stood second to last in a line of five seventh graders all dressed in Thurgood's standard gym uniforms: green shorts, green T-shirt—both with yellow trim. They waited behind a tall, orange construction cone that had had its top snipped off so that it could hold three fiberglass arrows. Tommy's line was one of a dozen such lines spread evenly in front of the gym's bleachers. Across the glistening gym floor were twelve thick archery targets and a floor-to-ceiling shroud of white netting.

"Take up your bows!" Mr. Phitzsinger bellowed. As he spoke, a strange clump of too-blond hair flopped around like a fish on his always-sweaty, always-red forehead. "And watch your spacing!"

Haley Shoop was first up in Tommy's line. He was glad of that. She'd surely make up for his poor scores. Haley scooped up her bow and gave the bowstring a practiced pull. She looked over her right shoulder at Mr. Phitzsinger.

"Nock arrows!" He yelled.

Haley selected a golden arrow with blue and orange fletchings and swiftly put it to the bowstring.

"Draw!" cried the P.E. teacher. Followed shortly by, "Release!"

Haley's first arrow sliced through the air in a blink and struck the target an inch outside of the bull's-eye.

Tommy loved the pop-thud sound of the arrow piercing the plastic target. *Just once*, he thought, *I'd like to hear that sound from my own shot.*

Haley seemed frustrated with her first attempt. She took up the second arrow, put it to the string, and lined up her shot. Tommy clenched his fingers and tried to focus on Haley's technique. Her feet were shoulder's-width apart in-line with the target. The elbow of her right arm came backward as she pulled the arrow back on the string, fingers to the corner of her mouth. Her left arm held the bow straight out, slowly leveling the tip of the arrow with her target. Then the arrow leaped from the string and buried itself several inches deep into the upper left quadrant of the bull's-eye.

"Yeah!" Tommy blurted out a little louder than he'd meant to. Haley turned around. Her surprised expression melted away into a sweet smile and a blush. She turned back to the target and loaded up another arrow. Her final shot slammed into the blue outer ring, uncharacteristically poor for Haley.

"Bows down!" called Mr. Phitzsinger. The shooting was over. Students put their bows on the floor and went to the targets to collect their arrows. Some students had to retrieve theirs from the netting behind the targets. Not Haley. She yanked her arrows out and marched over to the teacher.

The composite score appeared on the basketball scoreboard: 448.

"Decent score," said Mr. Phitzsinger. "Very decent! You know, you guys keep shooting like that, you might have a chance to beat the teachers."

The gym erupted in cheers. The first archers went to the end of the line, and a new group of students took up the bows.

Haley slowed down a bit as she passed Tommy. She looked at him a moment, smiled, and then stared at the ground. *That was weird,* Tommy thought. *Girls are weird.*

The next three archers went by way too quickly for Tommy. He waited a few moments and stepped up behind the large orange cone. It reminded Tommy of the cones that emergency crews set out around an accident scene. *Kinda fitting,* Tommy thought.

"Take up your bows!"

Tommy did. It was an awkward thing, all yellow and black with pulleys and loops of bowstring all over. He held the compound bow as if it were some kind of trap that might spring shut on him. Why couldn't they play soccer against the teachers? Tommy could play soccer. He pictured himself dribbling circles around his literature teacher.

"Nock your arrows!"

Tommy selected a golden arrow with orange and blue fletchings, the same arrow Haley had used first. He tried to balance the front of the shaft on his left hand while fitting the nock onto the bowstring. It slipped off.

"Draw!"

Tommy's fingers fumbled.

"Release!"

Tommy looked side to side. All the other kids fired their first arrows. Tommy tried again to nock the arrow. This time, he fit the arrow onto the bowstring, but as he lifted the bow, the shaft fell away from the bow.

Thwack! Thud! Thwack!

Tommy heard his classmates firing their second arrows, and he struggled to get the arrow back onto the bow. Sweat rolled down his back. His fingers felt clumsy and numb. But he got them to work well enough to at last get the arrow nocked. But in his rush, the back of the arrow was much higher than the arrowhead.

Tommy pulled back on the bowstring, felt the resistance of the pulleys, and pulled even harder. When he could not pull back any farther, he let go. The bowstring stung his fingers and grazed his forearm. "Ow!" The arrow zipped away and . . . clattered onto the hardwood gym floor.

"C'mon, Bowman!" Mr. Phitzsinger bellowed. "You'd think with a name like yours you'd shoot better'n that!" Everyone giggled.

Tommy reddened, grabbed a second arrow, and fit it to the string. He aimed quickly, seeing the gold bull's-eye, but it looked so far away. And Tommy couldn't make himself focus. It was as if the bull's-eye bobbed among the circles of blue, white, and red. Uttering an exasperated sigh, Tommy fired. But after putting the first arrow into the floor, he'd aimed the second way too high. It sailed well over the target and caught in the top of the white netting.

Chirrups of laughter snickered out of the line behind him. His shoulders sagged, and he stared at the floor. He wished he could shrink himself down, squeeze between the boards on the gym floor, and disappear. Most of the other kids had fired their third arrows, and Mr. Phitzsinger seemed to be staring at Tommy.

Tommy sighed and picked up his final arrow. Without thinking, he fit it to the bowstring. He raised his bow and aimed. As he drew back the bowstring, he felt a tingling in his fingertips of his right hand. It was as if his hand had fallen asleep, but only his fingertips. He raised the bow and aimed. The bull's-eye still seemed so tiny and far away, but it stayed relatively still for a change. He held his breath.

Tommy released the arrow.

It flew straight toward the target but just a little high. It bounced off the top of the target and flipped into the netting. More laughter from behind, but one "Awww," and Tommy was sure it was Haley. It didn't help. If anything, it made things worse.

20

Falcon Day

FALCON DAY. The thought hit Tommy during his third mouthful of cereal the next morning, and a brick of ice seemed to form in his belly. But that was nothing compared to the chilly, twisting knots he felt later that morning in homeroom. Haley Shoop, the seventh-grade archery ace, was absent.

The bell rang, and Tommy trudged to his first-period class. Without Haley, the seventh grade would have no chance at beating the teachers in the afternoon archery meet. Everyone would see how low Tommy's group's score was, and everyone would know exactly why the score was so low. *Maybe Haley is just running late*, he mused. *She could still show up in time.*

"Go, *FALCONS!* Go, *FALCONS! GO!*" Hundreds of sixth, seventh, and eighth graders stomped their feet on the bleachers in the gym and clapped their hands to the *Boom-boom-thwack* of their familiar fight song. Tommy stood last in his line of four. Four! Haley still hadn't shown up.

"Can you at least try to hit something on the target?" Brock Eastman jeered from the next line of archers over. "We're going to need all the points we can get, Tommy!"

Tommy scowled and was about to reply, but music, even louder than the din of the students in the stands, blared on the gym's PA speakers. Tommy recognized the music. It was the deep, brassy piece that played in the *Star Wars* movies whenever Darth Vader showed up. And suddenly, fifteen figures entered the gym from behind the targets. It was the seventh-grade teachers, and each one carried a long bow and wore a dark hood and cloak, like a band of villains. Led by Mr. Belanger, the science teacher, the teachers took their places on either side of the gym.

As the music died down, Mr. Phitzsinger came to the front of the gym and motioned for the students to quiet. "Welcome to the Falcon Day Teachers versus Students Archery Meet," he said. "The rules are simple. The first student in each of the seven lines will shoot first. Three arrows. Once all arrows are fired, I'll tell you to retrieve your arrows and add up your score. Ten points for a center ring bull's-eye. Two less points for each ring outside of that. Write your score on the score sheet and submit it to me. I'll post the scores on the basketball scoreboard. Seven teachers will take their turn next, repeating the same process. We'll alternate until the student lines are through."

"Archers ready?" the gym teacher called out. The students stepped up to the cone at the firing line. "Nock your arrows. Fire when ready!"

The first student in each line put an arrow to the string and fired. *THWACK, THUMP, WHAP!!*

No one missed the target. That was both encouraging and discouraging to Tommy. Lots of points for the students, but if this kept up, Tommy would look like even more of a dork when he shot one up at the ceiling or into the floor.

The teachers came next. Mr. Belanger had two ten-point bull's-eyes and a seven-point red circle. And even though some of the less-skilled teachers barely got their wobbly arrows to the target, the score at the end of the first round was Teachers 146, Students 142.

The next two rounds went by in a blur. The teachers led by sixty points, and Tommy found himself standing at the firing line.

"Archers ready!"

Tommy picked up the green bow at his feet, and something peculiar happened. The bow didn't feel awkward. No, indeed. It seemed as comfortable as sliding on his favorite pair of jeans. Tommy looked up at the target. The bull's-eye seemed unusually large . . . like a great big Frisbee just a few feet away.

"Nock your arrows!"

Tommy selected a silver arrow with white and blue fletchings. He nocked the arrow, and it didn't slip away from the bowstring. *What in the world?* He had never felt so relaxed with a bow in his hands. Tommy easily pulled the bowstring back until the fingertips of his right hand grazed his cheek. Then he took aim.

The moment the arrow left the string, Tommy's vision blurred, and he felt like he himself were blazing toward the target . . . as if his eyes were glued to the tip of the arrowhead, then . . . *WHUMP*.

There was an audible gasp from the crowd, broken a moment later by a roar of applause from the bleachers behind Tommy. Kids shouted and cheered.

Tommy shook his head, blinked twice.

It can't be.

Had he missed altogether? He must have. And someone from one of the other lines must have accidentally shot the wrong target, for there, plunged deep into the very center ring of the bull's-eye, was an arrow. His arrow? Surely not. That had to be it, because Brock Eastman was at the front of the next line over, and he was staring at Tommy's target. It was Brock's arrow.

"Good shot," Brock said, sounding surprised.

Tommy's head swiveled comically back and forth between Brock and the target. *A bull's-eye? Me?*

"How'd you do that, Bowman?"

Tommy shrugged. "I . . . I don't know."

"Whatever," said Brock as he selected his next arrow. "Just keep doing it."

Tommy took another arrow out of the cone. In one swift motion, he set the arrow to the string, drew his hand back to his cheek, and lined up the shot. *Amazing,* Tommy thought. Just the day before, he'd had no idea how to judge the distance and the height of the shot. Now, it seemed so clear. The arrow simply had no choice but to go straight into the bull's-eye. Tommy let it go. This time the sensation of his vision riding along with the arrow wasn't nearly as disorienting. Now it felt . . . normal. For a split second, all Tommy saw was a huge, yellow circle, and then, *WHUMP.* The arrow—*his arrow*—stuck out of the bull's-eye right next to his first shot. It couldn't have been closer if Tommy had run up to the target and rammed the arrow in with his hand. It was almost as if—

"Aaahhhh! Ow, ow, ow, OWWWW!!"

Tommy spun to his right. Brock was down on his knees. His face was beet red and he clutched his left forearm. Tommy saw the ugly, purple bruise spreading on Brock's arm and knew immediately what had happened. "Brock, are you okay?"

"No, I'm not okay!" Brock squealed. "The bowstring almost cut my arm in half!"

The crowd grew silent, and Mr. Phitzsinger commanded the archers to put down the bows and came running over. He knelt by Brock, saw his bruised arm, and grimaced. "I told you to keep a little bend in that arm," he said. "Think you can still shoot?"

"It hurts," Brock complained. "I need to go to the health room."

"Okay, Son," said Mr. Phitzsinger, helping Brock to his feet. "The show will have to go on without you though." But then he looked up and saw the two bull's-eyes in Tommy's target. He looked to Tommy. "Twenty points with two arrows? Who did that?"

Tommy blushed and said quietly, "Uh . . . I did."

"You?" Mr. Phitzsinger laughed. "You shot two—no, you're pulling my leg."

"No, he did. I saw him," said Brock. "Do it again, Tommy."

Tommy reluctantly picked out his final arrow and put it to the string. He pulled back the bowstring and aimed. For whatever reason, Tommy wasn't quite sure why, he felt like he shouldn't hit the exact middle of the bull's-eye again. The bowstring sang, and the arrow flew straight and true—into the second yellow ring of the bull's-eye. The students in the bleachers erupted again.

"That's a twenty-nine-point set, Bowman," Mr. Phitzsinger declared. Then he yelled over to the seventh-grade teachers. "Hey, Belanger! Tommy Bowman just beat your best set!"

Mr. Belanger, one of the most good-natured teachers in the school and never one to put down a student, couldn't help his astonishment. Tommy watched him mouth the words "NO WAY" and couldn't help but grin. The other kids in Tommy's line patted him on the back and asked him the same question over and over again. Tommy's answer was the same each time: "I don't know."

Mr. Phitzsinger helped Brock to the waiting assistant principal, Mrs. Rout, who ushered the injured boy out of the gym. Then he yelled, "Fire when ready!" At the end of the fourth round, the gym teacher collected the student score sheets and posted the scores. To the delight of the crowd, the students had the lead—410 to 394.

It was short-lived, however, for the teachers took their turn. With the teachers comfortably in the lead 504 to 410, Mr. Phitzsinger announced to the crowd: "One round to go! Students, take up your bows, nock your arrows, and fire when ready!"

Tommy and the three kids in his line stared at one another. Haley Shoop would have been their fifth. Now what would they do? Tommy ran behind the lines of student archers to the gym teacher. "Mr. Phitzsinger, we only have four in our line. We don't have to take a zero for the fifth set, do we?"

"No, Son, I went over this yesterday. One of you can just take another turn."

Tommy relayed the news to the students in his line. "You do it," they replied unanimously. Tommy swallowed. It felt like the collar of his shirt had just tightened two sizes. Maybe his new skills had been a fluke, like a first-time bowler getting a couple strikes in a row. And now the entire gym would be staring at him while he shot. He stepped up to the firing line and took up his bow once more.

Again, the bow felt comfortable in his hand, as if he'd used the same bow for years. And, in spite of the pressure, Tommy felt sure he could hit the bull's-eye. He turned around. Tons of smiling sixth and seventh graders, sprinkled with aloof eighth graders. A few teachers and parents, and . . . *Mrs. Galdarro!*

Tommy hadn't noticed her there before, seated among the students and a few parents at the top of the bleachers. But what was that look on her face? She was staring right at him. Worry creased her brow and lined the corners of her eyes. The absence of her confident smile felt to Tommy like the sun had just been covered with dark clouds.

Tommy gave her a half wave and saw a flicker of recognition in her eyes. He started to turn back to the target, but something caught his attention. At the top of the next set of bleachers, about forty or fifty students to Mrs. Galdarro's left, sat a man in a gray coat. Tommy couldn't see the man's features under his wide-brim hat but felt sure he was watching.

It's him! Tommy thought urgently. *The guy with the black car.*

He did have a visitor sticker on his coat, though. That meant that he had to have checked in at the main office, but still. Tommy shivered and turned around. His thoughts were all over the place, and it took him a moment to focus on the target. But once he locked on, the confidence began to build once more. He didn't just feel—*he knew*—he could hit the bull's-eye all three times. The question was, should he? *Why not?* Tommy wondered. *We need the points.*

Still, he kept thinking of the peculiar man. *But I'm safe, right? I'm in school. Nothing can happen to me here.* Tommy thought of Mrs. Galdarro's troubled look. He altered his aim just a fraction and proceeded to fire off three nine-point bull's-eyes, less-than-perfect center-ring bull's-eyes, but still satisfying.

By the time the students' fifth-round scores went up, the gymnasium was already rocking. Students hooted and hollered, declaring victory over the once-fearsome seventh-grade teachers. Mr. Phitzsinger posted the score: Students 570, Teachers 506.

"Go, FALCONS! Go, FALCONS! GO!" The chant went up. *Boom-boom-thwack!* The stomping and clapping began again. But the archery meet was not over. The teachers hadn't had their fifth round, and Mr. Belanger was part of that rotation.

They came forward, full of adult confidence. All they really needed was sixty-five points, and it seemed sure they would get it. Tommy and the other student archers sat on the bottom step of the bleachers and watched. The gym became quiet. The teachers began to shoot. The crowd groaned with every arrow that hit the target.

Tommy buried his head in his hands as Mr. Belanger got a bull's-eye. Still, some of the teachers had apparently lost their groove. Several of their arrows lodged in the two-point white circles or missed the target altogether. Hearing the cheers, Tommy looked up. He wished he could see the scores change as the arrows struck home, but he'd have to wait it out.

Brock, his forearm wrapped in ice, plopped down next to Tommy. "What's going on?" he asked. "I could hear the cheers from the health room."

"We tore it up during the last round." Tommy grinned. "Since Haley wasn't there, Mr. Phitzsinger let me shoot again."

Brock looked up at the scoreboard. "Cool! How'd you do?"

"Um . . . twenty-seven points."

"SWEET!"

"Ah, the teachers are finished," said Tommy. "I can't look."

One by one, the seven teachers brought their score sheets to the gym teacher. The gym filled with nervous whispers. Mr. Phitzsinger shook his head a few times as he entered the scores. Then, after an agonizing few seconds, the final score went up: Teachers 579, Students 570.

The seventh-grade teachers were victorious. A collective groan went up from the students. The teachers made a big show of bowing to the crowd and shaking hands with the student archers. Tommy couldn't believe how the day had worked out. He'd entered the gym hoping to at least hit the target once. And then Haley Shoop had stayed home sick, which meant his lack of skill would be that much easier to notice. But somehow, he'd shot well. No, that wasn't quite right. It was more like in the span of a day, he'd realized archery was something he'd always been meant to do. His shooting had gotten the seventh graders so close to beating the teachers, only to fall nine points short. "Bah!" Tommy shrugged. It had still been a memorable day.

When Tommy turned his head again, Brock was gone. He was over talking to Mr. Phitzsinger. *What's he up to?*

Mr. Belanger came over to Tommy. "So what's the deal, Bowman?" he asked playfully. "Your parents Olympic archery champions or something?"

"Uh, no," said Tommy, keeping one eye on Mr. Phitzsinger. "I don't think so."

"Well, that's the first time I've ever seen a student shoot a twenty-nine-point set." Mr. Belanger laughed that deep laugh of his. "And look what you did! You followed it up with twenty-seven! Bowman, that's amazing. If Haley had been here, the seventh graders would've ki—"

"Hold on just a minute!" Mr. Phitzsinger bellowed over the loud-speaker. "Teachers, please direct the students to sit back down in the bleachers."

Mr. Belanger looked up. He and Tommy wondered what was going on. Brock stood next to Mr. Phitzsinger and gave Tommy a little nod. The gym teacher waited until everyone was seated. Tommy noticed Mrs. Galdarro had changed to a seat closer to the gym exit. The man in the gray coat hadn't moved at all. Tommy looked away quickly.

"The Falcon Day Archery Meet is not over yet!" announced Mr. Phitzsinger. It took the teachers a full thirty seconds of hollering, finger pointing, and shushing to restore order in the gym. "One of our seventh graders," Mr. Phitzsinger went on, "did not complete his turn due to injury. He has one arrow left to shoot." Near pandemonium spread across the gym, teachers standing and shushing the students. "A nine-point bull's-eye would tie it up. A ten-point bull's-eye will win it for the students. But because Brock can barely pull back the bowstring right now, he's elected to have Tommy Bowman shoot in his place!"

"Ohhhh, no!" Mr. Belanger shouted, raising his hands and making a big show of the new threat to the teacher's victory. "We're in trouble now!" The students were beside themselves with delight, their roar deafening.

Mr. Phitzsinger beckoned for Tommy to come to the center of the gym. Tommy grabbed the bow he'd been using and walked toward the cone. The cheering from the stands made Tommy's mind swim. He'd never, *never* felt so appreciated. He couldn't recall anyone ever clapping for him before. *This is the best day I've ever—*

His thoughts scattered like ants under a magnifying glass as halfway to the center cone, he made eye contact with Mrs. Galdarro. Her porcelain-smooth face was not only creased with worry but paler than usual. Her placid smile was replaced by an anguished frown. She seemed to be trembling. Tommy mouthed a silent "What?" to her. She shook her head subtly side to side.

"C'mon, Bowman!" bellowed Mr. Phitzinger. "The target's waiting. We're *all* waiting."

Tommy stepped up to the cone and nocked his arrow. *What's wrong with Mrs. Galdarro?* he wondered. *She'd shook her head. No? No what? She couldn't mean . . .*

The students began the *"Go, FALCONS! Go, FALCONS! GO!"* foot stomping. Some of the teachers even joined in. The gym was as loud as Tommy had ever heard it. He took a deep breath, raised his bow, and took aim. As he drew the imaginary line that would send the arrow plunging straight into the bull's-eye, something gurgled in his gut. *Mrs. Galdarro couldn't have meant I shouldn't take the shot. Could she?* It was too late. He was at the shooting line. All the students were counting on him. And everyone was watching. Tommy turned his head just slightly. The man in the gray coat was definitely watching. He'd leaned forward. Tommy thought he could see the gleam of the man's eyes. Why was he wearing a hat inside the school building?

The bow suddenly felt heavy, and Tommy lowered his aim just a bit. "C'mon, Bowman," Brock whispered urgently. And a few kids in the stands right behind Brock began to chant: "Bowman, Bowman, Bowman." Then the whole section joined in. Soon the entire gym rang out with cheers. "Bowman, Bowman, Bowman!"

All images of the gray-coated visitor, of Mrs. Galdarro's worry, and of crazy warnings vanished from Tommy's mind. He had to come through for the crowd.

Tommy felt his pulse slow and locked his gaze to the center of the target. Not just the bull's-eye but the absolute center of the bull's-eye. He lifted the bow and lined up the shot. He decided to give it a little something extra, so he pulled the bowstring back beyond his cheek. And then he let it fly. As before, his eyes seemed to go with the arrow, but only for a split second. A puzzling kind of gasp from the stands behind him led Tommy to conclude he'd somehow missed the bull's-eye.

The murmur in the gym climbed in urgency. Tommy looked at the target. *No, I couldn't have missed the entire target.* But as Tommy stared, he noticed a black X in the center of the bull's-eye.

Mr. Phitzsinger loped across the gym floor to the target and stooped down. He looked strangely at Tommy and then turned to work at something behind the target. He was there, struggling for twenty, thirty seconds before pressing his knee into the target and giving a hard tug. A few seconds later, he emerged with Tommy's arrow.

"A ten-point bull's-eye!" he announced. The gym had been loud before. Now it was bedlam. Students ran down the bleachers, hooting and hollering. A crowd of hysterically happy sixth, seventh, and eighth graders surrounded Tommy, patting him on the back, high-fiving him, and even tousling his hair.

"Unbelievable, Bowman!" Mr. Belanger shouted. "You nearly shot the arrow through the target! Unbelievable!"

Mr. Wilson, the principal, even found his way through the jostling kids to congratulate Tommy. "You've just made Falcon Day history, young man," he said, patting Tommy repeatedly on the shoulder. "This is the first time the seventh graders have ever beaten the teachers at the archery meet. And they owe it . . ." Mr. Wilson went on, but Tommy became distracted and lost his words. Just above the principal's left shoulder, a gray figure descended from the stands. Tommy watched the visitor as he left the gymnasium. His gray jacket and hat filtered through the mass of oblivious students and disappeared around the corner of the bleachers.

Mr. Wilson patted Tommy one more time on the shoulder, and then took the mic from the gym teacher. "All right, students, that was quite an event. But Falcon Day isn't over. Your teachers and parents have been busy setting up the classrooms for your afternoon activities. You are officially dismissed. Enjoy the day you've earned!"

Tommy reluctantly wandered behind the departing crowd. His eyes darted left and right. Whoever that visitor was, he seemed to be gone. Tommy followed a line of students through the gym exit.

In a split heartbeat, from the corner of Tommy's eye, a swift, dark shadow approached. A strong hand seized Tommy's arm and pulled him toward the stairwell outside the gym. A voice said, "That was a mistake."

Tommy tried to jerk away, but the grip was firm. "Mrs. Galdarro?" He blinked at her. "I thought . . . I was afraid—"

"No, I am not him," she said. "And you are very fortunate that I am not, after your foolish demonstration in there."

"The bull's-eyes?"

She nodded.

Tommy smacked himself in the forehead. "That's what you were trying to tell me."

"Yes," she replied. "I thought I made it very clear that you should shoot more modestly. And I was not the only one, was I?"

Tommy's brow crinkled. "I don't know wha—"

"Oh, yes, you do, Tommy Bowman. There was a voice in your heart, was there not? An unspoken warning . . . you knew you were not supposed to keep shooting the bull's-eyes. But you did anyway. You even put an arrow so far into the target that your school's strongest teacher could barely loosen it. Your desire to be a hero to your class-mates overcame the warning in your heart."

"How . . . how did you . . . ?"

"Not here and not now," she said. A cheerful whistle cascaded down the stairwell. "Oh, good," said Mrs. Galdarro. "I hoped he would hurry."

Mr. Charlie, the school custodian, came *tip-tapping* down the stairs. He carried a long-handled mop and continued whistling until he stood beside Mrs. Galdarro. "How many?" he asked.

"One on the inside," she replied. "But certainly others wait among the trees. You will see to them, won't you?"

Mr. Charlie winked at Tommy. "Oh, I'll see to them all right. Uh-huh. But I'll have to visit my closet first."

"You'll need to get them all," she said. "If even one gets back to warn—"

"Leave it to me," he said. "Old Charlie gets the job done."

"You're a godsend, Mr. Charlie," said Mrs. Galdarro. "There'll be fresh scones and tea waiting for you when you're finished."

Mr. Charlie swept past Tommy and spun around with the mop as if it were a dance partner. "Yes, ma'am, I do like that tea of yours." With that, Mr. Charlie disappeared down the office hallway.

Tommy had been confused by plenty of adult conversations before. But this one topped them all. "Mrs. Galdarro, what's going on?"

"We need to have a long talk, Tommy Bowman." She paused and studied him for a moment. "Eight hundred years is a long enough wait."

"What?"

"Never you mind," she said. "We will talk soon. I need to check some things, and then I will call for you. For now, stay away from ALL strangers. You will listen this time, won't you?"

Tommy swallowed. "Yes, ma'am."

21

Unstoppable Force

JETT GRINNED as the announcer began calling the players for the home team. It'd been quite a challenge convincing his mom to let him play football this soon. But in the follow-up visits since the accident, all of the doctors had declared Jett 100 percent healthy. "Good as new," they'd said. "The Miracle Boy. Strong as an ox." Maybe stronger.

In the days that followed, Jett had cut seven cords of firewood. He'd removed the big tree stumps from their side yard. And he'd even fixed the fence around their three-acre property—the whole fence. Jett's dad had no idea how his thirteen-year-old son had managed that feat.

Given the test results, the professional opinions, and what they'd seen Jett able to do, Mrs. Green gave in at last. Coach Tucker was so relieved he sent Jett's mom a bouquet of roses. Jett was relieved, too. He wanted to play. Needed to play. This afternoon's contest was the regional final against their biggest rival. And it wasn't that the Raiders couldn't win without Jett, but he was certainly a huge part of their success.

Jett heard the cheers and watched his teammates charge out of the tunnel onto the field. He put in his mouthpiece, preparing for his entrance. He couldn't believe he'd been in the hospital just a week before. He felt too good. In some ways, he felt better than ever.

"And now Greenville fans"—came the tinny announcer's voice—"let's give it up for number twenty-eight, your Raiders running back, Jett Green!"

Jett tore out of the tunnel, smacked hands and pounded the fists of his teammates, and jumped all around. And to the crowd's surprise and joy, Jett did a back flip. He landed lightly on his feet and laughed. *Never done one of those before!*

Jett felt a hard pat on his shoulder pad and turned to find Kyle Merkel, the Raiders' quarterback, standing there. "Jett, lighten up on the high-fives, man," Kyle said, shaking his hand like it still stung. "I gotta throw with this hand, y'know?"

"Why throw when you can just hand the ball off to me!" The two pointed at each other and laughed.

To Jett's surprise, Coach Tucker didn't put him in on the kickoff team. "I know the docs say you're fine, but I don't want to wear you out."

"Coach, I'm good," said Jett.

"I'll use you when we need you." And then he turned and walked toward the assistant coaches. Coach Tucker was like that—few words, many decisions, and no one dared argue.

The Raiders kicked off. The ball sailed end over end and landed in the arms of Cleat Ferguson, Clifton's burly running back. They called him "The Brickhouse" because he didn't just run past his opponents; he ran over them. Cleat returned the kick past his team's thirty-yard line and found a seam between blockers. Then, like a locomotive train building speed, he charged across the fifty before the first Raiders' player got in his way. Cleat hit him so hard he spun around. The Brickhouse made it to the Raiders' forty-yard line before Raiders' players gang-tackled him.

Jett watched from the sideline but felt so full of energy he couldn't sit still on the bench. Besides, things weren't going well for his team, and he hoped Coach Tucker would put him in soon. It would prove to be a very long wait, and . . . a very long afternoon.

✳

Midway through the third quarter, the score was Clifton Tigers 24, Greenville Raiders 3. Every other play, Jett begged Coach Tucker to put him in. Jett's teammates tried, too. Even Jett's mother, who had originally been reluctant to let Jett play, found herself hollering at the coach.

But Coach Tucker ignored them all. He was like that.

Jett looked up to his parents, saw their frustrated expressions, and gave them an I-don't-know-either kind of shrug. Jett started to turn back to watch the game when one of the spectators caught his eye. It was the way he was dressed, too warm for a North Carolina afternoon, even in the fall. Dark trench coat, gloves, big, wide-brimmed hat. Jett thought the hat was cool, kind of like Indiana Jones.

"Jett!" called Coach Tucker. "Get over here!"

Jett took a last look at the oddball in the stands and then raced over to his coach. *Finally*, Jett thought, *I'm going in.*

But Coach Tucker wasn't ready to put Jett in. Instead, he rallied his troops on the sideline. "Wrap the Brickhouse up!" he challenged his defense. "You try to just knock this guy down, he'll pulverize you. But stop his legs from churning, and he'll go down like a ton of bricks. Ha!"

"Put Jett in," mumbled Derek Moody, a linebacker and one of Jett's best friends on the team.

Coach Tucker gave Derek a steely glare. "We are a team, not one player! We just need to execute our plays! Fundamentals: make your blocks, wrap up on the tackles—simple as that." Then he gathered the kids and did hands-in for a cheer.

The next few possessions went a little better. The Raiders scored on two of their first three possessions, and they were able to stop Brickhouse a few times. But with the third quarter winding down, the Chargers still led 30-17.

The Raiders kicked off, and the Clifton kick returner let the ball get away from him. It hit the turf and bounced between his legs before wobbling to a stop at the ten-yard line. The Raiders dove, but after the referees sorted through the mound of players, one of the Chargers had somehow come up with the ball.

The Chargers then began a long, time-consuming drive. And once again, it was Brickhouse dishing out the punishment. He barreled through the line for fifteen yards on one play and, while blocking for his quarterback, flattened a Raiders' defensive lineman. The Chargers sat on the Raiders' twenty-yard line, and they'd eaten all but the last three minutes of the clock. Coach Tucker knew even a field goal would put the game completely out of reach. Without even turning around, he yelled, "Jett, you're in at middle linebacker! Let's go!"

Jett sprang off the bench and raced out onto the field. The home-town crowd cheered. Even the Chargers turned from their huddle to see what all the noise was about.

The Raiders' defense huddled up, and Jett said, "All right, we know they want to chew up the clock. They're going to try to run it down our throats. And you know what we're going to do?" He looked each player eye-to-eye. "We're going to close every hole and give 'em no place to go but DOWN!!"

They broke their huddle almost chanting, "Down, down, you're goin' down. Down, down, you're goin' down."

The Chargers lined up with one running back in the backfield, the Brickhouse. They tried to spread the defense by putting wide receivers far out on both sides of the line and putting one of them in motion, but the Raiders' defense didn't bite. The handoff went to Brickhouse, and he lumbered toward the line. His offensive linemen were adept blockers, and they'd opened a hole. Brickhouse came charging through, and the Greenville crowd cringed, expecting another big gain. But something shot through the gap and hit Brickhouse. Not only did he stop, but he was driven backward five yards. He landed hard on his back on the turf. And Jett Green, grinning like it was Christmas morning, landed on top of him.

The crowd went wild.

"Get off me!" Brickhouse yelled. He shoved Jett off and clambered back to his feet. He eyed Jett. "You got lucky!" he said as he lumbered back to his team's huddle.

Coach Tucker called a time-out. The clock stopped at 2:18 to play. He ran out to the huddle where the defense was busy slapping Jett on the pads and whooping it up about his crushing hit on Brickhouse. The coach broke up that little celebration. "What you think? You win the Super Bowl?" He glared at his players, especially Jett. "All you saw was a player make a play he was supposed to make. Now, get your head in the game. We're playing for our play-off lives. You have to stop them right here and right now. Either get me the ball or drive them back out of field goal range!"

The Chargers came to the line of scrimmage. This time, they brought in a fullback and two tight ends. They weren't even trying to pretend they might pass.

One tight end went in motion.

The Raiders' defense shifted.

Jett kept his eyes on Brickhouse. *Man, I feel good*, he thought. He flexed the muscles in his chest and arms and even did a little hop. Then he got low.

The center hiked the ball. The Chargers' quarterback looked for a moment like he might actually pass, but at the last second, he slipped the ball to Brickhouse. Again, the offensive line cleared a running lane. But this time, Brickhouse had a fullback running ahead of him, trying to pick Jett off.

Jett saw the fullback, a big kid himself, rumbling his way. And he could see Brickhouse behind the fullback, following his lead block, ready to go the opposite of the side Jett committed to. But Jett had other plans. Jett surged forward with a burst of speed. He stayed low, got under the fullback, and put his shoulder hard into the fullback's chest. Jett hit the fullback so hard that he drove him directly back . . . into Brickhouse!

The stunned running back tried to spin around, but by that time Jett had detached himself from the fullback. Jett felt like he'd been holding back before, and so he hit Brickhouse with all his might, using his legs and driving his shoulder into Brickhouse's gut. The collision was terrible. The crowd *oobed*, and then instantly went silent.

The Chargers' running back groaned and flew backward, and the football came loose and bounced on the turf. Jett climbed over the fallen Brickhouse and scooped up the ball. Two Chargers players were there to try and stop him, but Jett was too fast. He split his opponents and raced eighty yards for the end zone.

"That's my boy!" Mr. Green hollared, slapping high-fives with everyone he knew and didn't know in the stands. The place went ballistic.

Jett's teammates surrounded him again. And again, Coach Tucker put an end to the party. Still, as the coach walked Jett back to the sideline, he said quietly, "Jett, they can't stop you. You hear me? You are an unstoppable force!"

Jett felt joy and pride bubble up inside. For once, he couldn't even talk. He just beamed at Coach Tucker and went to the sideline.

The extra point was good. That made it Chargers 30, Raiders 24. The score wasn't the issue anymore. Holding them on defense and going down to score was doable. But the game clock on the scoreboard stood at the end of the field like an immovable object. One minute and thirty-seven seconds. If the Chargers got the ball on the kick-off, they could simply run out the clock.

"HANDS!!" Coach Tucker bellowed. He needed the wide

receivers, tight ends, and anyone who was adept at catching the ball. The Raiders had to try an onside kick.

"Coach!" Jett yelled. "Coach, let me go out there on special teams!"

"It's an onside kick, Jett!"

"I know. C'mon, Coach, I have an idea."

Coach Tucker didn't answer, but he grabbed Jett by the shoulder and practically threw him onto the field.

Jett ran on and lined up between the kicker and his friend, wide receiver Bryce Tomlinson. "Bryce, c'mere!"

"What?" Bryce asked, looking anxiously at the referee.

Jett whispered in Bryce's ear. Bryce took a step back and said, "You're going to do *what*?"

"Look," Jett said. "Just follow my lead. I'll get it done."

"Okay, Jett . . . you're crazy."

Then Jett called the kicker over and whispered in his ear. The kicker stepped away. "Are you sure?" he asked. "But Coach usually has us—"

"Trust me," Jett said as he lined up. "I'll get it done."

The kicker shook his head and bent down to adjust the football on the tee. He took three steps backward and two to the side. The Chargers' players had to line up twenty yards away. Knowing an onside kick was the Raiders' only hope, the Chargers watched the kicker carefully.

The referee blew the whistle. The Raiders' kicker stepped toward the ball as if he might kick it sharply to the right.

The Chargers players adjusted.

But the kicker did not send it bouncing toward the right at all. Instead, he gave the ball a little pooch kick. It drifted over the head of the closest Charger. In that instant, as the Charger watched the ball go over his head, Jett slammed into him, sending him into an awkward backward roll. But Jett wasn't finished. Another Charger player loped back across the field toward the ball. Jett could never get to the ball in time, but he sprinted toward the opposing player and crashed into him.

Bryce Tomlinson did exactly what Jett had told him to do. When Jett took out the two Chargers' players closest to the ball, Bryce streaked right up the middle and dove on the football. Since the football had traveled ten yards and Bryce recovered it, the ball belonged to the Raiders.

The crowd was delirious. The Chargers coach threw his clipboard to the turf. And Coach Tucker's eyes bulged. "We got the ball," he said quietly to himself. "I don't believe it. We got the ball!"

The clock still loomed as the enemy. The Raiders had the ball on the Chargers' forty-yard line but only one minute and twelve seconds left to play. Coach Tucker grabbed Kyle Merkel by the shoulder pad. "After this play, Kyle, go no huddle. Watch the clock. Just remember what we've been doing all week in practice. Go get 'em!"

Kyle ran out into the huddle and looked at his teammates. "This is it, guys. No huddle from here on out. X Out, Slide, Y Wing. Go on three. BREAK!"

Jett lined up at running back directly behind Kyle. He knew he wasn't featured on this play. He needed to block so that Kyle would have time to hit the wide receiver deep or the tight end ten yards out near the sideline.

Kyle called out, "Hut, hut, hike!"

The center delivered the ball. Kyle dropped back about three yards and looked for a receiver. Bryce was covered by three defenders on the deep ball.

Kyle looked for the tight end.

No good. They had guys camped out at the sideline, waiting for the quick out.

Kyle started to panic. A Chargers' linebacker broke around the outside and sprinted toward Kyle's backside. Kyle didn't see him coming . . . but Jett did.

He dove backward and slammed the linebacker, knocked him to the turf, and he did not get back up. That hit bought Kyle the extra few seconds he needed to find his second wide receiver streaking across the middle of the field. Kyle threw a dart right into the receiver's chest. He caught it at the twenty-five yard line but was gang tackled there.

The clock was at one minute and counting, and the Raiders were out of timeouts. Kyle ran up to the new line of scrimmage and motioned for the line. Ten more seconds flew off the clock before they were all there and in position. Kyle got the snap and quickly threw the ball into the turf, the only way to stop the clock from running. He looked up at the white lightbulb numbers.

Fifty-three seconds left.

With the clock stopped, the Raiders huddled up. Kyle began to call the next play. "Okay, they are taking the sidelines, so we go with X Scat Fly, YZ posts!"

"Kyle!" Jett yelled. "Give me the ball."

"We can't run here. They stop us, the clock'll keep running."

Jett shook his head. "They won't expect it. Line up in shotgun and spread everyone out. Then give me the ball with a draw play."

"If the linebackers see—"

"I know, Kyle, c'mon," Jett urged.

Kyle looked at the receivers and the linemen. They shook their heads in enthusiastic agreement. Kyle shrugged. "This doesn't work, Coach'll kill me."

"It's one of the plays Coach gave you, right?" Jett asked. "Four X Slide, Y Delay Dive—Shotgun draw?"

"Uh, yeah, but we don't have enough ti—"

"C'mon, Kyle, I feel good."

Kyle shook his head. "I'm glad you do. I feel like I'm going to barf." Kyle turned to the rest of his team. "Four X Slide, Y Delay Dive, on two. BREAK!"

Kyle lined up behind the center and then took five steps backward. This formation, known as the shotgun, forced the center to hike the ball through the air rather than simply putting it right into the quarterback's hands. Standing that far behind the center and offensive line gave the quarterback a better look at the field, and so it was mostly used when the team wanted to pass the ball. Of course, the Chargers' coach knew this; the Chargers' defense knew it as well . . . and that was what Jett was counting on.

The wide receivers lined up three on the right side, one on the left. The Chargers' defense dropped all their linebackers and cornerbacks into deep-zone coverage. No one was going to go deep on them this time.

Kyle barked out, "Hut!"

His third receiver on the right went in motion, running left behind the offensive line and coming to a stop just behind the other receiver on the left. The defense watched the motion receiver the whole time, expecting him to try a quick cut underneath for an easy catch and run out of bounds to stop the clock.

But as soon as the motion receiver stopped, Kyle grunted, "HUT!!" Kyle held the ball for a second and scanned the field just as he would for a pass play. But suddenly, he turned and slid the ball into Jett's arms.

The Chargers' linemen had been busy trying to get free to sack the quarterback. They didn't even see the blur that was Jett racing up the middle. The linebackers and corners realized what had happened, and they moved into the middle of the field. Jett sidestepped a linebacker. Then he stiff-armed a cornerback, planting his hand on the defender's helmet and pushing him to the turf. The buzz from the crowd surged louder as Jett neared the end zone. He was at the ten when two defenders closed in. Jett spun around one, hurdled another, and kept going.

Two yards from the goal line, a speedy safety tripped Jett up, and another defender hit Jett as he fell into the end zone.

Jett heard the whistle. He got up just in time to be mobbed by his teammates. Even Coach Tucker came over. "I told you, Jett! You're an unstoppable force! That's what you are, Son! UNSTOPPABLE!!"

Coach Tucker turned back to the sideline to call for the kicker. They still needed the extra point for the win. But one of the referees kept blowing the whistle and pointing at the field. Jett looked up at the scoreboard. It still showed the Chargers ahead 30–24.

"What?"

The referee finally got Coach Tucker's attention when he yelled, "The ball carrier's knee hit the ground before the ball crossed the goal line! It's first and goal on the one-yard-line."

"You gotta be kidding me!" Coach Tucker ran up to the referee and argued, but it was no use. The referee made the call. There was no touchdown, and the clock was at twenty-two seconds and still running.

Coach Tucker screamed for his offense to get on the field. As they ran on, he yelled to Kyle, "Bulldog slam!"

Kyle lined up right behind the center and hurried a couple of his offensive linemen. Jett hunched down three feet behind Kyle and waited. The game clock ticked down. 5 . . . 4 . . . 3: "HUT, HUTTT!!"

Kyle handed Jett the ball. Jett felt it in his arms and tucked it in. He looked ahead for a hole, even a tight crack he could plow through.

But there was none.

Suddenly, two of the Chargers' defensive linemen broke through and slammed into Jett. They drove Jett backward two yards, but he did not go down. He just kept churning his legs. The Chargers' player slipped down and held on to Jett's left leg. Two more Chargers blasted in and crunched Jett between them. Still he did not go down.

At that moment, everything seemed to slow down for Jett. He'd scored touchdowns before, many of them. He'd broken tackles before and had even dragged another player across the goal line before. But he'd never felt as strong as he did this day. It was as if each time he thought he'd spent all the energy he had, more strength poured into him. He was carrying three defenders and was still moving forward. As he neared the goal line, more Chargers' players piled on. One, two, three more defenders slammed into the pile and pushed it back a yard. The game clock had run out. If the referee blew the whistle, or if Jett lost his feet and went down, the game would be over . . . and the Chargers would win.

But Jett did not fall down.

He kept his legs moving. He leaned forward and pushed with all his might. And the entire pile, now seven defenders all around Jett, began to move forward again. The crowd exploded with cheers. Everyone stood. Jett's parents screamed, cheering him on.

The pile lunged forward. Carrying some, dragging others, Jett surged ahead . . . across the goal line.

And everything went quiet.

The referees saw Jett score the touchdown, but they didn't signal. They just stared as Jett emerged from the pile. Even Jett's teammates and Coach Tucker were speechless.

The Raider's kicker, Neil Stefanik, was the first to speak. "Coach?"

Coach Tucker didn't answer.

"Coach?"

"What?" Coach Tucker replied as if waking. "What is it, Stefanik?"

"Uh . . . it's tied now, 30–30. You want me to kick the extra point . . . uh, so we can win?"

Coach Tucker's thick brows beetled, and he practically pushed his kicker onto the field. "What are you waiting for, Stefanik? Go win the game!"

Whooping and hollering, hugging and smacking, Jett and the offense loped off the field. They knelt on the sideline and waited breathlessly to see if the kick would be good.

The special teams unit marched toward the end zone and lined up on the five-yard line. The Chargers players lined up. Some of the linebackers and safeties jumped up and down to distract the kicker, but it was halfhearted. After what they'd just witnessed, they'd lost their fight.

The snap and the hold were perfect; the kick went up and sailed right between the uprights.

The fans in the bleachers exploded at last and stormed onto the field. Jett's teammates picked Jett up and carried him on their shoulders even as the crowds of exulting fans surrounded them.

It was some time before Coach Tucker could get his team away from their friends and family. Jett's mother had her son crushed in a bear hug. "Oh, you make me so proud," she said, giving Jett another squeeze. "My baby . . . my violet-eyed baby. Don't you take too long with 'em, Coach Tucker. We're takin' our baby out for pizza and ice cream."

"I understand, ma'am," said the coach, gently prying Jett away.

After the coach's usual postgame speech and the awarding of the game ball—to Jett—Coach Tucker took Jett aside. "That was a herculean effort, Jett." Coach Tucker shook his head. "I've never seen anything like it. Not even John Riggins or Earl Campbell."

"Who?" asked Jett.

"Ask your father," replied the coach with a laugh. He scratched the graying hair at his temples and repeated, "Nope, never seen anything like it. Now, go on home and rest up. We've got the championships next weekend. And I expect you'll run the ball quite a bit."

"Yes, sir!" Jett smiled from ear to ear, even as Coach Tucker turned and went back into his office.

Jett left the locker room and walked out into the tunnel. He turned left to head for the parking lot. As he walked down that shadowy concrete tube, he mused on the incredible game he'd just experienced. Nothing had ever felt as good. Maybe it was the adrenaline, but rather than being exhausted from a demanding game, he still felt energized. *I feel like I could play another game right now*, he thought. He looked back over his shoulder toward the field end of the tunnel. And then the agile star running back for the Greenville Raiders almost tripped over his own feet.

There was someone standing at the other end of the tunnel. He was tall and narrow and wore a coat that reached down to just above his ankles. But with the light behind him, he was just a silhouette. *A strange silhouette*, Jett thought. And though Jett couldn't determine just what it was, something about the man didn't look quite right. He wore a hat, too. "It's the guy from the stands," Jett muttered. "But what's he doing?"

Jett had a sudden urge to run to the parking lot, but instead he turned his back and continued walking. Slowly at first. And he listened intently, hoping he wouldn't hear the sound of distant footsteps mixing in with the scrape of his own cleats on the tunnel floor.

Jett sped up a little.

He turned and looked back just in time to see the man disappear from the mouth of the tunnel. Jett sped up a bit more.

By the time he approached fading daylight at the other end of the tunnel, Jett was moving a little faster than a jog. He took one last look over his shoulder and ran out of the tunnel . . . straight into a man in a long gray jacket.

The man caught Jett by the shoulder pads and absorbed Jett's impact with his own strength. "Whoa, Jett!" said the man. "You trying to score another touchdown?"

Jett looked up. "Mr. Spero? What are you doing here?"

Mr. Spero, Jett's new English teacher, raised one eyebrow and gave one of his famous, sarcastic smirks. "Well, let's see. Could it be that I thought I'd better make sure my favorite student is keeping up with his literature homework? Um, no. That wasn't it at all." He winked. "I was here for the game, of course. Quite a game, indeed."

Jett's eyes flitted nervously. "Uh-huh."

"After your accident," Mr. Spero continued, "I didn't think you'd be playing. Seems that fall you took was much less worrisome than was reported. Glad to hear, of course. That last run of yours—Jett, what is the matter?"

"Huh?"

"You are clearly very distracted, and you keep looking over your shoulder."

"You'll think it's silly."

"Try me."

"There was someone there."

"Who?"

"I don't know. Couldn't see, really. There was just a guy standing there on the field side. Dark coat and hat, kind of spooked me, 'sall."

Mr. Spero's cocked eyebrow flattened out. "Probably just an NFL scout, Jett," he replied with a wink. "But I suppose I should look into this. Your parents are waiting in the parking lot. I'm sure they're anxious to take you out for a celebration."

"Okay, Mr. Spero."

"Oh, one more thing, Jett. I wonder if your parents would mind if I dropped by your home later this evening."

"What? Why? Have I done something wrong?"

"No," Mr. Spero replied. The grin returned. "No, nothing wrong. There are just a few . . . things we need to discuss . . . a unique opportunity."

With that, Mr. Spero walked right by Jett and entered the tunnel. Jett watched him merge into the shadows. For a moment, it looked to Jett like Mr. Spero had reached inside his coat and removed something. *No way!* Jett thought. *Mr. Spero's packing? No way!*

Jett slowly walked across the parking lot, where he found his parents still exuberant, anxious to get going. Jett slid out of his shoulder pads, threw them in the backseat, and sat down.

As the Greens' big truck left the parking lot, Jett watched out of the back window. Jett blinked. He could have sworn he saw a flash of blue light near the tunnel. *Strange.*

Foresight

AFTER THE bizarre battle in the streets of Ardfern, Jimmy had raced home only to find an unwelcome guest sitting in his family's living room. It was the man from the pub. Jimmy was sure of it. But that was impossible! How did he get here so fast? Ahead of Jimmy, even?

"If yu don't mind," said Mr. Ogelvie. He stood with the help of a brown walking stick and covered his wavy white hair with a dark cap. "I think I best be headin' home."

"So soon yu be leavin' us?" Mrs. Gresham asked, clutching her plump, sweatered arms as if she'd caught a chill. She looked to her husband expectantly.

"Aye, so soon?" added Mr. Gresham, obviously just to please his wife; Mr. Gresham was just relieved not to have another hand picking at the dinner roast.

"Me pets need tendin', I'm afraid." Mr. Ogelvie smiled and looked to Jimmy. "Spiders don't feed themselves, yu know. At least caged ones don't."

Mrs. Gresham turned to Jimmy. "Mr. Ogelvie is an archenonologist."

"Arachnologist, my dear," said the neighbor.

Mr. Gresham chuckled.

"That means he studies insects," she continued, leering at her husband as if she'd gotten it right all along.

"Technically, that would be entomology," Mr. Ogelvie said gently. "You could say, I'm more of a specialist."

Mr. Gresham turned his head to stifle a laugh and avoid his wife's glare.

She frowned at her husband, but turned on a gleaming smile as she spoke about the new neighbor. "He's already given Geoffry a wee spider an' a beautiful cage." Jimmy looked to his brother, who sat in the corner of the room tapping on the clear plastic of a tiny box.

"I'm a sorry, lad." Mr. Ogelvie eyed Jimmy. "I was not aware there were *two* boys in this home or I'd be a bringin' another present with me."

"That's all right," Jimmy said hesitantly. "There b' plenty of spiders 'round here."

Mr. Ogelvie smiled like he'd just finished a fine meal. "Aye, that's true, me boy. And they all be needin' food."

And with those words, every nerve in Jimmy's body caught fire. The muscles in his upper back tightened, and his stomach churned. He couldn't understand why he felt so uncomfortable—even afraid—of the old guy.

Mr. Ogelvie had age spots all over his cheeks and white hair growing in patches like ferns out of his ears. His dark pullover sweater and pleated khakis fit loosely on his spindly frame. Now that Jimmy thought about it, this Mr. Ogelvie couldn't have been the man from the pub, the man fighting against Mrs. Finney. He clearly didn't pose a threat. But something about him made Jimmy nervous. He reasoned that the unexplainable encounter in the street had just rattled him.

Mr. Ogelvie walked to the door, and Jimmy stepped aside. "It's been a pleasure, Greshams," he announced. "And a pleasure meeting yu now, Master Jimmy."

Mr. Ogelvie towered above, and Jimmy felt a shudder travel

through his whole body. He nodded slightly in acknowledgment of the old man's farewell.

"I'll be seein' yu again," said the old man. Something hardened in his faded blue eyes. When no one else could see, he gave Jimmy such a penetrating glare that Jimmy stepped backward. Mr. Ogelvie hobbled over the threshold. With his walking stick adding percussion on the stones outside, he began to sing quietly, "Soon, very soon . . . I'll be coming 'round to meet yu again."

Jimmy bit on the sides of his cheek to keep from crying out and started to close the door, but Mrs. Gresham pushed herself into the gap between the door and the jamb.

"Thank yu for stoppin' by, Mr. Ogelvie." She waved. "It's been delightful!"

"The delight, dear people, is all mine." And with that, the man gave Jimmy one last glance and slipped around the corner of the picket fence. A sudden indignant fury boiled up in Jimmy. The moment his mother was clear of the door, he slammed it. Hard.

"James Lewis Gresham!" his mother yelled, a combination of anger and surprise shrilling her voice.

"Aye, what's wrong with yu, boy?" Mr. Gresham put in. Geoffry looked up at last from his spider box. Thunder rumbled outside.

"I—" Jimmy hesitated, now ashamed. *What is wrong with me?* "I'm sorry, I just—"

"To yur room, young man," ordered Mrs. Gresham. "I've had quite enough, what with you insultin' our new neighbor and all!"

"But, Mum—"

"I'm not yur mother!"

Jimmy's mouth dropped open. He half-choked on his next breath. She had never said such a thing before. Mrs. Gresham, clearly shocked at her own outburst, covered her mouth with her hand, and looked back and forth between her husband and Jimmy. Jimmy could see tears welling up in her eyes and felt them in his own. She fell into Mr. Gresham's arms and sobbed.

"Look what yu done!" he said. "Now get!"

A mixture of shame and confusion hammered Jimmy as he ran around the couches and up the stairs. He burst through the door to his room and landed on his bed. He buried his head in his pillow, face growing hot from frustration and wet from tears.

Yu knew the danger, now didn't yu? Jimmy chastised himself. *Believin' they might love yu the way real parents do . . . left yurself wide open. Now look at yu,* Jimmy growled. Sure he had known it would hurt, but he'd never dreamed it would hurt like this: unspeakable, excruciating pain, the kind of pain that twists your guts in knots and wracks your body with tremors. He lay there, shaking miserably, as rain pelted the roof overhead and time ticked by.

After his tears dried up, a numbing frustration settled in. He couldn't believe the day he'd had. If there had been anyone he wanted to tell about the fight he'd witnessed, it would have been his parents. But now?

Could it have really been Mrs. Finney and Regis out on the street? And what was . . . that thing?

Voices from downstairs, raised then hushed, then raised again. Jimmy turned around on the bed and leaned toward his door to listen.

". . . don't' understand," Jimmy's mother was saying. "We've done everything for him, but, he's so . . ."

"Strange these days," said his father.

"Aye. What's gotten into him?"

"Why are yu asking me? I dunno!"

"Well, *yu* said he might be bringin' a wee bit o' baggage with him, but we'd be able to handle it!"

"Oh, don't start that again!" Mr. Gresham slammed his fist in the table. "We both decided to get that boy! And now yu have yur very own, so I cannot help it if yur not wantin' him 'round anymore."

"I didn't say that, Roger."

"Aye, yu did, right to his face."

Jimmy flipped back over and buried his head in his pillow, unable to take anymore. He tried to shut out his crying, but it was impossible. He heard his mother sobbing, too. Or perhaps now she was just *Mrs. Gresham.*

✳

Although Lochgilphead is not far from Ardfern, the walk to school the next morning couldn't have felt longer. Jimmy's mother had handed him his lunch but said not a word. Jimmy saw her lower lip tremble and then the door to his home shut. The grief of the previous night weighed like a sack full of anvils and briars on Jimmy's shoulders. But now that he was outside again, the unusual events regarding the stranger and Miss Finney and Regis roared back to life once more.

Jimmy left the main road for a shortcut through the moors—vast, rolling plains carpeted with peat moss, patches of long grass, and sedge. As was often the case in the morning, the moors were shrouded in white mist. *Ah, nothing's right anymore*, Jimmy thought. *Nothing feels safe. Maybe I need to see the school psychologist.*

He moved north, away from the loch. Minutes later he rounded the last hill and saw Lochgilphead Central School. *If I hurry, I might be able to make it before these clouds dump rain on me*, Jimmy thought.

No such luck.

The rain came down in sheets, soaking Jimmy even as he sprinted the rest of the way. He emerged from the moors and raced down the hill to the teachers' parking lot. He saw some of his teachers balancing various colored umbrellas while digging in the trunks of their cars; others holding steaming mugs of coffee, huddled under the side door arch.

Jimmy searched their faces. No Miss Finney. He entered the building, shed his jacket in his locker, and squeaked down the hall. She wasn't in her classroom, either. *Must be a library day*, Jimmy thought as he glanced at the clock. He had ten minutes until homeroom. Plenty of time.

Jimmy eased open the library doors, and there she was, checking out books to a handful of underclassmen. Her dark hair was up in a high ponytail, thin glasses resting on the edge of her nose. She wore a dark-green sweater vest over a gray blouse. Nothing at all out of the ordinary. No medieval warrior princess like the night before. Maybe he was just mistaken, and it was someone else. After all that running through a driving rain, it could have been anyone. But Miss Finney had been there to help him up. And there was no mistaking her. She'd even said, "I'll handle this," right to his face!

It had to be her. But how to approach her? *Uh, Miss Finney, I was wondering . . . what were you doing out in the rain fighting a strange man-thing with long fingers?* That just didn't seem quite right. Not knowing what to say, he waited in line behind the underclassmen. Jimmy watched the clock. Only a couple of minutes left before homeroom. Little heads of blond and curly black bounced up and down in front of the check-out counter. Miss Finney smiled warmly at each one and then sent them on their way with a cherished new treasure. At last, it was Jimmy's turn.

He waited. Maybe she would say something first. She looked above the rim of her glasses at him.

He couldn't stand it. "Miss Finney, yesterday, in the rain yu—"

"Not here, Jimmy." She put a finger to her lips and glanced at the students who'd gotten in line behind Jimmy.

"But—"

"Not now." She winced.

Jimmy looked at her sweater near her waist. There was a small spot there, darker than the sweater. "I knew it," he said. "It jabbed yu, didn't it? Are—"

"Shh, Jimmy Gresham!" she said. "We're in a library, yu know."

"But yu . . . yu're hurt?"

"Never yu mind."

Jimmy started to speak again, but Miss Finney raised her voice and said, "Yu've come to pick up yur book, then?"

"Uh . . . I didn't check out anything."

"Of course, yu did, Jimmy boy. Why, yu put it on a reserve just the other day."

Jimmy stood there gaping as Miss Finney reached beneath the desk and removed a thick book with a dark-green cover trimmed in gold. She didn't scan it as she usually did a checkout book. Jimmy didn't see any barcode anyway. *What is this?*

"Here yu go, lad," she said, handing Jimmy the book. "I think yu've made a good choice with this one. It's a tale that goes right to yur heart, if yu get what I mean."

Jimmy took the hefty book in both hands. He read the title and didn't recognize it. "Who's it by?"

Miss Finney giggled. "Who's it by?" She laughed again. "Surely . . . no, of course, yu wouldn't. Let's just say, yu'll be gettin' to know the author right soon. Now be off with yu. Homeroom's about to start."

"But, Miss Finney, what about yest—?"

"Don't yu worry about that, lad," she said, her eyes full of warning. "Oh, and I've put a bookmark in there for yu. Hope it keeps yu . . . from losin' yur page."

Jimmy thought he'd seen a subtle wink in that last glance. He looked at the braided tassel hanging out of the pages and wondered. A rough knock to his shoulder scrambled his thoughts for the moment.

"Basketball in gym today, Gresham," said lanky Angus MacBain. "Think yu might play a bit?"

"I might," said Jimmy, knowing full well the gym teacher would make him play whether he wanted to or not. He only hoped that he could be on Angus's team. That was bad enough, but it was better than playing against him.

✳

Jimmy made it to homeroom just moments after the late bell rang. Mr. Duncan gave Jimmy a look that somehow spoke very clearly: "Sit down now, Jimmy lad, else I'll extend me full sarcastic wit and reduce yu to quiverin' jelly."

Jimmy flew to his seat. He welcomed the warmth of the radiator unit that was about six inches from his right elbow. He needed to dry out. The morning announcements were on, so Jimmy put his head down on the book on his desk.

The book!

Jimmy sat up so abruptly that the other students stared. He grinned back sheepishly and then looked at the book. *The History of Berinfell*. And beneath the bold title in a smaller font *The Chronicles of the Elf Lords and Their Kin*.

Huh, Jimmy thought. *Never heard of it*. He opened the cover and flipped through the first pages. An intricate piece of black and white artwork stopped him immediately. It was a bridge stretching from a deep wood to the side of a cliff and a stairway that climbed a high, pointed tower like a daring vine. It was so wonderfully detailed that Jimmy found himself tracing the lines with his finger . . . that's when something surprising happened.

Jimmy lifted up his hand to find his fingertips blackened and the artwork smudged. How could that be? He looked at the back of the page and found indentations from a pen, like the back of a sheet of notebook paper he'd written on. He turned a few more pages and sat back. It was all *handwritten*, the artwork *hand-drawn*.

What sort of book was this?

Jimmy kept flipping pages until he came to the bookmark. It was a chapter called "The Ruins."

He'd read just three words when the bell for first class rang. Math with Mr. Jastrow, and no one ever went late to Mr. J's class. Not unless word-problem marathons after school were your idea of a good time. No, the strange, handwritten book would have to wait . . . till lunch at the earliest. Gym was second period. Gym, basketball, and Angus MacBain.

✳

"Look alive out there, Gresham!" yelled Mr. Brodie, the gym teacher. And in the time it took Jimmy to register the comment, Angus MacBain snatched the basketball right out of Jimmy's hands. It was the fifth time since the game began. Jimmy hated basketball.

He dutifully raced after his opponent and tried his best to steal the ball back. He swatted here and there, but each time Angus easily avoided Jimmy's attempts. He spun Jimmy around and scored on a lay-up off the backboard.

"Stay on that one, Gresham!" Mr. Brodie hollered.

"Yes, sir," Jimmy replied. "I'm trying." But what Jimmy really wanted to know was: *How come he only yells at me? I'm not the worst one on the court. Am I?*

"Better luck next time, Jimmy," said Luke, his friend and teammate.

Jimmy smiled, waved, and puffed out his cheeks, doing his best impersonation of *No sweat. It's just a game. Doesn't bother me.* While his acting might win him an award someday, it didn't earn him much there in gym. And, of course, Jimmy knew.

He shook his head and ran over to get a drink from the fountain. It seemed everyone was out to get him. As he walked back onto the court, he wished he could just disappear. If anything, he just wanted to talk with Miss Finney and get back to that book. Jimmy was so lost in his thoughts that he didn't even hear Mr. Brodie blow the whistle to start play.

Jimmy's vision grayed at the edges and blurred. He suddenly felt lightheaded. Waves of nausea washed over him. Sounds became distorted. He thought he might lose his breakfast right on the court. "More water," he whispered. "I need more water." He began to wobble back toward the fountain.

"Jimmy!" someone yelled, and the ball was speeding toward him. He put up his hands and caught the pass, stinging his palms. His head still swirled, and he thought he might throw up. *Great.* The other team wouldn't need to steal the ball from him . . . just grab it after he barfed. *Just great.*

It was then, however, that the strangest thing happened. Jimmy watched those waving and shouting his name—Luke and the others, each demanding that he pass them the ball—slow to a near standstill. And as if seeing himself from above the game, he saw Angus MacBain charge in from the left and bat the ball out of the frozen Jimmy's hands.

The moment the ball hit the ground Jimmy's eyes snapped back to life, and his stomach settled. He stood holding the ball as before, his teammates screaming for the pass. He felt the leather in his hands and had no idea what had just happened. But, sensing movement behind him, Jimmy ducked to the right; he had moved a mere second before Angus's hand swiped at the ball.

Jimmy's teammates went wild as Angus tripped and fell from not having expected to miss the steal.

"'Dere yu go, Jimmy!" Mr. Brodie yelled. "Take the shot! Take the shot!"

Jimmy squared to the net and recalled everything he could about the proper form; he couldn't even remember the last time he'd had an opportunity at the basket. He held his breath and pushed the ball up, letting it roll gently off his fingertips. Everyone watched as the ball sailed elegantly through the air, bounced around the rim twice, and sank through the cotton net.

A hand slapped his back. "That was a good one!" said Luke. "Didna' know yu had it in yu!"

"Aye, neither did I," Jimmy said looking to Angus, who was picking himself up off the court. The lanky redhead now had a red face to match. He, like Mr. Brodie, was clearly shocked. But unlike the gym teacher, Angus was not speechless.

"Lucky, move, Gresham," he said, glaring at Jimmy. "Yu won't be scorin' on me again anytime soon, I can tell yu true."

Jimmy gave up a little grin and turned back to the game. He wasn't quite sure what had taken place, but something told him this was going to be a good day.

※

Fish and chips . . . yummm! thought Jimmy as he spied the trays of a few kids walking by in the school cafeteria. *My favorite.* Jimmy took one look at the sparse lunch his mother had packed him. Minced egg sandwich and sticks of celery just couldn't compare to the deep-fried splendor of Lochgilphead's fish and chips. His bag lunch sailed into the tall trash can, and Jimmy stood tenth in the lunch line. Angus MacBain, still very red in the face, got in line six places behind Jimmy.

The line moved briskly and Jimmy found himself in front of Mrs. Entwhistle, the kindest lady in the school. Considered everyone's grandmother, she spoiled her favorites with large portions. "Ah, Jimmy, me wee boy," she said. "Are yu hungry today?"

"Aye," Jimmy replied with a wink. "Like a wolf."

"I best b' fillin' yur tray then," she replied. With her silver tongs, Mrs. Entwhistle selected two gigantic crispy fish filets and plopped them onto the green tray. Then, utilizing one of those wide-mouthed scoopers that no one knew the name of, she piled enough chips on the tray to half cover the fish. "That'll do yu, then?" she asked.

"Aye, it will!" Jimmy said, eyes wide. He stuck a piping-hot chip in his mouth. "Delicious!"

"Yu're so kind, Jimmy me boy. Now don't forget the tartar sauce outside. Made it meself, I did. Special herbs, yu know."

"Thank you, Mrs. Entwhistle." Jimmy took out his wallet and fished out the last two pounds of his allowance. But it was worth it.

Steam rose from the golden brown bliss on his tray. He couldn't wait to sit down. He left the serving room and went straight to the condiments table. Mrs. Entwhitstle's tartar sauce was there, along with an assortment of bowls of mustard, ketchup, brown sauce, relish, vinegar, ranch, and even hummus. Jimmy took the spoon and gave himself a generous dollop of tartar sauce. He loved the stuff. He'd even dip his chips in it.

Then it hit him again.

The strange nausea that had overwhelmed him in gym came back with a vengeance. He dropped the spoon back in the tartar sauce and steadied himself on the edge of the table.

Whoosh. The kids entering and exiting the serving room slowed way down. Their images blurred. There was sound as before, distorted sound, very low in pitch. Muffled. And then Jimmy found that he could again see the scene from above.

There he was putting the spoon back in the tartar sauce at the condiments table. But from behind him, Angus MacBain left the lunch line, handed his tray to his usual partner in crime, Michael Murray, and rushed toward Jimmy. At the last second, Angus grabbed Jimmy's jeans by the belt loops and yanked them straight down to Jimmy's ankles. The roar of laughter from the kids pointing at his boxer shorts sounded monstrous and strange.

Whoosh. In a blink, Jimmy was back to himself. He knew what was coming. *No way I'm going to let that happen!*

He had only a moment to act.

Without turning around, Jimmy took a hard step backward and bent over at the waist. Angus came on too fast and couldn't stop. Being tall but light, he slammed into Jimmy and flipped over the smaller boy. Angus crashed onto the condiments table, causing an eruption of brown, red, green, yellow, and white. Mustard, ketchup, brown sauce, relish, vinegar, and tartar sauce splattered the floor, the cafeteria wall, even the ceiling. And Angus looked like he'd been the target of an army of paintball soldiers. "Ugh," he groaned, wiping mustard out of his eyes.

Jimmy approached him. "Thought yu'd pants me, did yu, Angus?" he asked.

"Wha—? How'd yu—?"

"If it makes yu feel any better, I spilled me fish and chips."

Mrs. Entwhistle and the kitchen cashier emerged from the serving room. "Angus MacBain!" Mrs. Entwhistle chided. "I spent all mornin' makin' that tartar sauce. Now look what yu've gone and done! I'll fetch yu a mop, a rag, and a bucket, and yu can just spend yur lunch cleanin' it all up."

"Me?" Angus whined. "But Michael helped me!"

"Did he now?" Turning to him. "Well then, Michael can help yu with the mop!" Mrs. Entwhistle looked to Jimmy. "Did that bully make yu spill yur lunch then?" Jimmy nodded sheepishly. "Just come back in here and let me fill yu another tray."

The events of the morning and the fresh fish and chips were enough to distract Jimmy Gresham from his more serious problems for a while. But those problems did not go away, and the book Miss Finney had given him still waited.

23

Cast into the Night

"MOM? I'M home," Kiri Lee said as she put her key in her coat pocket, turned the deadbolt, and waited for the bombardment to begin.

No answer. Then she remembered her parents were performing tonight. She plugged her cell phone in to charge, set her violin case down, traded her boots for slippers, and reluctantly began walking the hall to the kitchen. But surprisingly there was a delicious aroma in the air. Kiri Lee wasn't entirely sure what her mother had left her for dinner, but it sure smelled tasty. She poked her head around the corner to find place settings for three on the breakfast table. On the counter sat the classic white to-go containers from any one of a dozen Chinese restaurants. "Mom?"

Born Alyona Mihailov to Russian parents, Kiri Lee's adopted mother married a studious Majesty School graduate, one Myung Yuen. Upon completion of their degrees in music, they had traveled incessantly, taking up residencies with numerous orchestras, never landing the dream jobs they wanted, and thus continually struggling to make ends meet.

They had been unable to have children on their own, but Mrs. Yuen's deep desire for family eventually helped her convince her husband to adopt. When their adoption agency found them a Korean child just a few months later, they couldn't refuse. Though busily immersed in their music careers, neither felt like they could keep up the pace forever. Little did they know that their new baby girl would carry a an aptitude for music that was similar to their own . . . only more so.

Now, looking around the breakfast room, Kiri Lee saw no one. She turned to go toward the den when she heard, "Hello, dear." Turning around, Kiri Lee saw her mother standing before her. Mrs. Yuen brushed her long brown hair over her shoulder to keep it from dangling in the rice bowl she prepared. She was dressed for an evening orchestra show.

Hello, dear? Kiri Lee was a bit taken aback. She glanced at the clock, then to her mom. "You're . . . you're not mad?"

"Mad? Whatever for?"

Now Kiri Lee was stumped. Need she point out the obvious? "I'm late, and that's running you late to theatre."

Mrs. Yuen placed the bowl on the table and turned to look at her daughter. "Not by much. We can't control all the unexpected events that delay us, can we? I'm just glad you're home."

Not mad for being late? Something was definitely up here. The last time Kiri Lee had been three minutes late for practice, her mother had made her run through scales an extra hour before bed.

Kiri Lee knew her mother loved her and wanted to do the best by her, but there wasn't a bone in her body that wasn't strict to the core. From practices and timing to schedules and courtesy, Mrs. Yuen was as punctual and meticulous as a Swiss watch. And despite that, they were a close-knit family. Creating a family ensemble, practicing popular tunes together, and always making time to make one another laugh.

And then there was the Chinese food. Kiri Lee stood in the doorway watching as her mother dumped a box of sweet-and-sour chicken onto a plate. In her entire life they had never eaten Chinese food as a family. Kiri Lee's mother and father had always been radically strict about their diet. And while Kiri Lee had secretly enjoyed Chinese food with friends, nothing that even smacked of fast food or MSG ever entered their home kitchen.

"Chinese?"

"But it's your favorite." Her mom turned. Her eyes were questioning, but her smile was overly sweet and unnatural.

An awkward silence spanned between them until finally Kiri Lee burst out laughing. "That's a good one, Mom!" she roared. "Well, if you're okay with it, I sure am."

Mrs. Yuen smiled and then continued to empty the containers onto the plates. "Did you see Mrs. Allen today?" she asked.

"Yes," Kiri Lee answered.

"Did she say when she'd stop by tonight?"

"No."

"So, it could be . . . late?"

"I suppose."

"And when would that be?"

"Her usual time," Kiri Lee said, thinking it odd her mother wouldn't know. Mrs. Allen always stopped by to check on Kiri Lee on her way to her apartment when the Yuens would be late coming back.

Kiri Lee hopped up on one of the tall bar stools along the kitchen counter. A pile of mail sat untouched on the counter by the phone. She started flipping through the stack and mimicked her father saying, "Bills, bills, bills . . ." until she came to an envelope addressed to her . . . from the Edinburgh National Music Festival. In her mother's handwriting across the top was: CONGRATULATIONS! We should be back by breakfast. Love, Mom & Dad.

"Mom!" Kiri Lee held up the envelope. "Why didn't you tell me about this?"

"About what, dear?" Kiri Lee's mom never turned from her work at the table.

"About the music festival's reply to my application! My solo for the royal family this month!"

"Your solo?"

Kiri Lee felt a strange chill, but at the same time, simmering anger. "Is this some kind of joke?"

Her mother looked up dreamily and then back down to the food. Time slowed down. Kiri Lee couldn't believe it. First her mother completely overlooks the fact that she's late, then the Chinese food, now she doesn't even remember the royal invitation to Scotland. Kiri Lee watched her. "Hey, Mom?"

"Yes, dear?" Her mother flashed that strange smile once more.

"Is something going on? I mean, is everything cool with your orchestra?"

Her mother slammed down the serving spoon. She stared at the kitchen table for several intense seconds. When she looked up, she still had that smile, but the look in her eyes was so menacing that Kiri Lee took a step backward.

"You tell me, Kiri dear, is there something wrong?"

"N-n-no," Kiri Lee replied as she backed out of the kitchen. "Never mind. Where's Dad?"

"In the den." Kiri Lee's mom turned her back to her daughter and went to the brown take-out bag on the counter.

"Do not disturb, right?" But her mother didn't reply. "Uh . . . 'kay. That's cool."

Kiri Lee hurried out of the kitchen, but stopped a few feet from the den. *I must be missing something,* she thought. *Mom's never been like this. Maybe she and Dad got into a big fight. Maybe she lost her seat in the orchestra.* And then Kiri Lee thought, *Maybe I should apologize.*

Kiri Lee went back to the kitchen and found her mother still standing at the counter. But before Kiri Lee uttered the first syllable, she froze. Her mom had a red bottle, small, little larger than a tube of lip balm. Kiri Lee watched her mother remove its small stopper and pour several bright red drops into a bowl of won ton soup.

Kiri Lee's heart rate took off. She ducked back into the hall. Feeling tears well up, she raced to the den. "Daddy!" she called.

Her father sat in his antique practice chair, not reading a book, not scoring music . . . but watching television.

Myung Yuen did not often watch television; and when he did, it was concerts he'd recorded or occasionally a family movie. That was it. Now, her father sat watching some mindless French sitcom, and he was chuckling like an adolescent.

"Daddy?"

"Hello, sweetie," he mumbled.

Sweetie? He never called her *sweetie*. Her pet name had always been *Lee Lee*.

"Daddy, what are you doing?"

"Just watching TV, sweetie." He turned and looked at her, his eyes as empty and uncaring as if he were looking at a block of wood. Kiri Lee stumbled back through the door and turned. She bumped into her mother.

"What's wrong, love?" Mrs. Yuen asked.

"What's wrong, love? *What's wrong?*" Kiri Lee looked back and forth incredulously. "All of this is wrong! Dad was watching TV! And you"— she pointed a quivering finger at her mother—"you and your crazy Chinese food! There's nothing wrong with me! It's you! Both of you!"

"Calm down, sweetie," her father insisted. "Easy."

"I'm Lee Lee! Remember?"

The three of them stood there between the hall and the den, between rage and regret . . . as silent as death.

Kiri Lee wiped a tear and finally spoke. "Mom, Dad . . . I—"

"To your room. Now!" her father ordered.

"Not just yet," replied Mrs. Yuen, glaring at her husband. "The girl must eat dinner first." The two of them seemed to come to an unspoken agreement.

"Yes, sweetie," he said, "it would be unjust for me to force you to skip your meal."

"NO!" She cried, much louder than she'd meant to. "I saw you . . ."

"Saw me what?" Mrs. Yuen asked.

Panic bubbled up in Kiri Lee's throat. She blurted out the only thing she could think of: "I saw you plopping that stuff onto the plate. It looked disgusting. Besides, I've lost my appetite."

Her parents exchanged knowing glances. Kiri Lee didn't wait. She strode down the hall to her room. She quickly slipped inside, closed the door, and leaned against it as it clicked shut.

✳

Kiri Lee's breath escaped in rapid bursts. She walked to her vanity table and sat, looking at herself in the mirror. Her hands were trembling. Her eyes looked huge and fearful. "This is crazy!" she whispered. *Were they really trying to poison me? It can't be true, but what was the little red bottle? And why were they so adamant that I eat?* Between the strange, sappy looks and the weird conversations, Kiri Lee's home suddenly felt very foreign, even otherworldly. She glanced at herself in the mirror one more time and released a pained, ironic laugh.

In all the commotion she had forgotten to take off her coat. No matter. Somehow it made her feel safe. Protected. She still held the invitation from Edinburgh in her hand and fumbled with the torn side of the envelope. Performances. She could always rely on them. And this concert, playing for the royal family, was her most prestigious yet. Kiri Lee stuffed the invitation inside her jacket pocket and went to her bed. All her clothes still on, even her slippers, she slid under her covers. She tried to think of ways to explain away all that had happened. *Maybe the red stuff was hot sauce. Maybe they're overstressed. Or maybe they are getting a divorce.* Kiri Lee started to pray that divorce wasn't the case, but exhaustion claimed her before she could finish it.

That night she dreamed of the coming storm she had seen in her music. Lightning flashed as before, and the rains began to fall. But this time Kiri Lee could see under the clouds. Not much, but enough. The landscape was a tumultuous, heaving region of volcanic mountains, the red glow of fresh lava streaming in the lower valleys. But one specific peak caught her attention: a jagged mountain with a deep crag ripped right through the middle. It was as if a giant axe blade had cut into the ground and cleaved the summit in two, a red flow of lava within flowing like blood.

All at once the vision disappeared, and Kiri Lee woke. Her forehead was moist with perspiration, her pillow soaked through. Thunder rumbled in the distance. She opened her eyes and gazed up at the ceiling. A muted, gray light saturated the room from the window beside her. Her clock read 3:23 a.m. in red digits. She turned over and saw a shadowy figure holding a raised knife.

Kiri Lee screamed. *Robber!* The thought blasted into her mind as she thrust the covers off herself and into her assailant's face. She rolled off the far side of her bed and onto the floor.

A deep voice cut through the darkness, "Come here!"

Kiri Lee crawled toward her window and looked back over the bed. Suddenly, she was aware of another figure in the room, this one more slender. *A woman?*

"Stop!" the woman shouted.

"Stay away!" Kiri Lee cried out. "Leave me alone!" She tried to stand up—

Shunck!

A knife drove into the wall beside her head. Kiri Lee screamed and gained her feet. She had to get out. Now. But where?

She spun away from the knife and glanced at the bench and then let her gaze go to the big picture window.

"Lothriel, come here!"

Kiri Lee turned back to face her attackers. *Who?* "There must be a mistake! Please, don't—"

The gray blur of another knife whizzed by her shoulder and left a spidery crack in the window. The two figures advanced toward her, each carrying another knife. Kiri Lee was cornered.

She backed up against the window bench and screamed, "Mom, Dad, help me! Help!!"

"We're trying to help you, Lothriel," the male voice said.

Why do they keep calling me that? "You have the wrong person! I'm not this Loth—*whoever!* I'm Kiri Lee!"

Lightning flashed. She saw the intruders for a split second. Kiri Lee's heart stopped. Standing in the middle of her room, clutching knives, and wearing those weird smiles . . . were her parents.

"For the last time, come here!" they roared.

"No," she whispered. "No! This can't be real." Louder, "Please no!"

Knives held high, her father and mother inched closer.

Kiri Lee's heart raced as she turned and stepped up on the bench beneath the big window. She looked out through the glass, then back at her parents. She whispered, "God, please help me."

She heard the words of a familiar Bible verse in her mind and recited it aloud: "For I am persuaded, that neither death, nor life, nor angels, nor principalities, nor powers, nor things present, nor things to come, nor height, nor depth, nor any other creature, shall be able to separate us from the love of God, which is in Christ Jesus our Lord."

Her parents ducked and stumbled as if they'd been struck. They shook it off and raised their knives once more.

". . . nor height, nor depth . . ." Kiri Lee looked out the window and realized what she must do. In one swift motion, she leaped at the window, shattering the glass, and went flying out into the cold night air.

24

A Dark Cascade

KAT WAS buckled into her seat, sandwiched between Mr. Wallace and Anna. Aside from the three of them and a stewardess who walked by every now and then, they were alone in the front of the aircraft. Kat still couldn't believe this was happening. *What will my parents think when I don't come home?* she thought.

Kat turned to Anna. "You know, it might have been better to have me call my parents. I mean, the letter you left my parents might be convincing and all, but it won't matter. They'll call out the National Guard to find me."

"We know," Anna replied.

"You know? Well, . . . why didn't you have me write a note saying I ran away or was at a friend's for a sleepover or something?"

"Because that would be untrue," said Mr. Wallace, leaning in. "We try not to lie."

"What do you call these fake IDs?" she said, removing a handful of cards and a passport from her purse.

"You incorrectly deem them fake," said Mr. Wallace. "But they are actually truer than any identification you already carried."

"Right," said Kat with a smirk.

"It's true, Kat," said Anna. "Though Kat Simonson is the name your earthly parents gave you . . . it is not really who you are. California is not really your home."

Looking at her name on the passport, Kat shrugged. "Fat chance I'll

189

ever answer to the name Alreenia Hiddenblade. Alreenia?" Kat laughed. "Come on." She shook her head. "And, Anna, how did that last name not trigger a security alert?"

Anna shrugged. "I'm glad it didn't. Otherwise, it might have been awkward."

"We have four more hours in the air, Kat," said Mr. Wallace. "I suggest you continue reading. The more you understand, the better. You have eight hundred years of history to catch up on."

"Anna said that before," said Kat. "How can that be? I'm only thirteen."

"Thirteen years on Earth," explained Mr. Wallace. "But in Allyra, more than eight-hundred years have passed. As near as we can tell, one Earth year equals sixty-six in our homeland."

Kat squinted, working out some figures in her mind. "So how old are you two then?"

"Nine hundred seventy years," Anna replied.

"A thousand twenty-two," said Mr. Wallace. "And a half."

"A thousand twenty—what?" Kat laughed, but then she became quiet. As she thought, a smile curled in one corner of her mouth. "Are Elves . . . am I immortal?"

"Not immortal," said Anna. "We live two thousand years, maybe a little more."

Kat frowned, thought some more, and then asked, "Does that mean . . . if I stayed on Earth, I'd keel over and die when I turn thirty?"

"That was quick calculating," said Mr. Wallace.

"I've always been good at math," Kat replied. She cast a teasing smile at Mr. Wallace. "Much better than at social studies."

"So I remember from last year," said Mr. Wallace. "But no, you would not have died at thirty. While on Earth, you age as humans do."

"Oh," said Kat. "That's a relief." She started to open the book. "One more thing?"

"Sure, Kat, what is it?"

"How did you know to give me the book? How did you know that I was an Elf? My ears aren't pointed."

"They would be," answered Mr. Wallace, "had the Drefids not dared to put a blade to your flesh." He brushed a few strands of Kat's pink hair over her ear. "We hold out a slim hope that your ears may regenerate once you return to your world. But, to answer your question, it was your skin color that first drew my attention."

"The poly?" Kat scowled. "Ugh, I hate it."

"Why would you say such a thing?" asked Anna. "Your skin is striking."

"Strikingly weird." Kat smirked. "Ugly."

"Nonsense," said Mr. Wallace. "You are the daughter of Beleg and Kendie Hiddenblade, pureblood among the race of Berylinian Elves. In Allyra, your skin color is less rare, but nonetheless, it is considered exquisitely beautiful."

"You mean . . . there are others?"

"Thousands, Kat, just like you," said Mr. Wallace.

"Like me?"

"Well, not quite. They cannot read minds."

Kat sat in stunned silence. She'd never—NEVER—thought of her bluish skin as beautiful before. And to think that there were thousands like her . . . was almost too much to grasp.

"Kat?"

She blinked and found Anna and Mr. Wallace staring at her. "I'm sorry," said Kat. "I was lost in thought."

"Whose thoughts?" asked Anna.

"Just my own." Kat smiled. "I can't read minds whenever I want to. The only time it worked when I tried was with you, Anna, back at my house. The other times, it just kind of happened."

Mr. Wallace rubbed his now stubbly chin. "It may be that your gift has not yet matured fully. Perhaps it only manifests in times of stress or great emotion. Or great need."

Kat didn't answer. She stared at Mr. Wallace, concentrating every thought. "Bummer," she said. "It still didn't work."

"It will come," said Anna.

"Now, read your book, young Elf," said Mr. Wallace.

Kat smiled, shrugged, and opened the book, removing the tassel from where she had left off. She was ready this time. She took a deep breath and touched the text on the page. The cabin lights blinked, the air grew chill and drafty. An arrow shot out of the book and disappeared into the overhead compartment just as a flight attendant walked by. Kat laughed softly. *She didn't notice. To her, I'm just a passenger completely immersed in a good book.*

An arrow glanced off Cathar's iron helmet.

"Shrenleks!" The Gwar overlord growled out an epithet for the Elves. It meant *Treekissers*, and this small force guarding the northern tree gate was causing more trouble than Cathar thought possible.

Elf warriors held their positions on the grand set of stairs that led through the gate onto the hilly plateau of the deep forest. The gate itself was the opening to a vast tunnel formed by massive living trees—its pillars, large tree trunks—its roof, thick branches. Other Elf soldiers stood guard at the actual gate and waited for the onslaught that was only now on their doorstep.

The main host, thousands of infantry and dozens of Warspiders, continued to surge down the street devouring the forces of Berinfell like poultry pecking at corn kernels in a chicken coop. But it was not without loss, for the soldiers of Berinfell had taken out three Gwar for every Elf to fall.

Cathar's real objective—fleeing Elven citizens (mostly women and children)—was in sight but maddeningly out of reach. Cathar grunted. He had wanted to finish them off by himself. He turned and looked up to the top of the Elven cathedral, where six large, red Warspiders and their Drefid riders waited. Cathar loosed two short blasts on his war horn and motioned to the Drefin high commander that the time had come.

With eerie speed, the lethal red Warspiders clambered down from the cathedral's roof. Cathar watched them go to work using their swordlike forelegs to skewer their enemies; the red Warspiders driving straight through the fleeing Elves. Tyrith and the other Drefids fired arc rifles into the Elves at close range, causing many to be engulfed in perilous blue blazes. Between the spiders and the fire, a clear path had opened for Cathar's forces. And Cathar wasted no time leading his troops through it.

"Good. They see their doom coming," Cathar muttered. He watched the Elves emerge from the sewers and race madly toward the tree gate. *Odd,* Cathar thought. *The Elves are usually so protective and careful with their children. But look at them! They are in such terror that they drag their children like rag dolls.*

All in vain, thought Cathar as his line of Gwar and spiders caught up to the fleeing Elves. They didn't even turn to fight or ward off a blow. They just fell to the street and went under the claws of the rampaging Warspiders. *How easy it was!* Cathar exulted as his forces rode down the enemy. But halfway to the tree gate, something went wrong.

An arrow whistled past Cathar's ear from behind. Cathar reined his Warspider to a halt. Had one of his men fired an errant shot? He turned and looked back. The battle was still thick behind him. The Drefids and Gwar support troops continued to press the obstinate Elves. In the writhing melee it was difficult to tell, but it seemed to Cathar that his Gwar soldiers had been thinned by a third. And at least several Warspiders were gone. Still, in the waning moonlight, it was hard to tell for sure.

Cathar ordered a team of his soldiers into the sewers and then spurred his spider forward. He led his Gwar raiders to the foot of the tree gate and watched as a dozen or more Elven citizens climbed the steps and clambered awkwardly through the arched entryway. "What are you waiting for?!" Cathar bellowed to his troops. "After them!"

Ten Gwar warriors lumbered across the street, up the stairs, and beneath the boughs into the tree gate. Mere moments after the Gwar were out of sight, there came a great commotion from within. Cathar heard deep, throaty screams that could only come from . . . from his Gwar troops. The tree canopies shook, and from the outside it seemed as if the entire tunnel-like passage quivered and swayed. The agonized screams rose in pitch until, one-by-one, they ended.

But this could not be! Against women, children, and old ones?

"What is this?" Cathar muttered. He turned to see if the Drefids behind him had taken notice, but they were still busy with the Elves. *Good*, he thought. *I'll take no chances this time*. Cathar motioned to Vulmark, one of his commanders. "Take your Warspider and twenty lads. See what that's about!"

"Yes, sir!" Vulmark chose the Gwar infantry he needed and urged his spider-mount forward toward the tree gate. They entered. Cathar waited. If anything, the ruckus that occurred was even greater than before. This time, joining the howls of the Gwar, came a wretched *SCREE* from the Warspider and a horrendous *CRACK* like a large limb being torn away from a tree.

Then there was ominous silence.

Cathar waited a few heavy heartbeats. "Enough of this!" he growled. "Must I do everything myself?" Cathar gathered three more commanders: Marlock, Kreegan, and Skolch. Together with six Warspiders and more than sixty foot soldiers, they approached the tree gate. The soldiers fanned out on the stairs, and the Warspiders drove up the middle.

Nothing moved from the shadowy arched entryway. Slowly, Cathar advanced his team into the tunnel. The Gwar overlord held a Gwar hammer in one hand and a loaded arc rifle in the other. Once they passed into the darkness and their Gwar eyes adjusted, Cathar saw that scattered about the tunnel floor was the dismembered carcass of a Warspider and many still gray forms. And up ahead was a dark mass.

Cathar sneered. Something was there. He lifted his arm and fired the arc rifle. The arc stone kindled as it raced away, contacted something fifty yards ahead, and exploded in a massive blue fireball. The flash died away but left a whipping fire burning at the base of a large tree. Huddling in clumps on either side of the fire were many Elves. Cathar could see their large, frightened eyes glimmering. It was just as he had suspected, mostly women, children, and men bent with age. "Kill them . . . all!" he commanded.

Marlock and Kreegan spurred their Warspiders forward. Their Gwar infantry marched after them. Not twenty yards ahead, the Warspiders screeched and stopped abruptly.

"We are snared!" Marlock yelled. "Something's in the trees!"

Even as he spoke, more cables of dark rope sailed out of the woods on either side of the Warspiders. Each line had some kind of grappling hook on its end, and each one wound itself around and fastened to the upper leg of one of the spiders.

Cathar watched in a trance as more Elven citizens seemingly materialized between the trunks of the trees on either side. Teams of Elves grasped the ends of these cords that were wrapped around the sturdy trunk. They pulled the ropes tight and then . . . kept pulling. The Warspiders resisted but found their limbs overpowered and stretched; they fell hard to the ground and gnashed their jaws in pain as their limbs failed and tore free from their bodies. In that moment, the Elves dropped their cords and leaped out of the trees. They pounced on the spiders and their riders. A great spear pierced Marlock's breastplate, and he fell away. Kreegan jumped from his spider and tried to run but found himself cornered by three Elven women.

Women? The timid Elves from up ahead shrieked and charged into battle—the children, the old-timers, too. *This is impossible!* Cathar's mind raced through the succession of events, the carefully crafted ambush, and well-executed attack. He looked more closely at the Elves. Dresses, smocks, robes, plain clothing, and yet . . . their athletic build and agile movements? The Elf children looked strange, their faces expressionless, their limbs swinging limply at their sides. One of the Elf soldiers leaned down and incredulously grabbed the head of an Elf child and . . . pulled it off, revealing a large, round quiver full of arrows. "Not a child at all!" Cathar snarled. "What is—?" A grappling hook fell upon his spider's longest midleg on his right.

Another wrapped around its left foreleg.

"No! No!" Cathar growled.

His battle axe was out in a flash, and he whaled on the Elven rope. It took seven, eight, nine powerful cuts before the cable broke. The same with the other. And more hooks came flying from the trees. These were no peaceful townsfolk!

Even as he severed another cord from his spider's leg, Cathar felt pieces of a puzzle fitting together in his mind. *Why would these flet soldiers be defending the north gate dressed as common-folk, mimicking women and children?*

Thoughts flew through his head with every swing of his axe, as he tried to piece everything together. *They drew us away, that's what they did . . . to keep us from wiping them out. But drew us away from where? Where is the remnant of Berinfell? Not the South Gate. We only just left Sentinel Garden. Not east . . . not with our forces continuing to pour in through the Cliff Gate. West? The Forest Gate?*

Cathar knew the Drefids had taken out the Seven Lords and left the Great Hall in smoking ruins. But then . . . they pulled out. They left the Great Hall. The full picture became clear, at last.

Cathar raked his clawed hand across his chest. "Trickery!" he yelled to his soldiers. "Out of this deathtrap, Gwar! Retreat to the road!"

There were far fewer soldiers left to hear the command, but Kreegan and Skolch, both now on foot, followed their overlord out of the tree gate. Only two Warspiders emerged unscathed. What was left of their force bounded down the steps to the road. As he spurred his spider toward the Drefid high commander, Cathar loosed three blasts on his war horn.

— •• •• •• • •• •• •• •• •• •• •• •• — —

A Warspider barreled over the top of Travin as he lay near the bottom of the stairs. He'd barely managed to turn his body enough to avoid being crushed by a spider foot. Then he lay still again. *That was close!* Travin thought.

He had watched three groups of the enemy enter the tree gate. Several tense moments later, a throng of Gwar and two Warspiders raced back out and down the stairs. A war horn sounded three times.

"They know," Travin said, first to himself. Since he no longer needed to play dead, he yanked the half arrow shaft from his armor and yelled so all could hear, "They know! They know! Now, flet soldiers, NOW!!"

25

Fire of the Dead

Cathar halted his Warspider along the road. He and Tyrith, the Drefid high commander, sat upon their spider-mounts with just a few yards between them. Neither spoke, as they tried to understand what was happening.

Dead Elves in the road, on the stairs, and in the gutter . . . they began to stir. Bodies strewn in piles began to untangle. Figures—battered and bloody, sprawled awkwardly—rose up.

"We have been deceived!" Cathar practically spat at the high commander.

"The Great Hall," said Tyrith, his voice high and agitated.

Cathar growled. "YES, the Great Hall! Just as I told you. We left it unwatched for too long. And now, we have missed them!"

"Mind your words, Gwar!" Tyrith seethed. "We may catch them up yet."

Cathar growled and, as he drove his Warspider at the Elves, he thought of the warriors of Berinfell with a kind of grudging respect. It had been a brilliant ploy—diverting the Spider King's forces while the citizens of Berinfell escaped. *Still, it was likely all for naught*, thought Cathar, *for no matter where the Elves might hide, I will hunt them down.*

— ••••••• ••••••••• ••••••• —

Travin removed his spear from the thorax of a now lifeless Warspider. He felt a type of grim satisfaction, knowing that his efforts and the efforts of his flet soldiers had gouged out a fifth of the Spider King's invading force, and more importantly their diversion had bought his nation precious time to escape.

But they could do no more.

The bulk of the invading force had almost immediately withdrawn back south, and from there would no doubt march west to the Great Hall. They had left behind some four hundred Gwar. There were no more tricks, no more cards to play, and slowly, the outnumbered Elves were losing by attrition. It chafed Travin to the core to think of fleeing from battle. But Grimwarden himself had urged Travin to escape any way possible once the enemy had discovered the ruse.

Travin could not hesitate. The Gwar were advancing, threatening to flank them and, Travin guessed, tighten around them like a noose. . . . *Seek the trees and by the hidden ways, at last enter Nightwish Cavern. Whatever you accomplish, do not pursue the enemy back here.*

Travin knew the hidden ways, but few of his soldiers did. They'd need a rally point, somewhere in the deep forest. Travin could think of just one place the enemy would not know. "Hearken to me!" Travin yelled. "Make for the Moonlit Crown! All of Berinfell's faithful, pass the word: 'Make for Moonlit Crown!'"

He roared until he was hoarse, hoping his soldiers would hear him over the chaotic battle. Dodging Gwar hammers and axes at every turn, he reached every Elf he could find and sounded the retreat. As Travin fled the battle, exhaustion and emotion overtook him. His beloved nation of Elves was on the brink of extinction.

— •••••••• ••••••••• ••••••• —

Guardmaster Grimwarden stood with his back to the broken-out stained glass windows and watched the train of Elves moving across the floor of the Great Hall. Clearly Travin and Vendar had done their job. Five thousand Elves had escaped to the underground, but . . . he shook his head. *We need more time.*

A breeze from the quiet forest exaggerated the chill Grimwarden felt sliding along his spine as he watched a young scout named Fydelf entering the chamber. Fydelf looked from face to face before spotting Grimwarden. The scout ran to his commander.

"They are coming," Fydelf said.

"How far out?"

"Five miles, no more," Fydelf replied. "They move as if the Spider King himself drives them here."

Their feet are swift to shed blood, thought Grimwarden, words from the holy scroll kindling with new meaning. "We must hold them off still," he said.

"But how, sir?" Fydelf asked. "They bring many Warspiders. They will come through the windows once more. We have no barrier to hold them out, no weapon to deter them, no army to withstand them."

No barrier . . . no weapon . . . no army . . .

Key variables ricocheted aimlessly in Grimwarden's mind before at last coming together. He knew he had to act immediately.

"Stay here," he ordered Fydelf. "Do what you can to hurry our people into the tunnel."

"Wait, where are you going, Guardmaster?"

"To pick a fight with an irritating pack of arachnids."

Grimwarden ran for the main entrance to the Great Hall. He called on any flet soldier or able-bodied Elf he found along the way. He assembled the group at the mouth of a side passage near the main entrance.

"You," he spoke to three Elves, "bring torches. We're going to need them on the roof directly above us. And I want the five of you—no, make that the seven of you to the refractory. I want every jar of oil you can find. Every scrap of lard. Meet us above in twenty minutes. No more, or all is lost. Do you understand?"

Tentative nods from the soldiers. Fearful stares from the townsfolk. "Now GO!!"

The ten Elves scattered to their tasks, and Grimwarden turned to the others. "Follow me," he said, and he continued to speak as he led them back into the Great Hall. "The rest of you I chose because you look more or less strong. I just hope you don't mind getting your hands dirty."

"Master Grimwarden?" one of the Elves inquired with a raised eyebrow.

The Guardmaster smiled mirthlessly. "The only thing spiders hate worse than fire is water. Unfortunately, I can't make it rain. But I have plenty to burn."

———— •••••••••••••••••••••••••••• ————

The Spider King's army swarmed the streets, the walls, and the fortresses of western Berinfell like *cinder ants* on the carcass of a dead beast. Tyrith, the Drefid high commander, made certain that the Elves' so-called *Great Hall* was surrounded. And Tyrith himself led the bulk of his Gwar battalions onto the building's vast roof. There they came to an abrupt halt.

"I don't like this," Tyrith said, his voice the hiss of escaping steam. The large sockets of his eyes became mere slits as he tried to identify the strange mounds piled up along the far edge of the roof. It was impossible to tell. A half-dozen torches forty yards away ruined his night vision for anything on the other half of the roof. Unwilling to investigate himself, Tyrith called on three of his Gwar soldiers. "Mundruk, Jeer, Raspik, find out what that is."

"Yes, sir!" The three Gwar loosed their axes, spikes, and hammers, then lumbered forward.

Forty paces later, they stopped abruptly. "There is a smell," Raspik called back over his shoulder.

"What sort of smell?" demanded Tyrith.

"A horrid smell," said Raspik.

"Worse than the sewage river in Vesper Crag!" cried Mundruk.

"Aye," said Jeer. "But there's somethin' else . . . it burns my eyes."

There was a momentary pause. Then the three Gwar moved past the torch stands.

"By the Spider King's beard!" Mundruk exclaimed.

"There are bodies, sir," Raspik said over his shoulder. "Hundreds of our countrymen."

Tyrith scraped the bony blades of his hands together, and like the greased gears of some terrible machine the wheels of his mind churned. "Follow me," he growled to the rest of his troops. Some casting furtive glances at the soldiers on either side of them, others staring anxiously back over their shoulders, some five hundred warriors traversed the roof. The smell hit them as they neared the torches. A grim scene waited just beyond.

"Look at them!" growled Raspik. "They've stacked them like kindling!"

"It would seem the Elves wish to send us a message. Did they think they would scare us off?" Tyrith paused. "I think not. The last vestige of the Elves of Berinfell have taken refuge in the Great Hall below." He turned back to the masses behind him. "Bring the Warspiders forward! We'll need rappelling webs over the roof's edge. Fan out!"

Tarax's face contorted. "We're not going to . . . to trample the dead, are we?"

"Come now, Tarax," he replied. "They won't feel a thing."

The Warspiders clambered over the piles. The Gwar soldiers advanced as well, wincing at every squish. The odor became so strong that many became sick, mingling that intense, odd, stinging vapor with the other smells.

One by one, the spiders turned, so that their heavy abdomens hung over the walls, their thick strands of web soon dangling down. Gwar soldiers reluctantly trod over their fallen comrades and began to sling themselves over the edge of the roof.

Tyrith was amazed by the ingenuity of their opponents. The Elves had allowed their escaping citizens to be seen heading north and led the Gwar far away from their real sanctuary. A brilliant diversion. And the Elves had guessed the Gwar's next move as well, leaving a grim reminder of the toll this invasion had taken on the Gwar nation.

Tyrith looked at the bodies. He'd known some of them from years of training in the catacombs beneath Vesper Crag.

Wait!

Tyrith descended from his spider and drew nearer to the dead on the rooftop. At first, he'd thought the bodies were glistening with blood—there was plenty of that. But there was something else entirely, a yellow liquid dotted with small globs of white.

Suddenly, a strange wet *snap!*

Tyrith looked up to see several lines of thin rope jerk up from the bodies and then fall back. The ropes disappeared over the edge of the roof like the web rappelling lines. But at first, he couldn't see where the ropes ended. Once more the rope snapped up, and this time it pulled taut. Tyrith realized all at once what was happening. The other ends of the ropes were attached to the torch stands.

"Stop! STOP!! STOP!!!" he screamed. But the Gwar rappelling down the wall did not understand. They continued their descent, yanking on whatever trip wire the Elves had manufactured. The torch stands wobbled and slid closer to the piles of bodies.

Tyrith leaped back up to his Warspider just in time to see one of the torch stands jerk forward and fall.

FOOM!!

The piles of oil-soaked bodies burst into a raging inferno. Fuel canisters hidden beneath the top layer of Gwar exploded with thunderous fury.

BOOM!!

Tyrith was flung headlong from the saddle away from the fires but crashed into a pillar of stone and lay still at its base. The Warspiders on the roof flared up like dead wood. Gwar soldiers who had been waiting to rappel were engulfed in flames, or ran frantically about on the rooftop until the heat overcame them.

━ •••••••• ••••••••• •••••• ━

"There goes a Gwar," said Fydelf as the first bulky form hurtled past the broken-out windows.

"And another," replied Grimwarden. "They like to dish out the fire, but they themselves cannot bear it."

Then a flaming Warspider cartwheeled past the window. Grimwarden and Fydelf watched in silence for a few moments. They heard sheer chaos above. The blaze had done its work.

"We're almost clear," Fydelf said, looking to the last Elves about to enter the tunnel.

"Almost," Grimwarden replied, but his face shared none of Fydelf's enthusiasm. The screaming faded as the flame's victims expired, and soon sounds from the rooftop ceased altogether.

"Retreating?" Fydelf proposed.

"Would you?" Grimwarden eyed him. Fydelf shook his head. "They're coming, just not that way. We have precious few moments left."

Grimwarden and Fydelf helped Berinfell's very last soul, one of their most elderly, into the passageway, his first steps to Allyra's underworld.

The old Elf turned to the soldiers and said, "I will miss the sun."

Fydelf gave him a reassuring squeeze on the shoulder, and then led him into the depths. Grimwarden lingered a moment more. His face was ashen gray and streaked with blood. He wore a blank expression. The Guardmaster wondered if Travin and Vendar were still alive. He uttered a

204

silent prayer that they were, but the pang in his gut told him the odds were low. *I ordered them to their deaths,* he thought. *How many good Elves have died at my word?*

He shook his head.

It was foolishness to think of such things. He commanded Berinfell's entire military. An overwhelming foe had come upon the city without warning, and many good Elves died in its defense. So many. A number Grimwarden would not contemplate for fear that it would render him immobile.

Shrieks and growls snapped Grimwarden back to the moment. Shadows moved in the hallway beyond the main entrance.

Lots of shadows.

Grimwarden stepped into the passageway and sprinted to the first turn. He drew a large master key from his belt and turned it in a panel recessed into the stone. The small door opened with an audible creak. Within was a handle. Grimwarden grabbed it and turned. He heard a faint click.

It was armed.

He took one last look up the passage. He could just make out the ceiling of the Great Hall. He thought it might be his mind playing tricks, but for just a moment, he saw a flicker of sunlight. But then he heard growls and the scrabble of many iron-shod feet.

I too will miss the sun, he thought.

He pulled the lever and ran for his life.

26

Ringing of the Bells

"WHAT DO yu suppose the narrator meant by 'a multitude of bottled-up memories'?" Miss Finney asked excitedly after finishing a paragraph in the class's latest text. It was a B-schedule day, which meant she taught reading in the afternoon instead of her normal post at the helm of the school's library.

Lochgilphead Central School's pupils were generally motivated and eager to please . . . especially in Miss Finney's class. A number of hands shot into the air, each student keen to prove his or her reading comprehension prowess.

"Ellie Faust?" Miss Finney pointed.

"Is she talking 'bout past experiences . . . things she hasn' a told anybody?"

"Good, Ellie."

"And," Ellie went on, "she tried to tell someone, but whoever it was wouldna' listen. Maybe even humiliated her."

"And thus the tension of the scene," agreed Miss Finney. "Class, yu've come a long way in text analysis. Let's see if we can go even deeper. Tell me more about the tension."

As reading was one of his favorite classes, this would have been interesting to Jimmy, had it not been for the dramatic events of the past twenty-four hours, or for the weighty book that sat in the backpack under his seat. He could almost hear it calling his name. That and he was desperate to talk with Miss Finney in private. So consumed was he with his thoughts that he never did hear the question his reading teacher posed to him.

"Jimmy?" The sound of his name snapped him out of his daydream.

"Aye?"

"The tension?"

"I'm tense?"

The class giggled.

Mrs. Finney frowned. "Nay, Jimmy, the tension between our main characters."

"Right. I—"

The bell cut him off, and not too soon for Jimmy.

"Remember, class," Miss Finney yelled over the ringing, "chapters seventeen and eighteen for homework! We're covering them on Friday!"

Everyone filed out of the room except Jimmy. He sat staring at his desk, eager to talk with Miss Finney, but again not sure how to breach the subject.

She walked over to him and sat down in an adjacent desk. "Crazy day?"

"Yu could say that, Miss Finney."

"I heard the boys talking about gym. Said yu were a wonder."

Jimmy looked down, face slightly red. "I wouldna' go that far."

"Said yu faked out MacBain and scored a basket or two."

"I got lucky."

"Then yu gave him a bit of a hand into the condiments table at lunch."

"It's not like I have any special power or anything!"

Miss Finney's face went blank.

Neither of them spoke.

The whisper of a smile formed in Miss Finney's lips. A very peculiar smile.

"Miss Finney? What are yu smiling at?"

The bell rang, signaling the start of sixth period.

"I suggest yu make time after yur normal studies to study *something else* when yu get home." Jimmy saw her make a subtle gesture to the book she had given him in the library.

"What do yu know that I don't, Miss Finney?"

"Wait and see, Master Jimmy." She stood up and walked away from him toward the front of the classroom. "Wait and see."

✳

The rain hadn't stopped all day, so when Jimmy slipped in the front door of his house, the first thing he did was bolt for his room for a fresh change of clothes. Fortunately no one saw him; if they had, he wasn't sure *they* wanted to talk to him anyway. It had become all too clear that he had no real family.

He pulled on a dry sweater and opted for his pajama pants. He didn't plan on leaving his room for a long time. Sure, he'd miss dinner. But, at this point, he'd rather read than eat.

Jimmy unzipped his drenched backpack and dumped his books onto the floor. He scolded himself as he noticed each volume was also wet, the pages warped, covers blotted. And the book he was most interested in sat amongst the rest. Surely its handwritten pages were now utterly ruined. Jimmy reached for the large, dark-green tome, but to his surprise it felt dry. *But the pages will be soaked.* He cradled the book, admired its gilded title once more, and then carefully opened it up.

What's this then? He glanced back at the pile of study books on his bedroom floor, each clearly saturated from the rain. "Not a drop,"

208

Jimmy whispered. He flipped forward a few more pages, each of them just as he had seen them before, perfectly clear and devoid of blemish.

I don't understand.

He stood slowly and walked to his bed, eyes fixed on the writing within. He flicked off the room light and turned on his reading lamp before slipping under the covers. He dwelt once more on the intricate drawing, the vast bridge ascending across to a tower, and marveled at the detail. Almost photographic quality. *How can anyone draw like that?* Jimmy wondered. Only this time Jimmy thought the drawing had changed slightly—a different point of view perhaps, or the trees had changed position, or the clouds had moved. Something was different—something he couldn't put his finger on. Granted, his first glance at the mysterious book had been rushed.

He turned a few more pages until he spotted 9680 *Founding of Allyra.* "If this be typeset, I'm an aardvark," Jimmy said to his empty room. Someone had handwritten this text. But who? All the other books he had ever read were merely mass-produced, printed copies. This was one of a kind. And it looked old, smelled old, felt old. *Ancient* was a better word. For all that, Jimmy thought it best to be much more careful with it. With painstaking caution, he turned every page by pinching the absolute corner of the page. He made sure he never once touched the text.

Jimmy soon forgot about the hour, forgot about his hunger, and never did hear Mrs. Gresham summoning him for dinner. Mr. Gresham had come up and listened at Jimmy's door, but hearing nothing, assumed the boy was asleep.

Turning pages long after midnight, Jimmy found himself completely consumed with an ancient story of Elves and Gwar, epic battles, and evil plots. He had the oddest sensation while he read . . . a bizarre mixture of feeling as if he'd read it all before and a kind of creeping dread. It was so easy to see himself in this story. Somehow. *But that's crazy!*

And then he heard Miss Finney's voice in his head again. "Crazy day?" If only she knew just how crazy it was becoming . . . or maybe she did.

After all, it was she who gave him this book. Surely she must have read it, or else why recommend it? Better still, it was clearly not one of the library's books: no markings of *Lochgilphead* anywhere. *So it is her own. Wonder if she, wrote it?*

In that moment, Jimmy's heart began to thunder in his chest. He was on to something, putting clues together like a detective and closing in on the truth. And yet not all the clues added up. *But how could Miss Finney write something like this?* He knew she was a good teacher, and some teachers were known to write novels in their spare time. But this? This was a masterpiece!

Jimmy closed the book, leaned back against the headboard, and closed his eyes. His imagination churned, and he was nearly asleep when he heard a sound.

His eyes shot open wide, and he scanned his room.

It sounded like a cup or something had tipped over or fallen off— *the dresser!*

Jimmy glared at the top of his dresser, where Geoffry's spider container lay sideways, open, . . . and empty. *How'd that get in here?*

He jammed himself backward into the headboard and looked frantically around the room. He wasn't an arachnaphobe, but he didn't want the thing to crawl up into his bed in the middle of the night, either. Jimmy remembered reading somewhere on the Internet that, while sleeping, the average person ate thirteen or fourteen spiders every year. How anyone measured that, Jimmy had no idea. *What kind of sick scientists would just watch spiders crawl into some poor person's mouth?*

Jimmy squirmed in bed for a few moments, but his curiosity got the best of him. He leaned over the mattress to check the floor. He slid out of bed and walked gingerly around the room.

It wasn't on the throw rug.

It wasn't under the bed.

Jimmy even checked behind the dresser. No sign of it. Not finding it was somehow worse. Wondering where the little hairy booger had gotten to, Jimmy reluctantly got back into bed.

He struggled to stay awake for some time, but soon his willpower gave out. Jimmy blinked, nodded, and fell asleep.

The lights were out when he woke some time later. *Mom . . . Mrs. Gresham must have checked in on me*, he thought. He started to close his eyes once more when he felt something touch his right ankle. It was such a light, ticklish feeling that Jimmy ignored it at first. But in one sudden, heart-pounding moment, he realized what it was.

He flung off the covers, switched on his bedside light, and stared.

Brown and black, the size of a golf ball, the spider crawled slowly up Jimmy's ankle and onto his pajama pants leg.

"AII!!" Jimmy kicked his leg furiously, but the spider held on. Finally, Jimmy managed to fling it off. It landed at the bottom of his bed and made haste crawling back toward Jimmy.

"No yu don't!" Jimmy growled

He grabbed the only thing handy, his precious book, and slammed it down on the spider.

The first time he lifted the book, the spider was still there and very much alive. It kept coming. Again and again, Jimmy whaled on the spider.

Bam! Baam! Baaam!!

At last, it was dead.

He scraped the spattered remains off the book into the hallway toilet and flushed. A few globs and pieces of the spider decorated Jimmy's blanket, so he balled that up and threw it in the hamper.

It was a long time before Jimmy Gresham could fall back asleep, and an even longer night of tossing and turning.

✳

The next morning had gotten off to a great start. Geoffry cried all morn-ing long because "mean-old-Jimmy" killed his pet spider.

"Why'd yu put the stupid thing in me room?" Jimmy had asked.

"I thought yu were lonely," whined Geoffry.

Mr. and Mrs. Gresham had taken Geoffry's side, of course. And now, at school, things didn't seem to be improving.

"Did I write the book?" Miss Finney's expression gave away nothing.

"Aye. At least that's the only way I can explain it all," replied Jimmy. The way she looked at him now, Jimmy felt stupid for the question. It did seem absurd. But how else could he explain it?

"Tell me, Jimmy," she said. "Did it seem like an ordinary book then?"

"No!" Jimmy replied. "It was AWESOME. I was totally into it. But why'd yu write it by hand? Don't yu like the computer?"

"That's not what I mean." Her hands flew to her hips. "Stars, lad, did yu even touch the writing?"

"Touch it? No, I didn't want to mess it up."

"Mess it up—" Miss Finney's face reddened. "Yu can't mess it up, Jimmy." The two of them stood in the hallway between classes, kids rushing around them on both sides. Neither of them moved. Miss Finney just stared back at Jimmy.

Why is she so mad? Have I said something wrong?

Jimmy glanced around as students emptied the hall. Second period meant one thing for Jimmy: Mr. Brodie and more basketball.

"Yu can forget basketball today, Jimmy. I'll write yu a pass," Miss Finney said. "Yu must finish the book."

"What do yu mean—now?"

"Aye, right now. How far did yu get last night?"

Miss Finney was acting strangely. She seemed . . . frightened. Jimmy felt like his answer would decide whether he passed or failed. "Up to where the Drefids took the children to that Vesper place—"

"Not near enough. Yu *must* finish today. We haven't much time left."

"What, are yu entering yur book in a publishing contest or something?"

Miss Finney cast him a dour look that could have melted rock.

"Yu'd definitely win, Miss Finney. Seriously."

Distracted by voices, Miss Finney ignored the comment. She stared up the hallway. Coming around the corner with Mr. Donegal, the principal, was the last person Jimmy ever expected—or wanted—to see in his school. His heart skipped more beats than it hit; the tweed jacket, dark-green sweater, cane, and black cap—there could be no doubt.

Mr. Ogelvie.

"Jimmy, go to me classroom right now," Miss Finney ordered him with a whisper.

Jimmy was incredulous, looking back and forth between Miss Finney and Mr. Ogelvie. "Do yu know him? That's my neigh—"

"Jimmy! Yu must finish that book! Go to me class and lock the door, pull the shade over the window. Yu'll be safe."

"Safe?"

"Jimmy Gresham, yu have much to learn, but circumstances are now beyond me control, accelerating far too quickly, and I have only two objectives."

"Two obj—?"

"To keep yu alive and bring yu home."

"Alive?"

Miss Finney turned him by his shoulders and pushed him down

the hall, walking with him away from Mr. Ogelvie and Lochgilphead's principal. "Go read, Jimmy. And touch the writing this time. We'll speak when yur done."

"What's going on here, Miss Finney? I—"

"Yu'll know more than yu wish soon enough. But for now, yu're just going to have to trust me."

"Listen, Miss Finney, if I'm in some sort of trouble, just call me parents and they'll come get me. . . . at least I think they will."

She stopped him right there and spun him to face her. Jimmy peeked around her arm; Mr. Ogelvie was getting closer. His heart was racing. Miss Finney seemed out of her mind. But he was far more frightened of his new neighbor than he ever would be of her.

"Jimmy, don't yu understand? That's not the home I'm talking 'bout! The Gresham family cannot help yu now!"

"Miss Finney, I'm beginning to think that it's yu who—"

"I know about yur gift, Jimmy! Yu can see into the future!"

Jimmy was speechless, staring wildly at her now. He wasn't sure if it was the intensity of the moment, or being overtired from reading late into the night, but her very words provoked another wave of nausea to pass over him. And with it another vision . . .

He stood in the hallway with Miss Finney gripping his arms. A moment later, the principal and Mr. Ogelvie approached them. Words were exchanged. Mr. Ogelvie produced a small knife and, an instant later, Mr. Donegal was on the floor, blood pooling on the gray tile. Miss Finney reacted, but too slow, and the same knife plunged into her stomach, reopening the wound already present there. Mr. Ogelvie turned to Jimmy, the knife dripping with blood.

"Jimmy!" Miss Finney yelled.

Jimmy snapped back to reality.

"Miss Finney," Mr. Donegal spoke up from down the hall. "Whatever seems to be the problem?"

"Be careful," Jimmy said, panic tightening his throat. "He has a knife."

"Thanks for the tip." She smiled and winked at him.

Jimmy took off running down the hallway.

"Young man!" cried Mr. Donegal. When Jimmy failed to respond, the principal turned to Miss Finney. "Where's he going?"

"Detention," Miss Finney replied sternly. "Incorrigible wee lad, that one. And who do we have here?"

"Ah, right. Miss Finney, meet Mr. Ogelvie," he said, introducing the two. "Mr. Ogelvie is here to offer his services to our distinguished school."

"Oh?"

"He's a science teacher, or was for forty years."

"Is that so, Mr. Ogelvie?"

"I figured I'd come out of retirement for a spell," replied Jimmy's neighbor. "Yu know, help the wee lads and lasses."

"That's mighty kind of yu." Miss Finney covered her mouth and acted as if she were going to cough. She looked down, and spied a dark object in the man's *other* hand, the one not holding the cane.

Knife. Miss Finney locked eyes with the old man. This would not end well.

Ring! Ring! Ring! Ring! An ear-shattering bell rang through the air, and a beat later every door in the hallway burst open, releasing students from their classrooms like floodwater behind a broken dam. It was the fire alarm.

Within seconds, Mr. Donegal, Mr. Ogelvie, and Miss Finney were caught up in a sea of churning kids—all ecstatic their lectures had been interrupted for at least the next twenty minutes while the fire department checked out the building. Leaving his distinguished guest, Mr. Donegal strode away to attend to the mass of students flooding the wing.

In that same moment Miss Finney caught a movement out of the corner of her eye.

Mr. Ogelvie jabbed at her with his concealed knife. But, thanks to Jimmy's tip, Miss Finney was waiting for just such a move. She intercepted his wrist with a fierce hand lock and twisted the weapon around so it rested beneath his chin. None of the students or teachers seemed to notice the split-second attack as they scurried toward the closest exit.

Miss Finney leaned in to Mr. Ogelvie's face and whispered, "I know who yu are. *Il berne di wy blakkir nai letta wy feitbrill?*" (What place does the darkness have with the light?) Miss Finney knew the impact the words of Ellos would have.

As if struck by a bolt of lightning, Mr. Ogelvie was seized where he stood, his body rigid and shaking with energy. It was something in those words. Unable to move his head, he forced his eyes to glare at Miss Finney.

"And now we know where he is . . ." he hissed just before his entire body disappeared in a swirling cloud of dust.

Miss Finney placed the knife beneath her belt and swung around to see if anyone had noticed. Content that the students seemed oblivious to the strange scene and completely preoccupied with the commotion of the fire alarm, Miss Finney looked farther down the hall toward her classroom. There she spied her door cracked open ever so slightly and a small face poking out from within. Meeting Jimmy's eyes, she saw a hand shoot out with a quick thumbs-up sign.

"Well done, Jimmy, me lad," she whispered, praising the boy's ingenuity and quick thinking.

She knew there was no fire. The young man was already proving to be more Elf than human, and he still had no idea of his true identity.

"Well done indeed." She grinned.

27

A Dangerous Read

JIMMY STAYED put in Miss Finney's classroom for the remainder of the school day. While all the kids were milling about outside waiting for the fire department to secure the building, he crouched in a storage closet to read by the narrow band of light coming in from the cracked open door. "'Finish the book,' she says," muttered Jimmy. "And 'touch the writing.' Whatever for?"

Jimmy grabbed the tassel bookmark and flipped open the book. He looked at the beautiful script flowing across the page. Without a second thought, he pressed his thumb onto the first letter of the page and gasped.

The Drefids waited in their underground chamber, some forty feet below the Lightning Plains in the realm of Vesper Crag. They sat barely moving in their tall chairs carved from the living rock of the walls around the chamber. The seven stolen infants, children of Elven royal blood, lay silent or cooing quietly in the very blankets they'd been nestled in for their ceremony. As oblivious to the fate that likely awaited them as they were to the fact that they would never see their parents again, the babies seemed unusually content yet fully alert.

"Why do they not cry?" asked Bilec, the gleam of his large, white pupils just visible under his hood. As he spoke, he waved his bladed hand close to the face of the swaddled child at his feet. The child's expression remained unchanged.

"They are Elven Lords," replied Mobius, "raised in the cradle of Berinfell. They have not yet learned to fear."

"That might change," Bilec said bluntly. The other five Drefids hissed in approval. Thunder rolled somewhere on the surface far above.

"It might," said Mobius. "But perhaps not at your hands? In any case, we wait upon the Spider King's word. It should not be much longer."

There was another muffled blast of thunder, this time almost directly overhead, but the Drefids barely noticed it. Electrical storms were nearly ever-present in Vesper Crag. Lightning and thunder, but never rain. The Drefids looked up, their white eyes locked onto a section of bare wall on the east side of the chamber. Blue and violet sparks appeared and rippled on the stone. Soon the surface began to undulate as if it were not made of rock at all, but some sort of stretching fabric. It bulged, first at the bottom near the floor, then in other places. Soon the recognizable shape of a clawed fist pushed out from within the stone. And at last, like a creature escaping from a vault of web, a Gwar foot soldier tore through the wall. With a few last ripples of electricity, the stone wall snapped back into place behind the Gwar.

The Drefids recognized the Gwar as Kithrend Rhot, the high messenger to the Spider King. The Gwar flexed his massive square-jawed head side to side, eliciting a muted cracking of bone within his thick neck. "Threading makes my muscles stiff," he said with a grunt. "Why can't you have a normal door like everyone else?"

"We like to know ahead of time when someone is coming," said Mobius.

"And deny them access if their arrival doesn't suit our needs," added Grehl, his Drefid speech higher and more shrill than the others.

"Besides," Mobius continued, "the Spider King rarely gives gifts. When he does, it is best to use them." The Drefids hissed.

Kithrend chuckled. He thought it a shame that most Gwar—even the grizzled warriors—had such a fear of the Drefids. They could be quite witty. Mobius in particular had a deadly dry humor.

"Speaking of gifts from the Spider King," said Kithrend, extending the rolled scroll he held in his massive fist to Mobius. "It is for that reason I have come."

The leader of the Drefids flexed his knobby fingers, and his bony blades retracted into the clefts in his knuckles. Better to read a scroll without cutting it to ribbons, after all. Mobius broke the wax seal, unfurled the scroll, and began to read. The white pupils of his eyes grew smaller as the black surrounding them grew larger. "He cannot be serious," Mobius murmured.

"You may ask him yourself," Kithrend replied. "Though he rarely jests."

"He wants us to kill them?" Bilec asked. He lowered his hood and scraped the blades of one hand along the stone armrest of his chair. He knew the answer before it came.

Mobius nodded and received a chorus of angry hissing. He ignored his comrades. "We led the assault on Berinfell, and before we left the High Elven city in ruins, we went through the trouble of capturing these—" he extended the blades on his left hand with a *schiiing* and made a sweeping gesture over the Elven children "—as prizes for the Spider King. Let him roast them on a spit and feed them to—"

"Do you then refuse?" asked the Gwar.

The Drefids were silent. Killing was their very nature. But this was different. They knew the ancient curse all too well.

"Why kill them at all?" asked Grehl. "Let them reach the Age of Reckoning here in Vesper Crag. Use their realized powers for our purposes."

"They are Elves," answered the Gwar. "And that is enough for the Spider King. Need I remind you of ages past? Of fetters and chains."

"Spare us the history." Mobius let the scroll close and tightened its roll. "All of Drefidkind lives with Elven cruelty burned into our minds." Mobius was silent for a breathless moment. His eyes narrowed and he said, "When shall we do this . . . and by what manner?"

Kithrend Rhot replied as if rehearsing lines he had labored over. "Take the rest of this day, perform such rites as you know for protection, and then . . . slice them up, feed them to the fiery crevasses upon the Lightning Fields, or dash them on stones from the cliffs behind the stronghold. Just see to it that it is done before sunset."

Mobius silenced the hissing of his comrades. "It will be done as the Spider King commands," he said.

"Ah, very good, very good," said Kithrend, extremely relieved to not have to deliver bad news to his master. He turned on his heels, stepped toward the back of the chamber, and raised one hand. The wall rippled with sparks once more. The red tribal tattoo on the back of his gray scalp was the last thing visible just before the Gwar melted into the stone wall and vanished.

"So that's it?" asked Froth, the youngest of the Drefids. He had remained silent for too long. "Kill the firstborn Elven Lords before the Age of Reckoning? Defy the curse?"

Mobius was silent for a few moments. "It is our task because even the Spider King himself would not defy the curse. Are we greater than he?"

"Then we are snared," Froth muttered. "Caught between the ancient curse of the Elves and the curse of the Spider King." Thunder rumbled above.

Mobius's voice lowered to a gritty whisper. "We cannot defy the curse. I for one do not care for never-ending agony."

"But we cannot refuse the Spider King's order, can we?" asked Froth. "His wrath cannot be far beneath the curse. He might . . . he might give us to—"

"Do not speak it!" commanded Mobius.

"Then what shall we do?" asked Bilec.

"There is another way," said Mobius. He glanced at the Elven children and then back to his comrades. "Let us thread beyond Allyra, abandon them on one of the dead worlds."

"What?" Froth objected. "Thread without the Spider King's command?"

"Yes," Mobius replied. "Let the little Elven Lords perish of exposure, just not in our world."

"Think you that such a scheme will relinquish us from the curse?" asked Bilec. "If they die there, it will still be by our hand. We will not escape."

Mobius opened and closed his fist, extending and retracting the blades. "No," he replied with a hiss, "you are right. We must absolve ourselves of their blood entirely."

"Wait!" said Bilec. "The human planet!"

"What of it?" asked Froth.

"What if we give them to humans? Their children do not look much different from the Elves."

"The ears, you dolt," said Froth. "Or don't you think the humans will notice?"

Bilec held up his hand and extended his bony blades. "I will take care of their ears."

Mobius nodded. Hisses filled the chamber. "Once the humans take possession of the Elven babes, the blood will be on their hands."

"Still," asked Froth, "what if the Elven Lords grow up and return to Allyra?"

"How?" asked Mobius. "They will grow up to think they are fully human. They, like the rest, will never dream of another world so close to their own."

"Besides," Bilec agreed, "should they reach the Age of Reckoning on Earth and somehow discover their real home, what of that? Some eight hundred years will have passed here in Allyra. Berinfell has already been conquered. The Spider King will scour Allyra until all Elves are dead. The exiled Elven Lords will have nothing of their culture, nothing of their race to return to."

�֍

Jimmy was startled out of the story by a knock on the door. He shut the book, and the scene vanished. "Jimmy?" came a muffled voice.

"Who is it?"

The door creaked open, fluorescent light nearly blinding him. "It's me, Miss Finney. Are yu all right?"

"Aye, I'm fine, Miss Finney. Thanks."

"Do yu have any idea what time it is?"

"Time?" Jimmy pushed himself off the floor and stood. "Nay, why?"

"It's nearly five o'clock. I looked for yu all over school with no luck, so I came back here. I was at a loss until I noticed the closet door cracked open."

"I stayed put like yu told me," Jimmy said, trying to sound obedient but knowing full well he was terrified to come out should Mr. Ogelvie be there; while Jimmy had seen Miss Finney alone in the hallway after he pulled the fire alarm, he assumed Mr. Ogelvie had left with the students. He had no idea what had actually happened.

She helped Jimmy out and closed the storage room door. Jimmy couldn't help but look toward the hall and wonder.

"He won't be a bother to yu anymore," said Miss Finney.

"He won't? I mean, who?" Jimmy tried to act brave.

"Mr. Ogelvie."

"Oh, yu mean me neighbor."

"He's hardly yur neighbor, Jimmy. Still, yur quick thinking allowed me to kill him."

Jimmy was incredulous. "Yu killed him?"

"I killed a Wisp, Jimmy. I'm afraid Mr. Ogelvie, the *real Mr. Ogelvie*, has been dead for quite some time. I suspect the authorities will find his body in the basement of his home. Pity that. He was probably just a kind old man looking for a quiet place to retire."

"Hold on a sec, yu killed a *what?*" Jimmy's mind raced back through the story. "A Wisp? As in the *History of Berinfell* Wisps?" He tapped a finger on the book.

"One and the same."

"But—how is that possible?" Jimmy felt himself overwhelmed.

"I think we better go for a drive, Jimmy. In fact, I'm taking yu home to gather some things."

"Gather some things?"

"Aye. We're going on a bit of a road trip."

"A road trip? To where? Why? What's going on?"

Miss Finney gestured for him to sit down and then walked over to close her classroom door. She came back and sat in a desk across from him. "We need to go to Edinburgh."

"Edinburgh? Whatever for?" If Jimmy was confused before, he was truly baffled now. "I can't go to Edinburgh, Miss Finney. I mean, what about school? And me parents?"

"Are they really yur parents?"

Jimmy sat in silence.

"Jimmy?"

"What," he said indignantly.

"I know all about yu." She smiled softly.

"Sure yu do. Everyone's read my file."

"I know yu don't feel like yu belong, like yu are second rate. I know yu don't love easily because yu've been hurt by people yu were supposed to be able to trust. I know that yur brother is dearer to yur mum than yu are."

Hot tears began to well up in Jimmy's eyes. It was like she was reading his thoughts. But how?

"I know that all yu dream about is a place yu've never been, knowin' yu were destined for greater things than Ardfern, but never sure how to get there. And I know that yu can see glimpses into the future."

"Stop!" Jimmy blurted out, rubbing the heel of his hands into his watering eyes. Neither of them talked for a moment until Jimmy could compose himself. "How do yu know all this? I mean, who—who are yu really?"

"Do yu trust me?"

Jimmy eyed her. Everyone had let him down. Everyone had promised things only to change their minds when it seemed convenient. In their best interests . . . never his. But something in his heart told him that he could trust this lady. Something that felt like she was more family than anyone else had ever been. "Why do we have to go to Edinburgh?"

"For one thing, yu cannot stay here. They know yu're here now—"

"Who's *they*?"

"Never yu mind, Jimmy. Everything will be explained to yu soon enough."

"So many secrets! How do yu expect me to trust yu?"

"Jimmy, Mr. Ogelvie is dead because a Wisp killed him and took his place. But the Wisps are just the spies . . . the scouts. Soon this place will be crawlin' with somethin' even more fierce than Wisps. And they will kill anyone who gets in their way. Includin' the Gresham family and everyone one of yur friends in school."

"Drefids?" Jimmy inquired, thinking back through the story.

"The very sort. If we get yu out of here, there's a good chance they'll leave the Gresham family and the school be. They'll come after us. No time to waste. We need to get yu out of here, Jimmy. Now."

"But where?"

"Yu have just been selected for a special trip with me to attend a concert for the Queen Mum in Edinburgh in two days' time. We leave at first light to visit Dalhousie Castle tomorrow as part of this 'field trip'."

"That's what I tell me parents?"

"Aye; and that, lad, is the truth—as much of it as we dare tell them."

"And then where? Surely yu're not taking me just to see a concert for Her Majesty?"

Miss Finney stared back at Jimmy with a strange, otherworldly glow in her eyes.

"Miss Finney?" Jimmy asked. "Where are yu taking me?"

She leaned forward, just inches from his face. "Back to Berinfell."

Taken

AARON WORTHINGTON'S thirteen birthday had turned out to be a grand disappointment. He'd asked for thirteen presents—*a reasonable request*, he thought, *one for each year of life with such a wonderful son*. But his rich dentist parents had only come through for twelve of them.

Aaron couldn't believe it. And one of the gifts—the 10-gigabyte MP3 player—had frozen without ever having played a single song.

He had thrown such a tantrum (a justifiable animated complaint, he called it) that his parents had sent him to bed early. He'd begrudgingly brushed his teeth with that awful bubblegum-flavored medicine toothpaste they made him use and marched to his bedroom. He stood in the doorway and looked back over his shoulder at his father, a broad-shouldered, balding man whose prominent brow and square chin seemed to hang over Aaron like high cliffs.

"C'mon, Dad, can't I just stay up for one more hour?" he pleaded.

"You spat on the floor and kicked your new MP3 player halfway across the room," Aaron's father explained, his deep voice deepening to a growl. "Do you have any idea how much those things cost?"

Aaron didn't know and didn't much care. "But, Dad, it's my birthday." He had barely said the words when he was airborne, lifted up by the shoulders and dropped lightly into his bed by the window. He lay there, his fingers laced behind his curly, reddish-brown hair and holding his breath. But all that seemed to do was hurt his scalp and fill his mouth with medicine-toothpaste gas. He let out the air at last and felt ridiculous.

"You know, that stopped working on us when you were six."

Aaron glared at his father, who shook his head, flicked off the room light, and headed down the hallway.

Aaron sat in angry darkness for a few heartbeats until slowly, the frustration bled away to discomfort. "DA-AD!!" he yelled. "You forgot to put the hall light on!!"

"Turn it on yourself!" came the muffled reply.

Aaron bounced on his bed and crossed his arms. But the darkness was still there. Why his parents had to buy the creepiest old house in this stupid neighborhood, he had no idea. Actually he had some idea. It was the biggest house in the neighborhood, practically a mansion. But it was creaky, full of shadowy corners and chilly drafts. And no kids his age lived nearby, well, except that dweeb Tommy Bowman two doors down. Aaron couldn't be expected to hang out with someone who didn't even have cable TV.

The floorboards shifted in the hall. The wind kicked up outside. Aaron couldn't stand it. "DA-AD!!"

Yellow light at last filled the hall outside his room. "About time," Aaron muttered as he turned sideways and faced the window-side wall. A sliver of glass was visible between the drape and the window frame, and not far beyond, the Jack-knife tree loomed in the shadows. By day he could see that it was just an odd, gnarling bulge and a broken-off limb in the crook of the tree. But at night, it looked as if a man with a knife crouched up in that tree waiting for the right moment to come for him.

And the Jack-knife tree wasn't the only scary tree. All of them, especially when the leaves had mostly fallen, looked like dark, towering beasts, demons blacker than the night sky behind them. Aaron watched the trees sway in the wind a few moments more than he should have. He flipped onto his stomach, but that did no good. Aaron imagined one of the trees' branches, twisted, black, and groping. A gnarly hand reaching for the glass. Aaron turned on his other side.

That's when he noticed the closet door was still open.

"DA-AD!" he yelled again.

"WHAT?" his father yelled from far below.

"You left my closet door open! Could you please come close it?" He hadn't really meant to say *please*. It just slipped out somehow.

"Are you KIDDING me?" his father bellowed. Aaron could almost see the veins sticking out on his father's reddening face. "One more word and you'll be in bed early for the whole week!!"

Aaron kicked his feet and let out a whine anyway. It didn't improve his situation in the least. The bifold doors of the closet yawned open just a few yards away from the side of his bed. The hanging clothes dangled in the darkness like spirits jostling to escape. The shelving unit looked like waiting vaults of a crypt, and the jars of coins on the top shelf seemed now to hold slithery specimens, wriggling actively in their clear prisons.

CLICK.

Aaron flipped on his bedroom light. Just clothes. Just shelves. Just jars of coins. He darted over to his closet, banged his pinkie toe on the bottom of the bedpost, and somehow managed to slam the closet doors shut. He fell backward into his bed and howled.

"AARON ROTHCHILD WORTHINGTON!!!"

"I just shut the closet door, like you said, Dad!" Aaron clinched hot tears in the corner of his eyes and clutched his foot.

"That's IT! I told you what would happen. You're going to bed early for the rest of the week!"

"No, c'mon, Dad!"

"And do me a favor, would you, Son?"

"What?"

"Grow up a little."

Aaron threw a pillow out of his room.

"And get your light out!"

"How did he know—oh, never mind." Aaron hobbled out of bed. Just before clicking off the light, he noticed a little black spider on the floor between the bottom of the door and his dresser. That was okay. Spiders didn't scare Aaron. He grabbed a sock off his desk and tossed it at the arachnid.

CLICK. The light went out.

He turned back toward his bed and began to wonder if anything could be under it. Before his imagination could conjure up anything, Aaron leaped back under the covers and lay still.

His heart pounded as he lay there in the new silence. He pulled another blanket up to his ears. It was a hot evening for October in Maryland. Aaron didn't care. The blankets were protection, a hiding place. Aaron snuggled in farther and nestled his head in the down pillows. Then he froze.

There'd been a creaking sound. It wasn't the floorboards of the hallway this time. It wasn't a shifting of his bed. It wasn't the heat clicking on. Those creaks were bad enough, but Aaron knew all those sounds. This creak had come from outside. Aaron waited. There it was again, a high undulating sound like someone opening an old door or tearing a dead limb off a tree.

A TREE?

Aaron's mind took off like a bottle rocket, exploding in dark tree images. If he heard it again, Aaron would yell for his dad. He waited. Nothing but the *chirrup* of crickets.

Aaron exhaled.

This was just silly.

Here he was thirteen years old and afraid of night sounds? He laughed quietly to himself . . . and swallowed. He even glanced over his shoulder at the window. Now that his eyes had adjusted to the lack of light, it didn't look so dark.

Aaron shrugged and laughed again. *I bet I could even look out that window*, he thought. *It's just the outside, same as daylight.* Aaron sat up and let the covers fall from his chin. He looked at the still curtains and the vague printed images of baseballs, footballs, and basketballs. Aaron wiped a bead of sweat off his forehead and hunched onto his knees. He'd just take a quick look to prove to himself . . . and to make sure.

He reached both hands toward the curtains and grasped a fold on either side. Then, squinching his eyes shut, he parted the curtains. Aaron opened his eyes and saw the glass of the window, but the reflection of the hall's light kept him from seeing anything outside.

He moved closer and squinted into the darkness . . . it was really dark, as if someone had draped a tarp over the back of the house.

There was something there.

Aaron started to scream and back away. Huge gnarled limbs broke through the glass, and great knobby hands caught Aaron just before he would have fallen off his bed.

Aaron screamed a high, shrill wail as the tree branch curled hard around his waist.

"Si-lence!" came a deep, raspy grunt. Aaron screamed all the more and struggled against the pain.

"Listen to him whine!" came another voice. This one had an eerie whistling quality to it. Aaron turned his head and saw the shadowy form of a man. He had white hair that seemed to glow in the moonless night, and his hands . . . it looked like he had knives for fingers. Aaron screeched and flailed his arms.

"I told you this isn't the one!" the shadowy man hissed.

"But . . . he is the age . . . and has the curly hair."

Aaron felt his head clutched as if it were in a vise and saw finger-knives on either side. "No, there are no scars on his ears."

"Ugly . . . human . . . thing."

"Throw the brat back."

Aaron felt weightless for a moment, bounced off his bed, and crashed hard on the floor.

Aaron's father, red-faced and wide-eyed, came to Aaron's room a few seconds too late. He found Aaron's bed empty except for rumpled covers and broken, black twigs. Aaron lay weeping on the floor, trying in vain to squeeze under the bed.

"The Jack-knife tree . . ." Aaron sobbed. And that was all anyone could get from Aaron for a long time.

Rumor of Evil

TOMMY HAD heard the sirens late at night, eerie-wailing screams starting far away and then coming dreadfully close by. More than once, flashes of red or blue light pierced Tommy's curtains and danced on the walls of his room. He rolled out of bed and met his dad coming the other direction up the hallway.

"Dad, what's with all the sirens?"

"Not sure, Son," Mr. Bowman replied. "I've seen several police cars cruise by . . . some of them had spotlights."

"Looking for somebody? Have you checked the news?"

Mr. Bowman nodded. "Nothing on the news. But don't worry, Tommy." He rumpled his son's curly, brown hair. "I've double-checked all the locks and the security system. We're safe."

Tommy had no doubt that his house was secure. His parents had forgone their summer vacation to afford an upgrade on their home's security system. It was state-of-the-art, very high tech, and if Lockdown Global Security was to be believed, it protected Tommy's family from everything short of a nuclear bomb. Tommy went back to bed, but he wondered what had happened. When his father went back down the stairs, Tommy stole out of his room, tiptoed into his parents' room, went to their bedroom window that looked out from the side of their home, and peeked outside. He saw flashing lights aplenty, but it was hard to tell whose house. It wasn't the Palmers' or the Ledbetters'. Tommy's block curled to the right, and he couldn't really see past the wall of tall pines that separated the Worthington Estate from the rest of the neighborhood. It looked like the back end of an ambulance at the edge of the trees.

Tommy had never been friends with Aaron Worthington, not exactly. But a chill came over Tommy, and he became very afraid for his neighbors. Police cars and ambulances were always bad news. Before Tommy turned away from the window, he found himself watching the pines and the larger broadleaf trees of the Worthington Estate. In the eerie flashing lights, the trees almost looked as if they were walking.

✴

Tommy's mother dropped him at school just as the warning bell rang. He waved goodbye over his shoulder and joined the jostling crowd entering the building. But many in the flood of students turned and surrounded Tommy.

"What happened?" Andi Batten asked.

"Did someone get shot?" asked Brady Smith.

"I heard Aaron's in the hospital," said Lindsay Leggett.

"I don't know!" Tommy struggled to be heard. "All I saw were police cars and an ambulance!"

"I told you he got shot," said Seth Davis.

"Did not," argued Andi.

"My dad told me Aaron got *kilt*," said Sean Wood with a somewhat troubling grin.

"They don't take dead people in an ambulance, you goof," said Danny Harvey.

A shadow fell on them. Mr. Borman, the assistant principal, all six foot eight inches of him, stood directly behind Tommy. "What's all this talk of shooting and dying? Don't we get enough violence and bloodshed on the evening news?"

233

"I don't," said Sean.

With a stern look at Sean, Mr. Borman ushered the kids into the school. Tommy did his best to avoid everyone as he headed to home-room, but it was nearly impossible. It seemed everyone thought they'd heard something about Aaron, but no one knew for sure. After franti-cally grabbing books and such from his locker, Tommy hurried to his homeroom.

"Tommy?" called Ms. Willging. "Here's your pass."

"My pass—?" Surprised, Tommy looked at his homeroom teacher questioningly.

"You've got GT testing in the library's media center," she said, without looking up from her seating chart. She held out the blue pass. "Here ya go."

※

The media center was humming as usual during homeroom. Seventh and eighth graders hustled back and forth from the TV studio, get-ting ready to broadcast the school's morning announcement program: Falcon News Live. A steady stream of children lined up at the circula-tion desk. Mrs. Goetz was doing her best to check books out and in, collect fines, and give suggestions. But Mrs. Galdarro was nowhere to be seen.

Tommy heard the jingle of keys, and Mr. Charlie walked out of the media office. He glanced once at Tommy and started whistling. The tune was cheery, as usual, but Mr. Charlie's expression seemed pained. He interrupted his tune to tell Tommy, "She's in there." He pointed to the media office.

Tommy went inside and found Mrs. Galdarro at her desk. She did not immediately look up but was intent on her writing. She used a quill pen the color of blue flame and dipped it into a squat jar of ink.

Tommy thought he saw tiny wisps of smoke rise each time she put the pen tip to the paper.

"Cool pen," said Tommy.

Mrs. Galdarro looked up and smiled briefly. "Uh . . . yes, it was a gift." She put the pen back in the bottle of ink and then hurriedly rolled up the piece of paper. With a practiced flip of the wrist, she tied it up with a fancy red and purple ribbon. Then she said, "Tommy, I am very glad you've come. If you had been absent today, I don't know what I would have done."

Tommy held up the pass and looked at her quizzically. "Um, so when do I start the test?"

Mrs. Galdarro laughed. "You've already passed the test, Tommy. You are most definitely gifted and talented, the likes of which this school might never grasp."

Tommy smiled. *GT, who'd have thought?* He looked down at the pass and asked, "If I'm already in . . . then . . . why did you send this pass?"

"Are you quite sure you don't know?"

"You mean the book?"

"Yes, Tommy, the book." She studied him a moment. "You have read it, haven't you?"

Tommy rocked on his heels. "I read a lot of it."

"Uh, excuse me, Mrs. Galdarro?" A tall eighth grader peeked around the door frame behind Tommy.

"Yes, Max, what can I do for you?"

"I did a poster for my book report on *The Vanishing Sculptor*. May I hang it up in the media center?"

"Absolutely, Max. Just ask Mrs. Goetz for some tape."

"Cool." And Max was gone.

Mrs. Galdarro turned back to Tommy. "You did start at the beginning of the book, didn't you?"

"Not exactly—"

"Where then?"

"'Red Dusk.'"

"Well, that was foolish. Gave you quite a scare, did it?"

Tommy nodded repeatedly. "Mrs. Galdarro, how can . . . how can a book do that?"

"Did you ask your parents?"

"Yes, but when I told them the book came to life, they thought I was using a figure of speech. They look right at the book, and they don't see it like I do."

"Well, of course not, Tommy," said Mrs. Galdarro. She sighed. "They aren't Elves."

Tommy's eyebrows knotted over the bridge of his nose. "What?"

30

Identity Crisis

MRS. GALDARRO reached into her desk drawer and pulled out a large, suede-covered book. Then she stood and closed the door to her office. "There," she said, "we ought to have a bit of peace in here."

She held the book up for Tommy to see. "*The Chronicles of the Elf Lords and Their Kin . . .*" she began. "This is my copy, one of ten in existence. It is a history book of sorts . . . my history . . . and yours."

"You said something like that before," said Tommy. "What do you mean?"

Mrs. Galdarro took a deep breath. "Tommy, the reason you can read this book as it was intended, the reason the memories recorded here come to life when you touch them, the reason its contents are your history, is that you are not human . . . you are not of this world."

Tommy scratched his ear beneath a few curly locks. He blinked and asked, "What am I then?"

"Did you not hear me a moment ago?" She smiled. "You are an Elf."

"An Elf, for real?"

She nodded.

"Cool." Tommy grinned.

"You're taking this better than I thought," said Mrs. Galdarro.

Tommy bobbed his head left and right as if searching the room. "Look, Mrs. Galdarro, I don't know how you got my parents in on this, and I have no idea how you got the book to do all the special effects, but it's all very cool. I'm glad you picked me. So what is this, anyway, some reality–TV show? Where are the cameras?"

Mrs. Galdarro's smile vanished.

She seemed suddenly taller, and the fluorescent lights flickered overheard. Then she opened the book. "Tommy, you are the highborn son of Velaril Silvertree, one of the Seven Elven Lords of Berinfell."

She placed the tip of her finger on the page. The black servers and white cinder-block walls faded. In their place rose pillars of smooth stone, great burgundy banners, and seven marble seats. In them sat four men and three women. Behind the throne of each man stood a woman. Behind the throne of each woman stood a man.

No, Tommy realized, they were not human men and women, but merely male and female. Their skin, light and dark, was without crease or wrinkle, as flawless as cream. And their ears tapered to an angled point. Tommy felt a warm breeze flow over his shoulder. He saw Mrs. Galdarro's finger still touching the page of the book, but also hovering like a ghostly projection over the Elf in the center throne. "This is Velaril Silvertree," said Mrs. Galdarro, and her voice was rich and amplified with the resonance of a great hall. "Behind him is his wife, Tarin Silvertree. They are your parents, Tommy. Your *real* parents."

Tommy stared at the Elf Lord. Velaril's ears were partially hidden by long chains of curly hair. Curly hair just like Tommy's. "I don't believe this," Tommy said. "Close the book."

"I will not," said Mrs. Galdarro.

"Close the book!" Tommy commanded. He stepped forward. "I don't know how you knew I was adopted, but putting me through this . . . I mean, this isn't funny."

"No, Tommy, it is not funny at all."

Mrs. Galdarro turned a few pages. The room around them, the thrones, the lords and their spouses all looked the same as before, except that each lord held a small, bundled child. Mrs. Galdarro pointed to Velaril's child. "That is you, Tommy. You know, they let me hold you once. It was just a few days before this ceremony."

Tommy shook his head slowly but continued to watch and listen.

"I was there that night," she continued, "when the Spider King's forces attacked."

Tommy watched with horror as the tall, stained glass window to the left of the thrones shattered. He held up his arms to cover his face from the falling glass; it all seemed so real. A huge spider shape crawled through the opening. Armored warriors leaped down from the creature as even more spiders entered the hall.

Fire leaped forth from one of the thrones. A female Elf Lord stood with her hand outstretched, and a stream of white flame blazed into the oncoming enemy. Soon the vast and beautiful hall became a chaotic den of war. Barrel-chested Gwar soldiers and their monstrous Warspiders collided with the Elves. It was brute force versus skill, but the Elves were outnumbered.

"They fought valiantly, Tommy, on your—and the other children's—behalf," said Mrs. Galdarro. "But at last, they were overcome. And you . . . all of the children . . . were taken."

Tommy watched the children loaded like sacks of grain into satchels on the sides of the huge spiders.

Mrs. Galdarro turned the page, and the quiet of the room returned. Tommy's face was a wreck of emotion.

"I . . . I can't be an Elf. I mean . . . I just can't be. I don't even have—"

"Haven't you ever wondered about those scars on top of your ears?"

Tommy reached up and felt the rugged tissue on the top of each ear. He blinked and looked up at Mrs. Galdarro.

"Your captors, the Drefids, disfigured your beautiful ears," she said. "They should look like mine." She picked at a flesh-colored seam on each ear and peeled away the normal-looking section to reveal ears as pointed as the Elves in the throne room picture. "We've learned to use prosthetics," she said.

"We?"

"There are many of us—Sentinel Elves sent to look for you. We've become librarians, teachers, shopkeepers in this world—any profession where we can discreetly search for all the young lords. We've been searching here for a long time, hoping to find you before the Spider King's forces do."

"I don't know if I get any of this," Tommy said, rubbing his temples, "but didn't the . . . the Spider King . . . didn't he already have us?"

"Yes, but capturing you was never part of his plan." She paused. "The Spider King wanted you dead . . . all of you. The Seven Elf Lords are the most powerful warriors in Berinfell. They are also a link to untold years of tradition, a living testimony to the power of Ellos.

"Think of it, Tommy. The Spider King had you all in one place at the same time. He could break the spine of all the Elves in one vicious attack. That was his plan, but it went wrong.

"The bloodline of the Elven Lords—your bloodline—has been kept pure and unbroken for tens of thousands of years. Your royal bloodline is protected by the oldest and most feared curse in Allyrian history. The Spider King knew if he himself killed you—or any one of the seven child lords—before you reached the Age of Reckoning, he would have been doomed to disaster and misery for three generations.

"The Spider King is aggressive and calculating. He's driven by an unquenchable thirst for vengeance, but even he is not so foolish as to challenge the Curse of the Firstborn."

"Vengeance?" Tommy frowned. "What's he got against Elves? Aren't they good?"

"Good? Yes . . . but not perfect," Mrs. Galdarro replied, her expression distant and somehow very weary. "Our history, like the human history you've been learning during your lifetime here, is dotted with events we regret."

"Wait"—Tommy tilted his head and scratched in the whirls of hair near his ear—"there was something in the table of contents . . . a gap in the years. I wondered about that."

"You are very clever, Tommy," she replied. "There are few Elves in all of Allyra who know the full tale of those missing ages, and I dare not tell you what I know . . . not yet. Suffice it to say that the Spider King and the Gwar have reason to resent Elves, but not a license to make war against us or extinguish our race."

She allowed this to sink in and then said, "In his quest for our destruction, the Spider King wanted you dead, but he would not do it himself and risk the curse. Instead, he turned to the Drefids, his dark assassins, to do the dirty work for him."

Mrs. Galdarro opened the book to a new section. Up from the pages surged a very different scene: a catacomb lit in wavering angry oranges and reds. In this desolate place seven hooded figures stood, and the seven infant lords lay at their feet.

"I remember this," said Tommy. "I read about this. The Drefids knew of the curse, too, right?"

"They knew . . . and they found themselves in a merciless place: suffer the consequences of the Curse of the Firstborn or the Curse of the Spider King. In the end, the Drefids found an escape. The Drefids deceived the Spider King, telling him they had slain the infants, when actually they had abandoned them here in this world. You and the other six Elven Lords would grow up here, never knowing your true lineage. Their plan might have succeeded, but by the grace of Ellos, one of the Drefid commanders changed."

"Changed?"

"One day, Sarron Froth was a brutal and bloodthirsty assassin;

the next, he was changed. He simply could not continue as he was. We found him half-starved and near death in the ruins of Berinfell. If not for Froth, we would not have found you." Mrs. Galdarro closed the book once more, and her office reappeared.

Fingering the top of his left ear, Tommy whispered, "I'm an Elf."

"And not just any Elf," said Mrs. Galdarro. "You are an Elven Lord, endowed with spectacular power. Wait until you try your hand at the bows we make in Allyra."

"I'm going to Allyra?" Tommy took a step sideways and leaned on a metal rack full of DVD players and electronics.

"You must take your part in the rebellion against the Spider King. For eight hundred years the Elves in exile have hoped you and the others were alive. Searching for you has kept them going . . . has kept *me* going."

Tommy flinched and jerked his elbow off the metal shelf. "Spider!" he said, flapping his arm like a chicken's wing. A black thing fell to the floor and began to skitter away. "It was on my arm. *Bab*, I hate spiders."

"Move!" Mrs. Galdarro commanded. As soon as Tommy was clear, she pulled something out of her pocket and expertly threw it at the spider. It struck the floor a few inches from the spider, exploded like a dirt clog, and showered the spider in white powder. Instantly, the spider trembled and dissolved. There was nothing left on the floor but a brown smudge.

"Whoa," said Tommy. Then he made a face. "*Phew!* What's that smell?"

Mrs. Galdarro grimaced. "Nothing smells worse to Elves than burnt spiders."

"You, you vaporized it!"

"I had to. Spiders are his spies, the Spider King's eyes in this world. He and his Drefids can communicate with them."

Tommy looked again at the brown smudge on the floor. He

thought about spiders . . . and the Spider King. Then his eyes widened. "Then he knows, doesn't he? The Spider King knows we're here!"

Mrs. Galdarro put her slender hand on Tommy's shoulder. "Yes, Tommy. He has sent an army of Drefids and worse things into this world to find you."

"But the curse . . . they won't kill us because of the curse, right?"

She shook her head slowly. "The curse protects you only until your thirteenth year, the Age of Reckoning."

"But I don't turn thirteen for another month. I'm safe."

"Your earthly date of birth is not accurate. Your archery exhibition on Falcon Day revealed to me and to the Drefid in the crowd that your lordly gifts have begun to develop. There can be no doubt: you have reached the Age of Reckoning. That means there is nothing to stop the Spider King or his Drefid assassins from killing you."

"Here at school? They won't . . . they won't try—"

"No, I do not think they will attack you here. Too public. And Charlie is here."

"Mr. Charlie?"

Mrs. Galdarro nodded and replied, "Charlie is far more than a custodian. No, the Drefids will come at night . . . to your home. They have already tried once."

"What? When?"

"Last night, they took Aaron Worthington . . . they thought he was you, Tommy. Thankfully, they realized their error and spit him back out."

"Spit him out?" Tommy found himself breathing hard. "They eat people?"

"Not the Drefids. But as I said, the Drefids did not come alone. They have brought with them the black trees of Vesper Crag. Perilous and alive, the Cragon trees tore into the side of Aaron's house. Tommy, they now know exactly where you live. You cannot stay another night in your home. If not for your sake, for the sake of your parents."

"What do I do?"

Mrs. Galdarro strode to her desk and picked up the scroll she had sealed earlier. She handed it to Tommy and said, "Put this in your backpack. Do NOT open it. I will call your parents in an hour and let them know that I will be picking you up for another meeting at 4:30. I want you to pack a change of clothing—only 100 percent cotton, do you understand? Put the scroll on the pillow just before you leave."

Tommy nodded repeatedly. He had only one question. "Mrs. Galdarro . . . will I ever see my parents again?"

The librarian clutched her book to her chest. "I hope so, Tommy . . . but I can make no guarantees."

31

Gravity

AFTER SCHOOL, Tommy placed the scroll on his bed and zipped up his backpack. He put on a 100–percent cotton pair of jeans and 100–percent cotton long-sleeved T-shirt. He hadn't bothered to ask Mrs. Galdarro why the cotton. *Maybe Elves are allergic to polyester?* Tommy didn't know. And he had far more important things on his mind.

He felt heavy, like God had turned up the gravity. Year after year of memories poured out from every corner of his room. The mural he and his mother had spent the summer painting when he was ten, trophies from soccer and karate standing like a little golden army on his dresser, and of course Smores, his pet guinea pig—they weighed on Tommy's heart. A fur ball of tan, black, and white, Smores stood up on his hind legs and leaned on the rim of the aquarium. He gave Tommy his "red alert, I'm hungry" squeal.

Tommy lifted off the cover and poured a cup of multicolored pellets into Smores's feeding dish. The guinea pig emitted a happy trill as Tommy combed the hair on its lower back with his fingers.

Two sharp beeps outside.

Mrs. Galdarro.

"Bye, Smores," Tommy whispered. He hoisted his backpack and left his room.

His mother stood in the kitchen with her hands on her hips. "I don't think this microwave is working right," she said as Tommy entered the kitchen. "Tommy, you didn't put any metal in there, did you?"

Tommy didn't answer. He grabbed his mom around the waist and hugged her. He hugged her the way he did when he was seven. He smelled the cotton in her shirt, smelled her lilac perfume, and felt the warmth of her shoulder on his chin.

"Oh . . . oh," Mrs. Bowman replied, and at first she didn't seem to know quite what to do with her arms. But then she wrapped them around him and forgot all about the microwave.

When they separated, she asked, "What was that for?"

"I just love you," Tommy said. "That's all." He turned around so she wouldn't see him tearing up. "Where's Dad?"

"In the basement, playing bridge on the computer, I imagine." As Tommy went to the basement door, she said, "That backpack looks a little full for just a meeting."

Tommy froze in mid step. He wouldn't lie to her. If she opened the backpack, found all the food, the photo album, the clothes. . . .

Honk! Honk! Mrs. Galdarro saved the day.

"I've gotta go, Mom, but I want to say goodbye to Dad," Tommy said.

He ran down the stairs and found his father in front of the wide monitor, the blue light reflecting strangely off his father's glasses. "Hey, Dad . . . uh, I've got to go, so I just wanted to—"

"Just a second, Son," he replied, clicking the mouse. "I have a six-no-trump bid going here. Can you wait till I'm the dummy?"

"Mrs. Galdarro's waiting outside," Tommy replied. Not knowing what else to do, Tommy threw his arms around his father's neck and hugged him, too.

"Careful, Son, you knocked my glasses off."

"Sorry," Tommy said as he released his dad. "I'm in kind of a hurry."

"Oh, okay," his father replied as he slid his glasses back onto his nose. "Haven't had such a hug in a while. Thank you, Son."

"Uh, yeah, sure, Dad," Tommy replied. He turned back to the stairs. *Say it. Go on, Tommy. Say it. Why is this so hard?* At last, Tommy pushed out the words, "Love you, Dad."

Tommy was halfway up the basement stairs when he heard his father's words, tentative but warm, "I love you, Son. Be safe."

✳

"That was hard," Tommy said after they'd been driving for a while.

"I am sorry, Tommy. But it's for the best. With you in that house, none of you would be safe."

"But what if the . . . the Drefids and those trees attack anyway? They don't know you've taken me."

"Yes, they do. You may not have noticed several new trees in the woods across the street from your home. They were watching, Tommy. I made sure they saw me clearly before you came out. Even now, I suspect the trees are getting word to the Drefids that we are gone. That is well for your parents, though likely more unpleasant for us."

Scenery went by the windows in a blur. Tommy caught glimpses of familiar places: streets where friends lived, community pools where he liked to swim, favorite restaurants and the like. It was strange not to know if he'd ever see any of these places again. Even stranger to know that Seabrook, Maryland, was not his real home. But in spite of such uncertainty, Tommy felt something deep inside, a kind of peace with all that was happening. He trusted Mrs. Galdarro. And bubbling away in some distant corner of his mind was a thrilling sense of anticipation, similar to thinking of an upcoming vacation . . . only better.

Mrs. Galdarro brought her silver SUV to a stop in front of the school. The back hatch opened, and Mr. Charlie threw a large black satchel inside. It reminded Tommy of the bag Mr. Phitzsinger used for all the lacrosse sticks.

Tommy went to get out of the front seat so that Mr. Charlie could sit down. "No, sir," said Mr. Charlie, holding the door from opening farther. "You are the guest of honor. Now, just sit yourself on down." Mr. Charlie jumped into the backseat and shut the door. Reluctantly, Tommy closed his door.

"Yes, sir," Mr. Charlie continued. "I'ze been waitin' fer this day, a long, long time."

"You know, Merrick," said Mrs. Galdarro as she drove away, "you don't need to use that dialect any longer. We're all Elves here."

"Awww, shucks, Elle," Mr. Charlie replied, and then his voice changed. "Certainly I do not need to maintain colloquial speech for camouflage, but really, it's such a beautiful dialect . . . full of hospitality, comfort, and grace. I'ze might jest keep usin' it fer a while. Fact is, I've grown right attached to the name Charlie, too, if you don't mind."

"If it pleases you," said Mrs. Galdarro with a curious smile.

Tommy looked into the backseat at the man he'd always thought was the school's custodian. Since Mr. Charlie wasn't wearing his glasses, Tommy could see the depth of his eye color. "You know," said Tommy, "you don't see too many people with purple eyes."

"True 'nuff," he replied. He laughed deeply and winked at Tommy. "Not 'round here, that is." Then he began to whistle.

Tommy looked over Mr. Charlie's shoulder at the big duffel in the back. Then he turned to Mrs. Galdarro. "What's in the bag Mr. Charlie brought?"

"Tools," she replied.

"What kind of tools?"

"The just-in-case kind."

32

In the Shadow of Madness

SINCE THEY'D left the main highway, Tommy had gotten lost in the twists and turns. But finally, Mrs. Galdarro turned down a leaf-covered road and parked the SUV in the gravel on the side. A steep hill rose up to the left of the road, and a wall of tall trees towered above them. More dead leaves spiraled down from the heights and joined the others. They all got out of the SUV.

Shivering as chill air found its way under his jacket, Tommy said, "*Brr*, where are we?"

"Saint Elizabeth's Hospital for the Criminally Insane," Mrs. Galdarro replied. She'd said it as casually as if she were talking about a local grocery store.

A fleeting terror blew through Tommy. *How could I have been so foolish as to go with these strangers?* "What? Criminally insane?"

"Don't worry, Tommy. The hospital's been abandoned for more than twenty years. Besides," she said, gesturing, "Mr. Charlie brought his tools."

Mr. Charlie slammed shut the hatch and slung the big, black duffel over his shoulder. He unzipped the bag a little to show Tommy the contents. Tommy's eyebrows shot up. "Whoa!"

Mr. Charlie zippered the bag. "Just the thing in case old Mobius and his crew come to call." Laughing deeply, Mr. Charlie took to the hill. Even with the heavy duffel, up he went, one powerful bound after another, until he stood at the top. "C'mon, y'all."

Tommy felt it was weird to be hearing Mobius's name used . . . the same character from an ancient book . . . alive, and hunting *him*.

Mrs. Galdarro patted Tommy on the shoulder. "Merrick—er, Charlie is one of the Lyrian Elves," she said as she and Tommy climbed the hill. "Very strong. That and his Dreadnaught training have made him a formidable warrior . . . as you can no doubt imagine from his display of strength."

"Dreadnaught?"

"Among the races of Elves, few are selected for Dreadnaught training. Strongest of body and of mind, the Dreadnaughts learn a terribly difficult and profoundly effective form of combat called *Vexbane*. And, as their name implies, they fear nothing."

When all had reached the top, they traveled in silence between the hulking trunks of the tall oaks and elms and forced their way through a barricade of fat pines. They emerged to find the hilly campus and deserted buildings of Saint Elizabeth's Hospital.

A massive building of faded red and gray bricks was flanked on either side by smaller, colonial-looking brick buildings attached to the main by stone ports and fenced-in widow's walks. Few windows were left unbroken, and debris lay all around the perimeter as if an explosion had blown out the innards of the building but left its stone skeleton intact. And it seemed as if the landscape were intent on reclaiming the man-made structure, for leafless climbing vines practically engulfed the lower half of each eerie building.

"We have to go in there?" Tommy asked.

"I'm afraid so," said Mrs. Galdarro. "The portal is there."

Did she have to use the word afraid? "I've never seen a place so . . . haunted-looking," said Tommy. "Couldn't you have put the portal in a playground or something?"

"We had no control over the placement of these portals," she replied, "What little we know about the portals we learned from Sarron

Froth. The Spider King uses them to take slaves from Earth. It was the Spider King who put them in out-of-the-way places such as this."

"Slaves?"

"Another time, Tommy. There is too much to explain now."

Waves of wind swept through the knee-high grass as Mr. Charlie led the way across the deserted campus. They entered through a side door at one of the roofed ports of the main building. Once past a set of double doors hanging loosely from their frame, they stood at the end of a long hallway. Floor tiles that had once fit snugly into tight rows were cracked or shattered and scattered about the hall. Paint peeled on every wall. Water damage and rot had eaten jagged holes the length of the ceiling, and plaster dangled down like patches of old skin.

"Mr. Charlie," whispered Tommy, "could you take out the tools now?"

Shadow and pale light alternated up the entire hall. Doors from hospital rooms—some open, some closed—made Tommy wince as he walked by. Every creep, demon, zombie, and monster from every horror movie Tommy had ever seen waltzed into his imagination. At any moment, something would surely leap out from behind one of those doors.

Tommy positioned himself between Mrs. Galdarro and Mr. Charlie. They passed broken-out windows where the vines they'd seen outside had already penetrated and snaked into the hall.

Their footsteps did not echo, but there was so much debris on the floor that each new footfall cracked or crushed something. They certainly weren't going to sneak up on anything. Through another set of doors and they came to an inky, black stairwell. "A little light, Charlie?"

"Yes, ma'am," he said.

In a moment, he had a brilliant flashlight in his hand. He gave another to Mrs. Galdarro and one to Tommy. Obscene graffiti lined the stairwell. Tommy averted his eyes and stuck close to Mr. Charlie. At the bottom of the stairs, the double doors opened into a wide ward. A dozen small bed frames were tossed all about the floor as if a major earthquake had once hit the hospital.

"How much farther?" Tommy whispered.

"Not far," Mrs. Galdarro replied. "After this chamber, we've a short hall past several mostly empty rooms. The portal is in the strangest room in this building."

Tommy couldn't imagine anything stranger or creepier than what he'd already seen of the abandoned hospital. "What do you mean, *strange?*" he asked.

"Bunch of drawers," said Mr. Charlie.

"A little hard to explain," said Mrs. Galdarro.

They said no more as they passed out of the ward with the beds. Something wet dripped onto Tommy's arm. He shuddered and shined the light; a drop of discolored water trailed across his forearm. Tommy wiped it on his pants leg and shined his flashlight up at the ceiling. Gray and black stains blossomed sickly in the midst of the rotting ceiling tiles. *Disgusting,* Tommy thought as he walked along, continuing to stare at the blotches on the ceiling.

"TOMMY, WATCH OUT!!" Mr. Charlie grabbed Tommy by the arm just below the shoulder and kept him from taking another step.

Tommy's heart pounded so hard he thought his ears would pop. Mr. Charlie shined his light down at Tommy's feet. Part of the floor had torn away, revealing a gaping mouth into darkness. Tommy saw the water far down below, foul and green in the flashlight beam.

"I'm sorry about that, Tommy," said Mrs. Galdarro. "This hole wasn't nearly as large the last time I came this way."

Tommy blinked in the dim light. His breathing and heart rate made it all too clear what would have happened, if he'd taken just one more step.

The rest of the hall went without incident. They turned a corner, went through a wide door, and entered a square room. "This is the room," said Mr. Charlie. "See all the drawers?"

Tommy turned his beam on the walls of the chamber. There were square openings in vertical sets of three on either side of the chamber. Each opening had a thick door hanging open and inside a long tray, almost like a deep pan. There was soot or ash all over the drawers and the floor. Tommy suddenly realized what this room had been.

No Exit

"WHERE'S THE portal?" Tommy asked, staring at the abandoned hospital's crematory. He was convinced there were spiders—or worse things—all over him, and his skin crawled. Tommy wanted out of there, and fast.

"It is on the far wall," Mrs. Galdarro replied. They walked across the chamber to the wall. "Charlie, put the light on the wall for me."

"Yes, ma'am."

Mrs. Galdarro said, "Tommy, as you pass into the portal, you will feel very strange sensations on your skin—like running through millions of feathers. But there is also a steady current, like your electricity . . . not strong enough to shock or harm you, but enough to feel its presence. I will go first." She took a step forward and stopped. "Wait, this isn't . . ." She reached up and touched the stone of the wall.

"Elle, look," said Mr. Charlie, shining his light onto the floor. There were footprints in the dust and ash.

Mrs. Galdarro pounded a fist on the wall. "They've closed the gate!" she growled.

"Who?" Tommy asked.

"Drefids," said Mr. Charlie. "They are the ones who really know how to work these things. Got here before us."

"Why?" asked Tommy.

"To keep you from escaping," she replied. "I must contact the other Sentinels."

"Cool," said Tommy. "You have some kind of magic mirror, crystal ball, or like a pet owl or something?"

"Yes, I have just the thing." Mrs. Galdarro frowned and reached into her pocket. "It's called a *cell phone*." She flipped open her phone. "Oh dear, I'm not getting a signal."

"Maybe you should get ya'self a pet owl," said Mr. Charlie, and he smiled at Tommy.

"I didn't ask your opinion," Mrs. Galdarro huffed. "We need to get back to the surface."

They fled the strange room with all the drawers. Their flashlight beams danced all over the hall as they hurried ahead. Not taking a chance of falling into that ghastly hole, Tommy made sure to stay to the far right. They increased their pace and raced through the ward with all the tumbled bed frames. At a dead run, they hit the stairs and bounded up.

Night had settled over the hospital grounds while they were below the surface. Cloud-veiled moonlight through broken windows cast pale, intermittent light into the long hallway.

Mrs. Galdarro checked her cell phone as they walked. "Come on," she urged the phone. And then she stopped. "It says my mailbox is full."

"That can't be good," said Mr. Charlie.

"Shhh!" said Tommy. "What was that?"

There was a creaking sound above them. "Uh, Charlie," said Mrs. Galdarro. "I think it would be a good time to get out the tools."

"The just-in-case ones?" asked Tommy, looking to Mr. Charlie.

"Yes, indeed," Charlie replied, letting the black duffel slide off his arm to the ground. He reached inside and pulled out several items. "Miss Elle, here's your sword." He gave her a thin-bladed weapon that reminded Tommy of a samurai sword. "Tommy, I hope this short bow works for you." He handed Tommy a black compound bow and a quiver of long silver arrows.

"What am I shooting at?" Tommy asked, a tremor in his voice. The creaking above them turned to a rapid scratching and a horrendous rip. Pieces of wood and crumbling drywall fell from the ceiling.

"Run!" Mrs. Galdarro yelled. Tommy sprinted away, Mrs. Galdarro just behind. Even as he ran, Mr. Charlie dug into the bag. He seemed to be having trouble getting something out.

Tommy looked back over his shoulder and saw the former custodian pull a long shield out of the duffel bag. But then something tore through the ceiling behind them. A dark figure dropped to the ground twenty yards back. Tommy stifled a scream. He'd seen a shadowy figure with fiery points for eyes. Tommy turned to look where he was running, stumbled, but by lunging forward he kept from falling.

"Drefids!" Mrs. Galdarro yelled. "Charlie!"

"I see them!" he growled back. His dialect was gone and his voice had deepened. "They won't touch a curly hair on Tommy's head!"

THEY? Tommy stopped short. A shadow moved in the moonlight across the floor up ahead. Tommy saw something at the window, a human form, there just for a moment. But then with inhuman strength, it crouched and leaped up past the top of the window, disappearing from sight.

There came a keening screech from behind. Tommy didn't turn because the ceiling up ahead began to collapse. A massive piece of drywall fell to the floor. When the billowing dust and debris cleared, another dark figure stood there, just twenty yards away. Tommy had seen the Drefids as he read *The Elf Lord Chronicles*, but it was always from a distance and slightly vague—like watching through a thick windowpane. Now, a creature stood before Tommy. For real!

The Drefid was the size of a large man. He stood in a kind of half crouch and clenched his pale fists, repeatedly pumping his fingers as slowly sharp, bony blades emerged from his knuckles. Four of these lethal killing spikes grew from each hand to almost a foot in length. The Drefid slid his claws together, scraping them back and forth as if sharpening them.

"Shoot, Tommy!" yelled Mrs. Galdarro. "Aim for his eyes!"

Tommy looked at the creature's face. Pale skin; large, dark sockets; and luminous white eyes . . . they seemed to stare and yet see nothing all at once. The Drefid wore a black cloak, and his mane of white hair floated freely about as if the creature were underwater.

"What's the matter, boy?" it hissed at Tommy. "Lost your nerve?"

"SHOOT!"

In a heart's beat, Tommy nocked an arrow, lifted the bow, and fired. The shaft leaped from the bow, and for a moment, Tommy rode with it, heading straight for the Drefid's right eye. But the arrow pierced nothing but air until it stabbed the drywall at the other end of the hall. The Drefid had leaped up in the air toward Tommy. With his arms and clawed fists spread wide like wings, the creature plummeted toward the paralyzed thirteen-year-old.

Mrs. Galdarro raced in front of Tommy. Her sword blade flashed across the creature's midsection even as she shoved Tommy backward out of the way. The Drefid fell in a heap and landed facedown. Before he could rise again, Mr. Charlie was there. He grasped the bottom of his shield and slammed it down on the prone Drefid.

At last, when the creature was still, Mr. Charlie turned his shield upside down and brought its sharp upper edge down like a guillotine's blade on the Drefid's bony claws.

SNAP!

Mr. Charlie's shield severed the bony spikes from its fists.

"Charlie!" Mrs. Galdarro yelled. There came another shriek from behind.

The burly custodian spun in place. The second Drefid had been joined by a third. One sprinted straight at them up the hall. The other

Drefid scrabbled on all fours along the ceiling and nearly kept pace with the one on the ground.

Heedless of the Drefid above, Mr. Charlie raised his shield and bull-rushed the other head-on. A liquid chill ran down Tommy's back as he watched Mr. Charlie surge forward like a locomotive. Tommy thought with horror, *He doesn't see the one on the ceiling.*

Both Drefids came on.

The next three seconds turned to slow motion. Mrs. Galdarro yelled to warn Mr. Charlie, but her cry was cut short. The clawless Drefid may have been beaten down, but he had not been killed. He rose up on his knees, drew a slim dagger, and plunged it into Mrs. Galdarro's lower leg.

She grunted, spun her leg off the Drefid's weapon, and in the same motion, drove her own blade into the eye socket of the creature. In that moment, an arrow from Tommy's bow sang out and hit the Drefid on the ceiling square in the forehead just above the eyes. There was a peculiar spark, and the arrow sprang back. The force of the impact, however, knocked the Drefid off of the ceiling. He fell at Mr. Charlie's feet.

This time, Mr. Charlie didn't go for the claws. He plunged the sharp edge of his shield down on the back of the creature's neck. Something blue and faintly luminous sprayed up from the dying Drefid. But Mr. Charlie wasn't finished.

The final living Drefid had just gotten back on his feet down the hallway, when Mr. Charlie flung his shield. It hit the creature full in the chest. There was a swift cracking noise, and the Drefid fell to the ground.

"Mrs. Galdarro!" Tommy yelled. He stared at the fresh blood on her lower leg.

"I am fine, Tommy," she replied, sliding the sword into her belt. "It was only a scratch from an earth dagger. Had it been one of the lethal blades forged in Vesper Crag . . . well, best not to think on such things. Charlie, we need to——"

"I'm comin', Elle!" Mr. Charlie ran up.

With Mrs. Galdarro listening to messages on her cell phone the whole way, they hurried out of the hospital, across the grassy campus, through the trees, and down the hill.

Once safe in the SUV, they sat in silence for some time. Tommy shook his head. Wishing it had all been a nightmare hadn't worked. He had seen otherworldly things. And the notion that Mrs. Galdarro and her tale of Elves might yet be a fraud was blasted right out of Tommy's mind.

Mrs. Galdarro was still listening to messages, so Tommy leaned around his seat. "Mr. Charlie?"

"Mmm?"

"Those things . . . those Drefids, they'd have killed me and my parents if I'd stayed in my home?"

Mr. Charlie nodded slowly. "Expect so," he replied. "They'll watch for you there till they're sure you aren't coming back."

"The trees?" Tommy asked. "The black trees you said were watching my neighborhood. Will they leave?"

"I just don't know, Tommy. They should. I'm just glad there weren't any Cragon trees here. That would have been close."

Tommy turned back to the front seat. He'd nearly been killed. How much closer could it have gotten?

Mrs. Galdarro sighed and leaned her head against the steering wheel. Her cell phone lay limply in her hand on her thigh.

"Mrs. Galdarro?" Tommy tilted his head. "Are you okay?"

"Elle?"

Mrs. Galdarro sat up. "Those messages . . . they are from other Sentinels all over your world. The Drefids have closed all the portals."

"What does that mean?" asked Tommy.

"It means we cannot get home," she said. "We're trapped."

She lifted her hand up as if she'd been stung. Her cell phone vibrated and lit up like a Christmas tree. *Incoming call.* She flipped open the phone and said, *"Goldarrow."*

"Gold-arrow?" Tommy glanced in the backseat.

"It's her Elven surname," Mr. Charlie explained.

Tommy laughed. "Galdarro . . . Goldarrow . . . how did I not get that?"

"I understand," said Mrs. Galdarro. A moment later, an "I see." Then with a courteous "Thank you," she closed the phone. "Charlie, would you mind driving? I have some plans to arrange."

"Not a problem, ma'am," he replied.

Tommy waited as they switched seats. "What's going on?"

Mrs. Galdarro smiled as she pecked out texts on her phone. "Have you ever been to Scotland, Tommy?"

"Scotland? Uh . . . no."

"Well, we're going there now," she said without looking up. "Mr. Charlie, we'll need our nest egg. And then to Hangar A47, please."

Charlie started the SUV. "It would be my pleasure."

"Scotland? Really? But . . . how? I mean, don't I need a passport or something?"

"We have friends, Tommy . . . very useful friends."

"Uh . . . ooookay, I'm cool with that." Tommy shook his head. "What's in Scotland anyway?"

"The last open portal."

34

When the Music Calls

WHEN KIRI Lee leaped from the window to escape her knife-wielding parents, she thought it was her only escape. But once airborne, she felt sure the fall would kill her. She braced for the sudden, searing pain. She felt the wind whipping at her hair. A light rain sprinkled her face. She heard glass shatter against the concrete far below. Angry shouts from her room were still very near. Too near.

Kiri Lee opened her eyes and looked down. Her slippers felt as though they were on a solid surface, but there was nothing to hold her up. Yet, she was not falling . . . she was standing outside her window . . . on air. She did notice, however, that she was moving down ever so slightly . . . more like sinking through the air. *A very bad dream*, she concluded. *First, my parents try and kill me; next, I'm standing in midair outside my window.* She continued to sink slowly; whatever *this* was, it would not last long.

She felt something thud against the side of her arm, and then a sudden stinging pain. Something clattered on the street below. Kiri Lee grabbed her arm, felt the blood, and saw the knife blade reflecting in the streetlight.

Without thinking, Kiri Lee put her other foot out in front as if to step down. Six inches below her right foot, her left foot stopped. She had little time to be amazed as her mother flung the last kitchen knife through the window. Another step and it was as if Kiri Lee were walking down an invisible staircase. Like walking . . . on the wind.

Kiri Lee was just five feet above the sidewalk when the final knife missed her head and clattered along the pavement. Instinctively she jumped and found herself on solid ground. She turned back and looked up. Lightning flashed again, and Kiri Lee saw her parents race from the window back into the house.

Kiri Lee had to get away from here. But where? How could she possibly explain this to any of her friends? Her parents might just play it off and make *her* look like the weird one. Plus, at this hour? Who would answer their door? No, she had to get away . . . far away. She turned south down her street and started running. The Paris Metro was just up ahead. She thanked God that she'd worn her coat and clothes to bed.

"Lothriel! Come back!"

Impossible! How did they get downstairs so fast? And why do they keep calling me that peculiar name? Kiri Lee didn't even bother to turn around; she could hear their shoes against the concrete, gaining on her. Oh, she so desperately wanted to wake up. . . .

Just up ahead lay the subway entrance, a fancy, red awning waved overhead of the sublevel staircase. Kiri Lee reached inside her right jacket pocket and fumbled for her wallet. She pulled it out and removed her EuroRail pass, holding tight to the plastic.

"Stop!" came another shout behind her.

A second later Kiri Lee was bounding down the steps three at a time, almost tumbling over herself. She turned the corner and raced down the escalator deeper underground. She covered the next thirty feet in a matter of moments and eyed the turnstile up ahead.

Heavy footfalls echoed down through the corridor above.

Kiri Lee swiped her unlimited pass through the card reader, feeling as though it took an eternity for the red light to shift to green. It beeped.

Green.

She shoved her hands against the cold steel bars and pushed her way through. Feeling at least a little secure now, she chanced a look behind her. They wouldn't have their passes on them . . . would they?

Beep.

Kiri Lee screamed as the turnstile moved, allowing first her father through, then her mother. She looked around for the signs; even though she had ridden this line a hundred times before, she still needed to know where she was headed. She could take this line, the M4, directly to Gare du Nord. And from there . . . anywhere.

Kiri Lee raced around the corner and followed the signs to the northbound line. What time was the next train leaving? How long would she have to evade her parents on the platform? Her heart beat wildly.

She emerged just then through the grand archway and stepped onto the platform, the deep tracks just a few feet in front of her, and filling them, the train to Gare du Nord. Kiri Lee prayed a silent *Thank You, God* and bounded through the closest set of doors. As if the car had been waiting for her, a woman's voice came over the loudspeaker and announced that the train was departing and to please stand clear of the doors.

At the same moment her father and mother came blasting around the corner beyond.

"No!" Kiri Lee screamed.

"Stop!" cried her father, his face red and horribly stretched.

The doors started to close.

Kiri Lee stepped back and fell into an empty seat.

Her parents' hands strained, grasping for a hold around the rubber door liners . . . but never quite made it before the doors shut.

Kiri Lee sat trembling, her knees bouncing under her palms. Her father and mother hammered the glass with their fists, trying to get in the train, running along its side until the train was traveling too fast and they began to lose ground. Kiri Lee wanted to look away from the black, mindless rage in their eyes, their anguished screams. She couldn't stop watching, not until they were gone. But suddenly, their faces began to change . . . to dissolve. . . .

In a dozen rapid heartbeats, nothing of flesh and bone remained. But a pair of misty, vaporous faces stared into the accelerating car. Then the faces unraveled into two snaking strands of mist. They seemed to slither on the wind. One of them found purchase at the seam of the doors. Kiri Lee watched with horror as a thin tendril of mist wriggled through. The other fell away as the train continued to pick up speed.

"No, nooo!" Kiri Lee cried as the length of the thing that was through the doors began to take the shape of the upper torso of a man . . . a man reaching out with arms of mist to clutch for her. It was inches from her now, swiping at the air and growling.

At once, it seemed to be straining, struggling to get free of the doors; the train was approaching its top speed. More and more of the mist creature was sucked back out, and it began to lose its form. With a haunting moan, the rest of the vaporous thing vanished and was lost in the darkness of the tunnel.

❋

The train rumbled on, stop after stop. The doors opened; the doors closed. And no one got on or off.

Kiri Lee fidgeted incessantly, wringing her hands, her mind running wild. All at once her fingers stopped along an envelope in her pocket. Her invitation to Scotland. She pulled it out of her pocket and removed the letter. She found great comfort in the piece of paper, its fine quality, the signature of the dean . . . even the postmark on the envelope. Everything was as it should be. Safe.

Content that she would be safe as long as she stayed ahead of her parents or whatever they were, Kiri Lee thought long and hard about what she would do next. She had a few friends with whom she might stay, but that would put them in danger, too. Until she could figure out what these things were and what they knew about her life, she dared not go anywhere they might expect to find her.

One of her teachers? That was a possibility, but what would they say to her story? Certainly, they'd suspect she'd lost her mind. They'd alert her parents, perhaps even the authorities. The last place she wanted to end up was some psycho institute for teens who had delusions of their parents trying to murder them in their sleep.

"Scotland," she said under her breath and eyed the invitation.

She was invited, after all. And it seemed just the thing to keep her mind at rest, perhaps even let everything wash over. If she was going mad, doing something she loved would only help right the situation, wouldn't it? Give her time. Space. It might help. It might not. *Mist creatures . . . trying to kill me . . . and where are my parents?*

A cold chill snaked up her spine. She pulled the collar of her jacket up around her neck. Over and over she considered her options: friends, teachers, Scotland. And over and over thoughts of her parents intruded. *Where are they? What happened?* Her eyes began to fill with tears, and she fought them back. *How embarrassing . . . sobbing like a toddler.* She let her head rest against the glass window and felt the hum of the train. With every rhythmic bounce of the car, her mind began to fill with colors. And then the colors turned into melodies, and melodies into song. Harmonies formed as more colors danced through her inner vision.

The music.

It was calling her . . . calling her forward.

Her answers were not in Paris.

Scotland. The idea was there in her mind as clear as a billboard. The music told her, she was sure of it. She would go to Scotland. It would be an early arrival, but, if past experiences had taught her anything, she knew her hosts would only be too delighted to have a world-renowned child prodigy such as herself take up residence in their abode. *More time to see the sights*, she would insist. *Edinburgh is far too wonderful to see in just a day*. No one would think to counter her.

If all went as planned, and Kiri Lee felt sure it would, she would have time. Time to think about what she should do next. Time to think about what would happen after the concert. Time to think about what has happened to her parents and time to think about how she walked on air. She had no answers, but thought that maybe the music would. And now . . . right now . . . music was calling. Before long, Kiri Lee was lost to the melodies in her mind, leaving the train car—and the night's horrendous events—far behind.

35

Rags to Royalty

MANY HOURS, many trains, and a few euros later, Kiri Lee found herself on a large blue bus crossing into Edinburgh, Scotland. Scotland had always held a certain untouchable mystery for Kiri Lee. She had been once before with her father by royal invitation, and the memories never left her . . . the green countryside filled with ancient ruins, the cliff faces of the highlands, gray skies looming over endless strands of beach, and its ever-present history.

Somehow Kiri Lee always felt connected to the Scots, to their passion for freedom. She thought, like William Wallace she, too, would give everything she had if it came to it. Then she noticed a well-dressed elderly man talking on a cell phone. *He was on the last leg of the train, too.* She felt as if he might be watching her. . . .

"Parliament Building," came the metallic voice of the bus driver. When Kiri Lee raised her hand, he asked, "Right in front, wee lass?"

"That's fine, sir, thank you," Kiri Lee said.

The driver cast her a long look. He didn't open the door. She asked, "Is there a problem?"

"It's just that I picked yu up from the station, fresh from France, now I'm droppin' yu off on the street here. No bags. No nothin'. And yu got slippers on yur feet. Are yu sure—?"

"Thank you, sir, for your concern. You are most kind. But I assure you, I'll be fine."

"If that's what yu say, lass." The driver moved the lever, and the doors parted. Kiri Lee thanked him, descended, and then watched the doors close. He smiled once more from his seat before pulling the bus back into traffic. At least someone cared, and she was relieved that she was the only one who got off the bus.

Kiri Lee drew in a deep breath of the autumn air and felt Edinburgh rise around her. A recent rain had soaked the stones giving the air a rich, earthy smell. But just ahead, shrouds of steam rose from the ground and floated ominously across the road. Kiri Lee, frozen in place, fixed her eyes on the whirling, writhing vapors. She waited until she was certain it was safe and then merged with a group of people walking across the street. She kept her distance and watched everyone around her. A woman stopped abruptly and turned to walk back. Kiri Lee dodged awkwardly and bumped into someone.

A gangly teenager stared at her darkly and said, "Steady on! What's the matter with yu?"

Kiri Lee muttered a quick, "Sorry!" and hurried away. She turned and scanned the road. *Where did she go?* At last she saw the woman. She stood on the corner and hugged another woman like they were old friends.

Kiri Lee continued walking. A man just four feet in front of Kiri Lee shoved his hand into his coat pocket. *Knife?!* Kiri Lee's heart took off, but the man was only taking out a cell phone. Danger seemed to lurk all around her. Strangers' glances felt threatening and mean. Conversations around her seemed secretive or angry. Even a toddler's cries sounded creepy and unnatural. So when most of the crowd turned right to head to the car park that bordered the garden, she turned left and aimed for the massive front gate trimmed in black and gold.

A royal guard stood watch at the palace gate. Kiri Lee took a deep breath and looked down at herself; her clothes from the night before, still damp with rain, a cut on her sleeve, and her dirty bedroom slippers. No one in their right mind would let her into a hotel, let alone the Royal Palace of Edinburgh. But she had come this far. She prayed the invitation would do the rest.

Kiri Lee felt the man's cold eyes follow her as she neared the gate. Just as he was surely about to dismiss her, she raised the invitation and saw his attention shift to the gold-embossed document in her hand.

"M'lady? May I be of service?" he said, his voice deep and strong. Kiri Lee got the impression that if he ever yelled "STOP!" everyone within a mile radius would immediately freeze.

"Aye," she tried her best Scottish just for fun and handed him the invitation, as well as her photo ID from her wallet. Then came the tough explanation. "My presence has been requested by the Royal Family for a solo performance at this week's concert . . . well, as you can see. I'm afraid, however, that I needed to respond to the request early, as circumstances beyond my control—"

"Say no more, m'lady. I will fetch a steward at once. Please wait just inside here."

Surprised, Kiri Lee slid inside the gatehouse and took a seat as the guard walked across the grand driveway leading to the palace. "I'm in," she said quietly to herself. She was so tired. Tired, confused, terrified, anxious, and grief stricken. She leaned forward and sobbed into her hands.

✳

Across the street, standing in the shadows between a tavern and a small confectionary selling the city's finest traditional Scottish sweets, stood a man in a charcoal gray coat. He spoke into a cell phone palmed in a black gloved hand.

"She's here," he said.

A pause.

"Inside the palace now."

A much longer pause.

"Difficult but not impossible." He closed the phone, placed it in his coat pocket, and removed a small plastic container. He unscrewed the lid and shook the contents into the palm of his hand: three black spiders with very long red legs. The man in the gray coat whispered something to the spiders and they crept up onto his sleeve. Then he crossed the bronze brick road and walked directly in front of the palace gate. As he passed, the spiders dropped off of his sleeve and began a long, stealthy crawl.

Mr. Barnabas, the steward, was a portly, balding man with a thick handlebar mustache and a heavy English accent. He reminded Kiri Lee of the little cartoon guy in the Monopoly game. He said something like, "Follow me," and then several mumbled syllables Kiri Lee did not understand. He led her to a room—a suite, actually. It was so beautiful that Kiri Lee almost gasped when she entered. Thick carpets as soft as velvet, fine oak and cedar furniture, even a big Narnia-like wardrobe. Kiri Lee thought there must have been some mistake. Clearly this was one of the royal bedrooms.

But the steward said, "Will this—*mumble, mutter*—meet your needs—*mutter, mumble*—Miss Yuen?"

Kiri Lee nodded repeatedly. After the steward left she took a closer look around the room. The bed had one of those fully enclosed canopies like the princesses always had in the storybooks. But as exhausted as she was, she dare not flop onto the bed and dirty the sheets. She needed a shower.

As Kiri Lee folded her dirty clothes and slipped into a bathrobe, she didn't notice a tiny set of eight eyes peering up at her from the heating grate in the floor beside the wardrobe. When she started the water running in the shower, she didn't notice the red-legged spider waiting in the gap beneath the bathroom door. And when she began to wash the grime away under the pulses of very hot water, she didn't notice the small shadow moving up the outside of the shower curtain.

As Kiri Lee showered and shampooed, her thoughts turned again to her parents. *What could have happened to them?* Those mist creatures were some kind of impostors. Of this, she was sure. Even though they looked like her parents—well, except for those strange smiles—they didn't know the first thing about her family.

Kiri Lee was lost in thought under the warm water when a spider moved stealthily along the top of the shower curtain. It paused, its venom-filled fangs protracted, then crouched, ready to spring.

Kiri Lee spun, and in one quick motion, turned off the water and pushed the shower curtain along the bar to the far left. The spider found itself surrounded by the curtain. It managed to clamber out of the folds and back up onto the shower rod. It raced along the chrome rod and leaped for Kiri Lee's exposed back. It sank its fangs deep into . . . the thick collar of a bathrobe. Kiri Lee pulled her wet hair out from under the collar and, with a practiced turn of the head, tossed her hair behind her. The abrupt motion knocked the spider off onto the floor.

Kiri Lee left the bathroom, and the spider skittered after her. To her surprise an elderly woman in a blue business dress stood near the open wardrobe busily hanging garments. Her white hair was done up with pins, and she wore eyeglasses that made her look both gentle and wise.

"Miss Yuen, I am Mrs. Sherman." She gave a smart dip of her head and continued in her strong Queen's English. "I understand you might be in need of some wardrobe expansion." She smiled for a moment, but it was replaced by a half-angry, half-embarrassed scowl. Mrs. Sherman marched around Kiri Lee and slammed her foot down on the floor, making an audible crunch. "Dreadfully sorry, Miss Yuen," she said, grinding her heel into the floor. "A spider. I'll have Mr. Barnabas check the room for you later."

Kiri Lee stepped quickly away from the spider remains. "*Eww*," she said. "I don't much like spiders."

"Nor do I," Mrs. Sherman replied. She held out a hand to Kiri Lee. "As I was saying, Miss Yuen, I've brought you some clothing and a selection of shoes. I hope it suits you."

Kiri Lee was speechless, but her mind was busy. *I thought sure they'd refuse to let me in, or even call the police. But instead, they give me a huge room and extra clothes?*

"I also brought some food and tea." She pointed to a tray of cheeses, crackers, fruit, a pot of tea, and water. "I will be your personal chaperone for the length of your stay," Mrs. Sherman continued. "That is not to say that you will not have your personal freedoms, but seeing as you came alone."

There was an awkward pause just then.

Mrs. Sherman tilted her head and took a step forward. "Though I cannot help but ask . . . you come to us unannounced, a week ahead of schedule, and without any belongings save the clothes on your back and"—she eyed the dirty bedroom slippers on the floor—"your *shoes*. Are not your parents planning on—?"

"Mrs. Sherman," Kiri Lee said, "I'm not sure how to say this." Her mind raced along, trying to think of words to describe . . . to convey . . .

"Go on."

"When you are the child-prodigy daughter of aspiring musicians, you . . . well . . . sometimes I find that I am, uh . . . they are so dedicated to their craft that—"

"Peace, child," interrupted Mrs. Sherman. "I understand all too well."

Thank You, God! Kiri Lee thought to herself. She sighed with relief.

"Make yourself at home, Miss Yuen. I'm sure you are quite fatigued after your trip. Tomorrow we can set up a practice schedule and find you an appropriate instrument. Perhaps you would like to do a bit of sightseeing, too."

"Can we schedule a visit to a castle?"

"A castle? Of course, my dear." She gestured toward the window. "Of course, Edinburgh Castle is—"

"It's magnificent," Kiri Lee said. "I came once a few years back. But I was hoping to see a different castle, if I could."

Mrs. Sherman smiled and went to the drawer of the big mahogany desk by the window. She took out a half inch notebook and handed it to Kiri Lee. "I suspect you will find something you like in here."

Kiri Lee looked at the notebook and grinned. *Castles of Scotland*, it read. "I think you're right."

"My number is by the phone. Ring me when you find one you like. I'll have Collin, my chauffeur, take us tomorrow."

"Thank you, so much," Kiri Lee said. "Things have been . . ." Kiri Lee choked up.

Mrs. Sherman put a tender hand on her shoulder. "I understand . . . believe me I do. Let nothing trouble you now. Relax and enjoy the castles."

"Thank you," Kiri Lee whispered.

As soon as Mrs. Sherman was gone, Kiri Lee changed into a casual outfit, slacks and a dark-green, long-sleeved shirt, and got crackers and cheese and some water. Then she flopped onto the cushy bed and opened up the notebook. Page after page of magnificent castles were not enough to bring her comfort. Mrs. Sherman was kind, but wrong. There was no way she could understand what Kiri Lee had been through.

She continued to page through the castles until she came to Dalhousie Castle. No sooner had she seen its massive central turret, its vast gabled roof, and its formidable keep than she began to hear the first sweet notes. Soon that elusive melody poured into her mind, and she felt as if Dalhousie Castle was a place she had always been meant to go. Yes, she would call Mrs. Sherman and see if they could travel to Dalhousie Castle. She lay back on the bed and fell asleep with the open book on her chest.

The two remaining red-legged spiders, one on either side of the bed canopy, began to descend on invisible threads.

36

Dalhousie Castle

A LOUD knock on the door woke Kiri Lee with a start. The castle notebook fell onto the floor as she bounced out of bed just as one spider landed on her pillow and the other was still dangling on its web near the foot of the bed.

"I say, Miss Yuen—"came the voice, followed by a few mumbles. "It's Mr. Barnabas. May I come in?"

"Just a minute," Kiri Lee said. She quickly made herself presentable and then opened the door. Outside stood the Monopoly guy. "Miss Yuen," he said, as he stalked into the room. "I've heard yu've a bit of a spider problem in 'ere."

"It was just one," she said.

"Never just one—*mumble*—Mrs. Sherman asked me to see to it. *mutter, mumble*. And so 'elp me, I will—*grumble, mumble*. Oh, and Mrs. Sherman requests the honor of yur presence in the main dining hall. It's down the hall, first stairwell on the right. Can't miss it."

Kiri Lee thanked the steward, stepped into a pair of shoes, and left. Lingering in the hallway on the other side of the door, she heard a great deal of muttering, and the almost continuous *SHHHH* sound.

✳

The meal had been delightful. And Kiri Lee confirmed plans with Mrs. Sherman for a trip to Dalhousie Castle. When she returned to her room late that evening, Mr. Barnabas explained that she was to have a new room. All of her clothes had already been moved. Apparently in the process of making the room unhealthy for the spiders, he also made it very unpleasant for humans as well. In her new room, Kiri Lee slept soundly and had no trouble with creatures of any kind.

The next day, their car bounced along the single-lane road that weaved back through the countryside. At last the driver turned onto a private drive. There rose a majestic, reddish castle, its signature tower reaching for the stark blue sky. As they pulled through the gate and parked, she gasped at the sheer size of the structure. Collin, the chauffeur, came around and opened her door.

"Dalhousie Castle, Miss Yuen," he said.

"It's fantastic!"

"I've always enjoyed Dalhousie," said Mrs. Sherman, walking around the car.

Collin waited behind with the car as the two ladies marched up the long, curving path to the front doors. The property was busy today, Kiri Lee noticed. A group of schoolchildren about her age were in a class down at the falconry cages, while a wedding reception was taking place on the back lawn.

"There are a lot of people here," said Kiri Lee.

"Dalhousie was converted into a bed-and-breakfast years ago, complete with a chapel for weddings. The grounds have been adapted to teach children about life in the Middle Ages, thus it's a popular destination for those who know about it."

"I can see why." For a few moments, Kiri Lee could almost forget the recent tragedies in her life. She scanned the beautiful grounds and admired everything, from the flowerbeds and grand trees, to the sweeping spans of lawn. She wanted nothing more than to leave Mrs. Sherman behind and run through the grass, exploring every nook of the property—forgotten gardens, hidden passageways in the castle, maybe even a treasure or two missed by the proprietors.

They walked into the entryway, two staircases leading up into the dining room, another straight down into an office, and a third to the right where the ancient armory had been turned into a quaint chapel.

"Mrs. Sherman, so good to see yu." Kiri Lee glanced up as a well-dressed elderly man descended and offered his hand. *The man from the bus.*

"It has been too long, Edward."

"My thoughts precisely," he replied. He turned to Kiri Lee. "And who might this young lass be?"

"Edward Rengfellow, I'd like to present to you Miss Kiri Lee Yuen."

"*The* Kiri Lee Yuen?" he asked. "The prodigious solo cellist due to play at the festival?"

"The very same," Mrs. Sherman said. "She's come to us early enough to do some sightseeing."

"Ah, so very pleased to meet yu, Miss Yuen," Edward said, taking her slender hand with a feather-light touch as if he were afraid he might harm her gifted fingers. "I do so love the cello. I play a little myself, but I've heard yur playing is divine."

"Well, thank you." Kiri Lee gave a slight curtsy. "I'm pleased to meet you, Mr.—"

"Edward, please. Just Edward." He paused awkwardly and seemed to be staring. He blinked and said, "Those are very pretty earrings yu're wearing. Unusual."

"Oh, thank you." Kiri Lee brushed the hair off one ear and turned her head so he could see better.

"Yes," he said, "remarkable."

"Would you be so kind as to give us the standard tour, Edward?" asked Mrs. Sherman. "Kiri Lee has a practice at three o'clock this afternoon."

"Does she now?"

Do I? It was news to her.

"Right, then. Off we go!"

Though Edward was well on in years, he moved swiftly through the castle, Kiri Lee doing her best to keep up with him. Over six feet tall with a squirrelly nest of white hair, Edward seemed more like a teenager than a grandfather, apparently taking as much delight in telling Kiri Lee about the castle as she did hearing it. He focused far less on endless dates and politics and more on events and people, the reasons they built certain additions, where secret stairwells led, and of course, all the mysterious stories he could work in that had been passed down through the generations. Mrs. Sherman kept close behind her, never missing a step, but never saying a word.

The trio had toured most of the castle when Edward led them to his favorite spot—the turret of the castle's grand tower. The old staircase curved along the inside wall of the musty tower, until finally leading to a small trapdoor in the ceiling. Edward rammed his shoulder into it, and the cover popped open, a shaft of brilliant light blinding them momentarily. They emerged onto a wide platform with gap-toothed stone-edged ancient crenelations.

Kiri Lee walked to the edge and placed her hands on the stonework. "The view is spectacular," she sighed. Her eyes looked out over the whole valley, in awe of the sweeping fields that adorned the hills. Directly below her sat the parking lot and the falconry cages. A few of the students noticed her and began waving; she waved back with a broad smile.

She backed away and walked across the tower's summit to the opposite side, now mesmerized by the lush forests that enclosed the back property. The trees looked like broccoli tops, all cloistered together as if she could reach out and pluck them for the eating. And there on the back lawn stood a white reception tent bustling with people. "What a beautiful day for a wedding."

"Aye, 'tis that, m'lady," replied Edward.

Kiri Lee was just about to turn away when she noticed something odd in the trees just beyond the lawn. Poking up from among the leaves was a discolored area . . . of stones perhaps. In the woods?

"Pardon me, Edward, but what is that . . . there in the trees?" She raised a finger and pointed off in the distance.

"Why, those are the old *roons*, Miss Yuen." Edward smiled, actually saying the word *ruins* in his wide brogue. "Perhaps, when yu return, I can take yu to see them?"

"Oh yes!"

"Thursday is open," said Mrs. Sherman. "Will that do for you, Edward?"

"Quite nicely," he replied. "And yu, Miss Yuen?"

"I would like that." Kiri Lee was thrilled. She thought about the ruins all the way back down to the castle's front entrance. Renovated castles were certainly marvelous, what with their extravagant suits of armor and decadent dining halls. But there was always something about ruins . . . and about those ruins in particular . . . there was music there. She was sure of it.

"You've gotten faster with your tours, Edward," remarked Mrs. Sherman. "We've still an hour."

"Comes with practice," he replied. "Much like yur scales, eh, Miss Yuen?" Kiri Lee smiled. "With the extra time, perhaps Miss Yuen would like to stroll the grounds a wee bit? There's not time to visit the roons, but yu could certainly enjoy the estate. Mrs. Sherman and I could catch up on old times while yu explore."

"Would that be all right, Mrs. Sherman?"

"I suppose that would be fine," Mrs. Sherman replied. "One hour is all you have."

❈

Kiri Lee strolled first around the northern perimeter of the castle. Then, before she knew it, she found herself running, practically skipping, across the vast lawns. Feeling the wind against her cheeks and through her hair was exhilarating. Kiri Lee ran right past a group of schoolkids, first graders by the look of the students. They were so cute with their multicolored balloons and banner flags. Some of them saw Kiri Lee and waved.

Kiri Lee waved back and kept on running. She turned the southern corner of the castle and found a gorgeous expanse of grass bordered by dark evergreens. She stopped running. Just thirty yards away was a child all by himself. She thought he was dressed in the same uniform as the others, and he had a red balloon. There was no one else around. *He's not supposed to be back here by himself*, Kiri Lee thought. She walked over to him.

He turned, startled at first. "I just wanted to look, that's all," he said nervously. She thought his little Scottish accent was so cute. "I'll go back, I will."

"It's okay," said Kiri Lee. "I was afraid you were lost."

"Connor told me there be graveyards behind all castles, and I wanted to look," he said. "I have not seen any graves." Just then, he lost hold of his balloon. The wind caught it at once, and up it went. "Nooo," wailed the little boy. "That's me balloon. Oh noo!"

Kiri Lee simply reacted. The balloon was off and climbing. She went after it. Her first step was awkward. She half-expected to fall flat on her face. What happened the other night . . . well, it was all mixed into a nightmare. But her foot caught hold of something . . . like a step made of air.

She kept climbing. The little boy gasped as Kiri Lee grabbed the balloon's string and turned around. She was much higher than before and felt a combination of fear and exhilaration. She began to sink, so she quickly walked back down.

Kiri Lee handed the balloon to the open-mouthed boy. "Uh, it'd probably be best if you didn't mention what I just did to anyone."

"How'd yu do tha'?" he asked. "Yu . . . yu flew!"

"Not exactly," she replied. "Now you best get back to your class. They're going to be worried."

"Aye, it's a trick!" he said. "Can yu teach me?"

"Sorry, it's a secret. Now off with you." She gave him a warm but firm push and sent him on his way. As soon as she was sure the boy had turned the corner, Kiri Lee ran the rest of the length of the greenery behind the castle. Actually, she ran on the air.

❋

"Did you see that, Lexi?" asked a tall blond woman leaning on the parapet of the castle's tower.

"Ellos smiles upon us, Ril," replied her willowy brunette friend. "It's the last one. Has to be."

"She walks upon the wind," said Ril Taniel. "We need to tell Edward."

❋

"I had a wonderful time," said Kiri Lee to Edward back inside the castle. "I can't wait to come back."

"Thursday, correct?" asked Edward.

"That's right," said Mrs. Sherman.

"Excellent. Then we will visit those roons yu spotted from the tower. Very good view from up there, aye." He was quiet while he escorted them down the castle's front steps. "You know, Miss Yuen, I'm part of a string quartet. We're playing for some special guests who are flying in on Thursday, as a matter of fact. I wonder, Mrs. Sherman, would it be permitted to let Miss Yuen sit in with us? I'm a cellist myself, remember. I'd gladly give up my seat for Kiri Lee."

"Well," said Mrs. Sherman. "The festival isn't until Saturday, and we will already be here. Kiri Lee, what do you say?"

"I say yes, absolutely!" Kiri Lee clapped and bounced on her heels. "And you don't need to give up your seat, Edward. I much prefer the violin anyway, though everyone knows me for my cello. Miss Sherman, could you get me a violin?"

"Of course, dear," she replied. "There are several back at the palace."

Kiri Lee looked back to Edward and she said, "What shall we play?"

"I am fond of Mozart," said Edward.

"Me too!" said Kiri Lee. "Mozart it is." Kiri Lee knew by memory every note of every piece Mozart ever wrote.

"Ah, Miss Yuen, yu've made me very happy today," said Edward. "You have no idea what a special night this will be." As the two ladies walked farther away, he muttered, "No idea indeed."

✳

"Goodbye, Edward!" Kiri Lee waved once more as she and Mrs. Sherman made their way back to the parking lot. Just as their driver was climbing out to open their doors, the class with the falcons let out and entered into the parking lot to the right. Suddenly, kids were everywhere, talking about their field trip and how cool it was handling the raptors. Mrs. Sherman tried to steer clear, but Kiri Lee got knocked over by a young man a head taller than she.

"Ouch!" she cried out as she landed on her rear.

"See here, young man!" Mrs. Sherman scolded.

"I'm so sorry," replied the boy, instantly kneeling beside Kiri Lee. He reached out his hand. A woman knelt beside Kiri Lee, too, offering to help her up.

Kiri Lee hesitated, both her backside and her pride a bit sore, but eventually she took hold. And when she did, it was as if an electric current rippled through her body. She looked up at the young man, shocked.

What is this? Kiri Lee noticed his red hair and pale complexion. "Do I know you?"

✳

Jimmy felt terrible for knocking a stranger over. But not just any stranger, a girl! And worse, a *pretty* girl who was clearly from a rich home. Her chaperone and driver now eyeing him, he felt completely ashamed. He thought they would be justified in whatever they were about to say. Miss Finney was by his side in an instant.

"Are you all right, Miss Yuen?" asked the woman with the girl.

"I'm fine," Kiri Lee said brushing off her clothes.

"As for you, young man—"

"I'm horribly sorry, mum, honest I am," Jimmy said, his face now the color of his hair.

"Are you sure you are all right?" Mrs. Sherman asked. "And your hands?"

"Yes, Mrs. Sherman. My hands are both okay. It was just an accident." She turned to the boy. "My name is Kiri Lee."

"Jimmy Gresham," he said. "And this is my teacher, Miss Finney. I can't say as I know yur name, but I do feel like I've seen yu before."

"Perhaps you've seen her onstage," piped up the driver.

Jimmy looked to the man, then back to Kiri Lee. "An actress?"

"A world-famous musician, my good fellow," corrected Mrs. Sherman. "Now then. Off we go." Mrs. Sherman ushered Kiri Lee back toward the car.

"Sorry about all this," Jimmy replied, certain he had met her before. *But where?*

"It was nice meeting you!" Kiri Lee said over her shoulder.

Before he knew it, Jimmy called to her. "Perhaps we'll meet again." Then his face turned red. *I can't believe I said that,* he thought as Kiri Lee looked back at him and smiled.

37

Deadly Proof

QUIETLY SIPPING a glass of sweet tea with lemon, Mr. Spero sat in an armchair in the Greens' family living room. Jett, sitting on a couch just a few feet away, was as nervous as he'd ever been. Of all the teachers to make a house call, Jett would have never expected Mr. Spero. Mrs. Genresset, the math teacher, maybe. Mr. Midgley, the civics teacher, sure. But English was Jett's favorite class, and Mr. Spero was one of those cool teachers who made things easy to understand.

Did I forget to make up a paper . . . a test?

Jett couldn't recall anything. Jett's parents sat on an adjacent couch. Their questioning eyes bounced back and forth between Jett and his teacher. Feeling inexplicably guilty, Jett looked away. He stared at the trees swaying outside the living room's expansive picture window.

"This is terrific tea," said Mr. Spero. "Old family recipe?"

"Instant," said Mrs. Green.

Mr. Green spoke up. "Look, Mr. Spero, you're keeping us in a little bit of suspense here. What's this all about?"

Mr. Spero placed his glass on an end table. "I'm sorry about that," he said. "It's just not the easiest thing to talk about with—"

"Oh, he failed a test, didn't he?" said Mrs. Green, glaring at her son. "See, Austin, I told you Jett was hiding something."

"Ma, I didn't fail anything!" Jett protested.

"No, no, Mrs. Green, that's not what this is about." Mr. Spero removed a handkerchief from his coat pocket and wiped his brow. "Jett continues to be one of my best students. He's remarkable, really.

"It's not about school," said Mr. Spero. "I've been thinking about it for a while, but when I saw you at Jett's football game this afternoon, then I knew I—"

"Oh," said Mr. Green with a huge smile. "Ohhh, I know what this is about, heh, heh, heh." He got up and went to a drawer. "You're a big Panthers fan, aren't you?"

Mr. Spero cocked his head sideways. "Uh . . . yes, I . . . uh, follow the Panthers, but that's—"

"Don't say another word," said Mr. Green, taking a large permanent marker from a drawer. "Back in my playing days, I used to do this all the time. What do ya want me to sign? A football card? We could do a picture together and print it on the computer, if you like?"

"Mr. Green," the English teacher said, holding up a hand. "With all due respect to your playing career, I'm not here for an autograph."

Jett's father's cheeks burned red. With the marker still in his hand, he sat hard on the couch. "Oh. Well, I guess just say your piece then."

"Mr. and Mrs. Green, I believe Jett's life may be in danger."

"WHAT?!" Mrs. Green exclaimed. "My baby?"

Jett's father mouthed, "What on earth?"

"This afternoon, after the game, I met Jett on the other side of the visitor's tunnel."

"Yeah, I remember," said Jett. "There was this creepy guy watching me. Did you blast him?"

Mr. Spero swallowed. "No, I didn't blast him. I don't think he expected to see me there, and he ran off."

"Jett, why didn't you tell us about this?" asked Mr. Green.

"Mr. Spero, did you call the police?" asked Mrs. Green.

Mr. Spero shook his head. "In this matter, the police will be of no use."

"What . . . what do you mean?" Mrs. Green had her hands on her hips now.

Uh-oh, Mr. Spero, thought Jett. *You better do some explaining. Ma's getting upset now.*

"Okay," said Mr. Spero. "Here it is. Someone is stalking your son, but . . . he's not human." The English teacher held up his hand. "He is a Drefid, an assassin sent to murder your son because of who he is."

"That does it," said Mr. Green, standing up. "I'm calling the cops."

"Dad, wait," said Jett.

"Naw, Son, I don't know what kind of drugs your teacher's on, but he's as cra—"

"Mr. Green, do you know why your son's fatal accident did not kill him?"

Mr. Green froze.

Mr. Spero waited.

Jett's father sat down.

Mr. Spero went on. "I spoke to one of the paramedics. He told me Jett's neck was broken, said he was sure of it. Broken ribs, pelvis . . . he was paralyzed. He should have died."

"Don't you say such things!" said Mrs. Green. "The Lord healed my baby."

"I believe you," said Mr. Spero. "But it was not a momentary healing. Jett was born with . . . certain gifts. He's always been a special ballplayer, but have you ever seen him play like today? Have you ever seen any teenager play like Jett did today? Jett just about knocked Brickhouse into the next zip code. He carried eight young men over that goal line. *Eight*."

"What are you saying?" asked Mrs. Green.

"This is not going to be easy for you to believe. But short of leaping off the Empire State Building or being burned alive, Jett is nearly indestructible. He has superhuman strength as well because . . . he's not human, either."

"Get out of my house right now!" Mr. Green shot up and towered over the English teacher.

Mr. Spero stood and faced the ex-Carolina Panther. Then he reached up and tore away the rounded tissue above his ears. He lightly scratched at the tips of his pointed ears that were now revealed. "You have no idea how good this feels."

"Oh my!" Mrs. Green looked like she might faint.

"Mr. Spero, you got pointed ears!" Jett exclaimed.

"What in the wor—what are you?"

"I am an Elven warrior," Mr. Spero replied. "But I am nothing compared to Jett. He is one of seven Elven Lords, stolen from our world and left here to be forgotten."

"Hazel, call the police," said Mr. Green. He stood menacingly close to the teacher. "Elves? You've lost your mind!"

"No, Mr. Green. Though I cannot fault you for disbelieving me, I insist it is the truth." He paused. "What do you know of Jett's birth parents?"

"Birth parents? We're his rea—" Mr. Green stopped short. Mrs. Green's hands flew to her lips.

Jett looked back and forth. "Ma? Dad? What . . . what's he talking about?"

Mr. Spero closed his eyes and massaged his temples. "You haven't told him."

"How dare you come into our house—" Mr. Green leaped to his feet. "Get into our family's business—"

"No, Austin!" Jett's mother cried. She was on her feet and between her husband and the teacher in an instant. "Don't raise your fists in our home."

Mr. Spero stayed out of Mr. Green's reach but continued

explaining, "I am sorry. I didn't know any other way to tell you. Jett is the son of Elven Lords from a world called Allyra. He is now one of seven living Elven Lords. If he doesn't come back to his real home, our race may perish forever. These Drefids, they are deadly, and I don't know how many there are—"

At that moment, several things happened. Mrs. Green lost hold of her husband. In a blind rage, he flew at Mr. Spero and slammed him into the living room wall.

Surprising them all, the picture window exploded.

Glass flew everywhere.

Jett tackled his mother to the floor just as a massive, dark tree limb reached into the room through the window. It flailed about, smashing picture frames and keepsakes on the mantel and slashing the couches.

A massive tear opened in one corner of the ceiling. Timber, drywall, and debris fell, and the crack opened wider. A cartwheeling piece of wood cracked Mr. Green on the head. For a moment, a twisted face with huge, dark eyes appeared in the crack.

"There . . . you . . . are," came a voice like the wind and cracking timber.

Just as Jett got to his feet, the first dark limb closed like a vise around his waist.

Jett screamed.

"Fight, Jett!!" yelled Mr. Spero as Mr. Green slumped unconscious to the ground. "FIGHT BACK!!"

Jett abruptly stopped screaming and squirming. He grabbed at the barky finger constricting around his midsection and ripped at it with a might he had never known before.

Jett tore a chunk of hard flesh away.

A deep, rasping howl rang out, and the hand dropped Jett immediately. He saw his mother. She was shaking, her back against the double doors of the study.

"Ma!" Jett yelled. "Get into the basement! Call the police!"

"But, baby!"

"Go, Ma! Now!" His mother moved tentatively at first, but then raced for the basement.

Jett turned just in time to witness two dark figures leaping through the window. Just seeing them sent a wild, paralyzing chill blowing through Jett. Shrouds of whirling white hair. Cruel blades extending from each fist. And the eyes—*the eyes*—heartless pupils of ice, floating in seas of depthless darkness.

"Drefids!!" shouted Mr. Spero. Jett watched his teacher charge, producing a pair of hand axes from beneath his long coat as he dove at one of the creatures. The other Drefid came at Jett.

"Come to me, *Violet!*" the creature hissed.

The Drefid reached at Jett with both clawed hands.

Jett jumped backward, destroying an end table.

Again and again, the Drefid stabbed at Jett. Each time, Jett dodged or ducked out of the way. Then he drove at Jett so hard he embedded his bony blades into the living room wall.

Seeing the Drefid momentarily trapped, Jett balled his fist, pulled back his arm, and unleashed a crushing punch. Jett hit the creature square in his pale jaw, so hard that the creature's head snapped sideways and his body twisted so awkwardly that his trapped arm snapped. The Drefid slumped to the ground and was still.

"Call me Violet!" Jett growled. The whole room shook. The tree thing had both its twisted hands inside the torn ceiling and ripped free a ragged section, tossing it out into the night. Where once there had been ceiling, there now was dark sky and an even darker shadow bending down and reaching into the room.

Axes meeting bony blades, Mr. Spero and the Drefid still sparred. But the tree creature swept down its fist. It slammed into Mr. Spero, sending his axes clattering to the floor and knocking the teacher onto one of the ruined couches to Jett's right. He rolled off the couch and rose unsteadily to his feet.

The tree's grasping hands and the other Drefid closed in on Jett and the now weaponless teacher. Their backs to a pair of high bookcases, Jett and Mr. Spero had nowhere to go.

The dark, gnarled hands reached forward, and the Drefid sprang. A blast rang out.

The Drefid fell backward as if he'd been pulled on a string. The tree creature roared and started to jerk upright. It struggled in vain to twist, to reach around its trunk as if something was attacking it from behind.

"Finish 'em off," said Mrs. Green. She held a shotgun and stood in the doorway to the living room.

Just then, the tree beast spasmed and fell, head, shoulders, arms, and upper limbs into the living room. Mr. Spero charged for his axes, found only one, and leaped on top of the tree creature. The wide blade bit deeply into the beast's timber flesh, and soon its roaring stopped, and the living room was covered in a sticky, black liquid.

The gunshot had only stunned the Drefid. He regained his feet and turned just in time to meet Jett's round kick. The creature staggered backward toward the window.

Unleashing a barrage of heavy punches, Jett went to work on the creature's midsection. The moment the Drefid doubled over, Jett lifted a violent knee under the creature's chin, and he flew back, out of the window from whence he had come. Wanting to make sure, Jett went to the window.

"He's not getting up again, Son," said Mr. Green from down below in the lawn. Holding Mr. Spero's other axe, he stood over the dead Drefid.

"Dad, how did you—?"

"Take more than a knock on the head to keep me from helpin' my boy. I woke, saw you havin' trouble with that tree thing, so I took one of the axes outside and went to work on its trunk. Go figure. Thing fell just like a regular tree."

✵

"If I hadn't seen these creatures with my own eyes . . ." said Mr. Green. He stood in the doorway to the study and motioned to the wrecked living room and the dead. ". . . I never would have believed you. I mean, you could've faked the ears, but those things . . ."

"I still can't believe it," said Mrs. Green. She rocked slowly in a desk chair. The shotgun was at her side, leaning against a tower of CDs and DVDs.

"I'm really an Elf?" asked Jett, rubbing the scars on top of his ears.

"Yes, Jett," said Mr. Spero. "You really are. And I've traveled between worlds to find you."

"What do we do now?" asked Mr. Green, sitting on a stool next to his wife. "We can't leave these things here."

"No," said Mr. Spero. "That would be unwise. Your nearest neighbors are close to a mile away, and you've got a large piece of property here. I'd suggest burying these creatures where they'll never be found."

"Bury them? That'd be some serious work. Why?"

"Mr. Green, can you imagine what would happen if the people of Earth learn of another world beyond their own?"

Jett's dad shook his head and whistled. "It could change everything."

"It *would* change everything," said Mr. Spero. "Now, Mr. and Mrs. Green . . . we've won a small victory here tonight, but there are more Drefids and more tree creatures—Cragons we call them—out there. As long as Jett is here, your home will not be safe. They will not stop until your son is dead. And, as you saw here tonight, they are prepared—even eager—to kill all who stand in their way." He turned and looked into Jett's violet eyes. "I need to take Jett back to Allyra."

Mrs. Green lowered her head to her husband's shoulder and wept quietly. Jett's father was very still. His eyes took on a frozen, faraway look. "He's . . . he's our son."

"Yes," said Mr. Spero. "You adopted Jett and have raised him well. Even with his immense strength, it took a lot of heart for him to go after those horrific creatures. You are good parents and good people. I will not take Jett against your will . . . or his. But you must know this: Jett was born in Berinfell, the capital city of the Elves. He was stolen from his birth parents and abandoned here on Earth. If Jett and the other six lords do not return to Allyra, the Spider King will destroy the Elven race."

"W-will he ever come back?" asked Mrs. Green.

"If Ellos . . . if God wills it," replied Mr. Spero.

Mr. Green took his wife's hand and rubbed it. Then he stood and went to Jett. "Son," he said. "I don't see how I can let you go . . ." A long silence followed. Mr. Green hastily wiped his eye. ". . . But I don't see how I can rightfully make you stay, either."

"Austin!" Mrs. Green objected. "Oh, Austin . . ."

"Hazel," he said, "this is beyond us. Even if he'd been born our . . . our natural son, he's God's property, loaned to us . . . for a time." He turned back to his son. "Jett, Mr. Spero says he won't take you if you aren't willing. And where you'd be going is a dangerous place, is that right?"

Mr. Spero nodded.

"So, what you need to decide," Mr. Green continued, "is if you are willing to step out there, in spite of the danger, in spite of the unknown, in spite of what you . . . what you're leaving behind."

Jett didn't answer right away. He went to his mother, hugged her fiercely, and whispered something in her ear. Then he went to his father. "Dad, if I can help save . . . I mean, there are a lot of peo—Elves who will die if I don't. There must be a reason I survived that bike wreck; there must be a reason I have this kind of strength. So I guess what I'm saying is, I'll go."

Mr. Spero's nod spoke infinite respect. "Jett, you should go change—those stains will attract attention. Oh, and wear all cotton."

"Why?"

"When we travel between worlds, only organic materials will pass through."

Jett scrunched his brow. Then he realized the meaning. "Right, wouldn't want to show up in a new world in nothing but my birthday suit."

When Jett left, Mr. Spero turned to the parents. "Mr. and Mrs. Green, I pledge to you, I will protect your son with my life. I . . . my people are grateful for your sacrifice." The teacher glanced over his shoulder at the living room and then said, "Now I have one more thing to ask of you. Please do not report Jett missing right away. Give us two days."

"Report Jett missing?" Mr. Green asked.

"You have to," said Mr. Spero. "You will tell them that I took Jett on a trip to the Folger Shakespeare Library in Washington, D.C. I'll give you a permission slip to sign and leave it on my desk as evidence."

"But the cops will think you kidnapped him," said Mr. Green.

"It's for the best," said Mr. Spero. "If the police do not have a legitimate lead, they will suspect the parents. It'll be hard to explain the damage to your house as it is."

"No, I'll take care of that," said Mr. Green. "I've been meaning to cut down that dead oak in the front yard. I'll just let part of it fall the wrong way . . . into our living room."

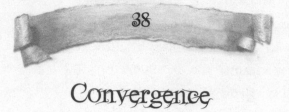

Convergence

AFTER A quick stop at the school to plant the permission slip, Mr. Spero drove Jett out of Greenville and looked for the interstate.

"Route 95 North?" Jett noted the sign at the exit. "Is that how we get to Allyra?" he asked.

Mr. Spero tried to frown, but laughed anyway. "No, Route 95 takes us to Baltimore/Washington International Airport. We're going to catch a flight to Scotland."

"Scotland?"

"The Drefids have closed every portal in the U.S. If we are to get home to Allyra, we must go to the last open portal in Scotland. Other Sentinels and those of your lineage wait for us in Baltimore."

✺

Mrs. Galdarro closed her cell phone. "I've now heard back from everyone except Nelly," she said.

"That's unlike her," said Gabriel Sandow, a Sentinel who had just arrived from Virginia. "With two of the seven in one place, it may be that the Drefids and Cragons concentrated there."

"I fear this also," said Mrs. Galdarro. She looked at the faces gathered in the hangar's waiting area. The group was made up of Sentinels and Dreadnaughts . . . and, of course, Tommy. "But . . . if anyone can take care of her wards, it's Nelly."

�֍

Later, Mrs. Galdarro found Tommy at the soda machine again. "But isn't that your fourth?"

"Free soda," Tommy said with a grin.

"But all that caffeine. . . . doesn't that it you jittery?"

"Not at all," Tommy replied, purposely blinking like crazy. "It has no effect on me whatsoever." They both laughed. "I can't wait to meet the others. Do you know anything about them?" he asked.

"The other Sentinel told me a little," she replied. "I suspect you'll know more about them after our flight than I know right now."

"Can't you tell me something?"

"Well, Kat Simonson is the young lady coming from California. Her plane is due any minute now. I know she is one of the Berylinian Elves, the only daughter of Beleg and Kendie Hiddenblade."

"Berylinian Elves?"

"Yes . . . you'll know them by the bluish cast of their skin."

"Blue? Really?"

She nodded. "But be careful not to offend her with your thoughts. She reads minds."

"Oh." Tommy made a mental note of that. "Okay, who else?"

"Jett Green is a football star from North Carolina."

"Football star . . . great," said Tommy.

"Do I detect a lack of enthusiasm?"

"I like football, but jocks can get kind of an attitude."

"Well, I hope not. We are counting on Jett for big things. He is a Lyrian Elf . . . dark skin, violet eyes, like Charlie. But unlike Charlie, Jett is an Elven Lord. His gifting is twofold: unimaginable physical strength and rapid healing. His Sentinel seems to believe he is a noble lad . . . I hope he's right."

"I guess I won't challenge him to arm wrestling," said Tommy.

"That's a wise decision." Mrs. Galdarro wore a hint of a smile and was lost in thought for a moment. "Two more: Jimmy Gresham and the newly discovered Kiri Lee Yuen wait in Scotland. But we are most worried about the two who remain here in America: Autumn and Johnny Briarman."

"Brother and sister?" Tommy thought for a second. "But I thought each one of us—"

"You're quite right. They were raised as brother and sister, but they are not really. I don't know if their Sentinel has told them this yet. Oh, I do wish we'd get news from them."

When the news finally came, it was not good. Five Sentinels from the Northeast arrived at Hangar A17. None of them had heard anything from Annelle Brookeheart. Kat Simonson had arrived on schedule, as had Jett Green. But Johnny and Autumn were missing, and the private plane bound for Scotland was scheduled to leave in less than an hour. They couldn't risk delaying the flight lest someone at the airport get suspicious.

Tommy wondered what was taking Mrs. Galdarro so long. She'd been debriefing Kat, Jett, and their Sentinels for more than an hour. At last, the business office door opened. Mrs. Galdarro strode wearily across the hangar. Behind her were several adults and two teens.

"Tommy Bowman of Seabrook, Maryland," she began. "I'd like to introduce you to North Carolina's own Jett Green."

The first thing Tommy noticed was Jett's eyes. *Just like Mr. Charlie*, he thought. Jett wore a long-sleeved cotton T-shirt and jeans. *He doesn't look that strong*, Tommy thought. As he reached out to shake Jett's hand, he thought he heard a giggle from the girl.

"Hey, Jett," said Tommy. "Nice to meet y—ya-a-a-a!"

"Mannn," said Jett, releasing the handshake. "I am SO sorry about that. It's, well, . . . I'm stronger now."

Tommy rubbed his throbbing right hand. "Glad you're on our side," he said.

"I warned you," said Mrs. Galdarro. "And Tommy, this is Kat Simonson from Los Angeles."

Tommy looked at Kat for the first time. She wasn't blue like a crayon, but looking at her was like looking through the blue lens of 3-D glasses, only it was just her skin. Tommy searched for something to say as he held out his hand, but what he came up with was nowhere near what he'd meant to say. "You're . . . you're blue," he said. "Cool."

Kat held out her hand and shook Tommy's fingertips for the briefest of moments. A bit of crimson mingled with the blue on her cheeks. "You meant that." It wasn't a question.

"Yeah," said Tommy. Then he mumbled, "How was your flight?"

"I was reading through most of it," she said.

"Well," said Mrs. Galdarro. "I've got to discuss some things with the other Sentinels, so I'll give you three some time to get to know each other."

The three teens stood in a loose triangle and stared at one another. Sentinels and Dreadnaughts moved about them like worker bees in a hive. And still they stood . . . awkward and silent until Tommy spoke up. "They have free sodas over there."

"Great," Jett and Kat said simultaneously.

After they each got a soda, Tommy sat on a folding chair and held up his drink. "This is my fifth one," he said, making his eyes bulge. "But don't worry. The caffeine has no effect on me whatsoever."

Kat snickered and snorted. "Ah! My soda went up my nose!"

Jett couldn't hold it in anymore. He misted the floor to his right with a mouthful of soda.

To all, it seemed like a good start.

Hours later, the entire team cruised at 33,000 feet over the Atlantic Ocean. The private jet was owned by one of the Sentinels charged with establishing the Elves's monetary base on Earth. No one had been certain how long it would be until the Sentinels found the seven, if at all—the Elves knew that the majority of the Sentinels would need to focus their attention on searching for the lords, not making money. Thus a few of the Sentinels? did nothing but accumulate wealth through gold trade, the only real form of money used in Allyra. In this they served the greater good, giving the rest of their team the resources necessary to continue their quest without fear of monetary limitations.

Kat, Jett, and many of the other Elves were sound asleep. Tommy had only flown once before, but he'd never flown over the ocean. But that wasn't why he was awake. No, the sixth bright-yellow soda might have had a little more to do with his alertness. He munched a handful of peanuts and looked around the narrow cabin. He wondered what had happened to the other two Elven Lords, Autumn and Johnny, and their Sentinel. He knew Mrs. Galdarro was afraid that the Drefids had gotten to them first.

What if they did? Tommy wondered anxiously. *What if only five of the seven young lords return to Allyra? Would the Spider King win?*

Tommy felt something strange, a feather's touch, as if someone was staring. He scanned to the right—two of the Sentinels he hadn't met personally peered over the headrests of the seats about eight rows ahead. They quickly looked away and slumped down into their seats. Tommy didn't like that at all. He'd read about those Wisp-things, the shape-shifting mist creatures. He wondered, *What if some had disguised themselves as Sentinels?* . . . Tommy stayed awake the rest of the trans-Atlantic flight. And it wasn't because of the soda.

39

When Darkness Falls

WET AND exhausted, Johnny and Autumn returned from the cave and found their father waiting on the steps of the front porch for them.

"This can't be good," Johnny whispered to Autumn as they neared the barn. The cool October night sent shivers down their arms and legs. The two siblings were reluctant to move out of the shadows, sure they were about to be punished for coming home so late after dark.

"We might as well face it head-on and get it over with," Autumn said. She took a deep breath and tucked the book under her arm. They crossed the yard and moved into the porch light, then up the steps.

"Hey, Dad," Johnny offered up with a smile. "How's it going?"

Mr. Briarman was not enthusiastic. Johnny and Autumn expected the worst. *Grounded. But for how long?*

"Have a seat, kids," Mr. Briarman said.

Johnny and Autumn gulped and walked over to the porch swing. The old wood creaked as they sat down.

"I'm not sure how to put this, but . . ."

Autumn noticed tears in his eyes. *What was wrong?*

". . . Uncle George has passed away."

Mom's brother. The news was not at all what the kids expected, but it wasn't too much of a shock, either. Uncle George had been sick for more than a year, battling cancer. The kids loved their mother's jovial older brother and felt terrible. Every visit from Uncle George came with presents and really cool stories. But more than that, Autumn and

Johnny felt for their mother. For, like the two of them, their mother and Uncle George had always been best friends.

"Your mother and I are leaving in the morning for Denver."

"Us, too, right?" Autumn asked, wiping tears from her cheeks.

"No, sweetie. I'm afraid you have to stay here."

"We what?" replied Johnny.

"Dad, we have to come!"

"I'm sorry, children. But you have to stay here. We just don't have enough money to buy—"

"I'm coming with you," Autumn declared, her lips pursing together and her brow furrowed.

"Now, Autumn—"

"He would want me at the funeral," she added.

"Autumn, we all know he would. But there's just no way we can afford to buy you a ticket on the flight."

"Then we'll drive."

"Then we'd all miss the funeral, Autumn," Johnny said, wiping away his own tears. "Be real."

"You're going to stay here with Aunt Norma," said Mr. Briarman firmly.

"Aunt Norma?" Autumn whined. "But she's so old!"

"She's my sister," Mr. Briarman contested, put off only slightly by the inference.

"She's the same age as Uncle George *is*," Johnny told her. Then realizing his mistake he quietly added, "was."

"In either case, Aunt Norma is going to take care of you while we're gone. We'll be back in four days. You can handle that."

Johnny and Autumn both looked down at the wood planking on the floor and listened to the bugs crash into the porch light above their heads. "I still think I'm supposed to come with you," Autumn said.

Mr. Briarman pushed her over a little to make a place for himself on the swing. The wooden seat protested. The chains stretched. "I know, sweetheart," he said, hoisting Autumn up into his lap.

She suddenly started crying as if a dam had broken in her heart.

"There, there . . ."

She buried her face in his neck and wept, betraying every air of strength she normally carried. Johnny sat hunched over until he felt his dad's arm wrap around his shoulders and give him a squeeze.

When Autumn's tears eventually subsided, Mr. Briarman held her back and looked between the two of them. "Now, you know who really needs your comfort and your prayers right now?"

"Mom?" said Autumn.

"Right. Inside, both of you. She's upstairs, and I'm sure she'd be very grateful if you were by her side."

✳

Johnny and Autumn woke to find their parents long gone and Aunt Norma cooking bacon and eggs.

At least she is a good cook, Autumn thought.

In spite of Aunt Norma's promptings the kids didn't speak much at the breakfast table.

That night, they ate dinner in near silence and decided to watch a made-for-TV movie to get their minds off Uncle George's passing. But the production of the film was poor, and Johnny was annoyed with all the commercials, wishing they had just watched a DVD instead.

When bedtime finally came, Aunt Norma tucked them in, not knowing any of their family's normal evening traditions, which made Johnny and Autumn feel even more uneasy. She said a quick prayer and then flicked off the light in each of their rooms.

It took both children a long time to fall asleep. Everything felt so strange. And it all started when they visited that bookstore yesterday.

Life was normal up until that visit. Meeting Nelly, a book for a gift, the changing title, the trip to the cave, and whatever weird thing happened in there. Then Uncle George dying. It felt almost like a dream. A bad dream. Even Sam was out on one of his adventures, which made the house even quieter without his *tip-tapping* nails and frequent barks. Johnny and Autumn closed their eyes. They each hoped for a peaceful night's sleep and that when they woke up in the morning, everything would be back to normal.

"Johnny!" Autumn whispered urgently as she entered her brother's room. "Johnny, wake up!" She shook her brother's shoulder.

Johnny opened his eyes and propped himself up on an elbow. "What is it, Autumn? I'm sleeping here!"

"Shh! Don't make any noise! Something's wrong!"

Johnny rubbed his eyes. "Autumn, seriously. You're just having a bad dream."

Then they both heard something crash downstairs.

Johnny jumped up. "What was that?"

"I told you!"

Two more crashes, each from different parts of the house. One was the sound of something wooden cracking in the den. The other sounded like an entire drawer of silverware had been thrown to the kitchen floor.

"The phone is downstairs. What are we going to do?" Autumn asked.

"Get under my bed," Johnny ordered. He pressed her head down and forced her beneath, then noticed she was visibly shaking. "It's going to be okay, Autumn. I promise. I'll protect you."

She looked at him, fear and question in her eyes. He strode to his closet and pulled out an aluminum baseball bat.

"What are you going to do?" Autumn asked from underneath the bed.

"I'm going to get these thieves out of our house, that's what." Johnny said.

"Johnny!" she whispered urgently. "What if they have guns?"

"I'll be smart, okay?"

"Please, please be careful." She pleaded.

Johnny walked to the door and cautiously turned the knob. Autumn covered her eyes and scooted farther under the bed. Johnny slipped through the crack and closed the door behind him.

Holding his bat, Johnny tried to keep his nerves under control. His dad had taught him many things on hunting trips in the deep woods, but the one thing that came to mind was how dangerous adrenaline could be. Shaky, unsteady hands were the hunter's nightmare. Johnny couldn't afford a slipup now.

He crept down the stairs avoiding the creaky spots in the floor with each step, and listening. Seconds later, another crash came from the kitchen, followed closely with what sounded like a bookcase falling over in the living room. At least two intruders for sure. Then someone screamed.

"No, get out of our house! Stop now!"

Aunt Norma! Johnny jumped down the last two steps, turned around the banister, and charged down the hallway into the kitchen.

"STOP!" he blurted out, brandishing the bat at . . . *at what?*

There, holding Aunt Norma to the refrigerator door with one hand, stood a large man in a trench coat. He wore a fedora hat and . . . sunglasses. *Sunglasses in the middle of the night?*

The man turned his head to face Johnny. The view Johnny got of the man's surrounding face left him feeling like he was looking at an old man . . . pale, shriveled skin, and wispy white hair. Yet he held Aunt Norma against the fridge—off her feet—with one hand?

"Put her down, NOW! . . . Or I'll crack you with this!"

The voice that spoke back was hoarse and gravelly. It reminded Johnny of Uncle George's cancer-ravaged voice the last time he called. But the voice of this intruder had no trace of kindness. "Are you Albriand, son of Elroth and Tisa?"

Johnny winced at the otherworldly voice. "You got the wrong guy, m-mister." He reared back with the bat. "Now, for the last time, put my aunt down."

Aunt Norma fainted, her body hanging limp against the fridge. The man released his grip, letting her crumple in a heap on the floor, and then started toward Johnny.

"I'm warning you!" Johnny tightened his grip on the bat.

The man cocked his head sideways, glaring at Johnny through the sunglasses. Just then another figure, dressed the same as the first, stepped into the kitchen from the living room. Johnny's eyes shifted between the two, a million questions racing through his head. Now the two men started moving toward him from different directions. They were hemming him in.

"Don't come any closer!"

The first one was now skirting the cutting board island and coming toward him.

Johnny wavered a moment. He'd been in scrapes and fights at school before. But he'd never hit anyone with the intent to kill. He felt like the contents of his stomach had curdled. Sweat rolled down the back of his neck. Everything in his world slowed down. He saw Aunt Norma on the floor. He could imagine Autumn shaking with fear under the bed. And it was then that he made his decision.

40

Nowhere to Hide

WITH BRUTAL force Johnny slammed the bat against the left arm of the first man. The blow sent shivers up Johnny's arm as if he'd just hit a tree.

The man didn't crumple to the ground as Johnny had hoped. He grabbed his upper arm and rubbed it like someone who'd been stung by a bee. Then he held up his pale right fist. His knuckles seemed to bulge, and at first, Johnny didn't realize what was happening. Slowly, four bony blades protruded from the fist.

Johnny took a few steps back . . . right into the other prowler. The intruder wrapped both of his arms around the thirteen-year-old. Johnny struggled, but it was like being bound with cables. Still, he managed to shove the bottom of the bat into the man's abdomen. The man let go for a moment, and Johnny ducked out of his arms . . . just as the other man swung his clawed fist. The blades missed Johnny entirely and slashed the other man's face. His shades and hat flew off. He screeched and doubled over.

When the man stood erect once more, Johnny gaped in horror at what he saw. The man had a skullish face, sallow skin, wild white hair, and eyes like white points of fire in huge black sockets. Three gashes marred his face, and luminous purple blood dribbled freely down his nose and chin. He roared at the other and turned back to Johnny.

Johnny spun around and bolted for the stairwell. His mind

whirled as he bounded up the steps. *Drefids, like in the book! But here? Now? It can't be!*

Wiping purple blood from his eyes and face, the wounded Drefid strode out of the kitchen. The other, flexing his left arm as he walked, followed as fast as he could. By the time they reached the stairs, both Drefids had their claws extended.

At the top of the stairs, Johnny twisted around the corner and yelled, "Autumn, get out! Through the window! NOW!"

Johnny clutched the bat and looked back down the stairs. It was just in time to see the first Drefid leap. The creature seemed to float up—seven, eight, nine steps, at least—and landed near the top. He put a clawed hand on the balustrade. Johnny moved fast and whipped the bat down as if he were chopping wood with an axe. The blow crushed one of the Drefid's bony blades, and the creature expelled a shriek that rang in Johnny's ears. He didn't wait around for the creature to recover but raced to the end of the hall. Johnny burst through his bedroom door, closed it, and twisted the lock. Autumn was already lifting the window open. "Johnny, what's going on?" she asked, her voice tense. "I heard some kind of growl or scream . . . what—"

"Just get out the window!" Johnny looked to the bedroom door. "We'll walk the roof and climb down the old maple!" It was an act they had performed a hundred times. Johnny walked backward from the door and kept the bat on his shoulder.

"What about Aunt Norma?"

There was a heavy thud against the door. Autumn screamed.

Another strike, this time rattling the hinges. Johnny yelled, "Autumn, GO!!"

A third blow and the wood split. Four razor-sharp bones punctured the door, and a gnarled, bony fist broke through. Autumn trembled so severely she could hardly get herself through the window.

Another fist burst through the door, extended the same kind of knives from its knuckles, and then curled around the rest of the wood, ready to rip the door apart.

Johnny dropped the bat and ran toward Autumn. "Go, go, go!"

Autumn jumped out the window and Johnny slid out after her, feet first. But he moved too fast and knocked into her. Autumn lost her balance and fell sideways. Johnny reached out, but it was too late. Autumn cleared the edge of the roof and sailed into midair. She let out one final scream.

"Autumn!"

"I have her!" came a voice from below.

Johnny clambered to the edge and stared down in disbelief. *How . . . ?*

"From the bookstore?" Autumn asked, staring up at the woman who'd caught her. "I—I—don't—"

"No need to understand it all right now," Nelly replied, setting Autumn down. "Come on, Johnny. You next."

"But I'm too big. You won't—?"

A crash echoed in Johnny's room. The creatures were in.

"Now, Johnny!"

He leaped from the roof, grabbed the thick bough of the maple trees, and dropped. With surprising strength Nelly caught him and set him on the ground. "Both of you, into the SUV," she said, pointing to the vehicle idling in the driveway. "And whatever you do, don't come out."

"What?" Autumn exclaimed. "You're not going in there, are you?"

Johnny stood in front of the bookstore owner. "Just call the police!" he said. "Call an ambulance. My aunt's hurt, and those things—"

"The Drefids are dangerous," Nelly agreed. "But so am I. Now, get in."

Brother and sister obeyed, and both peered over the backseat as

Nelly walked around to the back and opened the hatch. She retrieved what looked to be a long, thin sword in a sheath.

"You have a sword?" Johnny blurted out.

"No questions," said Nelly, lowering the hatch. "Answers later. Lock the door!"

"Did she just grab a sword?" Johnny asked, face glued to the SUV window.

"I think so," replied Autumn, still in shock. They watched Nelly bolt into their home.

Seconds later, Johnny's bedroom window—glass, frame, and all—exploded in a flare of blue flame. The Drefids, hair wild and eyes full of fury, appeared in the gaping hole and began to clamber out onto the roof. One was out, but the other seemed stuck. Suddenly, he fell backward and disappeared into Johnny's room. The remaining Drefid turned and, with a shriek, dove back into the house as well.

"What just happened?" asked Autumn.

"Uh—" Before Johnny could finish, there was a tremendous crash from within. Even through the SUV's window, Johnny and Autumn heard sounds of ringing metal, the crack of timber, and anything that could break . . . breaking. They heard shouts in some unrecognizable language, and then grunts, followed by the most horrific screams either of the two children had ever heard.

Autumn squinted. "There's not as much noise."

Yeah, by half, thought Johnny.

Two bodies locked in a struggle appeared in the gap where the window had been. In another instant, they were gone, back inside the room and out of sight. More clashing of weapons, a final yell, and then a scream that faded away into eerie silence.

"Is it over?" asked Autumn.

No sooner had she asked than a figure appeared on the front

porch. It was Nelly. She no longer carried her sword, but cradled Aunt Norma in her arms.

Nelly strode around the SUV and opened the front door. "You kids all right?" Both just nodded.

"What about Aunt Norma?" Johnny asked.

Nelly gently laid Aunt Norma in the front passenger seat, leaned it back, and fastened the seat belt. "I think your aunt will be fine," Nelly said. "Still, I think it's best that we take her to the hospital. In any case, I'm not going to leave her in your house."

Nelly shut the door, ran around to her side, and got in the driver's seat. She started the SUV and then fished around in her coat pocket. She pulled something out and growled, "Blasted Drefid trashed my cell phone." She banged a fist on her steering wheel. "Just when I needed wisdom."

"What?" Autumn asked. "What's wrong?"

"Everything! But nothing we can help now," Nelly replied, putting the car in drive. She did a tight U-turn in their lawn, heading back for the road.

The two siblings were at a loss, their minds blank one moment and then tornadic the next. They drove in tense silence for several minutes. Autumn spoke first. "Those . . . creatures, they're the ones in the book, aren't they?"

Nelly nodded.

"Drefids," Johnny muttered.

"Yes," Nelly whispered.

Autumn folded her hands and glanced out of the window. Streetlights went intermittently by. "It's not an accident that you gave us the book and then the Drefids came to our house . . . is it?"

"No," Nelly replied. "They were hunting you."

"Hunting us?!" Johnny exclaimed. "Why? What did we ever do to them?"

Nelly laughed sadly. "It's nothing you've done . . . but something they are afraid you will do." Nelly looked in the rearview mirror and saw the confusion on their faces. "Ah, now see," she muttered as much to herself as to the kids. "All this I would have explained to you when you came back to my shop."

A bright orange glow appeared in the distance off to the right. Many flashing lights, too. Johnny leaned forward. "A fire!"

Nelly was silent. She crept along in traffic, passing fire engines and police cars. In spite of the firemen's best efforts, flames engulfed one of the buildings on the right. Autumn had to squint because the fire was so bright, but she recognized the shape of the store. She leaned forward, "Nelly, your bookstore!"

"What happened?" Johnny asked.

"The Drefids attacked me . . . six of them. They wanted to keep me from coming to your aid."

"Six?" Autumn swallowed. "You beat them all?"

"Barely," she replied with a deep sigh. "They used arc stones . . . to burn me, but they underestimated how the books would burn. I escaped through the back door and locked them in with the security doors. A few escaped, but I took them out. That was when I raced to—"

"Uh, . . ." Aunt Norma blinked at the flashing lights.

"Aunt Norma!!" Johnny and Autumn cried. "You're all better!"

"Not quite all better," she said, smiling weakly and looking around. "Are you okay?"

"We're all fine."

She looked at the driver. "Who are you?"

"Annelle Brookeheart, but call me Nelly."

"Nelly," Aunt Norma repeated. She put a hand on Nelly's forearm and looked on her kindly. "You're the one who fought those . . . things and rescued us." She coughed harshly, turned her head, and started to close her eyes. "Thank you. Thank you."

"We're taking you to the hospital," Nelly said. "We want a doctor to see you."

"I won't argue." Aunt Norma whispered so low the kids in the back could barely hear her. "Please, Nelly, take care of Johnny and Autumn."

"I will," said Nelly.

�֍

After getting Aunt Norma admitted to the hospital and making sure she was okay, Nelly tried making a call on a pay phone. She tried three times. "I don't understand," she said to the kids. "I can't reach any of them."

"Any of who?" asked Autumn.

"It's a long story," said Nelly.

"This the stuff you were talking about?" asked Johnny. "The stuff you would have told us if we could have come to your shop again?"

"Yes," she replied. The moment she answered, she had Johnny and Autumn making a scene, begging her to explain. "We have a bit of a drive ahead of us," Nelly said. "That will give us time."

41

Kinship

AT 3:00 a.m. the private jet carrying the Sentinels, Dreadnaughts, and the three young lords touched down at Edinburgh Airport. After a short bus ride to Dalhousie Castle, and a brief introduction of Jimmy to the rest of the Elves who had gathered in Scotland, the four young lords had been escorted to their chambers while Mrs. Galdarro and a handful of the senior Elves met with Edward to plan for the day to come.

"Are you tired?" asked Kat. She lay in the dark in a tall bed in between Anna's bed and two Sentinels she'd come to know as Ril and Lexi.

"I'm exhausted," Anna replied. "But you already knew that, didn't you?"

"Not this time." Kat laughed.

Ril sat up in her bed. "Can you read minds all the time, then?"

"It was off and on at first," Kat said. "But it seems to be getting stronger. I still have to try . . . have to concentrate."

"Does it have a range?" came Lexi's muffled question, her chin resting deep in a pillow. "Or can you just think of someone wherever they are and hear their thoughts?"

Kat scratched her head. "The farthest I've ever been was about thirty yards."

"Still, that would be quite an advantage in battle," said Ril.

"Battle," Kat repeated. She'd played many battle-oriented computer and TV games, but she couldn't imagine physically engaging and trying to kill an enemy hand-to-hand. The very thought of it soured in her stomach. "When we get into the Elf world—"

"Allyra," said Anna.

"Allyra . . . when we get there, are you going to teach us how to fight?"

"Grimwarden will take you to Whitehall," the Dreadnaught replied. "There you will learn many things: weapon-craft, combat technique, and most important how to use your powers in concert with the other young lords."

Kat was quiet a moment. She wasn't really used to working together with others. Mostly, when it came to friendships, she'd found herself on the outside looking in. "When will the other girls get here?"

"Kiri Lee will be here Thursday," said Lexi. "She's staying at the Royal Palace in Edinburgh."

"We saw her yesterday," said Ril. "She's quite extraordinary. Walks on the wind."

"Is she pretty?" asked Kat.

An awkward silence followed. Lexi turned on a bedside lamp. "Kiri Lee has silky, dark hair; huge, brown eyes; and a perfect complexion. She is stunning."

"Great," Kat replied.

There, Anna felt she needed to speak up. "Kat, you've no doubt been wounded by very mean and shallow people . . . people who don't realize how beautiful differences are. In Allyra you don't need to worry about such things. You know, we have a saying in our home world: 'Ellos cares not for garments, flesh, or any outward thing. Ellos cares for the heart.'"

"Ellos?"

"It is our favorite name for God," said Ril.

"Oh," Kat replied. She pondered that a moment. "I guess I understand what you're saying, but living on earth . . . things are different.

Guys don't even look at me except to make jokes. And now, it's just that . . . well . . ."

"What?" asked Anna.

"Do you think Tommy's cute?"

Anna and the two Sentinels laughed. "I see now," said Anna. "And yes, Tommy is very handsome."

"You have to love that curly hair," said Lexi.

"Great smile," said Ril. "Of course, Jett is quite the charmer, too."

"Don't forget Jimmy," said Lexi. "He's a romantic, I can just tell."

Kat burst into fits of laughter. The others joined in.

"I'm so embarrassed," said Kat. "I can't believe we're in here talking about the guys."

"Don't worry about it, Kat," said Anna. "The boys are probably talking about the same kinds of things."

"How much blood was there?" asked Jimmy.

"It was coming out of my mouth and nose," said Jett. "And the paramedics said a broken bone in my leg stuck right out of the skin."

"Cool!" said Tommy and Jimmy simultaneously.

Tommy shook his head. "Man-n-n, I wish my parents would let me ride a motorcycle."

"Yu got to ride in a helicopter, too?"

Jett nodded. "A medivac helicopter, but not exactly the way I wanted to do it. I was in a lot of pain."

"Gentlemen," said Mr. Spero, "I think you've heard enough about Jett's bike accident. You'd better get some sleep before the sun comes up."

They all lay quiet in their dark chamber for some time. Then Tommy asked, "What do you think the girls are talking about?"

"I dunno," Jimmy replied.

"Beats me," said Jett.

✴

The next morning, some two hundred twenty-one Elves (including a few Sentinels and Dreadnaughts who had arrived just before sunup) met for breakfast in the castle's cavernous dining hall. There had been no word concerning Nelly and the Briarmans. Kiri Lee wouldn't arrive until later that afternoon. But the four young lords who sat together at the end of a long table looked to have been in the castle since medieval times.

"Yu should have seen 'im," said Jimmy, half-choked with laughter. "Straight away into the ketchup, mustard, and tartar sauce. Looked like he lost a paintball fight, he did."

"Sounds like he had it coming," said Jett.

Tommy nodded. He'd seen his share of bullies, but his growth spurt between sixth and seventh grade had mostly solved that problem. Tommy stretched to see around Mr. Charlie and a few of the other Elves. *Where is that server?* he wondered. *I'm starving.*

"I'm curious about our special gifts," said Jett. "Kat, you read minds; Jimmy, you can see the future—"

"Just scenes so far," Jimmy clarified. "And not always when I want to."

Kat piped up: "Same with me."

"Okay," said Jett. "I've got strength and healing, Tommy's an expert archer, and this Kiri Lee kid, she can fly?"

"Walk on air, I heard," said Jimmy.

"She walks on air?" Tommy grinned. "How cool is that?"

Too cool, thought Kat, but she said nothing.

Jimmy asked, "Anyone know what the others can do, Autumn and . . . Jerry?"

315

"I think it's Johnny," said Jett. "No idea what they can do."

"Mrs. Galdarro said their powers haven't developed yet," said Tommy.

"I hope they're okay," said Kat. The rest nodded.

At last, the server arrived at their table. Tommy was just about to give his order when Jett interrupted. "Wait, Tommy," he said. "I want to try something." The rest of the table went quiet. "Kat can read minds, and Jimmy can see the future. Let's see who can figure out first what Tommy's gonna order for breakfast. Cool?"

Kat shrugged. Jimmy said, "Okay, but no guarantees, you know."

The Elven server looked at Tommy expectantly. Tommy started to speak, but Kat interrupted. "Western omelet and home fries," she said.

Tommy looked at her with a kind of curious amazement. He smiled and started to order, but this time it was Jimmy who interrupted. "No, he's not going to order that. He's going to get the sausage sandwich on a croissant with DOUBLE home fries."

"Is that true?" Jett asked, comically turning from Tommy to Jimmy and back again.

Tommy nodded. "As Jimmy would say, 'spot on!'"

Kat frowned. "But that's not what you were thinking at first," she complained. "You just changed it because I was right."

Tommy smiled at her. "Um . . . under the circumstances, I guess there's no point in denying it."

"Will you be having the sausage sandwich and the double hash browns, then?" asked the server.

"And the omelet," said Tommy. "I'm starved."

"I knew that!" said Kat.

"Oh, stop!" Jett laughed.

After they placed their orders, Jett smacked both of his hands down on the tabletop so hard that half the dining hall turned and stared. "Uh . . . sorry!" he said. But then he lowered his head conspiratorially and whispered to the other three, "I just realized . . . it's a Thursday. We're missing school!"

The four of them exchanged somewhat guilty glances—which turned almost immediately to wry smiles and then full belly laughs. Their laughter went on through the morning meal, especially when they saw how much food Jett ordered.

"And I thought I was eating too much," said Tommy.

"What?" Jett feigned innocence. "Doesn't everyone eat four stacks of pancakes, a half pound of bacon, quadruple home fries, and a whole cantaloupe?"

Breakfast went on like that until Mrs. Galdarro's cell phone chirped.

Everyone in the hall went silent and turned to their leader.

"Galdarro," she answered. She smiled as she listened to the reply. After a few moments and nods of the head, she announced, "It's Nelly! And she has Autumn and Johnny safe!"

A great cheer went up from the room and persisted until Mrs. Galdarro shushed them. Her smile was replaced with a thin-lipped frown, and her eyes narrowed. She spoke quietly, shook her head, and ended the call with, "No, we're waiting for you."

Mr. Charlie went to her when she closed the phone. The young lords were right behind. "What's wrong, Elle?" Mr. Charlie asked.

"No, it's nothing wrong, really," she replied. "Nelly thinks we should leave now, told me she and the Briarmans would come when their flight gets in at ten."

"But we don't even have Kiri Lee yet," said Mr. Charlie. "And she doesn't even know what she is."

"That's what I tried to explain to Nelly. It's better we wait and go together. Strength in numbers."

"I think you're right," said Mr. Charlie.

Mrs. Galdarro tried to smile through her worry. "We will wait for Nelly and her two wards. Looks like Kiri Lee will be able to perform her concert after all. Edward will be pleased. Would you be so kind as to spread the word?"

"Yes, ma'am."

"Oh, and Charlie, one more thing. The enemy has left one portal open. They must be near, must be planning something."

"I don't doubt it," Mr. Charlie said. "We've got two hundred strong Elf warriors here. And since Monday, Edward's had Sentinels patrolling the grounds, all 'round the perimeter, I think. But I'll tell 'em all to stay alert."

"Good, very good," she said, nodding. "I lost the lords once to the Spider King. I don't intend to lose them again."

�֍

Tommy found Kat leaning on a wall atop the castle's main gatehouse and staring downward. "What are you looking at?" he asked.

Kat flinched a little. "Oh, I didn't hear you coming."

"Sorry," said Tommy, joining her at the wall. "So what's to see?"

"Um, nothing really."

"Hey, is that the new girl?" Tommy asked, looking down at a sleek limousine. The chauffeur held the door for an older woman and a raven-haired young lady carrying an instrument case.

"I think so," said Kat, feigning disinterest. They both watched in silence as the new arrival entered the castle.

"There you are," came a voice from behind. Tommy and Kat turned and found Jimmy and Jett standing there, looking suspicious.

"We looked fer yu everywhere," said Jimmy.

"Yeah," Jett said. "We need to talk."

42

Crescendo

EDWARD, DRESSED immaculately as always, came bounding down the stairs. "Ready to visit the roons?" he asked, his voice every bit as sprightly and vivacious as the spring in his step.

"Yes, very much so," said Kiri Lee.

"I should say she is," said Mrs. Sherman. "She's done nothing but talk about it all morning."

"Well then, let us not delay another moment," said Edward.

"What's that?" Kiri Lee asked, pointing to a leather satchel under Edward's arm.

"Oh," he said, "something fer later on. Shall we?" He held out an arm and Kiri Lee slipped hers through it.

Just then, a tall, blond woman, dressed in a neat, gray business suit approached. "Hullo, Edward," she said. "Is this Claudia Sherman?"

Mrs. Sherman replied, "It certainly is."

"Ah, Mrs. Sherman," said Edward. "Allow me to introduce Rachel Tanner. She's head of public relations for Dalhousie."

"Yes," said Rachel. "I was wondering, Mrs. Sherman, if I might have a few minutes of your time. We've been looking forward to a visit from the governor for some time. As you may recall, last February, Major General McDowell himself expressed a desire to stay with us. I was hoping we could put that in stone today."

Mrs. Sherman smiled. "Well, I . . . I didn't bring my appointment books, but"—she fished around in her purse—"a BlackBerry will

319

serve, I think. Edward, would you mind terribly if I skipped the ruins? My ankle's been giving me some trouble anyway."

"No, think nothing of it," said Edward. "And rest assured, I will take good care of Miss Yuen."

✳

"What's this about?" asked Tommy. The four young lords sat atop the gatehouse.

Jett looked at Jimmy, neither one sure who was to start. "Yu know what we've gotten mixed up in, don't yu? Yu've read the book, right?"

Tommy and Kat nodded.

"Look," said Jett, "traveling by plane always seemed kind of weird to me, right? Before you leave there's snow on the ground. A few hours later, you're on a beach. Well, we're about to leave our *world*. Imagine what that's going to be like."

"You're having second thoughts?" said Kat.

"Not exactly," Jett said, relieved that Kat apparently was not reading his mind at this moment. "I know what we're getting into. I've fought Drefids and seen the dark trees. My parents did, too. They gave me permission to go, and they know why I'm going. And Jimmy here . . . he knows what—"

Jimmy put a hand on Jett's forearm. "I'll speak for meself, if yu don't mind. I'll tell yu, Tommy . . . Kat, I've got nothin' to lose here. I grew up in an orphanage. Misery, it was. Finally, I got a home, only to lose it when me adopted parents had a *real* son of their own. Probably the only two people in this world who cared about me turned out to be Elves . . . and I'm goin' where they're goin'. It's that simple."

Tommy glanced at Kat. Maybe she knew where Jimmy and Jett were going with this, but he sure didn't.

"So, we're in," said Jett. "But you two have families, and they don't

320

really know what's going on, do they?"

Kat blinked back tears. She'd struggled with her parents for a long time, ever since the *poly*. But she loved them. And now, she was abandoning them. Kat cringed, remembering how she'd brushed her mother off the last time she saw her.

"Do they?" Jett asked again.

"Mrs. Galdarro left a special note . . . a scroll behind," said Tommy.

"So did Anna," said Kat.

"Uh-huh," said Jett, taking charge. "What Jimmy and I need to know, what the Sentinels need to know is . . . are *you* having second thoughts?"

"You might not know this," said Tommy. "But I've experienced the Drefids, too. And while I don't exactly know if I'm ready for all this, I'm going. The Spider King wants to kill a whole race—our race. And who knows if they'll stop there. It'd be like having a chance to stop Hitler, but chickening out. I couldn't live with that. I'm going, . . . even though I'm afraid."

"Good," said Jett, nodding approval. "I like that. That's what heroes really are, right? They can be scared out of their mind, but still do the hard thing anyway. Looks like, ready or not, we're on our way to another world."

They stood up and went their separate ways for the rest of that afternoon. Kat was grateful that Tommy had satisfied Jett's and Jimmy's curiosity. She was incredibly relieved that Jett hadn't asked her again if she was having second thoughts. She would have hated to lie.

After a glorious walk across the oceanic green lawns on the castle grounds, Edward led Kiri Lee down into a wooded hollow. A well-defined path began its serpentine journey to the ruins.

"What exactly are these the ruins of?" asked Kiri Lee as they walked.

"A castle," he replied. "An outpost, really. It was built in 1712 by Jacobite Highlanders, led by Lord Drummond. They attempted an overthrow of Edinburgh Castle in 1715. They ultimately failed, and what with Dalhousie Castle so close, the old Highlander outpost fell into disrepair. Remarkable place really. Full of tunnels and mysterious staircases."

It was only a few minutes walk through the trees when they came to a tall, freestanding stone arch right at the wood's edge. "This," said Edward, leading Kiri Lee under the arch, "was the old entrance to the garrison. It used to have a tall, thatched roof through here. Of course, that's all gone now."

Kiri Lee found herself enraptured, touching the ancient stonework and listening to Edward's tales. He seemed to know so much about the history of each piece of stone. They traveled into dark halls where light invaded only from little, round windows high above. They hopped over hunks of stone and even walked across the lower walls. Kiri Lee continued to be amazed by Edward's strength and endurance. "I hope I'm in as good of shape as you when I'm your age," Kiri Lee said. "Oh, I'm sorry, I didn't mean to imply—"

Edward raised his hand. "Think nothing of it, me dear. I am quite old. But I come from a very strong bloodline. As do yu."

"What?"

"Nothing, Miss Yuen. Oh, here we are. It's just 'cross this bridge." He motioned, and Kiri Lee followed him across a bridge that connected two large, squarish stone buildings. On the other side, a narrow stair broke off from the bridge and led down beneath it.

"What are we going to see?" asked Kiri Lee.

"My favorite part of the roons," he said. Beneath the bridge, a long tunnel lit with intermittent porthole-size windows stretched far into the heart of one of the large, stone buildings. They came to the end of the tunnel, and that's just what it was, the end. There was no door or corner to turn. Just a solid stone wall.

There was, however, a pile of stones—some very large, some quite small. Edward gestured for Kiri Lee to sit. She did. The stone was cold, but not uncomfortably so. "Um . . . I guess I don't get it," said Kiri Lee. "What are we looking at?"

Edward laughed. "That's just it, isn't it?" he asked. "Not very impressive at first glance. But doesn't it seem odd that this tunnel would lead to a dead end?" Kiri Lee nodded. "Agreed," Edward went on. "One might wonder if the seeming dead end actually hides something of great worth . . . a treasure perhaps . . . or a secret passage."

Edward bent down, picked up a softball-sized stone, and tossed it at the blank wall.

Kiri Lee gasped.

The stone hit the wall, and the wall stretched away. There was a momentary bluish sparkle, and the stone vanished.

"What?" Kiri Lee exclaimed. "What happened? Where'd the rock go?"

"An excellent question," said Edward. "What yu just saw suspends reality as yu've always known it. And that is difficult to accept. . . . Kiri Lee, have you experienced anything else lately that yu thought was beyond reality?"

For a moment, Kiri Lee felt afraid. She didn't really know this Edward person at all. They were alone in a tunnel with no one else around for hundreds of yards. She stared at the leather satchel. For all she knew, Edward could be one of those mist creatures. He could have a knife in the case . . . or a gun or . . .

Edward put the satchel in his lap and unlatched it. Kiri Lee involuntarily jerked backward into the stone wall of the tunnel. But when Edward reached into the case and pulled out a book, she felt not only relieved but strangely at peace.

�֍

"They aren't leaving, are they?" The gravelly whisper came from beneath a hooded cloak. Two dark figures stood behind a tall, thorny bush and what was left of a chamber wall just forty yards from the bridge in the ruins.

"So what if they are, Lorex?" said the other. "We know what they'll find on the other side."

"Still. . . . Mobius, if somehow they crossed over and were able to return with news—"

"They would never return to tell the tale," said Mobius. "I've planned this down to the last detail. But we must be wary that others do not come sooner than expected, like these two."

"If they do?" asked Lorex.

"Kill them."

The two Drefids hissed and ducked down, just as the old man and the girl emerged from the tunnel.

✖

Edward took Kiri Lee back to Dalhousie Castle and showed her to a private chamber to warm up. She picked up the violin on the stand. It was a Baroque violin. It looked like a Martelle . . . very old and very expensive. She tucked it beneath her chin and began to play. The arpeggios, individual notes played not together as a chord but one after the other, flowed smoothly right into the beautiful Mozart sonata, the first movement of the piece she would play for the private concert that evening. As her instincts took over, she began to play without thinking of the notes. It all simply came, and in the melodies she began to hear hints of that otherworldly music that made her heart soar. And now, now she knew where the music came from: Allyra, her real home.

As the music enveloped Kiri Lee, her mind roamed freely to the earthshaking conversation she'd had with Edward at the ruins. At first she'd thought Edward had lost his mind. But he knew so much and guessed even more. He knew that she could walk on the wind; he knew that she was afraid to go home; he knew that she'd seen horrible, frightening things. He even put a name to them: Wisps. Edward guessed that the Wisps had driven her to flee to Edinburgh early, that she had no idea what she would do after the Royal Festival. Well, that was all settled now. Edward had given her a book, too, a very special book. It was the beginning of her life story and a history of her people.

Elven people, Kiri Lee thought with a smile. The notes came fast and furious now as she progressed into the minuet. Edward suggesting that she was an Elf Lord from another world was nothing short of insane. But given the events of the past week . . . given her new-found ability . . . given the strange portal in the ruins . . . and given the scars on the tops of her ears, Kiri Lee had no reason not to believe it. But it was more than what she'd seen with her eyes. Something deep within her testified that it all was true, that it belonged to her, and she belonged to it. Something about the news Edward had shared with her agreed with the music. It struck the perfect tuning fork that resonated in a place within her that Kiri Lee could not ignore.

As her fingering accelerated for the *rondo* at the end, her thoughts continued to wander in a kind of peaceful, meditative state. Kiri Lee couldn't wait for the impromptu concert with Edward's group to begin. It wouldn't be quite as exciting as playing for the royal family at the palace. Missing the festival concert was one small regret, a small ache from her old life. But Kiri Lee wouldn't dwell on such things. With no fear at all, she thought, *This will be the last time I ever play . . . on Earth.*

✶

The sun had gone down. It was a perfectly clear night—unusual in Edinburgh this time of year. The lights outside of Dalhousie Castle bathed its great barrel-turret and its walls in shimmering white. Lights shone on the temporary stage used for weddings. In front of it was a myriad of folding chairs, and every chair was full. Elves and humans chatted politely, the latter completely unaware that they were talking to beings from another world.

At last, the performers took the stage. Since Kiri Lee would play violin, Edward kept his spot playing the cello. His good friend Chuck Rogers and Chuck's brother Bob manned the double bass and the viola. The audience lights dimmed and went out, and the concert under the stars and moon was ready to begin. Everyone clapped, and the quartet wasted no time. Music filled the night.

Mrs. Galdarro sat between Kat and Tommy in one of the back rows; Jimmy and Jett, along with their Sentinels and Dreadnaughts, spread out in the rest of the row. With close to three hundred Elves—Sentinels, Dreadnaughts, flet soldiers, and the teens—the audience was much larger than usual for Edward's concerts. So he had the staff put hundreds of extra chairs in front of the portable stage. Mrs. Galdarro was content. Things had gone exceedingly well. Kiri Lee had accepted the news of her Elven heritage better than most of the others. Nelly and the Briarmans were safe and would arrive at the castle in a few hours. Elle Galdarro sighed. Soon they would all return to Allyra.

Mrs. Galdarro looked off to the side in the direction of the road. She could not see them, but she knew Sentinels and Dreadnaughts were out there, patrolling the grounds. It was a comforting thought. Then she turned the other way and looked toward the forest and the ruins. Through the trees, she thought she could see the moon shining on a piece of white stone. The portal was there. She'd often wondered what they would find when they returned to their homeland. After all, hundreds of years had passed in Allyra. But the very fact that the Spider King still felt threatened enough by the young lords that he would send his assassins after them on Earth—that meant that the surviving remnant of the Elves must still be alive. Perhaps they were all still safe in the Nightwish Caverns.

"She's amazing," whispered Tommy. "I've never heard a violin played like that."

"Kiri Lee is one of a kind," Mrs. Galdarro replied. "As are all of you."

Kat glanced sideways at Tommy, but she didn't focus. She didn't want to know any more of what he was thinking about.

The moon was high in the sky as the quartet began the third movement. Even though Nelly wasn't due to arrive for an hour still, Mrs. Galdarro found herself looking often to the winding driveway leading away from Dalhousie Castle's parking lot. She wouldn't feel at ease until she saw Nelly coming down that road.

For now, she tried to get lost in the music. But as good as the quartet was, Mrs. Galdarro couldn't immerse herself the way she wanted to. Elves and humans sat here in the audience . . . but did Wisps as well? Had Drefids somehow penetrated the Elven defenses? Were they lurking now in the woods surrounding them? She had a bad feeling about the whole thing; their entire operation was so fragile—so precarious—even one wrong note from the quartet on stage seemed like it might wreck it all.

She shuddered to think what would happen if the Drefids also managed to shut this last portal. Hundreds of Elves, including the young lords, would be trapped in a world that was not their own. But that got Mrs. Galdarro to thinking. To trap them on Earth forever, the Spider King would need to close the portals forever . . . giving up the ability to raid the Earth for slaves forever. *Would he do that?* she wondered. Perhaps there were other worlds he could travel to—but if Sarron Froth was to be believed, the Spider King had yet to find any other realm where serviceable slaves could be harvested.

Still . . . something didn't feel right—the portals closing . . . everyone here in one place at one time. Was it truly just circumstances that started this all?

The music reached its furious *crescendo,* and Mrs. Galdarro's thoughts raced with it. She looked at the beautiful, innocent faces of the young lords: Tommy, Kat, Jimmy, and Jett. And Kiri Lee up on stage. So much promise. So much power.

Tangible cold like a blade of ice slid down the Sentinel's back. She sat up straight and looked toward the road once more. No headlights. She looked back in the direction of the ruins. It didn't make sense. *The Spider King wanted the young lords dead, not just trapped on Earth. . . .*

Then it all clicked.

"No!" she gasped. "He left the one portal open on purpose . . . as bait! To draw us all here, get us together in one place so he could—"

A blue flash. An explosion.

Screams.

Too late.

An arc stone had landed near the front row. Mrs. Galdarro had no time to determine the damage, for more arc stones fell from the sky. Explosions rocked the area. She looked up to see darkness closing in on their flanks . . . Cragon trees from two directions.

To make matters even worse, she heard the terrible *scree* of Warspiders.

Elves and people ran in all directions, chairs toppling over by the dozen. Several of the Elves began to shepherd humans to the castle, to the parking lot—any place away from the attack

"Mrs. Galdarro!" Tommy yelled. "What's going on?"

"It is a trap, Tommy! The enemy is here!" She turned. "Charlie!"

"Right here!" said Mr. Charlie, appearing behind their row. "And I brought my tools."

⚹

"Kiri Lee!" Edward shouted. She had fallen to the stage at the first explosion. He knelt by her. "Kiri Lee, are yu hurt?"

She rose to one knee. The violin had been crushed beneath her, and her beautiful, new white dress was spotted with soil and ash. "No, I don't think so . . . what—?"

"No time, lass! No time!" he shouted. He picked her up and carried her off the stage . . . just as it exploded in a flash of blue light.

They fell into a section of chairs and tumbled to the grass. Edward rolled to a crouch and surveyed the scene; Kiri Lee stayed low beside him.

The enemy attacked from all sides, arc rifles firing, battle-axes and swords swinging. "Ellos, have mercy," Edward said, losing his Scottish accent. He helped Kiri Lee back to her feet. "They're everywhere."

We're going to need weapons, he thought, quickly scanning the area. *And much more than Charlie has in his beloved bag of tools.* "Kiri Lee, come with me, now! If something happens to me, I want you to steal away on the wind so that they will never find you."

⚹

Firelight glistened off the many eyes of a massive Warspider as it crashed into the midst of the crowd fleeing their seats. The creature turned its gaze to Tommy . . . a mistake.

In ten seconds, Tommy fired three arrows, instantly blinding three of its eyes.

Just then, Jimmy—pale with dread—yelled over to Tommy, "Look out!" But he was too far away to do anything about the frightening vision he had just seen in his mind.

The giant spider shrieked hideously, turned around, and lifted its huge abdomen. Like a silken spear, a strand of web shot out for Tommy . . . but Mrs. Galdarro guessed rightly from Jimmy's warning and made quick work of the projectile with her sword. Tommy rolled, rose to one knee, and drew back the bowstring all the way to his ear. He let the arrow fly, sending the shaft deep into the creature's spinnerets.

"That had to hurt!" yelled Jett.

"No kidding," Tommy added, and then looked to Jimmy and Mrs. Galdarro. "Thanks, guys!"

The Warspider screeched and began to quiver and buck. Its Gwar rider fell awkwardly to the turf, where a tuxedo-clad Sentinel stole its axe and finished off both mount and rider.

"We must get to the portal, now!" bellowed Mrs. Galdarro. "Run to the ruins!"

Mr. Wallace, Anna, Mr. Spero, Mrs. Galdarro, Mr. Charlie, Regis, and Miss Finney all formed a perimeter around the four young lords, and they ran toward the ruins.

"What am I supposed to do?" Kat yelled, ducking at the sound of a nearby explosion. "I don't know how to fight. I can't use—"

"Here!" Mr. Charlie put a short sword in her hand. "If a Gwar gets in your way, cut his legs first. Then finish him, chest or head. If there's a Drefid, you let me handle him."

"I definitely will!" said Kat, trying to keep up, fumbling with the sword.

Charlie lowered his shield, pushed ahead of them, and charged straight into three Gwar warriors. They all tumbled to the ground, but Charlie was up first. His shield rose and fell three times. In a flash, he tossed the dead Gwars' weapons to the Sentinels. For a time, they were able to push back the enemy and keep the young lords safe. They had put down a dozen Gwar and two Drefids as they raced across the wide lawn toward the woods.

But as they left the concert area another hundred yards behind them, the Elves realized how deluded they'd been to think they could escape to the portal so unhindered.

Mr. Spero exclaimed, "Wait! Where are Kiri Lee and Edward?"

But none of them replied. They were riveted to something ahead. The moon, now half-covered by shreds of cloud, cast a weak light on a dark mass moving across the field toward them . . . a *huge* mass like a mountain of shadow. "I don't like this," said Mr. Wallace.

"Nor I," Anna agreed.

"Stop! Wait!" bellowed Mr. Charlie as he forced the group to slow.

The Elves pulled up short. Fanning out around them were Warspiders, driven by Drefids, and Cragon trees. They were surrounded.

Just then, Jimmy doubled over. "Oh, this is not good!" He pressed his fingers to his temples, a horrific vision passing before him.

"They're going to kill us," said Kat.

Tommy hefted his bow and looked to his new friend. "Are you reading their minds? Is that what they're thinking?"

"No," Kat replied. "That's what I'm thinking."

43

Help from Above

A JAGGED blade tore through the hem at the bottom of Kiri Lee's dress. "Aah, it's behind me!" she cried. "Edward, help!"

The Gwar snarled and lunged again for the young lord. Kiri took one step, leaped up, and the sword missed, slashing beneath her. But Kiri Lee didn't stop. Three, four, five steps up, and now she ran on the air ten feet above her enemy.

Riveted to his prey and shocked at her impossible escape, the Gwar didn't see Edward coming. Being more than sixteen hundred years old, the elder Sentinel was no longer as strong as some, but he more than made up for it with experience.

Edward pivoted and ducked under Kiri Lee as she went up. Then he exploded forward, pushing with his legs while at the same time rotating his upper body to violently drive his elbow just beneath the Gwar's rib cage. The blow forced the air from the Gwar's lungs. His sword flung into the air, and he went down hard on the grass, lying on his back and gasping for breath. Edward grabbed the Gwar's sword out of the air and, in one continuous motion, finished him off.

"Now to make this a fair fight!" said Edward, looking above. "Kiri Lee, follow me!" With little resistance, they made it to the castle's massive barrel turret. Kiri Lee descended from the air and found Edward clearing away bracken, branches, and pine needles from a pair of storm doors. These he flung open and then disappeared below. He emerged with two very heavy-looking green canvas duffels.

"Can you carry one of these?" he asked.

She grabbed the handles of one and hefted it. "Yes, I think so."

"Good," said Edward. "I'll get one more."

✻

"I need more moonlight," Tommy muttered. He had only nine arrows left in his quiver, and needed to make every shaft count. His hand flew to the arrow, to the bowstring, and to his ear, again and again until every arrow was spent.

Pierced in the heart, two Gwar slumped to the grass. Three Drefids, shot through the neck, tumbled out of their saddles and writhed on the grass. The last four arrows blinded two Cragons, and howling miserably, they stumbled and fell to the earth. In spite of the dim light, Tommy's aim had still been true. His bow now useless, Tommy grabbed a blade from one of his fallen enemies. But he, like Kat, had no training in swordplay.

Fortunately, Mrs. Galdarro, Mr. Charlie, Mr. Spero, Mr. Wallace, Regis, and Anna had. They put themselves between the enemy and the young lords. Their swords, axes, and Charlie's shield took down many foes. But a Warspider sprang forward and, with a sweep of one of its forelegs, sent Mr. Wallace sprawling to the ground.

Mrs. Galdarro ran to his side.

As the spider closed in to claim its victim, Mrs. Galdarro dropped her sword. She reached into her purse and pulled out a tan cube the size of a toy building block. She flung it at the jaws of the creature, and the cube exploded in a vaporous cloud.

The spider screeched and reared as the chemical compound ate away at its eyes and face. It tried in vain to slash the pain away with its forelegs, but collapsed to the ground and began to twitch.

Tommy had now seen Mrs. Galdarro dispatch spiders with the

333

strange cubes twice: once with a little spider back at school, and once . . . with a monster. It gave Tommy an idea. But it would have to wait.

Mrs. Galdarro looked at Mr. Wallace gravely.

He stood, hefted his sword, and nodded to Mrs. Galdarro. "I'm okay."

"Are you sure?"

"Yes, I'll be fine," he said. ". . . and thanks, Elle."

"We've got to get to the portal!" she said.

But to do so meant going through a virtual forest of Cragons. And the Drefids, who had been content to let their Warspiders fight for them, now leaped into the battle.

One of the Drefids came behind Anna and went to stab her in the back. But Jett was behind it. He grabbed the Drefid by the shoulders and rammed his knee into the Drefid's spine. Then Jett flung the limp foe into the jaws of an advancing spider.

"It's no good, Elle!" said Mr. Charlie, wiping something black and sticky from his face. "There are too many!"

"Where are they all coming from?" she gasped. "With every one we slay, more appear!" Then she realized how complete the design of the trap had been. And she began to despair. For not only were there Drefids and Cragons already waiting in Edinburgh for the Elves to arrive, but reinforcements were pouring forth from the portal itself. That had to be it.

"We've got to fall back and regroup!" Mr. Charlie growled.

The wave of enemies pushed them farther and farther from the portal, and there was little they could do but try to stay alive. Soon they had been driven all the way back to an area near the concert stage. There the battle was even more intense. But of the hundreds of Sentinels and Dreadnaughts who were in the audience before the attack, barely more than seventy survived to fight. Bodies of Gwar and Drefid—even a few Warspiders—littered the ground. And though the enemy dead counted far greater in number, the losses for the Elves were daunting.

"We've got to help them!" yelled Mr. Spero.

"No!" said Mrs. Galdarro. "We must protect the lords. All is lost without them!"

Tommy and Kat watched Jett slam another Drefid to the ground. Kat looked at Tommy. "I feel like baggage," she said.

"We've got to do something," said Tommy. He held up his Gwar sword. "Come on." They ran ahead.

"Tommy, Kat, NO!" Mrs. Galdarro shouted after them. "You're not ready!"

But they were gone.

It's all coming apart, she thought.

✳

For once, Jimmy was glad he was short. He stayed low and out of the way, but still within the protective reach of Regis or Miss Finney.

"Ugh!" Miss Finney swept the legs of a Drefid. He fell on his back but continued to swipe with his claws.

Battling beside her, Regis leaped off the thigh of a Gwar and ripped his helmet off using *Vexbane* techniques she'd learned in the elite Dreadnaught training. Descending, she brought the heavy iron helmet back down with both hands, trying to hammer the fallen enemy, but he saw it coming and rolled to the side.

Coming back toward Miss Finney, the Drefid leaped up to his feet again and slashed wildly at her face. Armed only with a short, dull blade she had plucked from a dead Gwar, she couldn't fend him off. Soon she was fighting not only the Drefid but two more Gwar.

Regis clambered back to her feet, wanting to help her friend, but she had to deal with the helmetless Gwar behind her.

To everyone's surprise, it was Jimmy who came to the rescue. "Miss Finney, look out!" he yelled. "Duck! Now!"

She did, without hesitation.

A Gwar's axe *whooshed* through the space above her head. The axe stroke was meant to decapitate the Sentinel. It took one of the Drefid's clawed hands off at the wrist instead. The white-haired warrior shrieked in terror, holding the stump of his mangled limb with luminous, purple blood streaming from the wound.

Miss Finney thanked the axe-swinging Gwar by driving her short sword into the foe's stomach up to the hilt. As the enemy fell away, she wrested the Gwar's broadsword from its hand and plunged it into the one-handed Drefid in a single fluid motion.

It was over in moments.

"Thank you, Jimmy," she said. "That's the second time your gift has bailed me out."

"Are yu kidding?" Jimmy asked. "Yu're the one doin' it all! I can't believe yu can fight like that. All this time, I thought yu were just a teacher."

"Ah, Jimmy," she said, ushering him along. "What I wouldn't give to go back to that simple, lovely life of reading and sipping cups of tea."

"No time for conversation," said Regis, now free of her Scottish speech. "We're far from out of this scrape."

Jimmy couldn't help but grin at Regis. He still couldn't believe his luck of being near her.

Miss Finney scanned the castle grounds, what had now become an otherworldly battlefield. Fire. Smoke. Blood. And the enemy seemed to have no end to its reinforcements. "I . . . I don't see how—"

"Just wait!" said Jimmy. "I've seen it."

"What?" Regis and Miss Finney turned to their young lord.

Jimmy smiled. "Kiri Lee's coming," he said.

✳

"How long can you stay up?" asked Edward, pulling weapons from the green satchels they'd retrieved from the castle. The two Elves were hidden for the moment by a scruffy berm on the edge of the battle.

"I . . . I'm not sure," Kiri Lee replied. "The day the other Sentinels saw me playing behind the castle, I think I walked the air for a minute, maybe more. I have to keep moving, or I'll sink."

"You've felt how heavy these satchels are," he said. "These swords and axes, especially the maces, will likely affect your ability to stay aloft. You will have to make your leaps very strategically, so that you come down in safety each time. When you're empty, you come back behind this hill to reload, do you understand?"

She nodded.

"Okay, how does this feel?"

Kiri Lee hefted the satchel. "I've got it," she said. "I'll make shorter leaps until I've given out enough weapons to lighten the load."

"Very well," he said, admiring Kiri Lee's determination. "Our people need the help that only you can give. Be careful, and watch for enemy bowmen."

"I will, but . . . where are you going?"

"I'm going to look after the humans. I fear too many have seen too much here to deny it. Tonight's events will likely shatter the humans' illusion that their world is all there is."

"Would that be such a bad thing?" asked Kiri Lee.

Edward was silent a moment. "That, my dear, remains to be seen. Endurance and Victory!"

"What?" asked Kiri Lee.

"Never mind," said Edward. "You'll learn. Now, go!"

Tommy and Kat raced to the aid of a Sentinel who had been cornered by a pair of Drefids. It was Ril! She was wearing an evening gown and had no weapon to defend herself.

"I don't know!" Kat yelled as they ran.

"What?" Tommy scowled.

"In your mind, you kept asking, 'What are we going to do? What are we going to do?' Well, I don't know, either!"

"Would you get out of my head?!" Tommy growled.

They came up behind the two Drefids, and they could see that Ril was a bloody mess. She'd been gouged and cut, especially her forearms, her only defense against their slashes.

I'll get the one on the left, Tommy thought. Kat looked over at him and nodded. They gathered what speed they could and attacked.

Tommy took his short sword in both hands and went to drive it into the Drefid's back below the shoulder, but the blade did not pierce the armor there. It slid down the plate metal, and Tommy fell. But he recovered enough to plunge the blade into the Drefid's lower leg.

The Drefid released a low moan, swung around, and backhanded Tommy. In all his life, Tommy had never been struck like that. Not even when he'd lost control of his bike and ran into a pole.

Tommy landed on his back several feet away. His shoulder felt like someone had branded him with a hot iron. He looked and saw three streaks of blood beginning to spread, his shirt torn.

Kat fared little better. She had one of Mr. Charlie's swords, so it was plenty sharp. But she stumbled, throwing off her aim. Her blade sliced the Drefid's side rather than piercing it. Kat, too, fell.

The Drefid slammed down its clawed fist, stabbing six inches into the turf . . . but Kat had rolled away.

"Friend of Berinfell," came a voice from high above. "Catch!"

All turned and looked up in the sky. Someone, a young lady with dark hair, was running across the sky twenty feet above them. Thinking he was seeing things, Tommy shook his head. But still, there she was.

Wait, that's Kiri Lee! She can fly!

Kat replied aloud, "It looks like it."

Kiri Lee dropped two weapons to the Sentinel: a spear and a mace. She caught them, ducked a fierce swipe from one Drefid, and slammed the mace against the enemy's side. Ribs obliterated by the blow, the Drefid crumpled to one knee.

But the other circled behind the Sentinel to get a better angle.

The Sentinel raised the mace and blocked the Drefid's high attack that she heard whistling down from behind. With the other hand, she blindly swung her spear around her back and up under the Drefid's chin. In a devastating move, she pushed up with all her might. Lightning quick, she pulled the spear out, rotated it around, and rammed it into the chest of the first Drefid who sprawled backward. Both enemies lay side by-side, dead.

Tommy looked at Kat. "I need to learn how to do that."

Ril ran to Tommy. "You're hurt," she said.

"Barely," Tommy blurted out, looking at the nasty gashes the Sentinel had sustained. She helped Tommy to his feet.

"Hey, what about me?" Kat asked. "I think I scraped my knee!"

All three of them laughed, but both Tommy's and Kat's expressions changed quickly to anguish. Suddenly, the fears and hurts of all the recent events came spilling out. Kat put her head in her hands. Tommy's tears streamed down his cheeks.

"I know it is a hard thing," said Ril. "Come, there will be time to mourn later, but never in the midst of battle. We must find Galdarro!"

�֍

Having fought their way through the teeming combatants, Mrs. Galdarro, Mr. Spero, and several Dreadnaughts and Sentinels found a momentary reprieve, as well as a decent vantage point, on a modest hill near the castle parking lot. Mrs. Galdarro had been looking desperately for Tommy and Kat, but found herself entranced, watching Kiri Lee crisscross the battlefield through the air, dropping weapons to the Sentinels. "Surely the pure blood of lords flows in her veins," she whispered.

"That it does," said Mr. Spero.

"Elle!" Mr. Charlie and Jett were cresting the hill. "We've found them. They were with Ril."

Mrs. Galdarro turned and saw Tommy and Kat run up, Ril close behind. "Don't you ever run off like that!" Mrs. Galdarro scolded them.

"You sound like my mom," said Tommy. He was smiling, but his chin trembled. Kat's eyes looked distant and haunted.

"Oh, you poor dears," said Mrs. Galdarro, and she embraced them, one under each arm. Mr. Wallace and Anna joined the embrace.

"Ril Taniel," Mrs. Galdarro said, looking to the Sentinel. "It was by Ellos' hand that you found them."

"By Ellos's hand, yes," said Ril. "But they found me. In fact, if they had not intervened, I would be dead."

"Elle!" Mr. Charlie called.

Mrs. Galdarro didn't respond. She was listening to Tommy and Kat's account of what had just transpired.

"Elle!" Mr. Charlie's voice was high and urgent. "We've got trouble."

Mrs. Galdarro released the young Elves at last. She turned. The wall of Cragons they'd run into when they fled for the portal had finally crossed the field of battle and caught up to them. Around the tree creatures' trunklike legs, Warspiders teemed. Drefids and Gwar soldiers prowled in packs after them. It was a massive wave of enemies, but they did not yet attack.

Instead, their lines marched forward and curled around the hill. The Elves found themselves outnumbered ten to one and surrounded. And at the head of the pack, leading the charge, was a face the Sentinels and Dreadnaughts knew all too well.

"Mobius!" Mrs. Galdarro spat out the name. "I might have known."

The Drefid commander's words spilled out from his pale, cracked lips in a venomous hiss. "Galdarro . . . so you've come out to play?"

She stepped in front of the lords and said, "You won't take them this time."

"We don't want to take them," he seethed. "No curse restrains us now—not from the prophecies, nor from the Spider King. We have come for blood."

44

The Ruins

NEITHER THE Elves nor the enemy noticed the headlights winding through the woods and up the road leading to Dalhousie Castle. When the driver saw the fires, the destruction, and the bodies, he brought the cab to a screeching halt. Nelly, Johnny, and Autumn stared from the backseat. For several agonizing moments, no one spoke.

"Driver," Nelly said at last. "Call the police. Call for ambulances and help. And then . . . get away from here as fast as you can."

"What're yu doin', then?"

"We're getting out."

"What're yu crazy? Yu can't get out here in this mess!"

Nelly said nothing more to the driver. She led the Brianmans out of the cab and across the road. The driver wasted no time in leaving them behind, peeling out and shooting back down the driveway.

"What's happening?" asked Johnny.

"Ah, Galdarro," she said, "why didn't you listen to me?"

"What?" asked Autumn.

"I'm sorry," said Nelly. "This is not the way it was supposed to happen. Somehow, the enemy has found us out." She led Johnny and Autumn up and over several knolls, and they came to a taller hill that overlooked the field of battle.

"The trees!" said Johnny. "They're moving!"

"Those are Cragons," said Nelly. "Dark-souled creatures from our world. And none too few."

"Warspiders!" said Autumn.

"Gwar and Dreſids as well," said Nelly. "I see also our people there. Galdarro and others. They are surrounded." Then her Elven eyes narrowed. "And Mobius leads the enemy. Fitting." She glanced back to the children. "Listen, my young lords, there are weapons scattered all over the field. I am going to find a blade or two and play my part in this battle. I want you to remain here."

"Here?" Autumn exclaimed. "And not fight?"

"Autumn," said Johnny. "We don't know how to fight . . . not like this."

"He's right," said Nelly. "When you are trained, when your gifts are mature, you will be the greatest champions in our world. But that time has not yet come."

"But look out there!" Autumn cried out. "We're losing. We're not going to get out of here. We need to do some—"

"What you need to do," said Nelly, "is stay safe. Your survival is most important. If the battle goes ill . . . well, you see that beautiful castle over there? I want you to go inside, hide."

"I won't," argued Autumn.

"Autumn!" Johnny exclaimed. "You're not thinkin' straight. C'mon. Do what Nelly says."

"But—"

"No more arguments." Nelly embraced them both and then turned to leave.

"Nelly, please?" Autumn called.

Nelly turned, smiled sadly, and then walked away. Soon she picked up speed and raced toward the battle. They watched her stoop to pick up a weapon, and then she disappeared into the masses writhing in the conflict.

"How could you just let her go?" asked Autumn. "She's going to die!"

"No she's not," said Johnny. "You saw what she did to those two Dreh, uh, Drep—"

"Drefids," said Autumn. "Yeah, but this is different. Look at them out there, Johnny! The Elves—our people are surrounded by, by monsters! We've got to help them!"

"What, Autumn?" Johnny got right up in his sister's face. "What can you do that might help? Those are monsters out there, like bad dreams come to life. Do you honestly think you can go out there and kill one of those things?"

Her brows knotted, Autumn stared at the ground. "It didn't stop you. You fought those things with a bat!"

"And I woulda been killed, if Nelly hadn't come along."

"Something. I've got to do something," Autumn said. She turned abruptly and started walking.

"Autumn, no, don't!" Johnny ran after her.

When she saw Johnny, she, too, started to run. But something felt different . . .

Usually, her feet pounded the ground, the shock of each step hammering up her legs. But this time, she could feel her legs moving, moving fast . . . but there was no impact on the ground. It felt effortless, like blowing out a candle.

She glanced over her shoulder, and Johnny had fallen back . . . *way back.* That's when Autumn looked down and saw how fast the turf was going by beneath her. Her gift had come full on.

"*YES!!*" Autumn screamed.

She blazed across the turf until she spied a dead Gwar who still held a sword. She stopped long enough to pry it out of his meaty hand. The weapon felt awkward in her grip, but when she swung it, she found that her hands were just as fast as her feet. The sword became a blur in front of her. "Cool."

I will help them, she thought. And then raced on.

"Autumn!" Johnny screamed. "Wait!" Autumn had always been faster, but just by a little. The way she had pulled away from him, it was . . . well—it was her gift. It had to be. Feeling like he was running through an ocean of molasses, Johnny tried to catch up to his sister, and wondered what on earth his gift might be.

❋

When Johnny finally came within thirty yards of the actual fighting, he couldn't believe what he saw. Autumn—his little sister—**wreaking** havoc among the enemy.

With her newfound sword, Autumn whooshed back and forth throughout the enemy army. She darted in and out, slashing them from behind. A few of the Gwar turned to try to grab her, but they were too slow. Autumn gashed several of them across the chest and stomach, one even across the bridge of his nose.

"Go, Autumn!" he cheered. But then Johnny felt his entire world spin out of control. A Drefid emerged from the enemy ranks up ahead of his sister. Johnny saw what Autumn did not—a Drefid who had positioned himself with one arm lifted, the knifelike blades now pointed toward Autumn.

All this he saw in the time it took to yell, "Watch out, Autumn!"

But it was too late. Autumn's speed and momentum carried her right into the Drefid. His blades drove hard into Autumn's stomach.

Johnny heard her scream. He would never forget that sound. He leaped forward and raced recklessly toward Autumn. He covered the thirty yards in seconds, in time to see the Drefid pull his knife-fingers out of his sister. The foe stood up straight, looked at Johnny, and smiled. It was then Johnny felt something within him snap. Like releasing a cramp or cracking a bone, but it was everywhere all at once.

"*NOOOOOOO!!!*" The word burst from Johnny, and he charged at the Drefid.

The clawed warrior sought to impale Johnny, just as he'd done the other. He lifted both clawed fists and just waited. But something happened that neither the Drefid nor Johnny could have expected. Johnny lifted his hands to grab or maybe strangle the Drefid. But before he could reach the enemy, he felt a kind of burning along his lower eyelids and then a tingling on the palms of his hands.

All at once there was a flash of white light. Johnny felt the muscles in his forearms pulsing, and streams of white liquid fire blazed from his hands. The first pulse of flame knocked the Drefid off his feet. The enemy fell backward into a group of Gwar and struggled to quench the fire that burned on his chest. But this manner of fire, the Drefid had never experienced. It clung to him like sap and spread like water. The warrior soon was engulfed.

Johnny willed the fire from his hands to stop, and he stooped down to his sister. She was still. Her eyes were closed. Blood spread out from her wounded stomach. He touched her arm. She was cold. He brushed a lock of hair out of his sister's face. The sound that Johnny released next could not be described as intelligible language. It was a keening, primal scream that echoed off the side of the castle. Then he stood up and looked at the teeming brood of enemies waiting just ahead.

Rage consumed him. He lifted his arms and released such a pulse of fire that all the Gwar closest to him were flash-incinerated, leaving only smoking husks behind.

Johnny turned one arm in a different direction and began torching every enemy in sight. Cragon trees burst into flames at the root, and the fire spread rapidly until the dark trees were engulfed entirely. Warspiders fled the flames, but the fire was inescapable. As it caught up to them, their agonizing *scree* rang out. It was then the unthinkable happened: the enemy began to flee.

✳

"This could be our chance!" Mrs. Galdarro yelled. "Follow me, and beware the flames; Johnny is not yet in control of his gift."

The Sentinel led Tommy and the others through the widening gap in the enemy ranks. The other Sentinels and Dreadnaughts raked their scattering enemies with their blades as they ran between them. The fiery orange glow disappeared ahead, and at last they came to Johnny. They found Nelly Brookeheart there, kneeling beside a stricken Elf. The moon had emerged at last from the clinging shreds of clouds, and in its light, Autumn looked very pale.

Mrs. Galdarro went to their side. "How is she?"

Nelly nodded. "Autumn lives . . . but . . . these wounds." She shook her head.

"There are herbs and salves in Allyra that would help," said Mrs. Galdarro. She stood and went to Johnny. "Johnny, your, uh—sister—is in great need of aid, aid that can only be gained in Allyra, our real homeland. Do you understand?"

"Yes," he said absently.

Mrs. Galdarro pointed toward the ruins. "Through there is a portal. We must get through. But the enemy holds that ground. You must drive them out. Can you do that?"

"I'm tired," Johnny said.

"I know," said Mrs. Galdarro, her heart on the verge of breaking. "I know you're tired. There will be rest soon . . . for us all. But, Johnny, you must do this, and you must do this now—to save your sister's life."

Johnny's expression changed. He looked down at Autumn. He turned toward the wood, and the ruins beyond, and then he started to run.

Mrs. Galdarro stooped and started to pick up Autumn, but Jett came to her aid. "Let me," he said. He lifted Autumn as easily as one might lift a pillow. He cradled her and began to follow Johnny. "Mrs. Galdarro, lead us!" Jett yelled.

Mrs. Galdarro gestured to the others, and they followed the charred path Johnny left behind.

"Who are you?" came a weak voice.

Jett looked down. Autumn's eyes were open. "A friend," he said. "Now rest."

❋

Johnny threw fire at Cragon, Drefid, and Gwar.

But it was all the remaining Sentinels and Dreadnaughts could do to protect the young lords from the enemy's greater numbers. At the base of a deep hollow, they met Edward, Kiri Lee, Regis, Miss Finney, and Jimmy Gresham, who had been pinned down by a pack of Warspiders; but the pungent burning aroma in the air made it very clear what Johnny had done to those spiders.

The Elves burned, slashed, and hacked their way along the path through the woods. Cragons, hidden among the earthly trees, grabbed and crushed several Elves. But each time the dark trees from Allyra revealed themselves, they were cut to pieces by Dreadnaughts' blades or scorched to cinders by Johnny's unearthly flames.

And the bloody march went on until at last they came to the ruins. Kiri Lee thought they looked ghostly in the moonlight. And with all the Warspiders, Drefids, and Gwar roaming the ancient stones, it looked horrific indeed. Edward raced ahead and joined Johnny. "There, son," he said. "Clear off that bridge area, would you?"

Johnny did as he was asked. White fire leaped forth from his palms, sending the enemy running for cover. Burning Gwar dropped off the edges of the bridge like globs of molten glass. Fires burned everywhere. Even the woods around the ruins kindled. The night air became warm, and it was getting warmer by the minute.

Edward led the Sentinels and company across the bridge, everyone shielding their faces against the smoke and the heat. Including the young lords, twenty-one Elves survived the battle at Dalhousie and the passage through the forest to the ruins. Jett looked down at Autumn and silently prayed that she would not succumb to the cruel-looking wounds before they could get help.

"If you want," said Mr. Charlie, "I can take a turn carrying her."

"It's okay, she's not heav—"Jett saw the bright purple in Charlie's eyes and smiled curiously. "Are . . . are we family?"

"Matter of fact, we are. Your father, Vex Nightwing, was my older brother. Now, you sure you got her?"

"I won't let her fall," Jett replied.

"Then come on, nephew . . . there's a whole world waiting."

They came to the end of the bridge and raced down the stairs to the mouth of the tunnel.

"Is this it?" Mrs. Galdarro asked.

Edward nodded. "At the end of the tunnel, on the far wall, is our way home . . . at long last."

"You'd better go first," Mrs. Galdarro said to Johnny. "Anything gets in your way, burn it."

Johnny went in. Edward and a long train of others followed. Mrs. Galdarro said, "Mr. Wallace, Anna, and Mr. Spero, would you be so kind as to watch our backs?"

"With pleasure," said Mr. Wallace.

❊

Johnny met plenty of resistance, all Drefids, more than a dozen. But they could do nothing against Johnny's scorching, white flame in such a closed space. *WHOOOSH!* Flames consumed their corpses and the air pressure shot their ashes out through the porthole windows.

At the end of the tunnel, one lone Drefid stood in front of the wall. His claws were not extended, and he had his arms crossed.

"It is too late," he hissed at them. It was Lorex, Mobius's right-hand underling.

Mrs. Galdarro nodded to Johnny. Another *whoosh!* of fire, and the Drefid fell in a smoking heap. Looking at Lorex's ashes, Mrs. Galdarro couldn't remember seeing Mobius after Johnny had arrived. Perhaps he had died somewhere in the inferno as well? Somehow, though, she doubted that very much. They raced forward now, eager to be done with this . . . but at the wall they came to a strange sight.

"Edward!" called Mrs. Galdarro.

Edward came forward, Kiri Lee right behind.

"It looks different," she said.

Rather than the blank wall they had seen before, electricity rippled all over the surface, and each time it did, an octagonal shape like a window appeared. It seemed to be getting smaller. Edward looked closer, and at every corner of the octagonal opening, a small, red spider was slowly crawling toward the center.

"Oh no," Edward gasped. "They have begun to collapse the portal. Johnny, bathe this wall in flame. Everyone, step away."

Johnny unleashed several short bursts of white flame. Edward held up a hand. "The spiders are gone," he said.

But with each flash, the opening continued to shrink.

"I don't understand," said Edward. "It should have stopped. Everyone, we've got to get through now! *NOW!!*"

Mrs. Galdarro called back to the others still in the tunnel. "The portal is closing. We'll get through as fast as we can. Dive if you must, but do not delay."

"Ril—you, Johnny, and Edward go first," said Mrs. Galdarro.

Ril strode toward the door. She put her leg through and then her torso. It was as if the stone stretched inward and then sealed on Ril's form until snapping shut once she was through. Johnny looked nervously over his shoulder at Autumn. Somehow the idea that he was born in another world had become a kind of bad dream. He found himself missing his mother and father, and wondering if he'd ever see them again. But seeing his sister's stricken form and feeling certain she would die if she stayed on Earth, Johnny closed his eyes and stepped through. Edward came next, followed by Jett carrying Autumn.

Others followed one by one: always a young lord followed by a Sentinel or Dreadnaught. Kiri Lee was uncertain for a moment, but when she heard the first few notes of a beautiful melody coming from the other side, she followed the music and entered. Mrs. Finney and Regis passed through next. Jimmy Gresham looked back to Tommy and Kat and said, "I'll finally be at home." Then he was gone.

After a pair of Sentinels went through, Mrs. Galdarro said, "Go on, Tommy. We cannot wait."

Tommy nodded, but he couldn't stop staring at Kat. Her face was a mask of mixed emotion, and he wondered if maybe he was reading just a little bit of her mind for once. For the dominant emotion staring out from her wide eyes and trembling at her jawline . . . was fear.

Something surged up within Tommy, then an overwhelming desire—no, a need—to reach out, to reassure. He stood up straight, threw his shoulders back, and thought in his clearest mental voice: *Don't worry, Kat. I will protect you.* Then he reached out, grabbed her hand, and thought, *Come on, Blue Girl. It's time to go.*

He thought she must have heard him, because she didn't resist, and the two of them went through, hand in hand. The lords were all through, and many of the remaining Sentinels and Dreadnaughts. But not everyone and not fast enough. The portal was shrinking. Mrs. Galdarro, desperate now, yelled back to the others, "Now for it,

Children of Light! This is our moment, our return to Allyra! COME
ONNN!!"

✳

"We must go," said Anna, edging into the tunnel. "Did you hear? The
portal's closing!"

"Yes, come on," said Mr. Spero. "We're done here."

Mr. Wallace looked out at the ruins. Plenty of Drefids still lurking out there, but he figured there was nothing they could still do.

"Come on!" Anna called over her shoulder as she ran into the
tunnel.

"Let's go! Allyra's calling us home!" Mr. Spero disappeared into
the tunnel.

Mr. Wallace took one last look at Earth. He turned to follow, but
felt a sharp pinch in his lower back.

✳

"*COME ONNN!!*" Mrs. Galdarro screamed. The portal was just
big enough that a person could dive through. Some Sentinels and
Dreadnaughts were still coming. "Go, GO, GO, GO!!"

"You first," said Mr. Charlie.

"Always the gentleman," said Mrs. Galdarro. "But no, you go on."

"Remember my mission," he said. "I'll see you through, or I won't
go at all."

"Stubborn." Mrs. Galdarro dove through the portal.

But Charlie waited for the others.

"It's closing!" yelled Anna.

"Go! Go!" Charlie yelled to her, pumping his arm.

She dove through.

Mr. Spero dove next. He barely made it.

Charlie looked back . . . only one Sentinel left. But Mr. Wallace was on the ground, struggling to his feet back at the opening to the tunnel. He would never get to the portal in time. Then to Charlie's horror, another Drefid sidestepped the crippled Sentinel and lunged forward, flaming white eyes fixed on Charlie.

"Mobius!" Charlie shouted. For a moment, the two famed warriors regarded each other with silent fury. The intensity of each one's gaze spoke nothing short of the annihilation of the other.

Charlie broke the standoff, glanced at the portal, now just two feet across. Whatever he did, it would have to be quick. He heard a growl and looked up a moment too late.

Mobius crashed hard into Charlie, knocking him and his sword to the ground. But Charlie managed to grab the rim of Mobius's chest plate and yanked him down with him. The two rolled in the dirt, Mobius edging his blades closer to Charlie's face, Charlie pushing hard against Mobius's chin with one hand, his other clenching the enemy's wrist.

They writhed in the rubble of the ruins until Charlie was pinned down on his back, bested by the larger, heavier Drefid. But for Mobius to free one of his hands from Charlie's wrists to execute the deathblow would mean Charlie would be free to throw a punch. So for a brief moment, a stalemate was reached, both warriors glaring.

It was then, however, Charlie noticed the gate above his head . . . no more than ten inches across, and closing quickly. As broad as he was, he knew he would never get through. But that didn't matter now that the lords were safe on the other side. The portal, Charlie thought, might be able to serve one more purpose.

With a lightning-swift thrust from his legs, Charlie heaved with all his might, and plunged the Drefid into the portal headfirst . . . and that was all that fit through. Before Mobius even understood what had happened, the portal closed around his neck and did not stop. There was a sharp, buzzing noise; a shriek; and a loud crack. Mobius's headless body landed in a lifeless heap on top of Charlie.

A heartbeat later, Mr. Wallace arrived at the portal. Charlie pushed Mobius's corpse off, and Mr. Wallace helped Charlie to his feet. He looked at the portal, now just the size of a quarter, and remarked, "That was close, eh, Charlie?"

"Yeah," he said wiping dirt off his arms. "A little too close. I almost lost that fight."

"Correction," said Mr. Wallace, "you did lose."

At first Charlie didn't understand. Then Mr. Wallace plunged a knife into his gut. The Sentinel looked down at the handle protruding from his stomach, then, completely stunned, back up to Mr. Wallace. He stammered, trying to find the words. His lips moved, but nothing came. Charlie slumped to his knees, then fell onto his side. From that angle, he saw Mr. Wallace's entire form dissolve into a whirling strand of mist that snaked through the portal just before it snapped shut.

45

A Poison Splinter

WHEN TOMMY first stepped into the shimmering portal, it felt like he had walked right through a dense and very sticky web. But more than just clinging to his flesh and clothing, the web seemed to soak into him like a cold fluid. He could no longer feel Kat's hand in his own. But he felt tingles all over just before being catapulted forward at a tremendous speed—much like he'd imagine g-force on a launch into space would feel. Flickers of light raced by. Gravity was gone. There was no longer any up or down. Just a lot of movement.

Unfortunately, it was such a nauseating motion that Tommy threw up immediately. But once the vomit left his body, it was vacuumed away. Tommy had no idea where it had gone and wondered remotely if he'd just splattered poor Kat somewhere behind him. The flickers of light had slowed and finally stopped, and Tommy stumbled forward and collapsed.

✳

Tommy lay on his side on a tuft of thick grass and rolled over onto his back. Strange stars—purple, green, or blue—winked down at him from above. A cold breeze rustled the grass and tossed his curly hair. He closed his eyes and struggled to comprehend what he'd just experienced.

It felt like being absorbed. That was the only way Tommy could think to describe the journey. Someone touched his shoulder, and Tommy winced. The wound he had received from the Drefid outside Dalhousie still stung.

"Here's one!" an edgy, urgent voice called. Someone stood over Tommy. "Here, in the tall grass!"

Someone else was suddenly there, kneeling at his side. "Tommy, thank Ellos you made it through." Mrs. Galdarro helped him sit up. "How do you feel?"

"Like I just got hit by a cement mixer."

"That's normal for first timers," explained Edward as he and Mr. Wallace approached. "Very normal, wouldn't you say?"

Mr. Wallace did not answer at first. His head was still, but his eyes darted restlessly. "What?" he finally said. "Oh, yes, very normal, Tommy."

"What's wrong?" asked Mrs. Galdarro. "You seem distracted."

"I am," Mr. Wallace replied. "Four are accounted for, but I have not seen the other three."

Mrs. Galdarro looked nervously about the area. "That would be Kat, Jett and . . . and Autumn!" Mrs. Galdarro stood.

Mrs. Galdarro scanned the hillside, searching amongst her kins-folk. The grassy slope that everyone lay upon was the only soft area before the hill descended onto a forest floor thick with dead debris left over from a long winter. Small mounds of snow still hugged boulders and tree stumps, while dry leaves and old branches poked up from under their frozen white blanket. Pockets of Elves moved all over the hill, but she did not see Jett, Autumn, or Kat. After all they'd been through, to lose them in this—

"Over here!" cried a voice near the bottom of the hill.

"Go on," said Mr. Wallace. "I'll take care of Tommy."

Mrs. Galdarro ran down the hill.

"Tommy?" another voice came out of the grass about twenty yards away. A strange pink thing appeared. It was Kat's head. She stood unsteadily but looked none the worse for wear.

"Kat!" Tommy ran to his friend.

"Kat," muttered Mr. Wallace. He took several steps away from the young lords. "Good, good!" he called to the young lords. "I'm going to join Galdarro and the others. Come right down."

He didn't wait for Tommy and Kat to catch up. In fact, he hurried to keep well away from them. "Kat Simonson, the thought-reader," Mr. Wallace muttered to himself when he felt sure he was out of her range. Could he mask his thoughts well enough to establish himself among the Elves . . . like a poison splinter? Then he might at last learn the location of the Elves' secret home. That would be worth much to the Spider King. Very much indeed.

✳

Mrs. Galdarro pushed the group aside and found Johnny, nearly hysterical, trying to take his sister from Jett's arms.

"Give her to me!" Johnny yelled.

Jett took an awkward step backward. "Stop it, man. You're going to hurt her worse."

"We're going to help your sister," Nelly said quietly. "Everything is going to be all right."

"No!" Johnny cried, still trying to break Jett's hold.

"Jett's right, Johnny," said Mrs. Galdarro sternly. "You are only making things worse. We need to get Autumn help right away."

Mr. Wallace appeared behind her. And to Mrs. Galdarro's relief, Tommy and Kat joined the group. "What's going on?" asked Tommy.

Kat whispered to him, "Johnny's very agitated. He's not thinking straight."

"Johnny, we want to help," pleaded Mrs. Galdarro. "We can take care of her, but we have to move quickly. We cannot linger. . . . Wait! Quiet! I heard something."

A branch snapped somewhere behind them. The hill went deathly silent. Jett took the opportunity to move Autumn out of Johnny's reach. Hundreds of years of training taking over, the Sentinels and Dreadnaughts ushered the teens to cover in bracken, deadfall, tall grasses, and among the trees. Mrs. Galdarro's heart crashed against her ribs. An assault here would be fatal. Little cover, few weapons, and more than half their number wounded.

Mrs. Galdarro held her breath, waiting for the first sign of attack. Nothing moved.

Then the sweet song of a satin whippoorwill floated up from amongst the trees. Mrs. Galdarro placed her hands to her lips, cupped together, and whistled out the reply. They *had* come.

A breath later, flet soldiers emerged from hiding places in the depths of the forest, stepping out into plain view. Archers watched from their lofty nests in the treetops, while others equipped with rycheswords crawled out of holes covered with brush. They ventured forward, assembling as a most welcome sight before Mrs. Galdarro. And leading them was none other than the famed guardmaster himself.

"Guardmaster Grimwarden, I feared you were the Spider King's forces. Half scared me to death," gasped Mrs. Galdarro.

"You are wise to be afraid. They are very near," whispered Grimwarden. He motioned to his troops. They raced forward bearing woodland cloaks and boots for those who had returned from Earth. He paused, realizing they had brought with them six times the gear they needed. "You have not all returned . . . but what of the lords?"

"We've returned with all of the Seven, Guardmaster, but one is in great need—"

"We have secured a place nearby for such a need. Herbs, salves, medicine—it is made ready. And Claris Gilant is here."

"Claris? Ah, thank Ellos," said Mrs. Galdarro. "She is unmatched in the healing arts."

"Quickly and quietly, follow me." Grimwarden motioned for his warriors to surround the Seven Lords and the Elves returning from Earth.

The Sentinels helped the lords struggle through the shrubbery and trees to a vine-covered area. Once there, Grimwarden motioned in the direction of a treetop and suddenly the area sprang to life. Flet soldiers ran to his side. Grimwarden turned to Galdarro, "Bring the most wounded lord forward, and tell what you require."

They brought Autumn to an Elf maiden at the edge of the clearing. She had large green eyes and blood-red hair. Freckles dotted her nose and the tips of her ears.

She took one look at Autumn's wounds and frowned. "You already tried to heal her?"

Mrs. Galdarro shook her head. "No, Claris, we haven't had time."

"Someone did," Claris replied bluntly, glancing at Jett. "It is not enough."

Johnny caught his breath.

"I can heal her," Claris explained, "but not if we do not get her to our stronghold." She reached into a pocket of her cloak and withdrew what appeared to be a tree twig about the size of a pencil. She cracked it open and rubbed one of the ends across Autumn's wounds. "This will fend off infection," she said.

Grimwarden motioned to two of his stronger flet soldiers. "Marak, Ramius, put her on a litter and bear her gently."

"I can handle it," said Jett.

"Nay, young lord," said Grimwarden. "You have never trod these paths. We cannot take a chance on you stumbling."

"I don't stumble," said Jett bluntly.

"Did you say 'lord'?" Claris asked. She stared at Jett. "You are one of the Seven?"

Grimwarden nodded.

"Guardmaster," said Claris, "with all due respect to your command, I believe this wounded Elf would be much better off with the lord who carried her this far."

"As you wish," he replied. The guardmaster stole a moment to survey the young lords. He saw in their faces a resemblance to their parents he'd last seen many years ago. And Grimwarden could hardly believe they'd all made it home to Allyra. "There is much you all must do," said Grimwarden, "and no time to spare for proper ceremonies. But it is with great gladness of heart I welcome you back to your homeland . . . it has been a long wait."

Some of the flet soldiers began to bow.

Tommy blushed and turned to Jimmy. "Dude, what do we do?"

"Just keep smiling," he replied.

"Stop!" Grimwarden commanded his men. "The lords are due every bow, but to do so here is very dangerous. Even one spy of the enemy could witness your acts and identify the lords for assassination. Now, let's get them out of this clearing, get them changed, and get them some food. They must be starving. Move with haste!"

✳

Once she'd changed into her Elven gear, Mrs. Galdarro searched out Guardmaster Grimwarden.

"How long can we risk remaining above ground?" she asked.

"Not long. It is unsafe for us, especially here," he answered.

"How did you know where to find us?"

"We've been monitoring the enemy's movements near the old portals. He has abandoned all the others but this one. In fact, the Spider King stationed a formidable war band here. We drove them off, but they will return and in greater numbers. I feel even now we are being watched." Grimwarden paused and looked around. "Goldarrow, you and your team accomplished a task we thought impossible. All of Elfkind is in your debt. When we return to the Nightwish Caverns, we will honor you and all who served with you."

Quiet filled the air between the two.

"Goldarrow, have the young lords' gifts began to develop?"

"Yes, but they have not mastered them yet."

"And will they be able to keep up with us?"

Galdarro smiled. "They have surprised me with their strength—"

Suddenly, Grimwarden stopped her to listen to a distant bird's call. "That is from our scouts! The enemy returns! Flet soldiers, depart! Swift but silent running!" He turned when Mrs. Galdarro touched his arm.

"You're heading to the north, but that is a longer journey and will take us—"

"Past the Dark Veil. Yes, I know. But, Elle, you have been gone a long while. The journey north is not nearly as long as it once was."

"But—"

He held up a hand. "I believe our preparations will be more than adequate."

"Preparations?" inquired Galdarro.

"You shall see. Come." He hesitated and turned to the Seven Lords now gathered near him—Autumn opened her eyes. "And you, my good lords—your journeys have just begun."

Continue the Adventure
Solve the Riddle on Page 372

Acknowledgments

SO MANY people gave love, time, resources, and insight to make this book possible. Coauthoring is really new territory for us both, so we owe a great debt to many, many people for their support and prayers. So to all the family, friends, and readers everywhere, we offer heartfelt thanks.

Wayne's wife, Mary Lu, and Christopher's wife, Jenny, bore the brunt of our collaboration, taking many extra shifts at home so that we could be online, writing or on the phone or in Scranton, Pennsylvania. God really blessed us with amazing ladies, beautiful on the outside and within. Following the Lord, our thanks go to you as God-given gifts for which we could never repay Him.

To our own young Tribe: Kayla, Tommy, Bryce, Rachel, Eva, Luik, and Judah—thank you for reminding us that deadlines can sometimes wait, and that play is an essential part of life. May God make tender warriors of you all.

WTB: Mom and Dad, Leslie and Bob, Jeff and Shannon, and Brian and Melissa—what an adventure we've been on together! Thank you for everything. And to the students and staff of Folly Quarter Middle School—as always, you are my frontline editors and readers. Pip-pip cheerio!

CH: Hopper and Nesbitt Clans—how will I ever repay the Lord for getting you as kin? I am blessed among men. And to all my hometown readers at New Life Christian Church and 33 Live . . . even Jill at the post office—you are my greatest encouragers. Shine bright; nations are waiting on the other side of your obedience.

To Billy Jepma—likely the next Robert Ludlum, Stephen King, and J. R. R. Tolkien wrapped into one—may ideas continue to pour into your mind, onto the page, and into the hearts of many! All for Jesus . . .

La famille Sureau: Pascal, AnneMarie, Juliette, and Sophie—our "superfans," who constantly patrol the trenches before we make a landing.

The Meldrum family in Dalkeith, and Phil Springthorpe in Ardfern— for all your Scottish input and tours of legendary castles.

To Keith and David at Literature and Latte—for creating the most extraordinary writing software on the planet: Scrivener—we most definitely owe you gents a pint. How did we ever write without it?

Jeff Hanson—for creating the coolest dashboard fantasy name generator widget ever known to man (or Elves).

The Banshee—for being the home away from home, the creative hangout for these two little inklings. Special thanks to Kathleen, Melony, Bobbi, Jenn, Chuck, Karen, Taby, Jamie, Brita, and Katie.

The Radisson Hotel Lackawanna in Scranton—you were long overdue for a mention. We have found your place to be a writer's sanctuary.

His Way Books—Michelle Black; Barnes and Noble, Ellicott City— Amber Stubbefield; and Gifts from Above—for supplying us with books to sell for Pennsylvania events.

To Gregg Wooding, our friend—and agent—man, are we glad to have you as an ally. You are a Swordbrother of the first order.

Authors Donita K. Paul, Sharon Hinck, Eric Reinhold, Bryan Davis, Jonathan Rogers, L. B. Graham, Chris and Allan Miller, Andrew Peterson, Dean Briggs, Bryan Polivka, J. A. Konrath, and many others who have modeled excellence in writing—thank you for inspiring us by your example.

Laura Minchew, Beverly Phillips, June Ford, Jackie Johnston, AnnJanette Toth, and all our friends at Thomas Nelson—thank you for spending your skill and experience on us.

And last but not least, to Pam Schwagerl, for being the catalyst for our Fantasy Tours . . . and for giving Christopher permission (wink, wink).

Sneak Preview of
The Berinfell Prophecies: Book 2

DEEP IN the northwestern corner of the Thousand-League Forest, carved into the living rock of Mount Mystbane and shrouded by the fearless cliffhanging trees, Whitehall Castle, the Elves' long abandoned home, had tenants once more. Hidden and far away from the Spider King's stronghold in Vesper Crag, Whitehall was the one place the Elves thought it safe to conduct the secret warfare training of the returning lords. Once embedded within the castle, a team of Sentinels and Dreadnaughts began their urgent mission teaching the young lords the Elven art of fighting. With few breaks, the young lords endured the rigorous lessons—while the exiled remnants of Elven civilization anxiously waited hundreds of leagues away in the Nightwish Caverns.

✳

On those rare occasions when he was free from the brutal training schedule, Tommy spent nearly all of his time exploring the labyrinthine passages of Whitehall Castle. The intricate network of corridors, keeps, tunnels, and towers was an irresistible puzzle waiting to be solved . . . and Tommy loved puzzles. Most often, he'd make a wrong turn and wind up at a blank stone wall, or worse, right back where he'd started. But every once in a while he'd follow a passage and discover spectacular settings, like a chamber full of sunlit water fountains or a hall strewn with intriguing artwork. Or, like yesterday, a secluded balcony high on Whitehall's central tower.

Tommy had spent several hours reclining on the balcony's curving stone bench and quickly made it his own. Eyes open or closed, he found the spot relaxing and entertaining. Colorful birds crisscrossed in the air and disappeared into the dark green shadows under the canopy. Braided mimots—the striped, ghost-faced, monkeylike creatures that lived in the treetops—hooted and cackled as they leaped branch to branch after each other. And numerous driftworms–thumb-sized fuzzy, purple caterpillars—descended from the upper branches on gossamer parachutes of silk, to land wherever the breeze carried them. It was as peaceful a place as Tommy had yet seen in Allyra.

After a particularly exhausting session, Tommy couldn't wait to get back to his special escape. Traversing several large halls, climbing two flights of stairs, and racing blindly down a dark passage, Tommy turned a corner and . . . came to an abrupt stop.

Kat Simonson was sitting in his spot. She looked up at Tommy, her bluish skin purpling with new blush. But there was no smile. Just a sigh.

"You're kidding," they both said.

"I just found this place yesterday," said Tommy.

"I found it the day before," said Kat. She saw his shoulders fall and didn't even need to read his thoughts. "It's okay," she said. "There's room for two."

Feeling somewhat disappointed and very awkward, Tommy sat. He crossed his arms and leaned on the balcony rail. He didn't look at her but could feel Kat's stare. When she finally looked away, Tommy felt somehow lighter. He relaxed a little and absently watched the driftworms.

"Oh, look," said Kat. Tommy turned. A small purple piece of fuzz was crawling down her forearm. "It tickles."

"Reminds me of woolly bears back at home," Tommy said. "'Cept they're not so purple."

Kat smiled and held up her hand. The driftworm traveled the length of her index finger and seemed perplexed as to where to go from there. "Have you seen the moths that these things turn into?"

Tommy shook his head.

"Ril says they're as big as both your hands . . . and they glow."

"Cool," said Tommy. He imagined the forest canopy at night, alive with hundreds of luminous moths. "Way cool."

Suddenly, Tommy and Kat stiffened and looked up. They had heard a sound, a haunting . . . alien sound. Like a bird's cry, but it had gradually morphed into a voice. It trilled and then faded.

"What was that?" Tommy asked.

"Shh! There it is again!" Kat looked at him wide-eyed. "Did it . . . did it speak?"

"So you heard it too." Tommy gasped. "It said—"

"*CoO-oMmMm-mme.*"

"It's in the castle somewhere!" Kat said.

"Where?"

"This way!" Kat leaped from the stone bench and tore into the castle. Tommy sprinted after her. Hearing the sound again, they followed the echoes farther into the castle, and then veered off down a passage they had never taken before. The haunting call led them deeper and deeper into the cliff side of the castle. Several twists and turns later, Kat held up a hand for Tommy to stop. The passage they were in was lit only from windows at either end. They stood in the shadows between.

"Why'd you stop?"

"That last—whatever it was—it's here. I feel like we should see it."

Tommy pointed to the far side of the corridor . . . a dead end. "Maybe you just heard it echo."

"No, it was right here."

"But it's just a wall."

Kat let out a yelp and jumped back. Something moved at the base of the wall.

Something with eyes.

Tommy and Kat edged backward, squinting in the dim light. It was hard to see whatever it was, but something snakelike emerged, apparently squeezing between two stones just above the floor. It slithered toward them and squeaked.

"Oh, it's a frake!" said Kat. She stepped forward and, to Tommy's astonishment, picked the thing up.

Tommy looked at it curling around Kat's wrist and up into her hand. "A what?" he asked.

"A frake. Well, that's what I call it at least." She gave him a goofy smile. "It's like a furry snake. Fur-rake—get it? Nelly called it some Elvish name I can't remember. So I just call it frake. Here, hold it."

She let it slither into Tommy's cupped hands. Indeed it was like a snake's body, but completely covered in soft, shorthaired fur. It had huge eyes and a small, pink nose. It squeaked again and then emitted a low purring sound. Tommy looked at Kat. "Is this what we heard?"

"No," said Kat. "No way." She walked over to the wall, eyeing the stones. "But that little guy just came out of the wall. Which means . . ." She pressed her palms flat against the stone. "I bet there's something behind here." She pushed in several places.

"Yeah, right, Kat," he said. "That only happens in the mov—"

"Ah! This one." Kat found a stone that slide inward and then fell, revealing a gaping black hole.

"I don't believe it." Tommy stepped forward. "What's in there?"

"I can't tell. Hey, put the frake down and help."

"Oh, . . . right." Tommy placed the still-purring creature on the passage floor and pulled at the edge of the hole until he dislodged another stone. It was no little effort, but soon, Tommy and Kat had an opening they could crawl through.

Kat looked at Tommy. "Think we should?"

"Why not?" he asked, sarcastically adding, "I mean, if you hear a scary bird-scream-ghost-voice coming from a black hole in a stone wall, the only thing to do is investigate." Kat whacked him on the shoulder and then disappeared through the wall.

It was a little more awkward a fit for Tommy. When he was through, Kat said, "Stairs."

Still wiping dust from his tunic, Tommy looked up. About seven feet away, just visible in the inky dark, gray steps spiraled up and to the left.

"Come on," Kat said.

Placing each foot carefully and bracing themselves on the cold, dusty walls, Tommy and Kat began their ascent. "*Phew!* There's a ton of dust," Tommy said.

"Been a long time since anyone's gone through here."

"I wonder why it was bricked up."

None of the answers that suggested themselves were very comforting. They continued to climb in silence, Tommy assuming the lead and Kat right on his heels. Up and up and 'round and 'round it went. Eerie, gray twilight filtered down from somewhere far above.

The dust was powdery and thick. *How many years had it built up?* Tommy wondered. But he noticed that there weren't any cobwebs . . . not a single one. That was good. Tommy'd had enough of spiders. In fact, he ho—

Kat squeezed his shoulder like a vise. "Did you hear that?"

"No," he whispered back, his heart kicking into thrash-metal mode. "What?!"

"It sounded like . . . scratching."

"I don't hear any—" He stopped short. He did hear something. A scratching or a scraping . . . but not very loud. What it lacked in volume it made up for in creepiness. Tommy imagined a zombie locked away in a stone crypt, and though the flesh of its fingers had worn away long ago, it still kept scratching. Kat read those thoughts from Tommy's mind . . . and wished she hadn't.

The scratching grew louder as they climbed. Tommy went around a bend . . . and stopped. Kat bumped into his back. Tommy whispered urgently, "STOP! Don't move."

"What?" Kat looked over his shoulder. The spiral stair ended at a tower chamber, the entrance of which had once been bricked up like the opening far below. It was a jagged hole now, but on the other side, with the Allyran sky darkening behind it, was an immense bird. At least six feet tall, the avian creature had a raptor's profile, like a hawk or an eagle, only it was covered in brilliant, burgundy feathers, and its fierce eyes were gold.

Tommy blinked. It seemed to be staring directly at him.

"I think we should go back," Kat whispered from behind.

The bird screamed, and the sound was such that it made every tiny hair on Tommy's neck and arms stand straight up. And it was so loud it made both their ears ring.

The bird released Tommy from its gaze. It lifted one of its long, taloned claws and began scratching at the dark stone of the chamber wall. Its talons had to be ridiculously sharp to gouge the stone like that. Several strange symbols, scratched in white, were already there, and the creature was finishing another. It almost looked like a language of some sort.

Tommy noticed that the bird was standing in a bed of parchments, some open, some still rolled and bound. And behind the creature was a stone bookshelf filled with very dusty, very large books.

SCREECH. The bird had apparently finished writing on the wall, and it turned its golden eyes on Tommy. It made a kind of deep chirp and bobbed its head in the direction of the symbols on the wall. It chirped again, louder and more urgent this time.

Tommy took a step forward.

"What are you doing?!" Kat clutched at his shirt. Tommy didn't answer, but she knew what he was thinking. "Tommy, come back! I don't think you should get near it!"

Tommy looked back over his shoulder. "I think it wants me to look."

"I think it wants you closer so it can eat you! Tommy!"

But Tommy didn't listen. He turned and kept going. As dangerous and strange as it appeared, there was something about the bird that felt . . . right. The creature watched Tommy intently, staring down its beak with unblinking eyes.

Tommy stepped through the ruined entrance to the chamber. It happened too fast for Tommy to react. The bird's claw shot out and raked Tommy's forearm. Kat screamed and watched him fall backward, blood dribbling from the new wound. She reached Tommy's side just in time to see the fierce, burgundy raptor spread its vast wings and leap toward them.

About the Authors

 WAYNE THOMAS BATSON is the author of five best-selling novels: *Isle of Swords, Isle of Fire*, and the Door Within Trilogy. His books have earned awards and nominations including: Silver Moonbeam, Mom's Choice® Silver, Cybil, Lamplighter, and American Christian Fiction Writers Book of the Year. A middle school reading teacher in Maryland for more than eighteen years, Wayne tailors his stories to meet the needs of young people. When last seen, Wayne was tromping around the Westfarthing with his beautiful wife and four adventurous children. For more on Wayne, go to www.enterthedoorwithin.blogspot.com.

 CHRISTOPHER HOPPER, whose other books include *Rise of the Dibor* and *The Lion Vrie*, has often been called a modern-day renaissance man. Christopher is also a record producer and recording artist with nine CDs, a youth pastor, painter, president of a Christian discipleship school, entrepreneur, and a motivational speaker for conferences and schools across the United States and Europe. Christopher has dedicated his life to positively affecting the culture of his generation and longs to see young people inspired to live meaningful and productive lives. He resides with his wife, three children, and three horses, in the mysterious 1,000 Islands of northern New York. For more on Christopher, go to www.christopherhopper.com.

Follow the Clues . . .
Solve the Riddle . . .
Begin Your Own Adventure

For those who **search** the gathering place,

A realm now marked by **posts** and lines,

The oldest **date** will speed thy pace

And **link** thee closer to thy find.

To begin your own adventure, go to
The Prophecies of Berinfell series Web site

www.heedtheprophecies.com